SHORTCUT

ALSO BY BRYAN THOMAS SCHMIDT

The Saga of Davi Rhii series
   The Worker Prince
   The Returning
   The Exodus
The John Simon Thrillers
   Simon Says
   The Sideman
   Common Source
Shortcut *(Jason Maxx 1)*

Anthologies as Editor:

Beyond the Sun

Raygun Chronicles

Shattered Shields *(with Jennifer Brozek)*

Mission: Tomorrow

Decision Points

Galactic Games

Little Green Men—Attack! *(with Robin Wayne Bailey)*

Maximum Velocity *(with Jennifer Brozek, Carol Hightshoe, David Lee Summers, and Dayton Ward)*

Infinite Stars

Monster Hunter Files *(with Larry Correia), a #1 bestseller*

Predator: If It Bleeds, *a #1 bestseller*

Joe Ledger: Unstoppable *(with Jonathan Maberry), a #1 bestseller*

Infinite Stars: Dark Frontiers

Surviving Tomorrow

Aliens Vs. Predators: Ultimate Prey *(with Jonathan Maberry), a #1 bestseller*

Predator: Eyes of the Demon, *a #1 bestseller*

The Hitherto Secret Experiments of Marie Curie *(with Henry Herz), a #1 bestseller*

Robots Through The Ages *(with Robert Silverberg)*

Joe Ledger: Unbreakable *(with Jonathan Maberry)(forthcoming)*

Nonfiction

How To Write a Novel: The Fundamentals of Fiction

https://en.m.wikipedia.org/wiki/Bryan_Thomas_Schmidt
https://Bryanthomasschmidt.net

SHORTCUT

A novel by Bryan Thomas Schmidt

Based on Characters & a Story by

Hunt Lowry

& Bryan Thomas Schmidt

Interior Design and Layout: A. R. Redington
Cover Design: A. R. Redington
Author Photo: Arpit Mehta

DEDICATION

For Jonathan Madajian, my Personal Sheldon,
this story would never work without your genius.
You are the real Jason Maxx, and I am so honored
and humbled to know you.
For my kids, Kishi and Kenjie, study hard and I know
you can change the world too one day.
Thanks for already changing mine.
And as always, for May.

CHAPTER 1

*T*HUMP!

Five minutes.

For a moment, the world around Jason Maxx faded under the cacophony within. His heart might burst from his chest at any moment. *Why do I feel like a grade schooler about to make my first presentation in science class?* he thought as he watched from backstage left at the 2025 Lightspeed Conference—the global gathering of the brightest futurists, engineers, and space flight pioneers together in one place, rapt at a speaker giving his summary of a project. THUMP! Jason's stomach clenched. This was the single biggest moment of his thirty-seven year life. Everything he'd worked for, his future, would be determined here.

In just a few minutes, he'd unveil his own project—one that had consumed half his life—his game-changing vision for space travel. Jason's whole life depended on it. Jason resisted the urge to run a hand through his perfectly coiffed blonde hair, for the first time wishing his pale skin bore just a hint of the tan his wife, Laura, wore to perfection. The visionary leader's nervousness caught him by surprise. He turned his focus on the speaker again, who was explaining Breakthrough Starshot. *Their pride and confidence is certainly apparent in that title.* And the concept was indeed cool, but... Shortcut was better. And it promised piloted spaceflight in this decade. People weren't excited about space anymore, but they still loved heroes. *And damn if we don't still need them.* His project Shortcut could deliver much faster than Starshot. Space and heroes. Jason was going to give them both.

Starshot was headed by physicist and venture capitalist Yuri Milner, with a board of directors of heavy hitters, including Stephen Hawking before he died. Starshot envisioned launching a mothership of a thousand tiny spacecraft (on a scale of centimeters) into high-altitude Earth orbit and then deploying them to accelerate via laser driven sails at up to 100 hundred kilometers per second for ten minutes, which would achieve much higher velocities on the order of fifteen percent of the speed of light at speeds of 100 kilometers per second to Alpha Centauri, taking twenty to thirty years to make flybys of Earth-like planets in that solar system. The bigger the lasers, the faster the speeds, the bigger the payload. It could be decades before there were lasers with enough power to propel manned missions, and there was also the issue of how to get the data they gathered back to Earth.

Pete Worden, his brunette hair cut short and exact, a reflection of the discipline instilled during a decade of service in the Air Force, was making the presentation at Lightspeed. The former director of NASA's Ames Research Center and the project director, at the moment, was echoing earlier public statements made by Hawking almost verbatim. "Our physical resources are being drained at an alarming rate. Our only home is being devastated by the tragedy of climate change—rising temperatures, reduction of the polar ice caps, deforestation, and decimation of animal species— the result of our ignorance and unthinking actions. We are running out of space and the only places to go to are other worlds. It is time to explore other solar systems. Spreading out may be the only thing that saves us from ourselves. We are convinced that humans need to leave Earth. Breakthrough Starshot is the first step to taking us there."

The idea was sexy, Jason had to admit, but what people really wanted was to send humans into space. The concept that had once ignited the entire planet had somehow gotten lost in the tragedies of space shuttle explosions and ballooning budgets, not to mention a general malaise toward science and general ignorance of the great discoveries made on many space missions—discoveries that had real practical impact on people's everyday lives. And while Starshot depended on technological advancements that might be decades away, Shortcut operated on technology that already existed. Its reality was tomorrow, not in some distant, undefined future.

THUMP! THUMP! As Worden finished to thunderous applause and left the stage, one of the conference organizers stepped up to introduce Jason, hailing him as "one of the great minds of mathematics this century," and other lofty statements Jason knew were true but nonetheless found embarrassing when stated so directly. THUMP! He took a deep breath, shifting on his feet, and cleared his throat. So far, he had spoken very little publicly about Shortcut—his plan to cut the time factor of space travel down to days and weeks instead of months and years and make manned missions to Mars and beyond a reality in the next five years, not decades from now. It was much faster by years than NASA's Space Launch System Solid Rocket Boosters could offer, plus Shortcut could be used again and again. NASA believed in it so much that they had already signed on with funding and support, and the first unmanned test flights would begin the following week. But the project was hush

hush and not a lot had been said outside the project's immediate circles, especially not to members of the group he faced now.

As the organizer called his name, turned, and smiled, waving him onto the stage, Jason put on a smile and walked forward confidently. THUMP! THUMP! THUMP! Some of these people had laughed at what they had heard rumored about Jason Maxx, the math guru and his crazy polariton-fueled Shortcut theory. But they didn't know the half of it, and Jason and the project principals had decided now was the time to let the cat out of the bag. To wow them with a giant cannon burst across the bow, so to speak. To come out with a major development that was about to change everything.

Jason stepped to the podium and smiled at the crowd, taking a deep breath again. So many familiar faces looked up at him—from Richard Branson and Yuri Milner to Timothy Mack, Gwynn Shotwell, COO of SpaceX, Amy Mainzer, Alvin Toffler, Michio Kaku, and famed former astronauts Scott and United States Senator Mark Kelly, now in demand as highly paid consultants—the room was packed with experts, people who could and would tear his theory apart bit by bit from the moment he revealed the details. This time his heartbeat silently. Somehow, his nervousness had been replaced by confidence, a sense of surety. This was his element, leading an audience where he wanted them to go. He'd win them over with humor and then he'd blow their minds.

He licked his lips and took a slow breath. "Yeah, let's talk about polaritons," he began and grinned. The audience laughed, just as he knew they would. He could hear them wondering: *Is he actually poking fun at himself?*

"Polaritons, does he actually think he can make them do

what he wants?" he could imagine someone saying.

"Maybe he plans to outthink them or confuse them with math," someone else might reply.

"The great thing about a conference like this is the guy who's used to being the smartest guy in the room finally gets some humble pie," another might add. It had all been said before.

And they'd all be watching him to see how he swallowed it.

"Polaritons and quantum entanglement," he continued. "And what these two familiar concepts put together could mean for getting humankind to Mars not in thirty years but in five, certainly less than ten. And my theory, Shortcut, does this not with technology we may one day have, but proven technologies that already exist." The laughter died down. Now he had their attention. With the flick of a finger, he put two equations up on the projection screen:

$$i\delta_t \phi_X = \left(\omega_X + g|\phi_X|^2 \right)\phi_X + [?][?]\phi_C$$
$$i\delta_t \phi_C = \left(\omega_C - \tfrac{1}{2}\delta_{xx} \right)\phi_C + [?][?]\phi_X$$

"What if polaritons could make it possible for humankind to travel at speeds of 10,000 times the speed of light?"

There was a collective gasp then mumbled chatter as some shook their heads. Was he crazy? Impossible. But Jason had them just where he wanted them.

"Let me tell you how," he said and paused for effect, then continued, "If the universe were simple, a polariton could be described by the dynamic coupling of the photon and exciton wave functions..." And with that, Jason delivered the first detailed public explanation of his Shortcut theory.

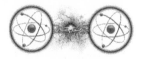

NASA CONTROLLER BOB Cooper's voice broke Jason out of his reverie, "Spacecraft reacquired, that's another successful Shortcut. That makes number nineteen, just one to go!" Red, green, orange, and yellow dots lit up the communications LED as images flashed across it matching those on larger screens hanging on the front wall overhead. Five years after the Lightspeed Conference, Jason was sitting beside his wife in a bustling Mission Control at NASA's Johnson Space Center. Crewless tests had provided amazing results and they'd finally reached the point of a short piloted test flight with two crewmembers.

Voices cheered around him as they had with every successful jump, their enthusiasm never wavering in the midst of a successful mission that was literally changing everything for the space agency and the entire world, though few outside this room or without access to NASA's private closed circuit feed would know it yet. Jason looked around him, still overwhelmed. As confident as he was with his Shortcut theory and his expertise in applied mathematics, when it came to most of the engineering stuff, especially the immense complexity of the world of NASA Mission Control, Jason felt out of his element, easily overwhelmed.

And on top of that, here he was in NASA Mission Control, a legendary place—a dark cavernous room filled with row after row of flat screens and keyboards controlling and monitoring every aspect of the current mission. Each station was manned by hundreds of controllers with backgrounds in various scientific and technical pursuits, all experts at their area of responsibility over the first piloted Shortcut test flight. Flags hung high on the walls representing each mission and crew that had been launched from here. And like NASA itself, the room was populated with employees of all shades and backgrounds—united in their mission as NASA Mission Controllers to launch each mission and bring it safely home. It was awe inspiring and intimidating at the same time. And although he was mostly an observer today, he was the star of the show.

"It's going pitch perfect so far, babe," his wife, Laura, said, her brunette curls hanging down to frame her full lips as they curved into a stunning smile. His palms were moist with sweat, his heart racing—she still had that effect on him that no one else ever had. If his mouth hadn't already been dry, it would have been now. When he failed to meet her eyes, she squeezed his arm where she held it and continued watching the controllers around them. At that moment, familiar warm flashes shot through Jason's body and his skin tingled. He had two great passions: Shortcut theory and Laura Raimey, now Laura Maxx. He loved their daughter Heather too, of course, but for Jason those two passions were what consumed him.

Unlike Jason, Laura, a former astronaut, was right at home here. She'd sat in this position many times and even more in the observation booth behind them. She'd been CAPCOM, guiding the crew as well, as every astronaut did. But today, she had one job: to be with her husband and usher him through his first experience in live Mission Control. And she was the picture of calm and totally in her element here. Jason envied her. Unlike Jason she was actually enjoying it. Whereas Jason's collar felt tight and his skin glistened with nervous sweat. Laura remained relaxed and aglow with confident excitement.

Jason ran a hand through his own short, precisely cut blond locks and took a deep breath as his eyes locked on the large view screen hanging at the center of the room. Two hours before, the spacecraft *Maxx-One* had left the launch pad 1,019 miles away in Florida, and left Earth's atmosphere for the Moon with a complement of two astronauts at the fastest speed ever attempted—its goal to circle the Moon, and return in record time— in sixteen hours, rather than the three days, one hour it had taken Apollo astronauts. His Shortcut program's future depended upon the success of this moment. He couldn't remember anymore what he'd thought this moment would be like, but what it actually was seemed completely different—surreal, childlike wonder, amazement, and an utter inability to process coherent thought, let alone words. Some genius he was!

Maxx-One was a round spaceship that achieved the fast speeds by accelerating using the Shortcut propulsion theory developed by Jason and designed to conglomerate polaritons and harness negative mass. Polaritons were quasi-particles formed by light interacting with a type of electric dipole, which appear to behave as if they have negative mass. It was complex science, but in effect, the solar-pumped polariton laser activated the Shortcuts that allowed the ship to jump through space at speeds upwards of 10,000 times the speed of light (6.7 trillion miles per hour). In between jumps, the astronauts would experience a g-force of a few g's as the spacecraft decelerated, despun, and cruised to the new jump point. Lasers excited particles at predetermined jump points—ten each way to the Moon and back to Earth. The spherical craft, which was surrounded by a shield of light, would then swap places with those particles, effectively jumping through space toward the Moon in large leaps, rather than a straight journey, using principles of quantum entanglement. In essence, by engaging its laser shield, Maxx-One would be creating a temporary light bubble around the spacecraft so that the whole ship behaved like a single particle that would then use a laser to entangle the entire ship with particles near the destination. Once entangled, the *Maxx-One* would then exchange its position with the equivalent number of particles at the jump point. These jumps were Shortcuts, the heart of Jason's theory.

Altogether, with the combination of speed and jumps, the spacecraft's travel time would be less than an hour. In between jumps, while cruising to the new jump point, the ship would decelerate to more normal speeds, still greater than three g's, so the astronauts' medical readings could be assessed and all systems double checked before engaging in the next jump. This was to ensure their safety and health as well as that of their spacecraft. Although several crewless test flights had occurred, astronauts in space had never before been repeatedly subjected to g's on this scale, not to mention the particle swapping. So NASA wanted to be cautious and ensure their personnel would return in the same condition as they left. Everything was going perfectly. The astronauts were orbiting the Moon seventeen hours after takeoff and sending back close-up images of the stark, cratered surface. The Shortcut Equation and everything Jason Maxx had dedicated the past fifteen years to had been validated. Now he just had to perfect the equation for longer distances.

He thought back to the time in Dr. Pope's Physics class when he'd started at MIT at age fifteen and made waves by proving a theory he'd become obsessed with.

"Jason, you have a question?" Dr. Pope had asked, after Jason had raised his hand several times.

Jason had nodded and stood, confidently stating his thesis: "There's no such thing as pure mathematics as presently defined."

"What?!" "Nonsense!" His classmates called out, mocking him.

Dr. Pope just tilted his head and smiled. "Why do you say that, Jason?"

"The applied mathematics branch concerned with physics, engineering, business, industry, and space is about practical problems and how everything works," Jason continued. "It can't exist simply for its own sake. It has a purpose. It requires problems to analyze and guide its course."

"Well, mathematics is certainly always concerned with problems," Pope agreed. "But its existence does not depend upon them. In the absence of our attention, it doesn't cease to exist."

"But that's just it, without problems what is it? It doesn't just exist for its own sake," Jason continued.

Dr. Pope chuckled. "Are you trying to put mathematicians out of business?"

Jason had smiled, then argued the point a bit, but no one seemed convinced. In the end, the young genius who'd scored perfectly on the SATs had rocked the campus of MIT with his theories and revelations, becoming an instant celebrity and focus of conflict and debate, and that had followed him throughout his entire career.

He'd gone on to attend six institutions of higher learning, including Rice, West Point, Oxford, Washington University, and Princeton, and managed to remain viewed as a dangerous rebel at all of them—not for outlandish behavior, but outlandish thought. So he was used to being a loner, feeling isolated. Yet here he was surrounded by hundreds at NASA all working for him: to prove his theory, to solve the problem he'd set out to solve. All sharing his goal and his mission. It was as surreal as it was exciting. It would have totally surprised and thrilled the fifteen-year-old who'd unleashed the firestorm all those years before.

Soon, the astronauts, Captain Dominick Creed and Lieutenant Matthew Wayne, would be returning home, again at amazing speeds. The first ten jumps had gone perfectly, taking them into orbit around the Moon. Ten more jumps and all they had to do was enter the atmosphere and land on the runway. The first Shortcut mission would be complete. Then funding would pour in like mad and make the rest of his plans possible at last.

Laura squeezed his arm as she stopped behind him, watching over his shoulder as he sat at the console, both watching the giant view screens on the wall in Mission Control. "It's like a dream," she whispered. His arm tingled at her touch and she leaned down to put her cheek next to his as they watched the monitor together.

"Better," Jason replied, the tension having totally left his body since the last time they'd been in Mission Control during a launch from the final crewless test flight. She laughed. Jason was at ease, feeling a sense of pride and relief mixed with excitement at the success of the mission. All the years of naysaying and controversy were over. He'd done it! No one could argue with it now.

An hour later, he was still watching with rapt attention when mission commander Dominick Creed's voice broke his reverie again. "Houston, *Maxx-One*—ready for the final Shortcut."

Jason scooted forward eagerly on his seat, despite the fact he was approaching twenty-six hours without sleep.

"Copy, *Maxx-One*," replied CAPCOM Scott Edmond, then turned to Propulsion.

"All systems go," Leti Najera said from the Propulsion console as she finished checking readings and making adjustments on her LED screen. She received laughter in response.

"Propulsion, got any clichés you haven't used yet?" Matthew Wayne, Creed's copilot, broke in to more laughter. As a former test pilot, he was used to fly-by-the-seat-of-your-pants thinking and improvisation on missions, and even enjoyed the challenge, and a little Mission Control humor always helped lighten the tension. Of course things were a go or they'd have already taken other action but the practice had always been to confirm each step as they went, just to provide checks and balances.

"Entering sequence code now," Creed, one of the first African Americans to rise to mission commander in NASA, confirmed, even as his fingers aboard the spacecraft flew across the keyboard providing the manual confirmation code for the last jump that had been programmed in for safety throughout the voyage. Just in case anything went wrong and they needed an extra precaution, he'd had to do so every time. NASA programmers had made it easier by giving him a rotating three code system, so he'd only had to memorize three codes. Even then, as yet another precaution, they were printed on a flight manual that was suspended overhead in easy reach from where he sat aboard the spacecraft. Creed's background included flying fighter jets for the Navy, teaching at the Navy's elite pilot training school in San Diego, and flying one mission to the international space station for NASA a few years before.

At this point, the code would initiate solar pumping of the laser, storing the energy that *Maxx-One* needed to establish the link. As the ship absorbed sunlight to pump the laser, its appearance would transition from that of a tessellated ball, like the eye of a fly, into a super black ball that was ready to Shortcut. Unfortunately, the charging process also blocked direct communication with the spacecraft from initiation until they made the jump. Blackouts in this case meant the blip that represented the spacecraft disappeared from monitors and radar and radio communications were interrupted for that period—currently around three minutes.

Jason and Laura exchanged smiles and his wife winked at him, tousling his hair. He felt like a little kid at Christmas right now, so elated, so in awe that it was all going so well. It had been a dream for so many years, but now it was so much more. Shortcut was a reality.

"Blackout in ten…nine…eight…seven…six…" Cooper, at the Comm station, counted down for the twentieth time as the numbers filled his LED.

"Here we go, Houston," Creed said as always, "Back with you in three minutes." And then they were gone—momentarily disappearing from screens like a glitch, radio silent—as the spacecraft made its leap from one location to another. THUMP!

And as always, Mission Control went mostly silent except for beeping LEDs and whirring AC vent fans, as they all waited, listening to Cooper at Comm:

"Three minute countdown…one eighty…one seventy-nine…"

This was the longest wait of their lives every time. A silence that lasted only a few minutes but felt like a lifetime. And for Jason, it was the one great moment of uncertainty in the entire sequence that made his heart beat a little faster. THUMP! Because no matter how perfect the math or technology, no matter how confident he was in himself or the team around him, real human lives were at stake, and for a few long moments, they had no idea what was happening to the astronauts. That was excruciating!

With the spacecraft shielded to function like a quantum particle, there was uncertainty in the speed and direction the spacecraft would be pointed after coming out of each jump. With all the tests and years of research, Jason had gotten pretty close, but some element of uncertainty still remained. This meant that with every jump, adjustments to speed, course, and alignment were required to reorient the spacecraft with thrusters between jump points. It was Jason's habit to manually calculate his best guess during each jump to see if he could beat the computer. Based on tests, he'd narrowed the variance down to generally three to five feet of the target each time. So his mind raced through the calculations.

He'd done the math hundreds of times; students in classes he taught had run millions of simulations as had the staff assigned to the Shortcut project; so he knew when he could get away with making assumptions. The math got very messy when anyone tried to account for all the variables at once; even the NASA's Aitken supercomputer had glitched out after several days spent trying to solve everything simultaneously. So Jason simplified the math and kept a running total of his margin of error alongside his calculations. He did this mostly in his head but pulled out an iPad and referred to it for notes and figures from time to time.

Given that Shortcut nineteen had used twenty percent more fuel from thrusters A3U and R1R than expected, that meant the craft would have three pounds less mass. Oh, and the center of gravity would move about... three inches to the left; too small to matter. *I'll just ignore that and add six inches to the margin of error instead.*

Taking into account the distance of the Shortcut, the megawatt laser operating at seventy-five percent power, the density of the destination particle cloud, the ship's mass and its forward velocity of 32,585 feet per second, he repeated the thought process for all six velocity vectors: forward, starboard, deck, roll, pitch, and yaw. That would place the craft—pitching violently, with almost no roll or yaw, and a velocity of around 30,000 feet per second forward and 2,000 feet per second toward the portside. He recorded his prediction on the iPad and then waited for confirmation as he turned back to the activity around him in Mission Control.

"Flight preparing to reacquire," Flight controller Matt D'Aunno confirmed as controllers sat stiff, leaning forward at their consoles, making minor adjustments or waiting with bated breath, all the while knowing they could expect no data.

Then silence again. Even having done it nineteen times in a row, Jason looked around wondering if anyone was daring to breathe. THUMP!

The pitch-black craft flashed in a brilliant pulse of light as the laser fired. Then it disappeared.

"Did you miss us?" Creed's voice broke through the silence and cheers erupted again.

Jason breathed again, not having even realized he'd been holding his breath or for how long.

"Welcome back, *Maxx-One*," D'Aunno at Flight said.

"Let's get you boys back home."

That's when things went to hell.

"Uh Houston, can you confirm coordinates of Shortcut Twenty target?" Creed said.

"*Maxx-One*, is there an issue?" Scott Edmond, the CAPCOM, said, looking puzzled. Then indicators buzzed and beeped as multi-colored lights lit up consoles around him. There were no klaxons, nothing blaring. It was all about helping people stay on task, focus, and work it through, not drowning them out.

"Houston, please confirm coordinates for Shortcut Twenty target," Wayne said.

"*Maxx-One*, Shortcut Twenty target coordinates are MidPac; 000, 153, 000; 290:06:32. 267: minus 00.71, minus 156.18; 06.9; 36196, 6.50; 1045.8, 36276; 290:23:32; 00:27; Noun 69 is NA; 4.00, 02:02; 00:16, 03:33, 07:43; sextant star 25, 151.5, 26.2; boresight NA," Flight answered.

"Spacecraft is not at the target coordinates," the Nav controller, Jamal Ammar, called out. THUMP!

"Houston," Creed replied. "We have our present coordinates as MidPac; 000, 153, 000; 290:06:32. 267: minus 00.71, minus 156.18; 06.9; 36196, 6.50; 1045.8, 36276; 290:23:32; 00:27."

The controllers exchanged concerned looks, then Edmond spoke into his headset and asked, "*Maxx-One*, CAPCOM, what is your current speed and trajectory?"

"Houston, *Maxx-One* is traveling at 30,075 feet per second on a heading of 3.82 degrees to port and 220 nautical miles altitude," Creed replied.

"Flight, Nav, confirm computer data for Shortcut

Twenty," Edmond said, then softly, off radio, "What happened, folks?" He watched as everyone in the room shifted to emergency protocols, trying to sort the problem and find a solution.

"CAPCOM, the space station is currently at that altitude," Ammar at Nav said with urgency to the room, staying off radio. "They're on a direct collision course. Impact in three minutes!" THUMP!

Panicked looks filled faces as Edmond scrambled, "Nav and Propulsion, we need evasive course now! Someone get the Russians on the phone!"

As the controllers went to work frantically typing into their computers for calculations, Jason got a sour taste in his mouth and his stomach rolled and his entire body tensed like a brick. Laura's hand tightened on his shoulder. Instead of coming out of Shortcut around a hundred nautical miles above Earth in position for reentry, the spacecraft had come out 220 nautical miles from Earth, directly in the orbital path of the International Space Station, which just happened to be presently on the same side of Earth as *Maxx-One*'s return. On top of that, preliminary navigation data indicated the *Maxx-One* was bearing toward the ISS, and its rate of speed was much faster than anticipated at this point in the journey. Since there is a tradeoff between knowing a particle's position or momentum, Jason and the engineers had decided to develop a system that would favor knowing the position of the *Maxx-One* after each Shortcut. Because the momentum would be "unknown" (not known as well), they'd developed a Rapid Reaction Control System that used artificial intelligence to determine the orientation and speed of the craft. Calculations were then completed in a split-second and then executed perfectly to undo any spinning, without causing the astronauts to blackout by maneuvering too quickly. So effectively, not only had the Shortcut coordinates failed somehow but the RRCS had malfunctioned.

"The RRCS misfired. We're pitching at 402 degrees per second. Attempting to manually despin." Jason translated in his head: The spacecraft was rotating at faster than once per second. They'd have to stop the rotation before trying any evasive maneuvers.

"We could try braking with the RRCS," suggested Laura as many called out solutions.

"Not fast enough," Leti Najera said dismissively from Propulsion. While the RRCS was malfunctioning, the standard Reaction Control System on the *Maxx-One* was designed for making small adjustments to velocity and wouldn't be any help. The astronauts had taken the only choice available: overriding the computers and slowing down the rotating spaceship themselves. THUMP!

"*Maxx-One*, after your despin, prepare to make an immediate correction," Edmond instructed over the radio, then turned to Najera. "Tell us what to do next, Propulsion."

The tension in the room was as thick as humidity in the Florida Keys in October, and Jason had a hard time staying in his seat. He wanted to be doing something, fixing the problem, taking charge. Needed to be involved. He was a genius, highly educated, highly competent, but at this moment, he was relegated to the sidelines. Everything depended upon others. THUMP! THUMP! THUMP! Laura reached down and squeezed his shoulders hard, signaling him to stay put and let the controllers do their jobs. Everyone was scrambling, calculating, checking readings, discussing adjustments, monitoring at an intensity level like never before.

Jason stood and hurried forward, his mind racing. He

could make most calculations faster than any computer but the near field phase construction of the laser made this calculation a bit more complicated.

"Jesus, Houston, *Maxx-One*, we have visual of the space station," Creed said, his voice breaking. "It's directly in our path!" THUMP!

"Flight, *Maxx-One* ready at thruster controls," Matthew Wayne, Creed's copilot, said.

"Have them manually Shortcut 2.87 feet at an angle of 0.02°, 84.4°, 000°," Jason said after examining star charts on overhead monitors and confirming data on nearby controller's monitors.

"That's less than a yard," Najera objected from Propulsion, even as she typed the numbers into a computer to double check them.

"At that speed and trajectory, it'll take them well clear. And we don't have enough time to charge the laser for a longer jump. So let's reduce their forward velocity, convert it into a deck momentum, and get them off the collision path. Who cares where they end up as long as they move down fast?" Jason said, fighting to keep the emotion out of his voice and stay professional. *Keep it together, Jason. The leader's confidence is the team's confidence.*

"There's no time to initiate sequence," Ammar said from Nav.

"They have to do it manually," Jason said. "It's faster. Trust me!" The controllers exchanged looks of uncertainty.

"NASA, we need instructions!" Creed urged.

Jason locked eyes with Edmond. "I know what I'm doing. Let me save them."

The CAPCOM nodded. "Do it!"

"*Maxx-One*, disengage auto. We want you to Shortcut immediately to 2.87 feet, roll 0.02°, pitch 84.4°, yaw 000°," Leti Najera at Propulsion instructed, reading from her LED. It would be a rough ride, but the ship could immediately relocate on manual without the built-in countdowns used by the computer before each jump. Jason held his breath again.

"Houston, confirming coordinates 2.87 feet, roll 0.02°, pitch 84.4°, yaw 000°," Creed said even as Wayne added, "*Maxx-One* disengaging auto for manual Shortcut."

"*Maxx-One*, Houston coordinates confirmed," Ammar said from Nav.

"Which code, Houston?" Creed asked.

Everyone looked at Propulsion. They hadn't planned for manual jumps.

"Any code," Jason said, releasing his breath. "We didn't specify one for manual."

Edmond nodded.

"*Maxx-One*, any code should work on manual," Najera said, even as her and her co-worker's fingers raced across the keyboard, frantically searching their database to confirm.

"Initiating Shortcut," Creed replied and then comms blacked out and the spacecraft was gone from the screens again. THUMP!

Everyone held their breath, several prayed, others simply froze, waiting. For the first time in years, Jason pondered praying. *Oh God, please, bring them home safe.*

Then, after sixty seconds, "*Maxx-One*, Houston, do you read me?" Cooper said at Comm. "*Maxx-One*, Houston, do you copy?"

All eyes went to overhead nav charts looking for the spacecraft's blip to reappear.

"*Maxx-One*, Houston, do you read me?" Cooper said again.

"Houston, *Maxx-One*," Creed's voice finally said. "You sound a little stressed there. But you're not through with us yet."

Cheers went up from all around as warning lights and alarms switched off or reverted to normal, and Jason let out his breath and closed his eyes in relief, the tension seeping from his body at last.

"Houston, *Maxx-One*, Shortcut successful, we are now at coordinates MidPac 000, 153, 000; 290:06:31, 267; minus 00.71, minus 156.18; 07.1; 36196, 6.54; 1051.0, 36276; 290:23:31; 05g, 00:27; Noun 69, NA; DO, 4.00, 02:00; 00:16, 03:31, 07:46; boresight sextant stars, NA; lift vector, up." Creed sounded relieved and they heard Wayne whooping behind him.

"Jesus Christ," Ammar muttered.

"*Maxx-One*, Houston, well done, gentlemen. Now let's get you home," Edmond said, then motioned to Propulsion, who were frantically doing calculations to get the spacecraft back on course.

Jason exchanged a relieved look with his wife as he breathed deeply and went back to stand beside her in the rear of the room.

"That jump took them feet instead of miles," Laura muttered, shaking her head with disbelief. "How—"

"We tested it at shorter distances," Jason said. "I can do the math in my head. It should be simple to correct course for reentry now, right?"

They checked the monitors together. "Looks like it's close enough," Laura whispered.

After that, it was all a blur as controllers got the spacecraft back on course and entered parking orbit to allow time to slow properly before reentry. An hour later, *Maxx-One* reentered the atmosphere, headed for a landing on the runway at Kennedy Space Center, and the mission was over. During the next few weeks, they'd get answers on what had gone wrong. But Jason's obsessing had already begun, his mind racing through all the possible causes he could think of for the Shortcut mistake. Shortcut calculations were never an exact science but this was a significant deviation from the planned location of the last jump. It wasn't the calculations. It just couldn't be. But what else was there? Navigation error? Computer or mechanical glitch? Computer virus? What had gone wrong? Whatever it was had almost cost the astronauts and the ISS crew their lives and just thinking about that left Jason tense and ready to explode.

After a few moments, he stood and hurried out, needing some air to clear his thoughts.

CHAPTER 2

AFTER JASON LEFT Mission Control, Laura stuck around a bit longer, hoping for whatever information she could glean. Afterward, as she wove her way through the parking lot toward her Lexus, she heard pounding music before she even saw him and knew it was her husband. Jason was in the Lexus' passenger seat, hands pantomiming drums, keyboards, and guitar licks, head twisting and flailing to the rhythm of U2's "Where the Streets Have No Name" blasting from the car stereo. He was totally in a zone, escaping his worries and stress in a way he always did in private. He would be embarrassed that she caught him, so she hesitated, slowing her approach and hoping he'd see her before she got too close.

Jason's pained voice matched the vocals of Bono note for note, in a decent blend, but his anguish was clear. He was feeling the song on a whole different level, singing it like an anthem of both confession and hope—a man shaken at his core, afraid, angry, confused, but determined. Jason tended to be so tunnel vision oriented on his goals, that when the unexpected happened it really threw him off, took him by surprise. Today's events would haunt him for a long time to come. Watching him, Laura wished she could just wrap her arms around him and fix it, but she knew that was impossible. She could listen, advise, and love him but he would have to find his own way through.

As the song ended, she passed the last car. He looked over, spotting her, and reached out to turn down the radio. She climbed into the driver's seat and their eyes met. Jason could come across as cold when he worked—being calculating, of course, was the nature of mathematicians. But she knew the real man, a man of deep passions and emotion, and she knew what the experience they'd just gone through was doing to him inside.

"They're safe, Jason," she said. The 2003 explosion of the space shuttle Columbia had rocked them both to the core. She'd been a high school senior lucky enough to earn an observation booth seat in Mission Control the day the *Columbia* exploded—February 1, 2003. And despite the horror of it, she'd never given up her dream of one day becoming an astronaut. Laura had lost friends and colleagues in various accidents over the years, though none of them particularly close, whereas most of the astronauts were total strangers to Jason, yet if anything he took such losses harder than she had. Like her own life had been threatened. Like he'd almost lost her. Since then, every time concern for astronaut safety came up in his project, Jason had treated it as nonnegotiable—the one variable that he wouldn't risk no matter what. And today, his astronauts' safety had been threatened. He needed to be reminded all was well, but even then the mere possibility was something he'd be obsessing over for months. "You can breathe easy again," she said. "Shortcut works!"

"Jonas Ross, Jim Haines, Agnes Cordovar—" Jason rattled off the names of old rivals, competitors, ex-employees, ex-lab partners. A few of the names had real beefs with him or he with them, she knew, but why was he thinking of them right now?

"What about them? It was an accident, Jason," she said. "It could be random cosmic radiation, computer or electrical malfunction—you have to wait and see what the evidence turns up. There are lots of possibilities."

"What are the chances the ISS would be right in the path?" Jason said. "They'd all love to see me fail. This will thrill them. They hate me. Jason Maxx: a failure!"

She sighed. Once he'd locked on a path like this, it would take a lot of proof to derail him from that line of thinking, but she had to try. "First, you didn't fail. And second, hate is a strong word," Laura said, keeping her voice soft, her words deliberate, as she absentmindedly reached up to brush back a stray strand of her brown hair. "Astronauts could have died. No one will be happy about this."

Jason nodded, sitting back against his seat hard. "I went over and over my math. Every single Shortcut calculation, the theory, everything on my iPad and packed in my head. I can't find anything wrong. The nineteen other jumps were all within my predicted margin of error. How could the last jump have been so far off?"

"It could be lots of things, babe," she said, frowning as his hand clenched tighter around the arm rest. "What about programming errors? A computer virus? Mechanical failure in the RRCS? So many possibilities. We don't know yet. But what we do know is Shortcut worked, and in the end, they made it back and the mission was a success."

"In the end, it's my fault. It's my baby." He slammed his fists so hard against his knees she feared they might leave bruises.

She reached over and cupped his cheek with a hand. "Take it easy," she scolded. "Don't hurt yourself. Shortcut and your reputation will survive this. And for your next trick you'll be solving world hunger."

"And then we'll finally see those streets with no name," he quipped and they shared a smile. "You know how concerned I am for the crew members' safety, but my whole life's work is at stake here," he said softly, then grew angrier again. "Why would the RRCS fail? There are so many fail safes…"

"The sensor and computer command data take time to verify," she said, gently setting her other hand atop his wrist. "There are still many uncertainties. Don't start making assumptions. We need more data." She sighed, her brow creasing with tension as her own anxiety reignited. What they needed was to rest and refocus. They could work on finding solutions in the days and weeks ahead. It wouldn't, couldn't happen tonight. But she knew better than to say that aloud. Instead, she said what she always said when he was feeling discouraged, "I believe in you."

Like her husband, Laura had been raised around Academia, and she'd turned it all into a game. Her charm and easy-going nature made it easy to make friends wherever she went, especially being the daughter of a legendary college football coach. Her father's work had its downsides but she'd grown to love the game and especially the spirit and philosophy of teamwork he taught as the basis of everything. That had served her well in her NASA career. It took a village, not just one crew, to make a successful mission, and like today, she'd seen that proven time and again.

Laura had become a decent athlete in her own right, ranked in tennis before a wrist injury ended her career early in high school. Not one to stay idle or give up, she'd made a late in life switch to dancing—late for a thirteen-year-old that is—and excelled at ballet through college. That led to a two-year stint with Cirque Du Soleil, another prime environment with teamwork at its core. But in the sciences she'd ultimately found her real passion and success. Her graduate studies in photonics research led her to pursue applications of lasers in space, which led to her first chance to connect with NASA. Once in the door, she'd never looked back, leveraging the opportunity to the fullest and gaining every experience she could, including learning to fly, and eventually earning her chance at the astronaut program. She'd first gone into space five years later and twice since. It was during this time that she'd met an exciting mathematician whose controversial formulas promised to change space travel forever and fallen in love.

Eventually, Laura's research in lasers had led her to a technological miracle: the invention of the laser cell. She had been developing the laser cell as part of a humanitarian effort to purify water by using concentrated solar energy. Her laser cells would collect sunlight, amplify it, and then focus the energy into a powerful laser beam aimed at a water tank. She had observed that, under certain circumstances, her laser cells would optically isolate themselves, turning into a near-black material, which could be used for both camouflage and solar energy collection. After she and Jason met, she worked to assemble the laser cells into a sphere and enhance their optical isolation capabilities. Her work was the engineering feat that allowed Jason to optically shield the spacecraft and treat it like a particle in his calculations. Collecting sunlight from multiple directions at once and transmitting laser light to one focused spot requires two different types of lenses, so she also developed the turnable lens, allowing laser cells to transition from one mode of operation to another. The Q-switch provides a jolt of electric power that alters the polarization of the optical isolator and releases the laser energy. As a bonus, since her humanitarian efforts took place partially in a radiological hazard zone after a fallout, they had confidence her device could function in an irradiated environment, which only increased NASA's interest and Jason's. So Jason wasn't the only genius in his field in their family.

Laura and Jason had always dealt with stress differently. By nature, she was easy going and Jason was the opposite. His love of math had started at a very young age and consumed his entire life. To him, it was the answer to every problem. For it to fail him—as he now feared it had—was Earth shattering. His expectations of its capabilities had been shaped primarily by a demanding father—a physicist and professor who settled for nothing less than perfection in himself and his students, and so, of course, he expected no less from his son. His father had passed on a love of math that exceeded his own to Jason, who'd become enamored of it almost from the first time he discovered its wonders and began to understand it, and Laura remembered once hearing him lecture on why he loved mathematics. That lecture had been the first time she realized she was falling in love with him. It had been in front of NASA employees after he'd come to present his ideas at a seminar and had been asked to talk to them a bit about why he loved what he did. Jason had spoken with such passion and sheer joy that Laura, a college intern, had been carried away by it. To this day, she remembered every word:

"I love mathematics because it allows us insight into the world around us and because you can take any real world situation and solve it," Jason had said, his voice rich with passion and emotion. "A lot of people think it's just a bunch of numbers and scary figures and formulas. But I love mathematics because it is the most powerful tool that human beings have in our possession. In physics, mathematics allows us to understand the orbits of the planets, to send spacecraft on journeys of hundreds of millions of miles in length and to land them in the right location. In engineering, mathematics allows us to design a steel building or a bridge or an airplane and to know that our design will work before it's even built. In biology, mathematics is allowing us to decode the mysteries of human DNA, to prevent disease, and to discover who we are. In business, mathematics allows us to do finance, to predict whether an enterprise will grow or fail, to do economics, and to know what we can do to bring prosperity and success to entire nations. It lies at the heart of our computers, our technologies, our electrical systems, the engines that drive our cars and fly our planes. And I believe in my core that mathematics is a pathway that can lead us to other solutions someday. Maybe even the end of poverty, the end of hunger, the road to peace. It's a conduit through which every answer to every problem can be found."

As he'd spoken, his voice had risen in pitch and enthusiasm with every word, until he'd almost become breathless. It wasn't like any speech about math Laura had ever heard. It was more like a love story, and as he finished, he paused to catch his breath and to look out at the audience and take in their reaction. After a moment, he continued, "Galileo said, 'The universe is written in the language of mathematics.' And God how I love being a coauthor of the universe. Don't you?"

The whole room had risen at once in thundering applause, caught up in his passionate words. Laura remembered NASA employees being inspired by it and talking about it for years after, quoting it even. But what amazed her more was how impressed Jason seemed with her from the moment they met. He asked poignant questions about her work and expressed his admiration, frequently commenting how impressed he was, as if his own work wasn't equally impressive. Laura couldn't help falling for a man with that kind of passion, and she wanted a man with that kind of passion to love her. Looking at him now, his face wrinkled from frowns and frustration. She knew his desperation and intensity could only be derailed by a distraction, a big one, so she tried a new tactic. "You're focused on the wrong thing, babe," she said and forced a reassuring smile. "Shortcut worked. The formula, the application—*Maxx-One* made it to the Moon in record time. The nav system can be fixed." She kept her voice soft and encouraging despite the tension they both felt. "Polaritons and quantum entanglement? Who would put all the pieces together like you did? And it worked! The mission was successful, despite everything that happened. Wonderful!"

She turned her eyes back to the road as she slowed for a light, then turned right and drove past the entrance to their subdivision. After a minute, realizing he hadn't responded, she wondered if he'd even heard her and turned, prepared to repeat what she'd said as she glanced at him again.

He was grinning and staring at her. Then he started to laugh. "It worked, by God, it worked! We did it!" Jason had never forgotten that Shortcut wouldn't have become reality without Laura's help. Years before, it was she, not he, who had built the first working prototype from his designs, and she had worked alongside him in the lab doing the experiments that proved polaritons were the energy solution they'd been seeking to make it all possible. Shortcut was in every way a family enterprise, and Jason would always be grateful for her partnership and support.

Laura laughed too, her body relaxing with relief. "Yes, you did." Jason was like this in whatever he did—his focus so intense, obsession so deep that he couldn't see anything else in the moment. The realization of what she'd said had clearly gotten through, though.

"Oh my God! This is going to kill Haines and the others!" Jason said, raising his eyebrow mischievously and shooting her a big grin.

"Well, at least you have your priorities straight," she replied, laughing again and shaking her head as she turned another corner a block from their home and relaxed her foot on the accelerator.

As they pulled into their driveway, an older man was backing out in his Lexus Convertible. Laura immediately recognized his neatly coiffed blond hair, clean shaven face, and slight tan. She found herself tucking loose hairs from her forehead behind her ear. Then he flashed what folks at NASA referred to as "the smile that set a million female hearts aflame." Colonel Jimmy Burnette, famous ex-fighter jock and astronaut, was the grandfather of Jason and Laura's ten-year-old daughter Heather's best friend. He headed down the road as she pulled into the drive. Though they'd barely interacted personally, his reputation for both his amazing flying abilities and effect on women was well known. As a pilot herself, Laura had been around a lot of fighter pilots, so it surprised her how long her eyes followed his Lexus as it disappeared down the road.

As soon as they entered the house, Heather threw herself into her daddy's arms. Blond with her mother's long, wavy hair and brown eyes, Heather was just the thing Jason needed to further stop his obsessing. Father and daughter danced around the living room for a minute, giggling and celebrating, as Laura and the nanny, Alice, watched with amusement. The way Heather was bouncing around reminded Laura of Jason when he was at his most adrenaline charged focus. Jason bounced a bit with her as they interacted, looking almost like two kids, instead of parent and child. Laura laughed.

"I thought you were supposed to be in bed," Jason gently scolded after a few minutes, looking up at their nanny, Alice. Alice was early twenties, thin, Vietnamese—a part time college student at a Houston university nearby.

"She wouldn't go," Alice said. "I tried and tried."

"Sounds like our girl," Laura said.

"She gets that perseverance from her mother," Jason teased as he kissed his daughter's forehead and paused, smelling the sweet, flowery scent of the shampoo in her hair.

Laura rolled her eyes and crossed her hands over her chest in mock disgust. "Take a look in the mirror sometime, daddy."

Jason laughed as Heather hugged him again.

"I wanna hear all about it," she eagerly pleaded. "We saw the landing on TV! It worked!"

Jason swung her up and over his shoulder like a potato sack and twirled around, humming. "It did! It did!"

"Put me down!" Heather yelled with fake enthusiasm. She loved every minute of their roughhousing and always had.

"You're flying like a spaceship, baby girl!" Jason cooed and laughed.

"Don't crash me!" Heather warned.

"Don't worry. My formula is perfectly safe. We proved it with real astronauts!"

"But they had trouble with the landing," Heather said, frowning and shooting her father a worried look.

"They did," Jason admitted, not allowing his own inner turmoil to show, but instead managing a reassuring smile. "But they trained for it and practiced a lot, like you do for your music and dance, and they were ready. The crew are home safe and so is the ship."

"Yay!" Heather shouted as Jason twirled her through the air again, making rocket engine noises.

Alice shot Laura an apologetic look as Jason carried Heather up the stairs.

"Don't worry about it, hon," Laura told the nanny. "We couldn't have done any better tonight. She's just like her father in that." Her words were punctuated by a scream of laughter from the hallway upstairs.

Alice relaxed, taking a breath. "Is he okay? He looks a mess."

Laura smiled. "Complications, which will be sorted out as more data comes in. He's obsessing, of course, but we know very little. She'll cheer him right up, thank God. Why don't you take the rest of the night and do whatever you need — homework, reading. We've got it from here." She patted Alice's shoulder then started up the stairs.

A MONTH LATER, the report on the conclusions of NASA's investigation was released, but details were withheld from the public. According to the official report, the Rapid Reaction Control System, which was responsible for unspinning the ship, had experienced a power glitch, causing the thrusters to misfire. The spacecraft returned to Earth with the original calculations intact in its memory banks. No mention was made of sabotage. Privately, whatever had caused the RRCS failure remained a mystery and there were so many questions unanswered. Jason had a pounding in his ears and his throat was so dry it hurt. They had to prevent this from happening again. Shortcut could not be the next NASA disaster.

Over the next few weeks Jason hardly came home and then just to sleep, and what sleep he got was restless. His mind never shut down, constantly calculating, aflutter. He poured himself into his work, both to investigate what might have damaged the RRCS or caused it to fail, and to find a way to bolster the craft to prevent such failures in the future.

"There has to be an explanation, something we can counter, build in backups, more fail safes, a defense," he said to Laura time and again.

For Jason, the revelation that something could so easily disrupt the spacecraft's avionics and effectively derail his moment of triumph had him both enraged and scared. He spent day after day working with NASA lab techs to try and determine exactly what had happened with the avionics and how they might possibly prevent it in the future, but they had made little progress, and until they diagnosed the issue, Jason felt certain it could and would happen again. He had to find a way around it. A week later, he went to the lab to check their progress, joining his lab manager, Dr. Paula Kim in walking through and talking to the various teams working on the problem. The lab looked like the *Maxx-One* had exploded in the most organized way possible: parts were being organized, sorted, and labeled in specialized holders, as the techs who built the spaceship slowly and meticulously disassembled and inspected each of them. The engineers who'd helped design *Maxx-One* worriedly scuttled back and forth, checking in with the techs throughout the lab, each wondering if their subsystem had caused the system glitch.

"Everything is shipshape," Kim reported. Barely five feet two, Kim was a Korean American in her late forties who'd risen through the STEM ranks the hard way, finally landing at NASA. She was a respected scientist, but less so for her interpersonal skills. She demanded as much from those around her as she did from herself, and not everyone appreciated it. Jason found her abrasive and bossy, and though Cline believed she was the best at what she did, he'd had his doubts. And making matters worse, Kim insisted everyone, except a few superiors, refer to her by her last name and title, creating a feeling of coldness and distant superiority with those around her. "Five separate power monitoring systems have confirmed that a power glitch did occur, but we still don't know where it came from. There were three power supplies; how could all of them have failed? We know that one of the three power supplies was damaged during takeoff; the second power supply was hit with a cosmic gamma ray right before the last Shortcut, but the last power supply seems fine and still works perfectly." She pointed to a vacuum chamber where a tech was test firing one of the thrusters.

Jason's eyes scanned the techs working around them, assessing both their attitudes and focus on their work. Everyone had to be giving it their all. Nothing less was acceptable. He grunted, pleased. "Good, good. No other theories or ideas?"

"Nothing of substance," Kim said.

Then a voice rang out, "I had an idea."

Kim groaned as they turned to see a young lab tech with long, disheveled brown hair moving toward them up an aisle. He looked frazzled, like he hadn't slept in days, which to Jason was a sign of the right kind of focused dedication. The kid reminded him of his younger self. His name tag read: Dr. Peter Edtz.

He said, "I designed and assembled the part of the power management circuitry that automatically switches to backup power."

Jason could tell that Peter Edtz took pride in this fact, even as his work was under intense scrutiny. Unlike his boss, Edtz was a tall, thin, European American and equally intense, but whereas Kim was abrasive, Edtz was warm and engaging—his passion obvious and dedication reflected in his work ethic. Jason had been impressed every time he encountered him.

"When the first power supply failed, my system worked flawlessly to transition power to the second supply," Peter continued, "But I think my system was hit by something at the same time the second power supply was hit. Look at this capacitor." He pointed to a component smaller than half a grain of rice. "When it was hit, it discharged and offset my timing circuit. I don't know the exact moment when that happened, but if it occurred exactly when the cosmic ray hit the second power supply, it would have taken a few seconds for the third power supply to come online. When the RRCS loses power like that, it shuts down and would be totally unresponsive until it reboots."

"Several observatories noted a solar flare in the area at the very time the incident occurred," Kim inserted quickly. "It could have hit both the second power supply and your timing capacitor."

"I don't think so," Peter countered. "I've examined the damage closely and I'm not sure it could occur naturally."

"What do you mean?" Jason asked, ignoring Kim and looking at Peter.

"I designed my circuit to resist the effects of radiation. I think it was hit by something stronger than a cosmic ray," Peter said.

"Peter, we've talked about this," Kim chided, her lips pursing as she crossed her arms over her chest and turned back to Jason. "He's the sole hold out." She made it sound like he was a rebel, someone out of line, but Jason never would have come up with Shortcut if he'd stuck to standard approaches. Outside the box thinking formed the basis of his whole career and success.

"Something pierced the spacecraft and caused the damage, I am convinced of it," Peter insisted as he stood tall and stepped around where he could look them both in the eye again. "And I don't think it was random cosmic radiation or a solar flare. What kind of freak natural event causes two cosmic rays to hit the precise components that would disable the RRCS?"

"There's an explanation, and we'll find it," Kim said but her eyes were dismissive.

Jason ignored her and looked at Peter. "Are you saying it was sabotage?"

"Of course not," Kim said immediately, shaking her head. "We have no reason to believe this was deliberately engineered."

Peter shrugged. "Yeah, that seems unlikely, but it's not impossible. Though we have no proof. I'm just saying that in all the cosmic event issues we've had, none of the results looked like this and it makes me wonder. In previous incidents of damage, the radiation was random. But this feels targeted. So it got me wondering. And if it was deliberate, we have no ability to create built-in protections to prevent further incidents in the future, especially not knowing the source. Sending astronauts out without that certainty leaves us exactly where we are now, and I'm not prepared to suggest it's worth the risk."

Jason noted a glint in his eye that betrayed the tech's confidence in his conclusions and stiffened at Kim's dismissive eye roll and cold glare at her subordinate. Peter was right, it was not debatable. But Kim was also right. They still needed more data.

"That's just wild conjecture, and we cannot proceed on such outlandish assumptions," Kim scolded. "The safety of our personnel has always been top priority, but everything NASA does has always had an unavoidable element of risk. But we are doing all we can to safeguard the issue. We feel confident additional protocols and revisions to the backup systems and sensors are the best course—"

"Well, lives are at stake here," Jason snapped, then took a deep breath, needing to control his emotions and stay professional. "We have to consider every possibility carefully—ideally, identify the exact cause—if we hope to prevent another incident."

"I know that, Dr. Maxx! That's all I think about, but we could go years and never fully understand what happened. And we won't get there assuming things with no evidence to back them up."

"We have a responsibility to at least spend long enough to be reasonably sure we've considered every possibility and fully investigated. We have to know what caused this."

"I know that. I care just as much about our people as you do," Kim insisted.

Peter led them back down the aisle toward his workstation. He stopped at his LED screen and pulled up some spreadsheets with his mouse. Jason read over the calculations even as Peter described them, his throat constricting. Then the lab tech showed him the images and circuit diagrams. He was right. The damage didn't look like random nature at all. They were too precise. Jason's stomach hardened as adrenaline rushed through his veins, his mind racing again through so many scenarios. He bit back a scream of frustration.

"Nothing like this has ever happened before. We're increasing security monitoring through the flight systems as well as physical security around all aspects of the modules and assembly," Kim said, her tone flat and unemotional. "We have years of experience with problems like this."

She sounded like every boss who'd ever tried to stand in Jason's way throughout his career. His lips tightened but he took a deep breath, fighting off the rising irritation he felt. "Well, that didn't save the *Columbia* or *Challenger*, did it?"

Kim stiffened, cringing. "That's not fair. We will always do everything we reasonably can—" Her voice rose in pitch as her face tightened in frustration.

Jason stiffened at her continued resistance. She of all people knew how much it mattered; every little detail. Was she really willing to take the risk? Jason wasn't, and he found his voice rising with the tension inside as he replied, "I will not have the deaths of astronauts on my head, Doctor. Not knowing we didn't explore every possibility, even the outside chance of sabotage. Anything less is unacceptable!"

He felt his fists clench involuntarily at his side and forced himself to relax, hoping no one had noticed. For him, the human factor was the one uncertainty he found hard to live with; the one element that disturbed his focus and fired up his emotions.

Kim opened her mouth to protest again but Jason cut her off. "I run this project, Dr. Kim. My name's on it. Not yours. And it has to be right. Every last detail."

"I know that." Kim had worked for NASA for two decades. She was more than aware of the costs of even small mistakes, let alone risky decisions. It had been President Reagan's insistence that the country needed another launch that rushed NASA to the choices which led to the *Challenger* disaster, after all. The whole culture of NASA had been haunted and informed by those mistakes ever since. "There are procedures in place—"

"The same procedures that still let astronauts die in the past, I know!" Jason's lip curled as he glared. He knew he wasn't being fair really. Kim wasn't some cold robot. Everyone at NASA had more experience with the cost of lives expended for science than Jason did, and the history of that echoed through the halls of Johnson Space Center daily, informing everything they did. Still, she sounded so cold, uncaring, and it irritated him.

"We have protocols to follow, put in place for a reason," Kim objected weakly, and even Edtz shook his head, looking ready to take her side.

"And I'm sure that's a real comfort to astronaut families when their loved ones have just blown up on a rocket, too!" Jason said.

"We've made a lot of changes since then," Peter added finally. "We all worry every day about it happening again."

"Tell that to Christa McAuliffe's widower!"

They all recoiled like he'd struck them. And in that moment, Jason realized he'd gone too far, but he'd had an incident in his lab a decade before that almost cost him everything when a visitor was injured, and her cold, matter-of-fact attitude about the risk to lives set him on edge. He swallowed and continued more calmly, "No chance is an acceptable risk. We have to get this right. In every area we can build a safeguard, we must do so. Every possibility will be investigated until we are sure we know the truth." Jason leaned toward them and they winced and backed off, as if afraid of physical attack. Jason noticed others around them had gone silent, staring at the drama unfolding in their midst.

Jason forced his body to relax, trying to project a calmer posture and appearance as he went on. "Whatever it takes, Dr. Kim. This is about the future of NASA and everything we've all dedicated our lives to. We're all on the same side, aren't we? What is the disagreement here?"

It was Kim's turn to glare. She stiffened, her shoulders rising, her forehead creased. "I know my job *for NASA*, Dr. Maxx. Believe me." Her eyes told him she meant she knew who she worked for and it wasn't him.

"Then do it. Lives might be at stake," Jason said, his voice calm and unemotional, but as he looked around him at the faces of the other techs, Jason knew he'd get no support there. He'd gone too far. He relaxed and took a deep breath, then motioned toward Peter. "Use everyone's ideas and keep searching 'til we find the cause. We'll bring in more people if we have to." For a brief moment, Jason considered an apology but they'd moved past it now. All that mattered was the mission. They'd get over it. They had to. Too much was at stake.

Jason turned and hurried off to run his own analysis, leaving them staring after him, the room still rife with anger and frustration not just his own.

CHAPTER 3

A S SHE FINISHED teaching a class to the latest astronaut trainees, Laura's mind went to her husband. Jason's gifts had set him apart from an early age. And with that had come challenges, especially when it came to relationships with others. His mind worked at such a frantic pace that others struggled to keep up, and, when forced to work with them, young Jason had blamed them for holding him back. In addition, Jason was prone to a kind of intense, tunnel-vision focus on whatever particular problem or issue he was endeavoring to solve at any moment. Nothing else was important that fell outside the scope of the immediate problem. This, of course, caused no end of consternation and resentment coming back at him from classmates, instructors, and peers, whenever this attitude showed itself. Who did Jason Maxx think he was, acting so entitled, so much better than everyone else? Who was he to scold or judge them? Who was he to push them? Because he evidenced little of the social skills good leadership demanded, his self-appointed role as their leader left him frequently isolated and lonely. But Laura had found it fascinating and admirable, given to her own bouts of intense focus. And instead of letting it drive her away, she'd embraced it and worked hard to find a way through, staying alongside him, despite his moods, and providing support and whatever assistance she could. That had been the beginning of their love affair and bond. For Laura understood and appreciated Jason on a level no one before ever had or at least had ever tried to.

Eventually Jason had learned to live with the loneliness and isolation from peers. After all, he had Laura and he had a few friends. Why did he need anyone else? But for those who loved him like Laura and his parents, it could be excruciating to watch. Jason had come to know this but still found it a struggle to restrain his demanding nature. He demanded no more of others than he demanded of himself, after all. How was that unfair? Dr. Kim was just the latest example. While she did her best to push things forward, the pace at which she and the others at NASA moved became more and more frustrating to Jason, so he pushed harder. And a pushy outsider was the last thing they wanted or respected.

Laura tried to keep an eye on his moods and stress to know when he might be reaching the point where he needed to pull back. But Jason had always been so intense, still, as she walked to her car in the parking lot, the call from NASA Director of Operations Phil Cline took her by surprise. They'd both started at NASA the same year and worked their way up.

She smiled, trying to imagine why he'd be calling as she heard the auto unblock click once she drew closer to the Lexus. "Phil, how are you?"

"We've had an incident, Laura," he said, his voice stilted. Built like the former UCLA linebacker he was, Phil Cline towered over most people and had the booming voice to match, but his staff all knew him for the teddy bear he really was, a man who preferred managing through encouragement and support than demands and fear. She'd rarely heard him stressed or upset like he was now, and it threw her.

"Jason? Has something happened?" Laura's hand tightened on the phone as she caught her breath, imagining the worst.

"Jason's fine, but he's got some of our staff in a bit of an uproar," Phil said.

Laura relaxed a little, slipping behind the wheel of her Lexus and sipping from the insulated mug she carried in her left hand. "What happened?"

"One of the techs brought up issues with avionics damage that might suggest sabotage, even though there is no evidence to make such a leap. The lab director and Jason got into an argument about safeguards and acceptable risk, then Jason dressed her down in front of her entire staff. He implied she didn't care enough about keeping astronauts safe."

"You know how Jason is about details," Laura said. "And he's been getting so little rest."

"But our people always care about the astronauts, Laura. You know how *Challenger* and *Columbia* affected everything they do. And they don't work for him. He has to understand that."

"I know, and he does, really, but this is a huge setback. And Jason views himself as ultimately responsible for any problems or failures in the project, so he's very worried." She took another sip of Brazilian brew.

"Of course. The lab director hasn't slept much either. But that doesn't excuse Jason from screaming at her in front of her staff. Or making unfounded accusations, even implying them."

"I'm sorry," Laura said, knowing how Jason got at times

like this. Still, NASA never tolerated contractors screaming at employees. The work was intense but etiquette demanded respect at all times.

"We've had complaints all week, but this was too far. We've sent him home, Laura," Phil continued. "I'm sending him an email. He needs to take a couple days at least while things calm down."

Laura sighed. Sending him home was clearly the right thing, but Jason would be furious. And keeping him away would take more than just an order. If anything, the interference could escalate his determination. There had to be a better way. "Phil, so much rests on this for him. He'll always want to know for sure what caused a problem like this. His work is his passion. And he's very emotionally invested."

"We share his concerns, Laura, you know that, but he has to control his temper and be professional," Phil said.

"I'm sure he'll apologize once he calms down," Laura said. "He appreciates what your people do, their invaluable contributions to making his dream a reality." She set her mug aside, looking at the clock on the dash and wondering if Jason would come straight home or drive around awhile. She'd call him as soon as they hung up.

"To be honest, Dr. Kim and several of her team asked to be taken off the project," Phil said. "We can't do that this far in, of course. It creates all sorts of complications. I've got to spend some time calming things down and trying to find a way for Jason to continue working with them."

Laura twisted her hair with a finger as she took a deep breath and leaned back in her seat. "I'll talk to him. Do my best to keep him home. But keep me updated."

"Of course," Phil replied. "You know I regret this as much as anyone."

"I know. Thanks, Phil." Laura sighed as he hung up.

When Jason got this intense, she'd sometimes made him sleep at the office to avoid subjecting their daughter to his moods. Honestly, his success at NASA the past few years had amazed her. He'd come a long way as a leader working with a team. This was a major setback. She wondered if her husband had realized yet how much. She plugged the phone into its charger and brushed back her hair. Something had to change, but she had no idea where to begin. Then a business card lying on a stack in the dash cubby caught her eye. Bearing the seal of the California Institute of Technology, it reminded her of the letter addressed to Jason she'd read two years before. She remembered every word. It took her all of two minutes to decide to pick up the phone and make the call. She and Jason had always agreed not to interfere in each other's professional lives, but it seemed to her a change was just what they needed, and this change could be the perfect solution.

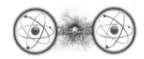

JASON WAS IN his Porsche 550 driving home when he got the call from his old friend Jack Matthews in Astrophysics at Caltech, who was also on the board of advisors for Shortcut. Two years before, they'd offered him the opportunity of a lifetime: his own lab, fully funded, fully staffed, autonomy in the great environment of Pasadena and Caltech. But he'd chosen to go to Houston and NASA instead. Of course, Laura's work as an astronaut had played a big factor in that. Now, she was no longer tied down. After a bit of chitchat,

Jack launched into the pitch again. He and Li Chin were Co-Chairs of a project with full outside funding, and they had enough to bring Jason on board and fund his work as well. They'd set aside the funding. They still wanted him. Would he reconsider their offer?

"It's been two years," Jason said. "Why now?"

"Well, we hear you've encountered some unexpected difficulties and could probably use another place to test out ideas, troubleshoot, make improvements," Jack said. "Caltech wants to be that place. It's the perfect opportunity for us, and we already work with NASA. We want to be a part of your success just as much today as we did two years ago. And it occurs to me that such a change might be just what you need to get a fresh perspective."

"Fresh perspective?" Jason frowned. The words sounded all too familiar and he grimaced. "Have you been talking to Laura or someone at NASA?"

"It's a small industry. Word spreads. We know there were complications," Jack said. "We want to help."

Jason almost believed him but a suspicion lingered in the back of this mind. Why now after two years? Surely, someone had put the idea in his head.

"You'd be a perfect addition," Jack said. "You can teach or not teach, but you can do your work. It's good for Caltech. It's good for you."

Did it really matter where the idea came from? Jason could do a lot with very little with the setup Caltech was offering. It had been really hard for Jason to turn down the first time let alone now. Teaching wasn't his main passion, but he'd been told he was gifted at it, and he enjoyed the stimulation of interacting with young minds and new ideas.

Besides, his team at NASA wasn't exactly fond of him, not that it mattered. He had to carry the mission through regardless. They needed him. But then Heather would love it, and Laura had often hinted she'd like a change.

No, he decided, now was not the time for Caltech.

"Look, Jason, I don't need your answer right now," Jack said. "Take a couple days. Think it over. If you want, I can call Phil Cline and run the idea by NASA as well. We don't want to cause more problems. We want to help with solutions."

"Yeah, yeah, I know, Jack," Jason said, and he meant it.

"Just think it over, okay?"

"Yeah, okay. I'll run it by Laura and Heather and talk it through, sure. It's an incredible opportunity." Despite his doubts, Jason's mind flooded with thoughts of possibilities, something other than his frustration with the potential sabotage or Kim and her stubbornness about NASA protocols. God, what he could do with his own lab! He felt butterflies in his stomach and his heart raced just thinking about it, as he found himself smiling for the first time that day. Damn it. He wasn't in the mood to smile. Suddenly, he realized he was coming up on the entrance to his subdivision. He didn't even remember how he'd gotten there, but he slowed down, anticipating the turn.

"Great," Jack said. "We're really excited to talk with you again. John sends his best." Dr. John Li, another old friend. "If you need to take a look at the facilities, we'll fly you all out here. Let us know."

"Absolutely. Thanks, Jack. I'll be in touch." Jason hung up the phone, his mind a whirl with a new and wondrous set of possibilities that hadn't entered his mind in two years. Then frustration hit him again. He couldn't let Kim or anyone else drive him away. Showing that weakness meant surrendering any leadership he had of the project. Sure, he didn't like her. He wasn't close to her team. They'd never trusted each other the way he'd hoped. It was the story of his life really: Jason being forced to lead, though he'd never really desired or felt the need of others, when his ideas became others' mission. Jason had always worked better with a handful of handpicked people in the past. Hand picking his own team, his own lab—it would be amazing! But it was impossible. Not now. He shook his head as he turned the corner into their subdivision, then debated whether to even go home or drive around a while longer. Heather and Laura would be expecting the usual engaging family chat at dinner and he wasn't in the mood. But they knew how much he loved them, and would surely understand if he had little patience for chitchat right now. Then it hit him. He needed to run this by Laura as soon as possible before he even seriously considered it.

Finally, he groaned, took a deep breath, and turned the car onto their street, headed for the house.

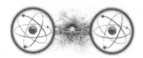

TO LAURA'S GREAT surprise, Jason arrived home in time for dinner. It was Heather's favorite time of day, a time when she had both her parents' full attention and both Jason and Laura made real effort to not miss it unless they absolutely had to. He started mentioning the Caltech offer but just as they got into it, Heather came running in all excited and they didn't want to discuss it in front of her until they'd agreed on a course of action. So, they exchanged a look of mutual understanding and headed into the dining room to eat.

As always, Laura sat at the head of the table near the archway leading to the kitchen with Jason on her right and Heather across from him on her left. Laura had made Swedish meatballs and noodles, one of Jason's favorites, and as they ate together. Heather filled them in on her day, asking questions about theirs. She was animated and cheerful and Laura joined right in, but Jason was somewhere else. He moved his food around with his fork, occasionally shoving some in his mouth like an obligation, with no joy in it. The couple of times Heather pushed him for responses, she got grunts or one-word answers, not even eye contact. She tried and tried, and though Jason would look up and nod or smile, he was clearly miles away. By the end of the meal, their daughter excused herself and sulked off to her room, and Laura had had enough.

"You know, I get that you had a bad day, babe, but it's not her fault," she said as Heather's door clicked shut down the hall. Jason continued staring into his noodles. "Jason!"

"What?" he looked up at her for the first time since they'd sat down.

"I made your favorite food and you're barely touching it, with no joy whatsoever. You ruined Heather's nightly ritual by tuning her out 'til she ran out of here thinking she'd done something wrong—"

"I'm sorry," Jason said and sighed, leaning back in his chair with a sad look. Jason would never do anything to hurt or let down his family, and they both knew that.

"What is it? The Caltech thing seems like good news," Laura said.

Jason sighed. "Yeah. Rough day at the office."

Laura nodded with understanding. "You wanna talk

about what happened in the lab today?"

Jason's brow furrowed. "You know?"

She nodded. "Phil Cline called, concerned."

"Phil told on me to my wife?" Jason snapped.

Laura shook her head. "He was concerned. You're an outsider with a limited understanding of NASA culture. He thought I might help you sort through the complexities."

Jason shook his head. "What complexities? There are still vulnerabilities we need to close up. Additional safeguards to apply. I got some pushback on looking at it from a new angle. It's handled." He bit back another sharp remark about Phil calling his wife to report on him. Phil and Laura were old friends and Phil was a people person manager. He liked to counsel, recruit opinions, and solve things as a team. It was his way.

"Handled, huh?" Laura said, shaking her head as Jason went back to toying with his food. She couldn't decide if he was wrestling with his emotions or running through formulas and calculations in problem solving mode. Either way he seemed to be somewhere else, but she tried again, "He said you lost it in the lab. Yelled at Paula Kim."

Jason scoffed. "We had a disagreement. A moment of passion. It's not like people don't raise their voices at NASA. Come on."

"In front of staff, questioning her abilities—"

Jason tossed his fork on his plate with a clang. "It's my project. A tech brought a legitimate problem and she was going to ignore it. Would you want that risk taken if you were a crewmember?"

"No," Laura agreed. "But to accuse her of not caring

about astronaut lives? Jason, that is too far!"

"I know that. I was upset."

"You've hardly slept since the landing. Worrying, anxious, paranoid. And now you lost it. You are exhausted."

Jason shook his head and wet his lips with his tongue. "No. We have to keep working. The mission goes on." He crossed his arms over his chest and leaned back in his chair but wouldn't meet her eyes.

"Well, it may be your project, but you have a team, and they are all experts at their jobs, so let them do them. You need to get some rest," Laura said.

Jason sat up straight again, his jaw set and dropped his arms. "I need to be there helping. I'll apologize to Dr. Kim tomorrow. It'll be okay."

"You do need to apologize," Laura agreed.

Jason took a deep breath and nodded. "I will. Heated moments happen in labs. She knows that." He pursed his lips as his eyes met hers.

She sighed. "You've been there, Jason. You have to show them you respect their work and abilities."

Jason looked away but that was acknowledgement enough.

"And you can start with your daughter. She didn't deserve your attitude tonight, so apologize. Plenty of time for making that up to her while you're home for a couple days," Laura said, locking eyes with him until his shoulders sank and he looked down at the table, nodding in agreement. Then she stood and began gathering the dishes.

"So Jack actually made you an offer to come to Caltech?" Laura said as she disappeared into the kitchen. "You know our agreement," she added sweetly moments later as she came back for more dishes and stacked them on her arm.

"It came out of nowhere," he called after her.

"So? It's incredible," she said with genuine enthusiasm as she returned for another load. "I'm amazed they still have the funding."

"Apparently they've been saving it."

"Ha! Told ya they really want you," she said.

"But why now? It's been two years," Jason groused.

"Sounds to me like it could be just what we need, babe," Laura said. "When you get like this, it's time to regroup. You can do your part just as easily from Caltech and commute when needed."

Jason shot her a look of suspicion, eyes probing. "Heather has friends, her school, your parents are here—"

Laura didn't respond as she carried another load into the kitchen.

Jason stood and grabbed a load of dishes, then carried them into the kitchen and set them on the counter. "You called them, right?"

She looked over from stacking the dishes in the sink as he leaned against the frame of the archway and smiled at his childlike look. It was cute and innocent, almost like the much younger, more naïve boy she'd fallen in love with. But she knew better than to admit it outright. It would come out eventually, down the road. For now, he was not ready, so she fudged. "I know how you hate me interfering." She focused on rinsing the dishes and loading them into the waiting dishwasher.

"Laura—"

"Just talk to them," she said as she began running water in the sink and reached for the soap. "They are working on key aspects for Shortcut too. Think of all the possibilities of two labs troubleshooting, double testing, coordinating."

"I'm needed here," Jason said.

Laura gave him a look that said it all.

"Okay, okay," he said, raising his hands in surrender as he took up position next to her and grabbed a dish towel.

She chuckled as she rinsed dishes then tipped her head toward the hall. "Your daughter needs you."

"Yes, dear," he said in the exaggerated tone husbands often use when they've been given an order and pretend to protest. He bowed submissively and set the towel back on the counter.

She grabbed the dish towel and swatted at him as he moved past her and headed for Heather's room. In a few minutes, laughter echoed down the hall from both Heather and her father.

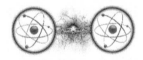

THE NEXT MORNING, Jason got an email from Phil Cline asking him to take a few days working from home while things quieted down. Jason honored both Laura's insistence and Phil Cline's order and stayed home, busily working in his den. He also lavished love and attention on Heather, who always craved it from her father. Although she tested genius like Jason, her aptitudes lay outside the sciences and mathematics along with her interests, so Jason had begun early on making math a game and Laura did the same with science. As a consequence, Heather had started school far advanced from her fellow students and had the teachers struggling to keep her focused. So Jason still helped her at home to keep her on task with the "simple, boring homework" while also continuing to advance her knowledge and abilities.

They were deep into college level calculus when the doorbell rang. Laura was out buying groceries, so Jason pulled himself away and went to answer. Phil Cline towered over him on the porch. "Hi, Jason."

Jason stepped back, shooting him a quizzical look. "Did I miss a call? Forget a meeting?"

Phil laughed. "No, relax. I just needed to talk with you and thought I'd save you the trip. I had an off-siter today myself."

"Oh," Jason nodded. Phil smiled but stood there waiting, and Jason suddenly realized he hadn't asked him in. Stepping aside, he made a sweep of his arm. "Come on in."

"Thanks," Phil said as he stepped into the foyer and Jason closed the door. Behind him, he heard the whisper of Heather's favorite bunny slippers on the tile as she came to see who'd arrived.

"Uncle Phil!" Heather sang as she ran to embrace the former linebacker.

"Hey, sweet princess," Phil said with a grin as he hugged her back. "What are you up to?"

"Calculus II," she said, looking to Jason, who nodded, "and we're learning about how to do modeling with differentials and infinite series! Those go on forever and ever and ever and ever..."

"God, the things kids do for fun around here," Phil teased, but his face showed a mixture of surprise and realization that he shouldn't be.

"Math, blech," Heather said, sticking out her tongue and making a face to play along.

"Daddy makes it fun," Jason said, tousling her hair.

"Yeah, but now we get to play with Uncle Phil," Heather said and grabbed Phil's hand, leading him toward the family room on the left.

"Actually, Uncle Phil needs to talk with Daddy," Phil said, sounding truly apologetic.

Heather stopped, releasing his hand and turned to put her hands on her hips as she shot him a scolding look that looked all too much like her mother. "You know, someone could come to see me sometime."

Phil laughed and pushed his palms together begging forgiveness. "You're right, princess. It has been too long. I promise not to keep making that mistake."

Heather pouted a moment longer, working him over with her guilty eyes, then sighed and smiled. "Forgiven. *This time.* But only if you come talk to me after you finish with Daddy."

"Promise," Phil said, raising his hand, fingers crossed.

"Good," Heather said, grinning again as she bounced off toward the study room.

Jason followed Phil into the family room as the NASA administrator chuckled. "What's up?" Jason asked.

"I got a call from Jack Matthews and John Li," Phil said as he settled on a loveseat, Jason taking the lounger across from him. Phil sunk into the luscious leather and groaned with pleasure. "We should have meetings on furniture like this at the office."

Jason laughed. "Maybe the Pentagon can get you gold toilet seats, too."

"Yeah, right, let's not tempt fate, huh?" Phil said, remembering what had become the all-time joke of government spending excess in the '80s. Oversight was much tighter now. No leather couches for him.

"So they told you?" Jason said, going back to the conversation at hand. He did his best to hide his frustration. He had wanted to be the one to talk to NASA first and thought he'd made that clear to Jack.

"Just a little," Phil said. "Putting out feelers. Making sure they won't piss anyone off."

Except me, Jason thought but kept it to himself. "Well, some people may be happy to see me go," Jason joked, then turned sincere. "I need to go apologize. Show them I didn't mean it how it came across." He locked eyes with Phil, hoping the regret and shame he felt would be clear.

Phil waved a hand dismissively. "Our people are the best. They do what's assigned, ego be damned, I make sure of it."

Jason shot him a skeptical look.

"I've already talked with them," Phil said. "There's stuff you and Paula can both work on. That's not the issue."

Jason hadn't expected that. He looked down, his lips suddenly dry, and wet them with his tongue as he asked, "What is then?"

"Are you happy, Jason?"

Jason stiffened, sitting up again and locking eyes with Phil. The administrator looked totally sincere, his eyes soft and genuine interest on his face. "Happy? What do you mean?"

"You know, happy at work, feeling good, satisfied?" Phil said. "Some people actually expect that of their work life, you know?" He chuckled.

Jason sighed. "Yeah, well, the first launch kinda failed, so I'm not gonna say I'm ecstatic here."

"Upsetting, of course," Phil said. "I mean before that. With the lab, coworkers, etc." He continued leaning forward to watch Jason intently.

"I hadn't thought about it," Jason said. "It's not a factor I give great weight to. I have a mission. That's what matters. I have a great family."

Phil nodded. "Hyperfocus. You do that, I know. But I want you to think about it before you give Caltech an answer."

Jason's stomach fluttered, and he felt a headache coming on. "What does that matter, Phil? We have work to do. We have to try again and soon."

"Of course," Phil agreed, "but that's going to take a bit of time and testing a redesign. Do you really have to be here for that?"

Jason frowned, crossing his arms over his chest. He had to admit he felt a bit like he was being pushed out the door, and it hurt. "So you want me to leave, then?"

Phil shook his head adamantly. "No. Not what I'm saying. I want you to be happy with your work because it will make it better. And I think just maybe a change of scenery might help."

Jason shook his head, leaning back. He didn't like to be pushed. It made him want to push back. "This is where NASA is. I need to be here."

"Jason," Phil said, smiling, "a state of the art lab, your own people, the chance to double check, experiment, and commute back here as needed, all while setting up a place that can carry you well beyond Shortcut to whatever the next project may be."

"The next project?" Jason said. He had no next project. Shortcut was his whole life. "Shortcut is my project, Phil. I'm the leader."

"You still will be, I promise," Phil said, his eyes not wavering. He meant it. "And there will be plenty of conference calls, Zoom, even in person meetings going forward. But I want you to take the family, go to Pasadena, and see what they've got. See if it might not be just the opportunity to shake things up, try new stuff, and find the best solution, so we can get this mother off the ground and keep her there."

Jason sighed. "But what about—"

"You can check in with daily reports, calls if required," Phil said. "I will make sure they stay on track as instructed. Just go take a look."

"Laura's family is here—"

Phil laughed. "For God's sake, Jason, we all love you! We all want what's best for you. Stop the worrying and just take a look." He smiled and locked eyes with Jason. They sat in silence for a moment, measuring each other.

Jason let out a heavy sigh and relaxed again. "Do I have a choice?"

Phil laughed. "Not really."

Jason grunted, almost smiling.

"But only because you always need a push when it comes

to big changes," Phil said. "You hate it, you're right back here. I promise."

Jason grinned. "Because linebacker or no, I can still outrun you."

Phil raised his hands in surrender. "I remember. God, I think my cardiologist would put me behind bars if I tried that again." They'd had an impromptu race at a NASA picnic a few years before when Phil was recovering from a heart attack. In part, Jason had egged it on because watching Phil act like an old man, slowing his own recovery because of fear, had worried him and he knew his friend needed a push. He'd also done it because they were both naturally competitive and he got a kick out of the reactions of their fellow staff. Phil had kept up with him half way, then given up, clutching his chest. Laura and Phil's wife, Karen, looked ready to kill Jason when the mathematician stopped and turned back, until Phil started laughing. He was faking, a sympathy play. Admitted he'd never felt better.

"Forget that Doctor, Karen would skin us both," Jason said and the men laughed heartily together.

Phil stood and extended his hand. "I'm behind you, whatever you decide, Jason."

Jason took a deep breath and stood, grasping his old friend's hand in a firm shake. "I'll talk to Laura."

Two days later, the Maxxes were packing for a week in California. Heather and Laura were ecstatic, despite Laura's parents trying to convince them all that taking Heather out of school for a work visit was unwise. She'd be bored. Fall behind in her studies.

"This is our first chance at a family vacation in six years, mother," Laura scolded, brooking no further argument.

Susan Raimey had kept arguing anyway, until Heather interrupted, tugging her arm.

"Alice is coming," Heather said excitedly. "She's taking me to see the ocean, to Disneyland, fun stuff. I've always wanted to, you know?" And then Susan melted under a look Heather had honed to perfection over the years and always employed when she wanted to bend an adult to her will.

Susan sighed. "Okay, baby. There's no arguing anyway when your mother gets like this."

Jason, Laura, and her dad, Roger, had chuckled as they watched Heather drag her grandma off, talking about all the wonderful things she'd be seeing and doing on the trip.

"Jason needs this, Daddy." Laura grabbed her father's arm in that daughterly way and worked her own finely honed magic. Jason always experienced a mix of amusement and annoyance at the way the strong, determined woman he married could so easily switch to the beloved daughter when she wanted to convince her father of something she wanted, but every time it worked like a charm.

"Just don't go doing anything crazy like moving," Roger joked then looked at Jason with an accusatory stare. Roger and Jason kept an easy peace, with Roger even treating Jason a bit like a son as they worked on various projects together around the house and cars on occasion. But when something threatened big changes to his family dynamic, Jason always got deemed the bad guy. Still, Jason admired the freedom Roger Raimey felt to express his emotions. Jason's own father had shown disdain for any show of emotion in his wife or his son, and except for occasional spurts of anger, had rarely shown any himself. Jason had always felt that had handicapped his ability to deal well with others. It certainly had resulted in Jason struggling with how to relate his own emotions when dealing with people.

Laura and Jason exchanged a look. Her parents were big family people and had grown quite attached to having their only daughter and granddaughter nearby. This change would be very hard, especially for her mother, so they'd agreed not to say anything until they knew for sure.

"We're just exploring the possibility on a vacation, Daddy," Laura said, smiling and rubbing his arm as she dragged him off too, leaving Jason alone with the bags and deeply touched by Laura's words. She hadn't said it because of her parents, but he'd seen it in her eyes. Jason had moved for her, supported her career once, she wanted to do the same for him. For the first time, he realized he really had his family behind him on the idea of a cross country move. It really wouldn't bother them. In fact, they were excited about the possibility. He'd been using concern for them as an excuse to resist the idea, deny himself the right to entertain any dreams of his own about it, but now...

He felt a fluttering in his chest as emotions swelled within. "God, I love her," he said aloud just as Laura appeared again in the doorway.

Laura smiled and kissed his cheek as she went back to packing. "You'd better be talking about me."

Jason wrapped his arms around her from behind and leaned in to nuzzle and kiss her neck. "You know you're my girl, babe."

They both laughed as their lips met and they settled into each other. In such moments, Jason always felt he could stay like that forever, but in a moment, Laura gently pulled away and went back to packing.

Her face was filled with love, even as she gently prodded,

"Come on. We have work to do."

CHAPTER 4

L OCATED ON 124 acres in the heart of Pasadena, California, eleven miles northeast of downtown Los Angeles, the California Institute of Technology, better known as Caltech, consists of a cluster of stucco buildings, houses, and modern architecture surrounded by trees and grassy landscapes amidst a residential district that looks straight out of middle America, not part of the mega-suburban sprawl of Los Angeles. In keeping with the surroundings, there's a heavy Spanish Mission influence to the architecture by design, lending the school a natural feel with its surroundings. Tennis courts and athletic facilities lie at the center, with a curving drive winding through as a main artery from the residential areas on all four sides.

Jack Matthews and Li Chin met Jason and Laura outside the rectangular Cahill Center for Astronomy and Astrophysics with its angular abutments highlighting its scattered windows and doors, one of the newest, most modern additions. Jason, Jack, and Li had met as fellow students at MIT in Boston, and the two cohorts had gone on to Caltech, where their first taste of success came with the creation of an intelligent toaster that paid for their first houses in expensive Pasadena. Li had met his future wife, Dr. Purva Diptha, on the project and all three served on the advisory board for Shortcut. Rarely a day went by when two or all of them didn't correspond via email or chat about something. Even so, Jason felt a surge of emotions at being with his old companions again—the giddiness mixed with comfort common to much younger men just starting out with hardly a care in the world. Jack was taller and broader with closely cropped dark hair and a full beard, while Li was shorter but thinner with his dark Asian hair tied in a ponytail behind his head. Purva was East Indian and taller than her husband, with striking beauty and an even more striking intelligence. She greeted them just inside the main entrance as Jack and Li led their old friends inside.

"We're so excited you're here," Purva almost sang as she hugged Laura and kissed her once on each cheek then did the same to Jason. All were smiling ear to ear.

"I was beginning to think we'd never get you out here," Jack teased, winking at Laura as they all looked at Jason.

"Well, a vacation seemed appropriate after the stress of the mission," Jason deadpanned, and they all chuckled.

"Vacation, right. What's that?" Li teased.

"He didn't know either," Laura said as they all laughed. "I had to show him on dictionary dot com."

"The internet is notoriously filled with errors and conjecture," Jason replied. "I'm not sure I can believe it."

Jack slapped Jason on the back. "Well, we won't argue with you as long as you do your vacationing here."

"Exactly," Li agreed.

"Come upstairs," Purva urged. "We just began a remodel. I can't wait to show you what we have for you." She pushed open a set of double doors and turned right, then made a U onto a stairwell, leading them upwards at a steady pace.

"You know, I thought this was a working institution, but it's so quiet," Jason teased.

"Students are attending classes and most professors and researchers are either well buried in their labs or not up yet," Li said. "Weird hours are a hallmark here."

"Ha! I remember that life," Laura said and exchanged a smile with Purva as Jason took it all in. One of the largest on campus, the building was polished and shiny like it was new, not the over a decade old, well-used building it was.

"Whose lab would I be inheriting?" Jason asked as they continued up past the second floor landing to the third.

"Some slouch who won a Nobel, got a big head, and left for private funding with some guy named Musk," Jack said.

"Isn't that a cologne?" Li joked.

"We're just getting started on the remodel, so hopefully you like what we've done," Purva said enthusiastically as Jack opened the double doors at the third landing and led them down a short corridor, then stopped to type a code into an access panel beside a grey door.

"We welcome your input moving forward of course," Li said and ushered them inside as Jack held the door.

The space they entered looked more like a small hangar at NASA than a lab. It was cavernous—that was the best word Jason could devise on the spot—with shiny white walls, bright LED Smart lighting overhead, and various offices, cubes, and lab tables scattered throughout. Jack led them toward the center so they could look around. A motel-like outer walkway wound around the room in a U with access to an upper level of meeting rooms, offices, and more. Jason and Laura exchanged a look of amazement as they took it in and Jason felt a new kind of giddiness born of possibilities he'd only dreamed of. *Oh, the things he could accomplish with facilities like this!* Painters worked on scaffolds and ladders at various spots around the room while electricians continued working on the lighting. The place smelled of fresh paint mixed with dust and cleaning solutions but was basically spotless. Probably as sterile as a medical facility, Jason mused.

Li motioned to the tables and cubes. "All this can be replaced or rearranged to suit your needs and preferences, of course, but we already started the painting and updated the lighting."

"It's both voice and remote controlled," Jack added.

"Well, it will be once they've finished installing," Purva corrected.

"State of the art computers and tech equipment, screens in every office and meeting space, a couple larger going in at each end here with projectors—all networked," Li said.

"You can pick your office, or we can combine spaces and make one where you want it, too," Jack said.

The space was so large Jason imagined doing an actual rocket test along one of the longer axes and shook his head in amazement. "All this for my lab?"

"Shortcut would be a major coup for us to increase the university's involvement," Jack said. "And we know that's just the beginning of what you can do here so we want you to have plenty of space and everything you need."

Laura grinned and elbowed Jason. "I can't believe you turned this down."

The others chortled. "That was a different space. We

upped it a notch when we made the new offer," Jack said quickly.

Jason was at a loss for words. The lab was three or four times the size of Chin's lab just on one level but the upper level just added more, and his imagination was going to work. The facilities could easily accommodate several dozen staff focusing just on Jason's projects. This would be a dream come true. He couldn't believe they'd offered it to him. "You're telling me I don't have to fight off more senior professors to get this?" he commented.

"Purva handled that," Li said. "She can be really scary." He smiled as Purva leaned against him and nodded.

"I had to be to keep Li and Jack on track," she said.

"This is truly amazing," Laura said, almost as excited and animated as Heather always got on their regular family game night or at their family dinners.

Jason grunted. "I can really have what I want?"

"Well, barring an actual spaceship, most likely yes," Jack said as the others looked on with amusement. Jason felt like a kid in a whole new world, and they were enjoying every minute of it.

"What I need most is a space to advance the formula and design engines that can maintain the thrust over longer distances, even indefinitely. The current rocket engines got us to the Moon but wouldn't make it to Mars yet. And what if we want to leave the solar system?" Jason posited.

They all nodded along excitedly.

"We would love to help make that a reality," Jack said.

"Let us help you, Jason," Li said, grinning.

Their enthusiasm was palpable and fed his own. "Well, I

wouldn't want to be locked up as crazy, would I?"

The others laughed.

"Does that mean you accept?" Laura asked, bouncing a little on her feet, clearly anxious for a response.

"Let Jack, Li, and I put our heads together," Jason said.

"Why don't I show you around the area so you can get ideas on housing and schools?" Purva suggested.

Laura smiled. "Great plan."

Purva took Laura's arm. "I can't wait to show you the bungalows I just stumbled onto. Oh, and you'll love the school where Heather will go."

"The hard part will be convincing my parents," Laura said as they turned toward the door.

Purva reached over and gave Jason's arm a squeeze as Laura walked on ahead. "Welcome aboard," she almost sang. Then she and Laura were out and their voices echoed from the corridor as the door swung shut behind them.

"Okay, let's talk design and recruitment," Li said, and the three old schoolmates went right to work.

THEY REUNITED THAT night for dinner at the Diptha-Chin's residence, a huge house with six bedrooms, a library, and two dens so each had an office. It had an exquisite dining room, a smaller kitchen dining area off a full kitchen that blew Laura's mind, two family rooms, a game room, and even a workshop where Li did woodworking and other projects in his "spare time." She laughed when she said the phrase to Jason, and he joined her. It was a foreign concept.

They spent several hours enjoying a luscious meal Purva and Li had had catered in of Mediterranean fruit salad, basted sirloin and chicken, potatoes and corn fresh from the family garden, and a luscious red Argentinian wine, while the scientists told old stories from school, many of which Laura had heard before though they did manage to sneak in a few new ones. Purva added to the fun by telling stories of Jack and Li's adventures which even Jason had not heard. They all laughed a lot, not venturing into any more discussion of business until the end.

As they finished a delicious tiramisu, Jack suggested, "Why don't you enjoy a couple days exploring the area. We have things to arrange. We'll get some samples for Jason to look at of both furniture and lab design elements and work on planning a press conference. Meanwhile, I'm sure we can arrange a visit for Heather to the school, if she'd like, and introduce her to a few faculty and staff kids so she knows she has friends when she arrives."

Laura and Jason both nodded, pleased with the idea.

"You're sure you don't need me?" Jason said, his features darkening with worry for a moment.

"I know you're used to running the show, Dr. Maxx, but trust us, we can handle the basics for you," Purva assured him. "We know the ins and outs of Caltech culture that have to be navigated, the best suppliers, and all that."

Li added, "We'll need you to approve stuff when the time comes. May even find a few potential staffers for you to interview, but we need a couple days, and I'm sure your wife and daughter would enjoy an actual vacation with you and exploring their new home, okay? Check out the bungalow and think about moving. We'll handle the rest."

"And how we're going to break it to my Mom and Dad," Laura said, her own face falling a bit at the thought. Roger and Susan were not going to be happy.

"I don't suppose you guys could handle that, too?" Jason teased.

"We'll handle a lot but not in-laws," Jack said. "I was never good at that." He'd been divorced twice and now had settled into bachelor fatherhood with gusto, enjoying regular shared custody of his three kids with his first ex-wife.

Jason and the others chuckled. "Worth a shot," Jason joked.

"Yeah, I wish," Laura said and snuggled against his shoulder. "You've all been so wonderful. Thank you for taking such good care of us."

"We're just getting started," Purva said and laughed.

THE NEXT MONTH was a whirlwind. They finished their week in Los Angeles by taking Heather to Disneyland then down to the beach to watch the sunset before showing her the bungalow. The next morning, they made arrangements with the realtor, then Jason interviewed a few candidates Caltech recommended before joining his friends at the press conference. Once they returned to Houston, Laura went to work packing and hiring movers and professional packers, while Jason met with Phil and his team at NASA. They agreed he could take five of the eight employees he'd brought on board with him provided three of them waited for replacements to be hired and trained before leaving. The other two would relocate to California as soon as possible to assist Jason and the Caltech crew with setting up the lab per Jason's preferences, hiring staff, and getting things up and running as smoothly and quickly as possible.

Jason also got permission to make an offer to Peter Edtz. The outside the box thinker in Chin's lab was just the kind of employee he wanted for his lab, and he figured he'd give him more appreciation and better opportunities than his present boss would. Laura and Jason determined that waiting to move Heather until the fall break was least disruptive for her, so she and Laura would stay behind while Jason went as soon as he was able. Purva arranged for temporary furniture to get Jason up and going at the bungalow. The rest would follow a few weeks before Laura and Heather did, requiring only two weeks of a rented apartment and disruption to their routine. Altogether, Jason was amazed how smoothly and calmly Laura took charge and managed most of the logistics at home. She even jumped in to help the two staffers with their relocation arrangements as well, and she was excellent at it.

One of the last tasks Jason made a priority at NASA was setting up a meeting with Dr. Kim and her staff so he could apologize. He thought his words came off sincere and convincing and Kim accepted it graciously, but in the end, he left feeling like the damage was done. A permanent barrier had been erected between Jason and part of his team and he knew no matter how long they worked together, he'd always regret that.

Although it was difficult, because Laura spoke with them daily, they waited until the following weekend to tell Laura's parents. Roger and Susan came over for their usual Saturday brunch with Heather. Jason and Laura had instructed Heather, despite many protests, to wait until they'd broached the subject before saying anything. Heather objected because of her excitement at all the new possibilities and friends, but they kept her busy and unavailable to talk with her grandparents by giving her extra time with friends in Houston so she could get used to the idea of saying goodbye and store up lots of good memories for the move.

The time finally came to take the plunge as they gathered around the table with Roger and Susan for the brunch Laura and Susan had prepared. Jason was in his office when they arrived, searching for some notes he'd made about the *Maxx-One* incident and left on his desk. He couldn't find them anywhere.

"Jason!" Laura called sweetly. "Dinner's on."

"Coming!" he called back, feeling a sense of dread. He would be the bad guy for taking not only their daughter but their granddaughter far away from them. Forget the opportunities it would create for Jason's career. He knew the Raimeys would be focused on what they lost, but they'd get over it in time. Finding his notes, he set them on top of his desk, then surrendered and went to join the others.

The Maxx family took their usual spots, while Susan sat next to Heather and Roger took the chair opposite his daughter. As they dug into scrambled eggs, sausage, pancakes, and fruit salad, Heather looked ready to burst. She met eyes with each of her parents then shifted impatiently and asked, "Can we tell them already?"

Susan and Roger chuckled. "Tell us what, dear?" Susan asked.

Laura took a deep breath and exchanged a look with Jason, who nodded his encouragement. *It was never going to be easy,* his eyes assured her, *but I've got your back.*

"Mom and Dad, we've made a very important decision,"

Laura said.

Susan smiled and finished chewing a grape before asking, "About what, dear?"

"We're moving to Pasadena to start a lab at Caltech," Laura said.

The change in her parents was immediate. Both stiffened, and Laura almost thought her mother would drop her utensils as their intense eyes locked on hers.

"What? Where did this come from?" Roger demanded, glaring at Jason.

"Caltech made Jason another offer," Laura said, upbeat and cheerful despite her father's expression.

"Well, kind of the same one," Jason added. "But this time NASA urged us to take it."

"NASA wants you to leave?" Susan looked confused.

Roger frowned, his brow creasing angrily. "What *did you do*?!" he demanded of Jason.

"Daddy, calm down. It was a mutual decision," Laura said. "You know about the trouble with the launch."

"So NASA is ending the program?" Susan said, her face showing shock and uncertainty.

"No, not at all," Jason said and smiled reassuringly. "We need extra hands to solve the problems and advance to the next stage."

"Right, and they are giving Jason the lab of his dreams, the staff and funding he'd always wanted, and coordinating with NASA," Laura said. "Phil Cline loves the idea. He thinks fresh minds will help move things along toward achieving the goals."

Roger cleared his throat, his eyes narrowing as he sat stiffly in his chair. "All of a sudden?"

"We've been considering it for almost a month," Laura said, wincing in anticipation of the explosion.

"What?!" her parents both demanded in unison as expected. Jason had always been amazed how the two teamed up almost as one person when facing adversity. They finished each other's sentences, falling into a coordinated, almost choreographed tag team as they confronted the problem. Jason wished his own parents' relationship had been so idyllic, but his father only rarely showed his mother such affection, at least in front of his son.

"Your trip to California was more than a vacation," Susan said, her tone making it clear she both knew the answer and felt betrayed by the deception. They hadn't lied, just withheld details, but to Susan Raimey they were one and the same. The Raimeys had always wanted to be involved with and know everything about their only daughter's life, and though it had taken getting used to, Jason got along with them well enough, so it had never seemed intrusive. But he had a feeling this would be more challenging. Jason and his father had a challenging relationship, so Roger and Susan were Heather's only ever present grandparents and, by default, Jason's surrogate parents, even if the relationship had its rocky moments.

In truth, he'd never been that close with his own father, and his doting mother had died of cancer when he was just a teen. Neither had been well prepared for the challenges of raising a son so much smarter than themselves. His father had even seemed to regard it as an affront to his own intelligence instead of the compliment Jason thought it should be, and so his natural curiosity and tendency to question everything constantly had come to be seen as a challenge and defiance rather than a natural extension of his gifts. In truth, he'd never known his father well enough to understand what made him tick. The Raimeys, on the other hand, weren't intimidated by his gifts at all. They had their own, as did Laura. Instead, they accepted the relationship and were mostly supportive, except when decisions conflicted with their sense of how they ordered the world, like now.

"In part it was, mother," Laura said.

"We went to Disneyland, checked out my new school, found this awesome bungalow, and did some shopping, City Walk, saw some stars' homes," Heather rattled off quickly and excitedly, her voice as animated as her body. "It was so awesome!"

Susan tried to smile, ever the cheerleader for her only granddaughter, but the hurt stayed in her eyes. "When were you going to tell us?"

"They're doing it now clearly," Roger said. He sat back in his chair and glared again. "I know this was my daughter's idea. Probably your plans are so well along by now that any objection is a moot point, but I don't like it."

Laura sighed. "I'm sorry. I knew it would be hard for you."

"Hard?!" Susan exclaimed. "Our only daughter and grandchild moving across the country away from us after all these years? Oh no, why should that be hard?" She rolled her eyes, crossing her arms over her chest, her shoulders rising in emphasis with the words.

"You accepted that my job involved travel to far places before," Laura said, "And Jason moved here to be with me. He's always been supportive. Now it's our time to be supportive of him."

"But it's so far away," Susan said, her voice rising with her irritation.

"Grandma, you can come visit as much as you want," Heather said happily. "The guest room is *amazing!*"

Susan forced a smile for Heather but turned back to shoot Laura a shaming look moments afterward.

"When do you leave?" Roger asked, his voice softer but no less intense.

"I go as soon as we can arrange it, to get things rolling," Jason said, keeping his own emotions in check for Laura's sake. "Heather and Laura will come after school is out for fall break."

"You're leaving before Christmas?!" Susan made it sound like it was a whole new crisis and injury.

"It's the best time to make the transition for Heather," Laura said, starting to show exasperation at her mother's dramatic reaction.

"It gives you a couple more months together," Jason said. "You can visit Heather as much as you want, take extra time."

"That's supposed to make up for not seeing her for months at a time?" Susan snapped.

"Susan, please," Roger said, irritation showing. She sighed but relaxed a bit, leaning back in her own chair even as her husband rested his elbows on the table and leaned forward.

"It's a dream come true for you, I guess," he said, looking at Jason.

"For both of us," Laura rushed to add and Susan looked wounded all over again.

"It will advance my work greatly and open new avenues through teaching and research," Jason said.

Roger grunted, nodding. "Well, then, I suppose we'll learn to live with it, even if we don't like it." Susan shot her husband a look that said she wasn't at all ready to be so accepting, but Roger ignored her and locked eyes with his daughter, his eyes softer and loving. "You know how proud we are of you all, and how much we love you."

"Of course, Daddy," Laura said.

"It's a big change," Jason agreed. "The decision was hard for me to wrap my mind around as well."

Roger smiled. "Well, we will be coming to California for Christmas and probably several times a year. Plan on it."

Laura and Jason sighed in relief, tension rushing from their bodies as they chuckled. "Of course," they said in unison.

And though Susan took time coming around, Heather immediately launched into regaling them all with tales of her adventures in California with both Alice and her parents and Susan soon fell into the easy banter she always enjoyed with her granddaughter as they went on with the meal.

CHAPTER 5

THE FOLLOWING WEEKS passed like a blur as Jason settled in at Caltech and began setting up and staffing his lab with great enthusiasm. For some positions, he brought in key people from his Shortcut team who had been working as contractors with the NASA team in Houston. Others, like Peter Edtz, he recruited fresh to fill various holes in skills and expertise that would bolster the team and its success. Some came over from the Jet Propulsion Laboratory at the recommendation of Jack and Li, their projects there having ended or being in transitional phases. The goal was to not only diagnose and resolve any potential issues with the RRCS but also to extend the distances capable via Shortcuts and the safety inherent in making longer jumps as well as planning and designing proper spaceships for longer voyages.

As expected, there were regular video conferences and calls with NASA leadership and personnel so that the two teams could not only get to know each other but coordinate their efforts to avoid duplication of effort. In some cases, like the RRCS work, both teams were working on the problem. Neither NASA nor Jason would have it any other way. In others, the work went in different directions, but everyone regularly shared notes and memos back and forth about what they were working on and how it might relate to the other team's projects as well as dialoguing about questions and issues that arose which might be invaluable to both. This was the normal day to day routine for most scientific work, including the coordination of teams at multiple sites. NASA sent a team out to provide secure links between NASA team computers and those of their Caltech counterparts, although access to certain areas was limited to need to know. NASA was, after all, still a government entity. Security clearance rankings applied to almost everything. In most cases, these functioned in name only as staffers with higher clearances used memos and conferences to inform their coworkers of needed information they might not have access to. With none of the work either military related or affecting national security, no one lost sleep over it. They didn't even try to track it. It was just the workaround people like them always used in such circumstances when they could.

Two weeks after settling in Pasadena, Peter Edtz notified Jason of new discoveries in the investigation he was leading on the issues encountered during Shortcut twenty of the *Maxx-One* test mission. Although Peter ran the investigative team, Jason had insisted on receiving all their raw data and regular reports and frequently commented or sent back suggestions or work of his own to add to or expand on theirs. As usual, they met in Jason's large office in the lab at 10 a.m. Located on the first floor of the lab in a corner, its glass window providing a great view of the lab and those at work outside, Jason's office was as precise as the numbers he loved to manipulate. Everything had its place, from filing to books to family pictures. It was clean and well-appointed and a clear reflection of the personality of its owner despite the intense hours he was spending at work. In contrast, the lab tech's hair and clothes were as disheveled as his workspace. It was clear he had spent more time at the lab than at home. His energy and focus revealed a man with great organizational skills and abilities, and one who possessed an endless reserve and didn't require sleep. Jason knew the sensation. Hyperfocus driven by adrenaline came with the territory when projects were in crisis. He appreciated, even admired, his people's genuine dedication. Jason did it because Shortcut was his baby, not to set an example. They did it because they shared his passion for getting it right, and knowing that excited him.

For this meeting, Peter brought with him a memo from NASA that concluded errant cosmic rays had fried the RRCS and other electronics, causing the failure. From the way he read it aloud, Jason could tell Peter found the idea laughable, but he followed along anyway on his own copy, taking it in. It was nice to have a fellow believer working alongside him, when he knew the majority of his cohorts at NASA felt his sabotage theory was too far-fetched.

"It's embarrassing to believe these people actually buy this crap," Peter said with obvious disgust when he'd finished reading the second half-page aloud. He shook his head. "None of that accounts for the specificity of the damage. Two errant cosmic rays exactly coordinated to strike the same location in perfect unison? That would certainly qualify as an act of God. I'd also classify it as a miracle. Let's notify the religious leaders at once!"

"I guess it depends what other electronics were affected and how," Jason commented.

"Oh, I believe cosmic rays could have done damage to the spacecraft's systems," Peter said. "I've seen it before, and in most cases it's the most likely explanation anyway. Especially programming glitches. But to explain the RRCS failure, based on the evidence we have, it makes no sense. I still think an outside force was used to pierce and disrupt the spacecraft."

"Do we need to call Mulder and Scully, Dr. Edtz?" Jason smiled.

"Yeah, I know how it sounds, but then again…while The X-Files seemed like complete bullshit in the nineties, when they did the new seasons, it was far more plausible. So who it was and what they used, I can't say, but that it was deliberate is the only conclusion I can come to from the data I've gone over a hundred times the past two months."

Jason nodded. "Okay, but we need more than your passion to convince NASA and the people funding the project. And that's the problem we have to overcome."

Peter sighed and leaned back in the chair where he sat across the desk from Jason. "Fucking money. It makes the world go round."

"Makes science possible at least," Jason said. There was no argument to be had. They both knew the realities, as frustrating as they might be at times like this.

"Oh, hell," Peter said, shoulders sinking. "I wouldn't believe me either, but I took a close look at both the hole we found in the fuselage and the damage to my power supply unit with a microscope and this…" He tossed several digital image prints on the desk.

Jason picked them up. They showed close ups of holes in *Maxx-One*'s fuselage and systems. These had been found weeks ago by NASA. "How many holes were there?"

"Three, that we've identified," Peter said. "But these are only images of the same two. I am convinced some kind of laser was used."

Jason's throat suddenly felt dry as he locked eyes with the tech and swallowed. "A laser? Not one of ours?"

"Well, it's possible if we have a Kennedy's assassination

magic laser theory, yes, but highly unlikely."

"But what other lasers were out there?" Jason asked, still hoping it was a very long shot. He needed to send the data to Laura for her expertise.

"Satellites have lasers, the ISS," Peter said. "Other spacecraft."

"What other spacecraft?"

"There are several possibilities is all I am saying. Look at the build up here around the hole." Peter leaned forward and pointed to one of the photos, where there was rough build up, like molten metal, around the hole. "Recast. It's a re-solidification of materials after melting that is common with laser damage. It's unevenly distributed, and note the HAZ width there." He pointed to another photo.

"HAZ?"

"The Heat-Affected Zone is the area around the hole that got so hot that it now has a different microstructure than the surrounding material. It's a result of thermal conduction. Kind of a side effect of extreme, centralized heat. Analyzing the properties of the HAZ can give us clues to the laser beam's diameter and power."

"These are common results from laser holes then?" Jason asked, knowing the answer already, his mind racing for explanations that would be easier to sell to NASA suits, but he was starting to buy into what Peter was suggesting. It made a lot of sense. And his fear surprised him—the tightening of his leg muscles, stiffening of his back, as if he were ready to run. The urge to protect himself and jump to worst case conclusions. Sure, he himself had thought of sabotage, even suggested the possibility, but to be staring at the very real possibility... THUMP! His heart pounded so hard he worried it might just explode right there in his office.

"Yes. And I haven't even checked for taper yet," Peter said, interrupting. The distraction was good. Jason's mind went back to what Peter had been saying. Off Jason's puzzled look, the tech added, "Taper is a variation in hole diameter along its depth. Tends to happen more with deeper holes at both the entrance and exit points."

"So you're saying someone deliberately fired a laser into *Maxx-One* to damage the RRCS system's power supply?" Jason said, summing it up.

"It's a strong possibility at least," Peter said. "No one else has come up with a better explanation, one that fits the evidence, unless you want to blame your calculations." He smiled.

Jason nodded, wetting his lips as he noted his stomach suddenly felt heavier, despite the fact he'd hardly eaten in sixteen hours. He had to troubleshoot before he could bring it up to Phil Cline or anyone in Houston. "Selling it to NASA is not going to be easy. I mean, if one of our own lasers somehow misfired…"

"It's too directional and precise," Peter said. "Someone would have had to specifically target the point of entry and move the laser into alignment. It's not something that could happen randomly by total accident."

"So, if a laser was modified before the flight left Earth? Sabotage…"

"Do you have a lot of extra lasers on the spacecraft that you wouldn't notice one was so far out of alignment after nineteen jumps?"

Edtz was onto something. The entire spacecraft was basically a giant integrating sphere with a solar-pumped laser for a shell. The entire surface was covered by laser cells. Of course, the laser could be turned electronically and precisely aimed, but astronauts sabotaging their own craft? It made no sense. Besides, Creed and Wayne were as invested in the mission's outcome as anyone. They'd become astronauts dreaming of being the first men on Mars. He winced, leaning back in his chair and attempting to relax and loosen the tension that had consumed his body as they talked about the holes. Deliberate sabotage seemed so far fetched but Peter was right about the precision targeting. Why? Who? What could they hope to gain? And proving it, that would take a lot more than what they had.

"We should at least mention it," Peter said.

"I can, but they're still going to point to our own lasers as the most likely culprit," Jason said.

Peter shot him a look that said 'idiots will be idiots.' They both knew how administrators thought. The easiest, most simple explanation was always their preference. Complicated explanations scared them.

"We need to have Laura take a look," Jason went on. "No one knows NASA's lasers better."

Peter nodded. "There's just no way someone would mistake cosmic ray damage and laser damage. There's too much research on both. They look totally different."

"That's why they'll blame our lasers for malfunctioning," Jason said.

"And there's always the possibility of spooky action at a distance, remember, though that would be virtually untraceable. I'm not done investigating." Einstein had famously used the phrase "spooky action at a distance" to describe quantum entanglement because it seemed to violate the speed of light. The phenomenon occurs when particles become linked by the strange quantum property of entanglement and become so deeply linked that they basically share the same existence. As a result, no matter how widely separated in space they became from each other, measurement on one would immediately influence the other. Einstein argued that special relativity made this impossible, but it was later proved experimentally by astronomers detecting gravitational waves.

"All right, good," Jason said, taking a deep breath and motioning to the photos. "Can I keep these?"

"Yeah. I sent copies to your email, too, just before I came in," Peter said. "And a written report summarizing what I found."

"Okay. I have a call with Cline in ten minutes," Jason said. "I'll forward them to him."

"He'll just be glad to be rid of me," Peter said, and Jason knew it was true. Cline was a smart guy and a friend, but even the idea of sabotage scared the hell out of him. "Good luck," Edtz added in sing-song as he glided out the door with a grin.

Before calling Cline on the landline in his hospital room, Jason poured himself a strong mug of coffee with extra sugar and sat back, savoring it for a bit as he gathered his thoughts. There had to be more to this than margin of error or even failed calculations. The holes alone were proof of that. And if they found no evidence of programming errors, viruses, or other system changes or malfunctions—which they hadn't so far—what other explanation could there be?

As expected, Phil Cline listened but immediately suggested the spacecraft's lasers. When Jason laid out the extreme scenarios that would have to be involved, Cline said it was "the most logical possibility" and left it at that. That meant "show me more evidence." NASA had to walk a fine line between accountability to the public and government oversight. Going to them with some alien or human outside interference theory would just cause more harm and trouble for the agency, not bring solutions. The response was anticipated, so Jason didn't let it rile him. Still, he wondered what it would take to prove answers his team's investigation might uncover that NASA wouldn't like.

"We'll obviously keep investigating the data, especially as anything new comes up, and we will work on new safeguards and fail safes," Phil said, "but I think it's time to meet with the department heads and get them started on the next phase. For all intents and purposes, except for this one glitch—"

"Glitch? A glitch that almost cost the astronauts their lives and destroyed a very expensive spacecraft," Jason snapped. He knew Phil better than to interpret the remarks as dismissive. He had a job to do and faced constant pressure to continue programs as efficiently was possible. But calling it "a glitch" trivialized it a way Jason found upsetting.

"But it didn't," Phil replied, unphased. "Thanks to you. And that's all anyone will care about. We have to approach this from a logical, well-reasoned place. Not wild theories. It's time to start thinking about where we go from here."

"Okay, call a meeting," Jason replied in a monotone, feeling helpless but controlling his inner turmoil. His first priority would always be keeping crews safe, and he knew it would be Phil's too, but sometimes the corporate agency entity didn't seem to act like it. He leaned forward with his elbows on his knees. "We have to make sure sabotage can't happen, Phil."

"Sabotage of a spacecraft is like a one in a billion risk," Phil said.

"Tell that to the Russians," Jason said. Until September 2018, few people had ever considered the possibility. Then Russia discovered a tiny hole it later determined was most likely deliberately drilled in a spacecraft attached to the International Space Station. The latter revelation caused a major stir, the worldwide press running wild at the possibility of spacecraft sabotage. In that case, a micrometeoroid strike had been ruled the most likely cause and the hole had been successfully repaired with sealant, but the possibility of human interference was no longer something anyone at NASA could disregard out of hand.

"Get me more data, Jason," Phil said, sounding frustrated for the first time. "And be ready for a meeting later this week." With that, he hung up the phone and was gone, leaving Jason to his resignation that the meeting had gone exactly as he'd imagined it would. Next, Jason went to meet with Jack and Li in their Caltech offices.

"Of course, NASA's skeptical," Jack said after Jason filled them in on his conversations with Peter Edtz and Phil Cline. "Why aren't you? I mean, how likely does it seem that someone in space could have fired a laser at your spaceship so precisely at just the right moment, when it was constantly jumping and moving through space at rapid speeds?"

"Well, look at the evidence," Jason said. "Wasn't it Sherlock Holmes who said, 'Whenever you eliminate the impossible, whatever remains must be true?'"

"You're not really dealing in impossibilities yet, at least not convincingly," Li said. "Just probabilities and oddities. So, of course, with everything they have at stake, they want to keep moving."

"And no one is saying they won't keep working on the problem and better safety precautions to ensure it doesn't happen again," Jack added.

"Right. You of all people should be excited by the success and wanting to move forward," Li said.

Jason felt a headache coming on as his chest tightened. Were his oldest friends on his side or NASA's? "Of course I do. The right way. The safe way. If we can't get crews to and from deep space safely, I don't want to do it, and Shortcut has no value to anyone."

"Agreed. No one disputes that," Li said. "But until there's more evidence, the only logical course is to work on protections against identifiable problems and press forward. They can modify the design to add additional shielding to prevent cosmic ray damage from affecting any electronics and they can improve their quality control to prevent defective or counterfeit components from infiltrating the supply chain."

"NASA has to focus on what it can fix, not what might be a problem but can't be proven, you know that," Jack said, then added, "And one of the problems it can't fix is you're a worrywart."

Jason leaned back in his chair, arms crossed. "I want to do it right."

"So does everyone else," Li agreed. He leaned forward and smiled. "We're on your side, but when you bring us a problem, our job is to talk you through it. That's all we're doing here."

"Even if you don't like what you're hearing," Jack said.

The comment struck home. They did know him well. Jason sighed. "Okay. I have never liked not knowing when major issues arise. Is that so bad?"

"Nope. And it is part of what people admire so much about you," Li said.

"It's a big part of why we've wanted you here for so long," Jack said. "But NASA has to consider a lot more than your discomfort in making decisions. Millions of dollars have been spent and switching course to another program would cost millions more. Holding would also cost money. Given their struggles to stay funded and keep the government and public interest, they have to make decisions fast and always make progress or at least the appearance of it."

"The next mission is a long time off," Li said. "Creed and Wayne are safe. The spacecraft came back to Earth in one piece. So there's time to identify and solve problems while still moving ahead and adding additional fail safes and design elements to make it even safer. Especially when the plan is to send humans millions of miles away for long periods of time. What we send with them is all they'll have."

Jason chuckled and put on a mock scolding tone, "You know, sometimes I just want you guys to agree with me when I vent."

Jack and Li laughed.

"Sorry. We have to show progress too, and keeping a good relationship with NASA is vital to us," Jack said, not even needing to mention the longstanding partnership between NASA's Jet Propulsion Lab and Caltech.

Two days later, on Thursday afternoon, Jason, Jack, and Li and the department heads of Jason's Caltech Lab participated in a conference call with Phil Cline and the Project Shortcut department heads at NASA about moving the project to the next stage: a voyage to Mars. A target of two to three years was established for the first attempt at such a mission as, in addition to current investigations and improvements, a new and larger spacecraft needed to be built to handle the longer voyage and a larger crew. With Shortcut, it was expected a journey to Mars would take six to eight months, depending upon the teams' progress with technological developments over the next few years. It would be decided if the craft would orbit Mars and take samples and run tests or actually attempt to land on its surface. Actual landing would require a bigger crew complement. NASA would make that determination within six to eight months from the meeting.

As various other priorities, assignments, and details were discussed and arguments erupted over whether Caltech or NASA teams would handle them, Jason's mind turned to his family, who were due to arrive that afternoon from Houston after reaching Heather's mid-semester fall break. Belongings and furniture, including two cars, had been sent with movers the week before and Laura and Heather had been staying with her parents. It had been two weeks since Jason last saw them, and he couldn't wait to greet them at the Burbank airport.

Their reunion was sweeter than he imagined. He hugged and kissed them both, reveling at the feel of having them in his arms again. *God, I love my girls.* And it was as if the stress he'd been carrying for weeks blew away on the light breeze at the tarmac. Just the presence of the two he loved most in life at his side made him feel calmer and more content. After helping them settle in then treating them to dinner out at Barney's Beanery, an LA staple with one of the largest and most varied menus of any restaurant he'd ever seen, Jason called to double check on the movers, who promised they'd arrive Saturday morning bright and early to unload.

"Nothing left for us to do but have some fun while we wait," Jason joked.

"You're on!" Laura replied, and she was serious. So they made immediate plans for a night out the following night after picking up Alice, the nanny, from her midafternoon flight out for a visit.

"Heather will have so much fun showing Alice the new house and area that she probably won't even miss us," Jason said and laughed.

Laura agreed, smiling. "Let's go back up to that awesome park we discovered when we were out here house hunting, okay? Arroyo something?"

"Arroyo Woodland and Wildlife Nature Park," Jason said. "You're on. Shall we pack a picnic?"

"Maybe just a walk and some nature sighting," Laura said. "I heard it might rain. But it'll be good just to be together and enjoy it again."

"You know it doesn't rain often out here," Jason said, thinking she was probably wrong, "But either way I sure won't pass up time alone with the love of my life."

Alice did a double take when she got off the plane and saw Laura dressed to the hilt. Heather joined her in making noises of admiration and funny looks.

"Come on you two, don't look at me like that," Laura mock scolded but her eyes sparkled with delight at their reaction. "You've seen me dressed up before."

"Never like that," Alice said with approval.

Jason took Laura's hand and raised his eyebrows, causing them all to laugh.

Within minutes of Alice's arrival at the airport, she was being overwhelmed by Heather's nonstop narrative of all that had happened since they'd seen each other last. Jason and Laura dropped them at the hotel, taking time only to leave Alice money for dinner, keys to a rental car, and a house key in case she wanted to check out their new home, and headed off for a romantic evening.

They dined on the rooftop balcony of Café Santorini in the heart of Pasadena's Old Town. A rectangular brick building at the corner of West Union and Holly, the romantic spot famed for its Mediterranean cuisine, had a glass walled second floor balcony that looked out over the streets below, which were lit up with colorful lights at night. It was quite romantic and the food was amazing. Jason and Laura had been foodies ever since Jason first made his name as the inventor of the smart toaster that perfectly toasted any size item inserted and popped it out afterward without need for prying or burnt fingers. The Thinking Toaster, T3 (Toaster Cubed) for short, made him a household name, literally, and also brought his first fortune. He and Laura made generous donations to various food charities and, in the process, found themselves hobnobbing with some of the stars of the culinary world from Wolfgang Puck to Rachael Ray to Guy Fieri. They both did the talk show circuit, with Laura gracing a few magazine covers much to NASA's delight, and Jason even applied his deconstructionist theories to cooking. He told one host that cooking was very much about deconstruction and the detours one made along the way, and that led to a friendship with Grant Achatz of the famed restaurant Alinea in Chicago, who became not only a friend but culinary mentor. Jason loved how the slightest change in one variable—hot, cold, covered, uncovered, evaporated, condensed, stirred, shaken, even the order of ingredients—impacted the others completely. Then there were the countless ingredients that changed the whole like adding chemicals to any lab formula. It was a new form of math and route to perfection and it filled him with new curiosity and excitement. As always, his drive was to understand everything and excel at it as much as one could, so he threw himself into the experience and found it fun, therapeutic, and creative all at once to form and create for those he loved a kind of primordial soup of flavors, aromas, and textures to discover.

After Laura started flying and with the arrival of Heather, Jason's interest had waned along with his free time, though they did trade off cooking for the family. He knew he didn't have the genius of Grant Achatz or Wolfgang Puck, but it had satisfied him a great deal just to invade their world for a while. Stepping inside Café Santorini and smelling all the delightful spices and aromas set his heart aflame again with passion and anticipation. Li and Purva had raved about it, and it had been a long time since they'd had any real opportunity to take in haute cuisine, so as they waited, Jason and Laura chatted like excited teenagers, filling each other in on all that had happened in their weeks apart and laughing at some of Heather's antics in her final days at school and with her friends in Houston. Later, they commiserated over Laura's parents' constant attempts to convince her that moving was either a huge mistake or tantamount to betrayal, and then talked about their own activities, from developments with Shortcut to the move to NASA.

As was their habit, once they'd been seated, they each ordered different items then shared them. Jason had the Fettuccine con Gamberetti, which was jumbo shrimp served over fettuccine in chili oil with roasted bell peppers, spinach, and garlic. Laura ordered the Moroccan Lamb Shank, breaded with dried fruit and served with herb couscous and balsamic vinegar. To accompany it, they ordered red sangria, which complimented the fruit of the lamb perfectly as well as the pasta. They devoured every bite in between endless streams of conversation and staring into each other's eyes. Jason found himself once again admiring her smooth round chin, the peaceful confidence in her warm brown eyes, and the dimples that formed in her cheeks when she smiled. He loved the way her brows knitted together when she was deep in thought and the way her voice rose in pitch every time her passions rose within. They'd been long overdue for a romantic evening and it was delightful. They both commented at various points how lucky they felt, that they couldn't be happier, and Jason's eyes misted a bit as he stared across the table at her, his mind flashing back through their life together: from meeting in college and realizing he'd finally found someone who could sincerely embrace all his interests and find fascination in them even if they weren't her personal passion, to celebrating her laser discoveries and advances and how even those she made with thoughts to how they might be useful to Jason in fulfilling his own pursuits. Whereas they were both only children, unlike Jason, Laura had been the center of her parents' universe and her thoughts constantly went to family as a unit, helping one another. From her and her family, Jason had gained a renewed sense of belonging he'd never had with his father, especially since his mother passed. He and Laura were truly one couple, not just two individuals spending time together, and the bond and love it had nurtured between them overpowered him as he thought about it. He stopped and took a deep breath as he felt tears forming in the corners of his eyes.

"Are you okay?" she asked sweetly at one point and reached across the table to lay her hand gently atop his.

He'd chuckled and motioned to his plate. "Spicy. Whew." Then fanned his face. She laughed it off, but he saw in her eyes she knew.

Jason finished the meal satisfied in every respect, from the warmth flowing through his body out of deep love for his wife, and the joy of being with her again, to the succulent meal. Afterward, they drove ten minutes down Avenue 64 and across Arroyo Verde Road to Arroyo Woodland and Wildlife Nature Park, where they slowly wound their way to a picnic and parking area near the center with remarkable views of scenery, wildlife, the surrounding mountains, and the Arroyo Seco tributary. The small three-acre enclave situated along the east side of the Arroyo Seco had meandering trails, native California walnut trees, and a lookout point offering views of the historical York Boulevard Bridge, Mount Washington, Verdugo Mountains, and the San Gabriel Mountains.

Parking, they left the car and walked, her hand sliding into his and fitting perfectly, like their hands were made for each other. As they took in the views, Laura pressed close against him as they talked softly and stopped to kiss from time to time. Unlike many parks, Arroyo was not heavily landscaped or planted, but more a preserve of natural southwestern landscape in the midst of urban sprawl. What they both loved about it was its rustic nature. It was so rare to see undisturbed natural areas in big cities, though there were some picnic tables, shelters, even playgrounds and a Frisbee golf course. Mostly it was natural. From deer feeding on wild grass at the park's edges to multicolored birds singing and butterflies fluttering between trees and flowers, there was plenty to take in. The smog was thin, unveiling so many stars that Jason felt like he was on a mountaintop instead of inside the Los Angeles metro limits; the natural beauty and wonder provided plenty of visual pleasure for their eyes. When they managed to look away from each other, that is. Anyone watching them would think they looked at each other like love starved teenagers, which was pretty much how Jason felt. God, he loved this woman. He could never find words to explain it. And that she loved him back so passionately was as amazing now as it had been all those years ago when they met. She was the most stunning woman he'd ever met then and he couldn't take his eyes off her. What his life would be without her was hard to imagine. From her genius laser cell invention and spherical design that had finally made the Shortcut theory become reality to Heather, to her astronaut missions and her intelligence, she amazed him every day. Constantly.

They stopped several times to read landscaped signs built on stands of rocks where large plaques told the history of the area, described the wildlife and plants, and park history, and at times each of them recalled memories of other natural beauty they'd observed together. Jason reveled in the reminder of the happiness they'd shared. When it finally started to sprinkle lightly, Jason pulled out his umbrella and offered it to Laura, but instead she leaned her head on his shoulder and pulled him closer and they sat on a picnic table with a great view of Mount Washington, necking like teenagers. They probably would have remained there for much longer if it hadn't started pouring rain. It came on suddenly and with a vengeance, and they huddled under Jason's umbrella and ran along a trail headed for the car.

The whole night they'd been mostly alone there, so Jason was surprised when they heard jocular voices—yelling, joking, laughing. Cutting across some grass, through a copse of trees in the direction of the parking lot, Jason and Laura stopped for a moment beneath a large walnut tree, attempting to stay dry. Jason squinted through the darkness.

"I thought we parked that way, but I can't see it," Jason said.

"Are you saying we're lost?" Laura said with a chuckle and smiled, squeezing his arm. "That old line."

"Don't worry. I have superpowers. Math will save us," Jason snapped back sotto voce and they both laughed.

"Look" said Laura, pointing at the full Moon shining brightly through the rainy sky, which had a surprising absence of clouds. "Where are the clouds?" A faint white-colored rainbow hung over the western horizon, arcing just above the skyline. Jason marveled at the rare Moonbow, its colors seeming to imitate the rainbow of emotions he was feeling. It made this time with his wife even more precious.

When the rain let up a little, they left the walnut's shelter and started across the grass, when they heard a male voice with a slight accent: "Awwww, look, they're in love. Los enamorados!" Other voices laughed, male and female.

Jason and Laura looked around for the source but it wasn't until they came around two large trees that they saw several Hispanics who looked to be in their twenties gathered under a picnic shelter staring at them. Several of the males wore similar denim jackets and red bandanas, gesturing and talking animatedly as if agitated or arguing. Was it a gang or something?

Tensing, Jason tightened his grip on Laura's hand and steered her left, away from them, picking up his pace. But then he bumped into someone hard.

"What the fuck!" a male said as Jason turned just in time to see a large, muscular tattooed man of Hispanic heritage wearing the same bandana and jacket as the others. The man shoved him. "Gringo pendejo! Watch it!" He glared, eyes cold, nostrils flaring.

"I'm sorry," Jason muttered and reached for Laura again, as she huddled under the umbrella nearby, eyes wide, lips pinched. He tried to reassure her with his eyes and a smile. "It was an accident. I didn't see you," Jason said calmly as the rain picked up again, soaking him and the angry man.

"Fuck sorry, asshole. Pay attention." The man stepped forward and shoved Jason again. "Why you smiling? You laughing at me?"

Jason wiped at his mouth. The rain was salty. Seawater rain?!

"Fuck yeah, Bene, he's mocking you," a woman shouted, interrupting his thoughts, as several of the others from the shelter moved toward them.

Jason looked at Laura, stepping between her and the men, his leg muscles tightening as he fought the urge. They were fanning out now to block his way. He felt Laura easing away.

"Someone needs to learn some motherfucking manners," the big man said, shoving Jason again.

Out of the corner of his eye, as he backed away and tried to keep eyes on him and away from his wife, who was ducking under a tree, still somehow dry, holding her cell phone as she called for help.

There was a glint in the moonlight. A knife? A gun? Then the jacketed men closed in a circle around him.

"Please, we're leaving. I'm so sorry. I apologize," Jason tried to say as he backed away but it came out soft, almost a whimper. And then Jason saw Laura looking at him through tears. Suddenly, her form went totally black, though he could still see an outline. "Laura!" he called out.

Punches landed in his gut as the men attacked. Sharp pain shot up from kicks to his ankles. He was falling even as his eyes tried to find Laura again. Where was she? Running? His lips were dry, his eyes tearing from pain.

Suddenly, a blinding flash of light filled the air and several voices cried out. "What the fuck?" "La Migra!" "Vamanos!" "Is it the Five-O?"

For a moment, his eyes blinked, trying to recover from the blinding flash and then he was lying on the ground, under assault, his arms and legs throbbing—his last thought was that one might be broken—and his vision faded to black.

CHAPTER 6

"LAURA!" THE HEAVY, oversized wood door slammed behind Jason with a bang and the click of the metal knob as he raced into the room and looked around for his wife. The bright glare of fluorescents overhead filled the space, reflecting off the bare, white, antiseptic walls as he approached the large, railed bed where she lay, the hiss of the breathing machine attached to her face ominous in his ears. An antiseptic smell filled his nostrils, as cold and ominous as the pinching in his gut. "Oh my God! Laura!"

He rushed to her side, clasping her cold hand in his and looked down toward her beautiful face, then screamed. The bruised, bandaged face lying unconscious on the bed wasn't Laura at all. It was Jason himself.

"Nooooooooooooooo!" Jason screamed, dropping the hand and backing away, and then someone was shaking him.

"Dr. Maxx, it's okay. You're safe," a female voice urged. "Looks like you had a bad dream."

Jason blinked, his eyes squinting against the bright glaring lights overhead. He was still there—in the hospital room with the antiseptic smell. Only he was the patient and his body ached all over. The beeping and hissing of the oxygen machine and life support machines in nearby rooms mostly drowned out the sounds of people and the intercom announcements from a speaker overhead. Through a window he saw darkness and stars. It was nighttime. Where was he? An ICU? Then he realized he had a tube down his throat to help him breathe and another running out of his chest, which throbbed with pain as if a semi-truck had run over it.

A young redheaded nurse smiled down at him, looking genuinely happy. "It's so good to see you awake. You've been in a coma for a while." The nurse was late twenties, pretty, kind blue eyes, her hair and makeup as fine-tuned as her starched white uniform.

Next to her, a male nurse who resembled a living Ken doll appeared, sporting a similar outfit without the hat and said, "You went through quite the trauma but you're going to be fine. Just stay calm and try not to move while I get the doctor, okay?"

As he hurried off, Jason grabbed the breathing tube and yanked—ignoring the redhead's protests—ripping away the tape holding it place and pulling it out. *Laura!* his internal voice yelled. The pain to his throat was sharp and quick, but it was the pain evoked by how moving his shoulder and arm disturbing his side and chest that caused him to really cry out.

"Are you okay?" the redheaded nurse asked, face filled with concern.

The male nurse appeared, looking worried and hurried back toward the bed. "Wow. Take it easy there," he said as a doctor entered the room behind him.

"Let me get you some water," The redhead offered and grabbed a yellow plastic pitcher off a rolling table beside the bed, pouring water into a matching cup.

Jason's throat was sore, raw and burned a bit as if from acid reflux. He tried to talk but went into a coughing fit. *Laura!* he cried out silently inside.

"Well, I'll bet that hurt like hell," the doctor said, eyeing the tube covered in torn tape that dangled off the edge of the bed.

"Yeah," Jason rasped, coughing again.

"Jason, I'm Dr. Brock. You're in Intensive Care at Huntington Hospital in Pasadena. How are you feeling?" The name badge pinned to a pocket that bore his smiling picture and a large bar code read 'Vaughn Brock, M.D., Trauma.'

The redhead held a straw to Jason's lips allowing him to drink a moment.

As soon as he could speak, he asked, "Laura! Where's my wife?" He tried to sit up but a pain in his side forced him back.

"Take it easy," Dr. Brock said. "You're gonna hurt a while."

"Where am I? What happened?" His voice came out as a rasp. Jason reached for the water again. The redhead grabbed it off the nightstand and held it for him as he took a long draw from the straw.

"They gave you quite a beating," the doctor explained. "Sustaining injuries to your head and upper body. Multiple rib fractures and contusions to your lungs are probably what you feel the most right now. You've had a pneumothorax, which means one of your ribs pierced your right lung, hence the chest tube to drain out the excess air that's leaking into your chest cavity. It's almost resolved now, and we'll be able to remove the chest tube soon, but it may hurt a lot while you finish healing."

Jason wet his lips with his tongue as the doctor finished and rasped, "My wife…"

The Doctor's face changed, his eyes narrowing as his smile disappeared. "I'm sorry. They only brought you in. My understanding from the detectives is they're trying to find her. But they had no witnesses to what happened. They'll want to talk to you. See if you can help."

"Laura's gone?" Jason's voice cracked as he panicked and tried to swing a leg over the side of the bed. Images flashed through his head of men in denim jackets and red bandanas, Laura under a tree looking afraid, and then he was being attacked as Laura seemed to fade and disappeared. THUMP!

Dr. Brock stopped him with a firm hand on his arm. "I wouldn't try to stand. You've been in that bed for two weeks. Your body needs time to readjust."

"Two weeks?!" Jason's eyes darted between the faces. "But my wife!" He started to get up again, but pain wracked his body, throwing him back against the pillows and mattress as tears flowed down his cheeks as his voice choked off. "My God. We have to find her." THUMP!

The doctor and the nurses looked at him with great sympathy. "I'm sure the police are doing everything they can," the male nurse said. He stepped toward the bed and supported his head with a palm as he leaned forward to drink from the straw.

"But we were together," Jason said. "She has to be here." He felt jumpy, his hands fidgeting at his sides, but yet it was hard to move anything else.

"I'm sure the detectives will be here soon to fill you in," Dr. Brock said. "I'm afraid we don't know much. We've been worried about you." He smiled.

Oh God, please let Laura be okay, Jason prayed. Then he thought of Heather. Had he really been here two weeks? What was the bright light? Laura had disappeared?

His mind raced with images and thoughts of the night in the park, reliving it.

"Take it easy, okay?" the redheaded nurse said and smiled again. "I'm your night nurse, Holly. Jan has you during days."

Jason raised his wrist and saw a red button clipped to a wrist band, an electrical cord running up to a panel above his head on the wall.

"That's to call us if you need anything, 'kay?" Holly said. Her starched white uniform was a perfect color match to the white coat the doctor at her side wore as he tucked his dangling stethoscope into its large front pocket and leaned over Jason, smiling.

"We're very sorry for what happened to you. But you were lucky. You're going to be okay."

"My daughter...Heather," Jason croaked.

Dr. Brock nodded. "Your in-laws flew out as soon as the news broke. They're with her and the nanny at your house. And the movers unloaded everything, I'm told. You're coming back to some big changes, but I promise we're going to get you well and back home as soon as we can."

Jason nodded, then turned away, as the sobbing started. *Laura!* She had to be okay. How could he face life without her? *My God!*

Within two hours, after the doctor and nurses had examined him and made sure he'd regained his composure,

Jack, Li, and Purva arrived, looking relieved and overjoyed to see him awake.

"Thank God!" Purva said as Jack and Li asked together, "How do you feel?" They all smiled, their eyes glistening with concern.

"Awful," Jason said. "Laura?"

Jack shook his head. "Nothing yet. But there were no witnesses. The park ranger found you after midnight, left there alone."

"What happened? Can you remember?" Purva asked.

Jason flashed back, picturing the bandanas and denim jackets. "I think it might have been a gang. It was raining hard. I bumped into one and he didn't like my apology. They were looking for a fight. Laura was under a tree, trying to call for help on her cell phone. They weren't paying attention to her. Then she disappeared."

"Disappeared?" Li said, puzzled.

"Like a black shadow and there was a bright light and she was gone."

The others exchanged puzzled looks that quickly changed to worry.

"Well, Phil Cline and the detectives are on their way," Jack said. "They'll want to know details, so we'll let you tell us more later."

Purva nodded. "We're just relieved that you're okay."

He could tell they didn't believe his story. "But Laura," Jason said again. "Please. Find her!"

"Believe me," Jack said. "Every resource we have is on it already. And we'll do everything we can to help the authorities."

"And you," Li added. They all reached out to squeeze his arm one-by-one, then turned as they saw Phil Cline and several men crowding around the doorway.

Purva leaned over and kissed Jason's cheek. "We'll be right outside if you need us, sweetie. Be strong." And then they all hurried out as Holly motioned for Phil and the others to enter.

Phil Cline had always been a man Jason thought handled stress amazingly well, but the man who hurried toward his hospital bed had haggard eyes, his brow creased with worry. "Thank God, you're okay," Phil said, looking down at Jason with deep concern.

With him were two men Jason didn't recognize but who both wore the badges of police detectives. One was short and stocky with black tousled hair and a raggedy mustache. The other was clean shaven, with neatly combed brown hair. Both wore cheap suits, though the neat one's suit looked newer and better cared for. The third man with Phil was Heather's best friend's famous grandfather, whom they'd met but only interacted with briefly on rare occasions.

Colonel Jimmy Burnette was an all-American hero known around the world. Everybody knew him. Everybody loved him—kids and men wanted to be him, and women swooned. A good ole boy from Oklahoma, he was a former astronaut. He'd also served in the Navy Seals in both Gulf Wars and was an ace fighter pilot to boot. He'd set records in the F-16 and Stealth bombers both before joining NASA, and he had movie star good looks. He was dressed to kill in a designer suit mismatched with slip-on loafers. They were new loafers though, and his smile almost sparkled as he joined the others. He stood beside Phil on one side of the bed, the detectives on the other, and they all looked at Jason.

"Jason, these are Detectives Connelly and Coben," Phil said. Connelly was the neat one. "And I'm not sure if you've met—"

"Howdy. Jimmy Burnette, Doc," Burnette said in a southern accent, reaching forward to offer Jason a firm handshake. The scent of his Paco Rabanne cologne filled Jason's nostrils. "We're all relieved to see you awake again."

Jason started to speak but his lips were parched, so he licked them first. "Everybody knows you, Colonel. I'm honored," Jason said as Burnette chuckled, then looked at Phil. "Laura—"

"Unfortunately, we have no idea where your wife is at the moment," Detective Connelly said. "But we did find her NASA badge, her purse, and an umbrella with her fingerprints and yours at the scene."

"We were hoping you could tell us more about what happened that night to aid our investigation," Coben added. The detectives wore traces of cologne, too, but far less expensive.

"If you're up to it," Phil added.

"Dr. Brock said it's okay as long as Dr. Maxx feels up to it," Holly said, standing watchfully just inside the door. "But no more than half an hour. He needs rest."

"Of course," Phil agreed and nodded to her. The nurse smiled with satisfaction then turned and left them alone.

"What can you tell us about your attacker?" Connelly asked.

"Attackers. I really only remember one of the guys," Jason said, trying to picture other faces but continually coming back to the one he'd bumped into. "The one who confronted me. But they all had the same denim jackets and red bandanas. He was Hispanic, huge, muscular. Lots of tattoos. Brown eyes, I think. Black hair in a ponytail. Late twenties, maybe. And one of them called him 'Bene.'"

Connelly's brow creased and he exchanged a look with Coben. "Puerto Ricans maybe?"

"Sounds like gang colors at the moment anyway," Coben agreed.

"How many were there?" Connelly asked.

"A dozen, maybe," Jason said, his brow furrowing as he strained to remember. "There were women in the group, too. None of them attacked me that I remember. It's a bit hazy, and the rain was on and off."

"Can you tell us when you last saw Laura, son?" Jimmy interjected.

"She was with me as I bumped into this guy, Bene, and then she moved away, under a tree. Trying to call for help."

"We found her cell phone under a tree, but 911 registered no call until the park ranger found you after midnight," Coben said. "I guess she didn't manage."

"Please take us through what happened," Connelly said.

Jason cleared his throat. "We had just left this shelter after a brief romantic moment. We were having the first date night we'd had in months, Dinner at Café Santorini then over to the park to look at the full Moon, stars, scenery. It started to rain—salty rain."

"Salty rain?" Burnette shared a puzzled look with Phil.

Jason licked his dry lips again and continued, "And we heard someone say something about 'oh they're in love' or something. And then we came around more trees and saw the group gathered under a picnic shelter."

"Did they look angry? Happy?" Connelly asked.

"No, but we did change direction a bit, not wanting to chance it," Jason said. "That's when I accidentally bumped into the big one, and he did not like that. Started cursing. Insulting me in Spanish, I'm pretty sure. I don't speak it."

"One of the few things you don't do," Phil joked.

Jason couldn't muster a laugh. "I apologized more than once, but he shoved me. Asked if I was mocking him. Some of the others said I was. He said I needed to learn manners. I backed away. Laura was ducking under a tree for shelter, a yard or more away. I kept trying to keep their attention off her. Then they were circling. I think I saw the glint of knives, maybe a gun or two and they attacked me. Punching, kicking, yelling.

"I kept trying to keep an eye on Laura, but then there was this blinding flash of light, people yelling out, wondering what it was. And she was gone. It was like she was a black blur and then disappeared. And they kept attacking, and then I blacked out."

Jason reached out to grab Connelly's wrist tightly, his voice cracking. "You've gotta find her. Please tell me it's a priority."

"Of course," Connelly nodded. "We're very anxious to find her."

"There's been no ransom demand, but we also haven't found her body," Coben said. "That's actually good. If someone has her, she's still alive."

"At any point, did you see any of them attacking her?" Connelly asked.

Jason shook his head. "No. I don't think so. They were so focused on me."

"Sounds like you were doing all you could to keep her safe, brother," Jimmy said, smiling reassuringly.

"But where is she?" Jason said.

"We'll find her," Coben said. "We're doing everything we can."

"And we are, too," Phil jumped in. "That's why Jimmy is here. He's the Chief Security Officer for NASA. We're adding our resources to the investigation to help in any way we can."

"And we've got extra security keeping an eye on your house and here at the hospital," Jimmy added. "We'll make sure no one bothers you."

"Did they act like they knew you? Or did it seem random?" Coben asked.

"I've never seen them before that I recall," Jason said. "I think it was wrong place, wrong time. Just people looking for trouble."

Coben grunted. "It does sound like that. But I wanted to ask."

"Do you remember anything else?" Connelly asked.

Jason shook his head. "You said you found her purse and badge?"

Connelly nodded again. "Yes."

"Can I see them?" Jason asked.

The detectives exchanged a look. "We'll check with our crime scene techs, but if we're done with them, yes. We will get them over here. Let you examine and tell us if anything's missing."

"They didn't take your wallet or anything as far as we can tell," Phil said. "Which is odd."

"It's almost like something scared them off," Connelly said.

"You mentioned you saw some kind of a—a bright light, right?" Burnette said.

"It was a flash. Just sudden, like the sun in the midst of night. Blinding."

"Could you tell where it came from?" Burnette asked.

"No. Out of nowhere. Very strange."

"Could it have been headlights? A spotlight?" Coben asked.

"Of course. Anything. But I have no idea," Jason said.

The men relaxed a bit, exchanging looks, then Coben stepped forward and pulled a business card from his pocket, setting it on the bedside table. "If you remember anything else, please give us a call, okay? Our cell and office numbers are on here. Day or night, someone will answer. We'll send a sketch artist over in the morning. To see if you can describe Bene enough to get a sketch. So if you remember anyone else, be sure and tell him."

"Okay, thanks," Jason said. "Just find my wife. Please."

"Of course," Connelly assured him.

"Well, I think that's enough for now," Phil said, motioning toward the door. "He just woke up. We should let him have some rest."

"We'll keep in touch as well," Burnette said as they all moved toward the door. "You can reach me through my men outside or Phil, okay? We'll talk again tomorrow."

"Thanks, Colonel Burnette," Jason said, licking his dry lips and reaching for the water cup.

Burnette saw it and came back over to grab it, holding it closer for Jason to take it.

Jason finished drinking and said, "Heather, I want to see her."

"We'll make arrangements. The Raimeys are with her at the house," Phil said.

Jason sipped water as Phil squeezed his shoulder, then he and Burnette turned and left with the detectives. Holly appeared quickly in the doorway to check on him with another nurse, taller and thin as a rail, with long blond hair.

"You okay?" she asked as she came over and took the cup, refilling it, then set it on the nightstand and began fluffing the pillows a bit and checking his sheets and covers, the other nurse going around to the other side of the bed.

"I will be. When they find Laura," Jason said.

"You love her a lot, huh?" Holly said.

"She's my whole world," Jason managed to say and then leaned back into the pillow as tiredness overcame him.

CHAPTER 7

THE DAY AFTER Jason awoke from his coma, a chest X-ray revealed the pneumothorax had shrunken to less than twenty percent. This meant they could soon remove the chest tube and sew him back up. The morning after the tube was removed and he'd been transferred from ICU to a medical floor, he awakened feeling stronger, more refreshed, and made his first attempt to get out of bed. The pain that moving his arms and chest caused sent him scrambling to grab the rail on the bed as he slid off and landed hard on the floor. He tried and tried to get himself back up into the bed, but his strength had left him, and he found himself lying sprawled on his side on the floor.

When his day nurse, Jan, finally came and found him, he had lain there for what seemed like an hour, but he was sure it was much less. Whereas Holly was a white redhead, Jan was black with piercing green eyes. She lifted him under his arms and helped him back into bed, then put her finger on the red button attached to his wrist. "Why didn't you call me?"

"I thought this was something I could do myself," Jason said, wincing as his body throbbed and he tried to calm his breathing again. It hurt every time his chest moved even slightly.

"Well, so much time unconscious with no movement leaves people deconditioned and weak, not to mention the residual pain," she said. "So just take it easy."

Jason groaned. "Yeah, I figured that out."

Jan smiled. "I'm sorry. Luckily, the pain should be fading every day now and you're about to start physical therapy, which will help get you back up and at 'em and ready to go home in a week to ten days."

Jason grunted. "How am I supposed to just lie here feeling helpless when my wife is out there?"

Jan's eyes narrowed, her eyebrows pulling down in concentrated concern. "I understand, but reinjuring yourself will just keep you here that much longer, so no stunts." On the final phrase, her eyes turned cold, her nostrils flaring in warning. "We'll get you out of here as soon as possible, I promise."

Jason raised his hands in surrender. "Okay, okay."

"You look like you've been through three wars and a goat roping. What happened?" Jimmy asked as he appeared in the doorway, frowning.

"Just a minor accident," Jan said. "He's fine."

Jimmy hurried over to the bed, a bearded guy in his thirties in tie-dyed t-shirt and jeans with a hippie-type beard close on his heels. "Trying to walk too soon, eh, pal?" Jimmy grinned. "Well, at least you didn't wet yourself or something."

Jason didn't respond. He hadn't considered that. Jan smiled as she tucked him in and fluffed his pillows. "He'll be just fine soon enough. No big deal. Now you two go easy on him."

Jimmy smiled and raised his hand, fingers crossed. "I promise, sister."

Jan shot him a stern look, but the sparkle in her eyes gave her away. She turned and smiled at Jason. "I'll be right outside if you need me. That call button is there for a reason." Then she gave the still-smiling Jimmy a quick glance and hurried out the door.

Jimmy motioned to the hippie. "This is Brett George. He's the sketch artist that the PD sent over. Why don't you describe that big fella who attacked you again."

Jason shifted so he was sitting up in bed. Jimmy started to help but Jason waved him off. "Let's give it a shot."

Brett sat in a chair beside the bed and ran Jason through a series of questions, sketching with a stylus on an iPad he'd brought along as he went. Within twenty minutes, they had a pretty damn good sketch of the big Latino who'd led the attack on Jason. Jason was impressed.

"All the things I can do, and I could never do that," he said after looking at the sketch.

Brett smiled. "Well, I went to art school, you didn't. We all have our gifts." He stood from the chair he'd been using beside the bed and nodded to Jimmy. "We'll get this in the system and see what we can find, okay? You get better, Dr. Maxx."

"Thanks," Jason and Jimmy said together as Brett headed for the door.

Jimmy pulled a badge out of his pocket and tossed it on Jason's chest. "I believe you asked for that. They're still doing forensics on the purse and cell phone, but they'll give it to you when they're finished so you can run your tests."

Jason picked up Laura's badge and examined it. He

immediately noticed the dosimeter indicated a few dozen counts above normal, and the value was climbing as he held her badge, indicating there was radiation nearby. He froze for a moment, scanning the room for potential contamination. Then it hit him: with all the medical scans he'd been through recently, Jason himself was radioactive enough to bump up the value on Laura's dosimeter. He looked at the polariton indicator, and it was high too. Unlike radioactive sources, polaritons are still experimental and a high dose like this couldn't have come from the hospital or a park for that matter. "Did you look at this?"

"Yeah, that's a whole lotta radiation," Jimmy said, lowering his brows. "Do you know when she was exposed?"

Jason shook his head. "She shouldn't have been. Not for years. Did the police mention it?"

"No, but I imagine their lab techs knew to check," Jimmy said, eyes narrowing as he glanced at the readings again. "It'll probably get their notice when the report comes through. What's the other number for?"

"There are two dosimeters in her badge; one's been modified to detect polariton exposure levels," Jason said. "All our people use them."

Jason's mind flashed back to the attack at Arroyo again and the moment Laura seemed to become a black shadow outline. His heartbeat accelerated, then it clicked and his jaw clenched, his senses heightening. Jason had witnessed that blackout phenomenon before, the shadowy blackness that formed just before a Shortcut jump. When Laura had been developing the laser cell for purifying water during college, she had observed that, under certain circumstances, she could tune her laser cells to optically isolate themselves. She never bothered with it until she met Jason and started enhancing the cloaking effect to help simplify his math. Once perfected, the laser cells, which were already optimal solar energy collectors, also acted like camouflage, isolating themselves from the outside world and turning into a near-black material. The phenomenon was observable on spaceships before executing Shortcuts. If it was a Shortcut, then the bright flash made sense too: that would be when the Q-switch fired the lasers.

Jason fought the urge to jump out of bed. A Shortcut?! Someone had Shortcut technology to swap people via quantum entanglement the same way Jason was using it for the spacecraft? If that was true, it was incredible technology. But how could anyone have beaten him at his own game? He was the leader in it, or so he thought. But the evidence was right there in front of him. He had to test the purse and get back to test the area of the park under the tree where Laura had disappeared as well. Jason did have one reservation though: if it was a Shortcut, why wasn't Laura surrounded by an optically isolating sphere? Her skin and clothes themselves had turned black, flashed, and disappeared. How was that possible without her being isolated inside a perfectly round laser shield?

"Tell me, son," Jimmy urged, watching his face. Clearly Jason's thoughts had played out on his face, though he doubted Jimmy could read their significance or even knew what a polariton was.

"Nothing," Jason said calmly. "Just rerunning the events in my mind again. She wasn't wearing this. It was in her purse. So unless it spilled from the zippered compartment she puts it in, she dropped it."

Jimmy pursed his lips, his eyebrows drawing together, as he took the badge and examined it. "Leaving us a clue? Smart." He looked at Jason again. "So what's she tryin' to tell us? And what are you not tellin' me?"

Jason stayed silent, uncertain if he was ready to talk about it. But his mind continued to race and Jimmy stared at his face.

"This ain't my first rodeo, son," Jimmy added, pushing.

"Nothing concrete," Jason said. "Just suspicions. I need to test the purse, and I need to get back to that park and the tree where she was when I last saw her."

"Well, the doctors say you need physical therapy for a bit first," Jimmy said.

Jason groaned. "We're losing valuable time. We have to find Laura!"

"I know, we're doing everything we can, brother," Jimmy said, handing Jason back the badge. "I'll talk to them. Speed it along if I can, but you're lucky to be alive, and your daughter needs you, so focus on what you need to do to get well."

Jason held up the badge. "Can I keep this?"

"Yes, for now," Jimmy said. "But I wish you'd tell me anything that might be of help. We're all trying to find your wife."

Jason nodded. "It's just a suspicion now. I'll tell you more when I have a better idea about it, I promise."

Jimmy smiled. "Okay. Please do. 'Cause I'm on your side, and anything you can tell us will help us find Laura."

"Of course," Jason said, locking eyes with Jimmy. There was suspicion there, something a little off, but the American hero was friendly, concerned, so Jason blew it off as his own paranoia.

"All right, you get some rest," Jimmy said. "I'll be back a little later. I wanna go talk to the police and see if that sketch can move things along for us. I'll talk to you soon, I promise." He turned and strolled out.

If Jimmy could read Jason's mind, Jason wished he'd return the favor, because he hadn't a clue what the man was thinking, but something about his demeanor still was unsettling. He leaned back into his pillow then, and a yawn came on. Within minutes, he was napping again.

THE NEXT TIME Jason awoke, he asked Jan for a microscope. She was puzzled until he explained he just wanted to do what he could to help find his wife and showed her the badge.

"We don't exactly leave them lying around," she said. "But I'll see what I can do."

A very long hour later, she brought one in and set it up on the long, rolling table that slid to sit over the bed on which Jason ate his meals.

"I can only let you keep it for an hour or two," Jan said. "The doctor whose office I borrowed it from will be out of meetings after that and looking for it."

"That's great," Jason said. "Thank you for finding me one."

Jason quickly set to work, his mouth dry and his chest suddenly light at the excitement of finally doing something. He carefully examined the badge and noticed some microscopic damage to the edges of the plastic lamination that reminded him of the minute marks Peter had shown him that lasers sometimes made. Plastic certainly would melt under a laser, so if this one had been exposed, damage was to be expected, though this was definitely far less than he'd imagined. Clearly Laura had tossed the badge away before the Shortcut lasers fully encased her in their field. Had she suspected somehow what was happening? If anyone knew lasers, it was Laura. And clearly she'd had some hint that something odd was going on for her to pull out the badge and leave it behind as a clue. The fact that she'd taken it out of the purse made Jason suspect she'd thrown the purse aside as an afterthought. Considering how fast it had all happened, it amazed him she'd been able to have such foresight at all, but then Laura was extraordinary. That was why he'd fallen in love with her.

Once again he felt a fluttering in his stomach that quickly changed to a feeling of emptiness. *I'll find you, baby. No matter what it takes.*

Jason set up a Zoom with Peter Edtz at Caltech and requested he conference in Jack and Li as well. He spent a few minutes explaining about the badge and what he'd found, having to stop several times and repeat himself when he talked too fast for them to follow. Then he asked them to arrange for someone to bring him equipment from Peter's lab so he could examine it properly as soon as possible.

"Jason, you're in a hospital and your job right now is to focus on getting out of there," Li said. "You've hired good people like Peter because of their expertise at just this kind of thing. Let them do their jobs."

Jason started to object, but Jack cut him off.

"Li's right. We insist. We promise to tell you everything the minute we know anything, right, Peter?"

"Of course," Peter agreed. "Should we wait for the

purse?"

Jason could tell they weren't going to give in on it, so he replied, "No. Let's get this going as soon as possible. We need all the leads we can get to find Laura."

"Okay," Peter agreed. "We took some samples at the park right after it happened when the police released the scene that we can run comparisons with."

When Jack suggested a courier, Li dismissed it. "I'll come get it myself. It's faster. I want to check on you anyway and make sure there are no delays getting you back on your feet."

So Li came by and peppered Jason with questions about how he was doing and his conversation with the detectives and Jimmy. Then he took the badge, sealing it carefully in a specimen bag as Jason urged, "Be sure he tests it for odd residues, materials, particles, whatever. If there was a Shortcut involved, those would confirm it."

Li smiled. "Peter knows what he's doing, Jason."

Jason sighed, leaning back into the twin pillows propping up his head. "Sorry. I just want to do all I can do to help Laura. I feel so helpless lying here."

Li patted his shoulder. "I don't blame you, but your job is to get well. We're on it. Let us know as soon as the purse arrives, okay?"

Jason agreed and then Li was gone and Jason tried to fight off another nap. He hated sleeping so much when Laura might be in danger. His senses were still heightened and his mind racing along with his heart, and his body was stiff with tension. There was so much to do. But in the end, he lost the battle and nodded off.

THAT AFTERNOON, ROGER and Susan Raimey brought Heather for a visit. As soon as she saw her father, Heather rushed to the bed and flung herself into his arms, sobbing. "I missed you so much, daddy."

Jason winced from pain as she briefly brushed against his ribs then his own tears flowed freely as he took large, savoring breaths and his nose caught the bubblegum scent of her shampoo mixed with baby powder. God, he'd missed that smell. "I missed you too, princess. I'm so sorry."

"I miss Mommy, too." Heather's voice cracked. "Where is she?"

Over her shoulder he saw the pain and sadness on Susan and Roger's faces, as tears flowed down their cheeks. Jason closed his eyes, gathering himself. He would not lie to her. They never did. But it was so hard. He'd never failed her before either. When he replied, it was through clenched teeth. "I don't know, baby. But we're going to find her. No matter what."

Heather sniffled and crawled up onto the bed to snuggle beside him. "Promise?"

"Yeah, baby, I promise." He snuggled her into him and buried his face in her hair.

Roger and Susan looked on, Susan wiping at her own tears. "We're sorry we haven't been by before," she said.

Jason waved it off. "No, you were taking care of Heather. That's exactly what we wanted. Thank you."

Susan nodded, smiling, then looked away as her eyes

glistened.

"They tell us you're going to be up and about again soon," Roger said.

Jason grunted. "That's what they say. I can't wait."

"Well, we've got the house in order for you," Susan offered. "At least, the best we could do. Hoping you like what we did."

"Heather made us change things," Roger said and laughed. "She was quite the task master."

"I know what they like," Heather said and smiled smugly.

Jason tousled her hair. "I'm sure it's fine. I'll just be glad to be there. How's school?"

"Oh, she's so great," Heather said. For the next half hour, overjoyed at both the reunion and the chance to escape from the constant hospital smell of antiseptic and industrial cleaning fluids, Jason soaked in the touch and smell of the daughter he loved more than life itself as she told him all about what she'd been up to the past few weeks: her new school, adventures with her grandparents, new friends, the neighbor's dog, and more. Jason loved every moment of it, the tension gone from his body, replaced by a warmth and peace he hadn't felt since he woke up in the hospital. For the moment, Heather's own worries seemed forgotten, and her enthusiasm was infectious.

When Heather finally started to waiver a bit, Susan stepped forward and ran a hand through her hair. "We should let daddy rest, dear. He's been through a lot."

Heather frowned. "Awwwwww, but I like snuggling."

Jason laughed as he gently eased her away. "I like it too, baby. So we'll do it again soon."

Heather kissed him and then slid off the bed, taking her grandmother's hand.

"I'm coming to see you every day until you come home," Heather said, as if it were nonnegotiable.

"Whatever the doctors say, dear," Susan replied.

Heather locked eyes with her father, offering a look that said *This woman is not the boss of me.*

Jason almost laughed but instead said, "Every other day, okay? I do have to get better."

Heather sighed, her shoulders drooping in defeat. "All right." She looked as if the world had come to an end.

Jason chuckled. "And stop trying to manipulate us, silly. We're onto you."

Heather grinned. And then as Susan pulled her toward the door, she waved in a way so cute and charming Jason almost melted.

As the ladies left, Roger lagged behind, shooting Jason a scolding look. "The police say you haven't been much help. Why is that?" His voice was tense, accusatory.

"I told them everything I can remember, Roger," Jason said. "I promise. I want Laura back as much as anyone. I'd be out there looking myself if I weren't stuck here."

Roger glared a moment more before relaxing. "She's been missing for three weeks now, Jason. They're going to find her body. Do you know what that will do to her mother?"

Jason knew he was talking about himself as much as his wife. "She's not dead, Roger. Don't give up on her. We *will* find her. I swear."

It was Roger's turn to sigh. "I hope so. I really do. But

that's a long time to be unaccounted for."

"I've got my lab people going over some of the evidence to see if we can add anything to the investigation," Jason said. "And I'm doing what I can from here, too. You know how much she means to me."

The men locked eyes a moment, staring in a silent contest of wills—as if one could prove he loved Laura more.

"That girl needs her mother," Roger said then and looked away, his voice cracking a bit. "Just find her. Find her fast."

And then he turned and marched from the room, conversation over. That was Roger. And for the first time in a while, Jason wanted to do exactly what his father-in-law had ordered.

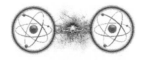

JASON FIDDLED AROUND on his iPad for hours that afternoon, reviewing what he'd discovered on the dosimeters, reviewing data about Shortcuts—all trying to wrap his mind around the idea that someone could possibly have taken his wife using the same technology he'd been developing for space travel. He couldn't imagine how it was safe. It was not impossible. But who would have that capability? Whoever it was had to have developed it beyond the level he'd reached with NASA at the moment. And why would they do it? What did they hope to achieve?

He was interrupted when Jan arrived with a wheelchair. "Put it down and let's go," she said. "Physical therapy time."

"Oh, man," he whined, teasing. "I'm working."

She smiled. "It'll still be here when you get back."

He set the iPad on the bedside table and scooted to the edge of the bed. "Okay, lift me over there, ma'am. I'll just lay here like a log and wait."

Jan laughed. "You wish. The wheelchair is hospital policy, but you can walk enough to get into it on your own, so hop to it!" She held out her hand.

Jason grasped it and twisted so both his legs dangled off the side of the bed beside the wheelchair.

"Okay, now the hard part," Jan said.

Jason took a deep breath and held it, his cheeks puffy, then stood, pausing a moment to steady himself before hobbling over to sit in the wheelchair, making a show of it.

Jan laughed, shaking her head. "You're just a big kid, aren't ya?" Then she stepped behind the chair, grabbed the handles, and wheeled him out the door.

Physical therapy was unpleasant. He hadn't realized how much the body goes through when it shuts down into a non-ambulatory state for several weeks. His limbs were like wet noodles, and the pain like daggers! It took him by surprise, despite what he'd felt when he'd fallen. The therapist was actually nice though, encouraging him and only pushing a little. She examined his cast a bit first, taking his legs and arms through a kind of warm up routine, gentle but firm, that covered a range of motions. Then it was his turn. He had to work hard, because he was absolutely going to get back up on his feet as soon as possible. She wanted him to succeed but not push himself beyond what he could handle. He quickly realized he had his work cut out for him. But that realization just made him more determined. He gritted his teeth and swallowed the pain like a trophy.

The therapist, Lynn Nelson, smiled when Jan arrived to

return him to his room forty minutes later. "You ready for more tomorrow?"

Jason looked at Jan. "You know she tortures me, right?"

"Yep," Jan said. "That's why we like her."

Jason started to protest that he didn't need the chair but then fell into it, exhausted and amazed at what a half hour had taken out of him.

When Jan returned him to his room, the phone was ringing. She helped him into bed and Jason answered. It was Peter Edtz.

Jason leaned back on the pillow, his arm tucked under his head and caught a sniff of his own sweaty armpit. "Good thing you can't smell it through the phone" Jason joked, crinkling his nose. "I just got back from PT."

"And I actually thought about coming in person," Peter replied. "But I figured you'd want this as soon as possible."

"What've you got for me?" Noting Jan slipping out the door, Jason reached toward the bedside table for his iPad, prepared to take notes, but as his hand fumbled around, feeling for it, he felt just napkins and the water cup. No iPad. He glanced over. Sure enough. It wasn't there. His eyebrows drew together as his eyes darted around the room, searching.

"Well, there are traces of elements, particles," Peter said, stating the obvious.

"What traces?" Where was that iPad? He leaned right toward the edge of the bed as his eyes searched the foot of the bedside table. The room was so bright there was nowhere for it to hide. Unless it slipped under the bed. Or maybe it was between the table and the wall.

"Niobium, copper, and nickel," Peter replied. "And

tridymite."

Jason sat up, his throat constricting as he clutched the phone. "Tridymite? Like Buckskin tridymite?"

"The one and only," Peter said. In 2016, NASA's Mars rover Curiosity collected powder from rocks at a location named "Buckskin." When analyzed using X-ray diffraction, scientists found significant amounts of a silica mineral called tridymite, a mineral which, while rare on Earth, had never been found on Mars before and was generally associated with silicic volcanism, requiring high temperatures and generous silicone deposits to form. It changed their concept of Martian geological history, hinting for the first time that the planet had once had explosive volcanoes.

"Okay, so she might be out on Mars or nearby?" Jason said. His muscles tensed as he felt an adrenaline rush. He'd ask Jan to look for the iPad as soon as she came back. He knew he'd put it there. Had he been robbed? He looked at the bureau where his wallet was tucked inside his street clothes. He could use the Find My feature if he had his iPhone, but they'd taken that, too, since the hospital forbade use of cell phones on certain floors.

"It's possible, but tridymite can also be found on Earth," Peter said. "But we also found traces of kamacite." Kamacite was a lattice polymorph of iron with nickel that occurred on Earth only at meteorite strikes, not natural formations. It was common to meteorites.

"So, she's out in space," Jason said. It seemed the only logical conclusion.

"Or near a meteorite strike," Peter said. "Either way, lots of possible sites. Not very helpful."

"It gives us a place to start," Jason said. "That's better

than nothing."

"I also found traces of potassium iodide and silver iodide," Peter said.

"Potassium iodide and silver iodide? What does that mean?"

"I don't know what any of it means, really. I'm just telling you what I found. We should probably go back and scan for radiation now as well. You never know."

Jan returned with his afternoon meds in a small paper cup and set them on the bedside table, motioning to him. He nodded in acknowledgement.

Then, cupping the phone, he whispered, "My iPad is missing. Could you please see if you can find it? Maybe it fell on the floor or something?"

Jan nodded and began a search as Jason went back to the phone. "Okay, well, so all we have to do is look for locations with kamacite and tridymite together and we'll find her." He laughed, because it was still equivalent to finding a needle in a haystack, but it made him feel better to have at least some clues.

"I'll run some more tests," Peter said. "See if I can narrow it down any, but yeah. Find the needle."

Jason sighed. "Well, thanks. Let me know if you find anything else."

"Of course," Peter agreed. "We also got the cell. We're going over it now to see what we can find. But the police said the GPS data was nonsense. Not sure what that means. More later."

The line went dead and Jason noticed Jan had a frustrated look on her face.

"I don't see it anywhere," she said. "Where could it have gone?"

"Someone took it?" Jason suggested.

She groaned. "It does happen, but I hope not. Your security guys were out there, not to mention a fully staffed nurses' station."

"It's small enough to conceal," Jason said. "And it currently has all the notes I've gathered since I woke up here about Laura's disappearance. We have to find it. Can you check the bureau? See if my wallet is gone too."

Jan walked to the bureau and opened a drawer, searching the pants where his wallet had been. She held up the worn brown leather mass. She knew it was there because she had showed it to him once, to let him know it was there. "Nope. It's still here." Placing it back, she slid the drawer shut.

"I have to find that iPad," Jason said, frowning.

Jan nodded. "I'll ask security and maintenance to look around. You can't search in your condition."

Jason smiled his most charming smile. "We could use the Find My feature on my iPhone, if you'd let me use that."

"I think the police have it," she said. "They were tracking your movements during the time of the attack. I'll get the other nurses and orderlies on it, and have the custodians keep an eye out too." She fluffed his pillow and set it back on the bed behind him, then motioned. "Now you take your meds and get some rest. That's an order." Her eyes narrowed, her brow furrowing in stern warning.

Surrendering to the inevitable, Jason leaned back into his pillow, taking a deep breath as he reached for the meds and the water cup. "Yes, ma'am." Then he grabbed a pen and jotted down what Peter had told him on a magazine beside the bed. It would have to do until he found his iPad. Where the hell had it gone?

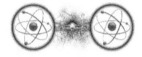

THE MAN HAD stumbled onto the Shortcut project buried in one of those encyclopedic daily briefings all intelligence officers got each morning for their review. At first, he'd blown it off as insignificant, but gradually, hints of its full capabilities filtered in and the man realized not only the potential but the importance a program like Shortcut could play in his own activities. Then came the October day when *Maxx-One* had a crisis prior to reentry. While NASA, as expected, leaned toward more traditional explanations for the causes of the associated systems failures, Jason Maxx from day one suspected something unusual, even sabotage. His first guesses were fellow rivals in the industry, but quickly, indications pointed toward a third possibility that really caught the man's attention: *aliens*. To Jason's colleagues at NASA and Caltech, the mere suggestion was ludicrous, farfetched, but to the man who had headed the top secret Project V for the past twenty years, it was anything but and he'd immediately assigned his people to keep a close watch on all aspects of both the investigation and the Shortcut program from then on out.

Stolen notes from Jason Maxx's home and office proved quite revealing. He had not given up his strong feeling that deliberate sabotage was the most likely cause of *Maxx-One's* issues, and though the fact the incident had occurred in space made the list of possible perpetrators small and hard to pin down, the man quickly realized the subjects of Project V were strong candidates.

Although Jason Maxx's strong insistence on such theories might cause a rift between himself and his colleagues, the Dr. never wavered, and the man became convinced the Shortcut project must be protected at all costs. In a memo to his superiors, he wrote:

The full dangers of Shortcut must not fall into the wrong hands, but Dr. Maxx must be allowed to complete its development so it can be acquired at all costs. I fully believe it is essential to our efforts against the V. It will take us leaps and bounds forward from present capabilities. Will attempt to assign an asset to close proximity with Maxx but, if unsuccessful, we have other options for infiltration and will exploit them, because we cannot risk the V's coming in and polluting our society or removing us from our rightful place as the world superpower. No matter what, that order must be preserved. It is our destiny to be the greatest in the universe one day, I have no doubt, and so whatever it takes to ensure that will always be my mission no matter what it costs or who gets in the way.

Other possible means ranged from dispatching techs to bug Jason Maxx's home and office to the installation of keylogger apps on his computers and iPads that would allow Project V to monitor everything he did. His people had managed to swipe the iPad from beside Jason Maxx's hospital bed and installed both a keylogger and a custom operating system with built-in backdoors and reporting subroutines. The modified OS's special features blended in with the iPad's normal functions while going around all of Apple's carefully built-in security features that made their products so difficult to hack. Even if Jason Maxx took the iPad to an Apple store for customer service, the extra algorithms the custom OS ran would blend in so well with the existing functions, the customer service people would have to be experts and know what they were looking for to even find a hint of something suspicious.

From that moment on, they could follow Jason's every email, diagram, file, calendar entry, and more from almost the instant he created them, the custom OS encoding and embedding them inside outgoing data the iPad used to regularly operate and communicate with networks, iCloud, and the internet, etc. Jason would have no idea, of course. In a day or two, his people would return the iPad, giving the appearance it had been taken by accident. In the meantime, the man was, as always, thrilled and amazed by his people's competence and expertise.

When something happened with Laura Maxx and Shortcut, he'd be the first to know and the first to respond. Then when the right opportunity presented itself, NASA and Jason Maxx would invite the Project V people right into their midst without hesitation.

CHAPTER 8

J ASON'S IPAD WAS still missing when Jimmy and the two detectives came back a few days later to fill Jason in on the case, and Jason was tense and frustrated. He'd checked in with them daily, but so far they hadn't had much news, and he wanted desperately to see progress.

"We found the man in the sketch," Coben said as they stood around the hospital bed.

"Bene Rodriguez," Connelly added.

"He's the leader of the Estradas Buenos, a Puerto Rican gang," Coben continued. "He denied any knowledge of Laura's whereabouts."

Jimmy scoffed. "There's a surprise."

Connelly shrugged. "Actually, we believe him. He said they were drinking and having fun with their families that night, not out on gang business. This gang isn't known for petty crime and robbery, though it does happen. They have too big of a narcotics operation to jeopardize it over petty side crime."

Jason listened but remained silent, brooding about the iPad, though he did note it was almost as if they were talking amongst themselves.

"They actually punish members who get caught doing

street crime," Coben added. "Bad for business."

"Regardless, we got warrants to search his home and their headquarters, and there was no evidence that they had any involvement," Connelly said. "And no one we or our gang unit undercovers talked to had any information. Holding a rich white woman, especially an ex-astronaut, would tend to generate some intel. Word spreads fast amongst these types and—"

"I don't think they took her," Jason interrupted, after debating what to tell them about his own discoveries.

All three men looked at him with surprise.

"Why's that?" Jimmy asked.

"I had people at my lab examine the badge and purse after I found evidence of polaritons on the badge and some microscopic damage similar to what lasers might cause," Jason said. "They found evidence of some minerals and elements that indicate she is not here locally." *Outer space. She's in outer space. No, they'll think you're crazy. You need more proof.* Inside, he knew how it would sound to them and how they might react, but the science pointed him there, and he had Peter and his team for confirmation.

"Then where is she?" Coben asked, puzzled.

Jason hesitated a moment, searching for an explanation. "That I don't know. Somewhere else."

Jimmy was watching him and looked suspicious, but the detectives nodded.

"You're saying whoever took her brought some of this with them that rubbed off on the badge and purse she left behind?" Connelly said.

"It's a possibility," Jason said. "I'm not sure how she

would have been exposed to these particular elements or minerals any time recently. It would really help if I could go to the park and walk through the scene, have my people look for other types of evidence that your forensics people might not know to look for."

Now the detectives looked amused.

"You know, our people have a lot of experience with this," Coben said. "It's a real science. They are very thorough."

"Did their reports mention kamacite or tridymite?" Jason asked. "My lab team found traces of it. And more."

"Never heard of them," Coben muttered.

"Well, one is only found in meteorites or at locations where meteorites have struck Earth," Jason said, forgetting the iPad for a moment as he focused on the scientific evidence. "The other requires heavy silica volcanic activity to form."

"Which means what?" Connelly asked.

"I don't know, but it's unusual," Jason said, brow piercing as his mind raced through many possibilities too complicated for most laypeople. "They're planning to go back and scan for radiation as well, just in case."

"Well, we'll talk to the doctor and see what can be arranged," Jimmy said. "Bet you can come along in a wheelchair at least. Show us where it all occurred."

"Great. Soon as possible," Jason said, smiling. He was sure it could really help, even if it was just by allowing his team an excuse to search. They needed him to pinpoint the exact locations in order to avoid endless hours of searching blindly. And he wanted his team there to take some more measurements and readings, and scan for more evidence, too.

The detectives exchanged a somber look with Jimmy.

"What is it?" Jason asked, but none of them would meet his eyes.

After a moment, Connelly looked at him. "Dr. Maxx," Connelly said, "your wife has been missing almost a month. The likelihood of finding her..."

"I know the odds," Jason said, cutting him off.

"We just think you should be realistic," Coben said.

"I can't give up on her," Jason said, shaking his head. "She would never give up on me. And there's no proof she's not alive."

"We're not giving up," Connelly said. "There's still room to investigate a bit, but that doesn't mean you shouldn't prepare yourself for the real possibility—"

"I know," Jason said, nodding. "It's constantly on my mind, detective."

The detectives nodded, then moved on to discussing charges against Rodriguez and his unknown cronies. They hadn't identified them all, but they had suspicions and would be working on that angle. When detectives wished him well and excused themselves, Jimmy lagged behind.

"What is it you're not telling us?" Jimmy asked.

Jason looked away, shaking his head. "I told you all I know."

"Bullshit, brother, I didn't just fall off a turnip truck. I can see it in your eyes," Jimmy said.

Their eyes met, as Jason debated how much to say. Jimmy did have more knowledge of space than the detectives would. But that didn't mean the man wouldn't declare Jason to be losing it and dismiss him if he fired off some outlandish theory. And what he was thinking was out there. He couldn't risk being sidelined as a mental case. *Laura needs me.* Still, he had to tell someone...

After a moment, he took a deep breath. "I think a Shortcut jump was used to kidnap her," Jason said, finally giving in. It seemed the least outlandish of his suspicions to start with.

"A Shortcut? Polaritons?" Jimmy repeated. Apparently he'd been reading up on Jason's theory.

"Yeah, the evidence traces suggest perhaps it could have been involved—lasers, polaritons, radiation," Jason said.

"But who would jump an uninsulated person without a ship? Isn't that dangerous?" Jimmy asked.

"Yes, but if they have that technology, they'd be working at a much higher level than we are with the Shortcut theory right now," Jason said. "It's not impossible."

"Someone else is working at far more advanced levels of your own theory?" Jimmy shook his head. "It sounds like bunk."

"If I thought it was bunk, I wouldn't be pursuing it," Jason said, pursing his lips as he locked eyes with Jimmy. "It's the only way to explain the blacking out of her figure before she disappeared, the evidence traces, and why the gang knows nothing about her and she hasn't been found."

"But who's got the technology to do that?" Jimmy said, frowning.

"If I knew, I'd be working with them, believe me," Jason said. "They could advance us years, I suspect."

Jimmy sighed. "You didn't tell the detectives because

they'd think you're a couple cards short of a full deck, right?"

Jason shrugged. "The way you're looking at me, you seem to be close to that, so yeah."

Jimmy grunted. "It's out there, brother. I mean, it's not like you're suggesting aliens did it or that she's not on Earth, but it's out there."

Jason smiled. Aliens were foremost on his mind, in fact. *But that I'll keep to myself...for now.* Time to stop sharing until he had more evidence. "I'm just doing what I can to help find any clue, anything that might suggest a lead."

Jimmy nodded. "Okay, we'll make some inquiries about other research on polaritons and similar theories to yours, if there are any. But you'd think they would have made themselves known. This has huge significance."

"I know. It's not the kind of thing most scientists would keep to themselves, which makes me wonder about private enterprise," Jason said.

"Private sector? Like some rich guy trying to make his own spaceship?" Jimmy laughed. "A few years ago that might have sounded crazy, too, but now there's Richard Branson, Elon Musk..." He watched Jason a moment, noting his sincerity. "Let me see what we can dig up. But do me a favor, keep this to yourself for now, okay?"

Jason grunted. "Yes, sir. But before you go, can you get my iPhone back? I need the Find My app to locate my missing iPad."

"I'll ask the detectives about it." Jimmy smiled and then took his leave, so Jason's mind went to work. They had a theory and enough science to lend it weight to scientists, but they had more work ahead of them. How could he find more evidence? Evidence that would convince not just people in the know like Jimmy or even Phil Cline, but civilians like the two detectives?

Jason couldn't get his mind off the smartphone. *Why would there be jumbled GPS data? The park would be easily marked on any GPS or Google map. Where did the jumbling occur? What had the police said about her not getting a signal — jamming?* Jamming might explain jumbled data. Could whoever had taken her have gone so far as to jam her phone to prevent calling for help?

No matter where the science led him, he'd explore it to the very end to find his wife, this much was certain. But this was *his Laura*. He needed others to join him. He picked up the phone and dialed Peter at Caltech. As he waited, he thought he heard an odd clicking on the line.

"Hello?" he asked. "Is someone there?" More clicks but no response. Was someone listening?

As he considered it there was a louder click then Peter picked up. "Hello?" he sounded cheerful.

"I need an update on what your people found with Laura's smartphone. Is there anything to that jumbled GPS data the police mentioned?"

"We've got people on it," Peter replied. "The police took forever just negotiating privacy issues with the cell phone company to crack it. We're trying other things."

"The GPS. Did you analyze the data?" Jason asked, having forgotten all about the clicking.

"That would be one thing, yes," Peter agreed.

"What did you find?" Jason demanded, impatient for answers.

"Let me check, okay?" He put Jason on hold and came back two minutes later, but to Jason it had seemed an eternity. "There is additional GPS data after her phone logged her location in the park that makes no sense."

"What is it? Is there something in the metadata?"

"We're not sure," Peter said.

"Let me know what you find as soon as possible," Jason said.

"Will do," Peter said and hung up.

God, Jason hated the waiting. The love of his life was somewhere out there, possibly injured or in danger. He had to help her. He was all she had. *She was all he had.* And all he wanted.

He shifted anxiously in the bed, struggling to get comfortable despite the tension of his body and anxiety of his thoughts. They'd told him he'd be going home in a day or two and his impatience grew by the day.

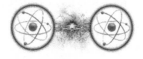

THAT AFTERNOON, JIMMY met with the detectives and Jack and Li in Jack's office at Caltech to discuss the investigation. The room was neat as academic offices go but it smelled of industrial cleaners, air fresheners, and paper dust. Bookshelves lined every available wall space filled with books of all shapes, sizes, and designs, a few models of rocket and other space paraphernalia displayed strategically among them. A large desk was centered in front of a large bay window overlooking the campus with tall file cabinets to either side, one pair supporting a large printer. The men were gathered around a round conference table across the room.

"It sounds like he's absolutely convinced there's some kind of unusual, even supernatural explanation for his wife's disappearance," Connelly was saying. "The doctors insist the head injury was just a concussion but I'm starting to wonder."

"Jason gets like this when it comes to Laura," Jack said, unperturbed. "Laura was on a space shuttle mission that encountered problems and kept them stranded in space for ten extra days. He won't admit it, but we all know it scared Jason to death. Drove him to the brink of exhaustion."

"It went beyond exhaustion, "Li grunted. "We thought he was losing it. When they landed and Laura got off that shuttle, Jason looked totally elated as he took her in his arms, but seconds later, he completely collapsed. He was on the ground for less than a minute and insisted he was fine, but the possibility of losing her just took everything out of him."

"He's so used to being in control of most situations he deals with and this was something he could do nothing about," Jack said.

"Like the present situation," Coben said.

"Exactly," Li agreed.

"So he could fall apart at any time?" Jimmy asked.

Li leaned back in his chair. "Laura is his whole world. They have a real love affair, not just a marriage. They're everything to each other, inseparable. The emotional strain he's under must be unbearable. Plus he has Heather to worry about and he's stuck in a hospital."

"All that makes it sound to me like he can't handle this," Jimmy said. "Phil Cline can interfere—"

"No," Li said. "He was way worse then. Doctors tested him for months and got him on a fitness regimen and therapy with a psychiatrist. They never really put a finger on what caused it."

"He's doing much better this time for sure," Jack added. "None of the short-term memory loss, lack of focus, or low energy we saw then. We think he'd just burned out and the fear of losing Laura was the final straw."

"He's a bit paranoid, isn't he?" Connelly asked, his doubt apparent. "Is he always like that?"

"What? The sabotage? Aliens?" Li said and exchanged an amused look with Jack. "His mind is always running full tilt with every possibility, every angle. It's out there, we know. And we're keeping an eye on it, but the thing that makes him such a genius is he can see possibilities from evidence nobody else sees. That's how he came up with his magic toaster and Shortcut and all his other incredible theories and successes."

"So you're certain he's not losing it again?" Jimmy said, meeting their eyes each in turn.

"He'll calm down once he gets home to his normal routine and sets to work on the problem," Li said, confident, unfaltering. "He's not good about letting others do the work. He wants to be at the center of it, thrives on it. But this is just Jason."

"Just Jason," Jack agreed. Both looked undisturbed by either Jason's behavior or his wild theories, but the looks Jimmy caught them exchanging as he glanced back on his way out the door left him certain they were keeping their own doubts to themselves. He resolved to keep a closer watch on Jason for the time being.

"HERE," HOLLY SAID, waking Jason from a light nap that evening. She tossed an iPad gently on his lap.

"Is this what I think it is?" Jason said through a yawn as he shook off the drowsiness and examined it.

"Yes," Holly said. "One of the custodians found it in a linen cart. It must have fallen off when they were changing sheets and got tangled."

Jason breathed a sigh of relief, tension draining from his body. He could get back to work with his own notes and data now. "Thank you. I've been missing this." The first task was to be sure he backed up the latest notes on the cloud, something he'd foolishly forgotten to do before the iPad disappeared.

"Well, let's lock it in your bureau for now, we have to go," she said.

"What? Where?" he mumbled, squinting against the bright fluorescents overhead.

"We've got work to do," she said, smiling as she pulled back the sheets and pushed the meal cart into a corner, then took the iPad and carried it over to the bureau, locking the drawer and bringing the key back over to Jason.

"Work? Isn't it almost dinner time?" Jason said, still drowsy.

"You're the one who wants to go home soon, right?" she said, hands on her hips. "So get up and let's go."

"Where are we going?" Jason asked as he sat up and shifted, sliding his legs over the edge of the bed, then waiting as she helped him slip the key's chain around his neck.

Holly motioned to the corridor that ran past the nurse's station and other rooms. "Practice walking. Make sure you're ready to leave tomorrow when you go to that park. We need to be sure you can handle yourself, Mr. Bigshot. So show me your stuff." She grinned.

Jason stood tenderly then slowly and cautiously made his way to the door as she stood waiting and watching. He felt less pain with the movement and his legs were steadier though clearly out of practice. Adrenaline surged as he realized he was out of bed and wondered how soon he could make that permanent.

Holly smiled. "Good. Now walk." She motioned to the corridor.

"You going to walk beside me; make sure I don't fall?"

She shook her head. "Not unless you need it. We need to see what you can do on your own."

"You're kinda mean," Jason teased and frowned. But inside, he was smiling. Joking and bantering with his nurses made him feel normal. It also distracted him from his worries and problems. After all, studies did show laughter was really good medicine.

Holly laughed, "Whiner."

Jason made a face then started strolling slowly down the hall past the nurse's station toward a window at the far end, walking awkwardly at first—one leg at a time—then picking up speed and steadying as he built his confidence. The physical therapy had really allowed him to make quick progress.

His mind went back to when Laura had been injured by a falling payload crate that accidentally slipped off a walkway above during shuttle training. The workers had yelled out, and the astronauts had tried to duck aside, but with three of them bunched up together at the time, Laura had to wait on the others and had lagged just enough for it to strike her leg. She'd wound up in a cast and had to switch places with a crewmember on the next mission while she recovered. That had really been a disappointment.

Jason had been by her side the whole time, encouraging, supporting, doting. He'd been the one to help her practice her crutch walking sometimes as well, though he hadn't been as teasing as Holly. He could never get away with that. Instead, he'd tried to coach so much it pissed Laura off. She was as much of an emotional wreck as he felt at the moment and Jason had borne the brunt.

"Stop sounding like Roger," she'd snapped.

"Your dad?"

"Yes, coach," she replied.

"I'm just trying to cheer you on."

"You're driving me crazy," she said. "And it's distracting. I have to concentrate here."

He'd sighed, feeling nothing but tenderness for her. "Sorry. You know I just want you up and about because you want it so badly."

"Just shut up and let me do it, okay?" she'd scolded again.

Jason had shut his mouth and watched. Laura had struggled too, wincing with pain, but gritting her teeth and pushing herself harder with every step. He wondered more than once if she was pushing herself too hard, but kept his mouth shut knowing she was determined not to be in that bed any longer than necessary. In the end, he swelled with pride at her determination and after a few days, she was making clear progress.

He shook off the memory as he reached the window, then spun with a bit of flair, and headed back toward her. She just watched him, showing no emotion, arms crossed over her chest. As he passed the nurse's station, several nurses looked up from their paperwork and monitors and grinned at him. One even applauded. "Way to go, Dr. Maxx."

"Well?" he asked as he strolled back up next to where she was standing outside his room. It felt good to be on his feet again without using any PT devices, and he smiled at her as their eyes met, hoping for encouragement.

She looked at her watch and shrugged. "I've got rounds to do. I think you're good."

"Wow, you're some cheerleader there, nurse," Jason teased. "Really encouraging."

The other nurses laughed. Holly stepped aside as he walked past her into his room. "You need me to come tuck you in and read you a bedtime story then?" she teased back. Again, laughter erupted from the nurse's station.

"Tough love, I got it," he said. She relented and reached for his arm but he scurried out of reach. "No, I got this. Maybe bring me a mint later for my pillow though," he said and smiled, then turned and headed back for the bed. Holly followed, just making sure he made it okay, then bent to quickly adjust his covers over him as he settled into bed, leaned back onto the pillow, and stretched out his legs.

"You can take the wheelchair to the park if you want to be lazy," she said, "but with the ground you might cover, you may get tired, so the chair is still a good idea, okay?"

"So this is it? I'm outta here?" he said hopefully.

This time she cracked a smile as she nodded. "Yep. Dr.

Brock signed off this afternoon. They'll pick you up for the park, then take you home. Congratulations."

Jason danced on the bed a bit before she laughed and hurried off to visit other patients.

Dinner arrived twenty minutes later, and soon after, Susan and Roger brought Heather for another visit. She brought with her a backgammon set, one of her favorites, and Jason helped her set it up on his rolling table. She sat on the bed between his legs facing him across the table as they played. Susan and Roger kindly took leave and disappeared. This was father-daughter time and much needed.

"So how's school?" Jason asked as they finished setting up the board.

"We're doing a unit on calculus word problems," Heather said immediately, knowing math was her father's favorite go to. "A satellite traveling in the y-direction at 17,000 mph ejects a payload that flies in the x-direction at 1000 mph. Two hours later, the satellite has completed its orbit and returns to the same position where it launched the payload. We're supposed to figure out how fast the two objects are moving away from each other fifteen minutes later. Ignoring curvature."

"Ah, geometry and derivatives, nice," Jason said, smiling as Heather made her first move. She was playing brown and he was white, as usual. Heather always wanted the most colorful pieces.

"Yeah," she said with a sigh as her eyebrows knit together lending her a striking resemblance to her mother as she slid pieces across the board. "Basic stuff."

Jason laughed. A ten-year-old conquering calculus was hardly basic, except maybe in a family like theirs. Luckily, at

Purva's recommendation, Jason and Laura had been able to enroll Heather in the school that served most Caltech professor's kids. It offered far more advanced classes than the average grade school, including higher level math. "So, what's the answer?"

"Well, first I need an equation to define the positions of the two objects over time." She wrote down y=17,000t and x=1000(t+2). "Next I'll need the distance between the satellite and the payload. Since their paths are perpendicular, I can use the equation for the hypotenuse of a right triangle," Heather said, explaining the equation that would form the basis for her diagram: $\sqrt{17000^2 t^2 + 1000^2 (t+2)^2}$. Taking some time to compute the derivative, she used the chain rule and got $\dfrac{1000(145t+1)}{\sqrt{\frac{145}{2}t^2 + t + 1}}$. Plugging in 15 minutes for t gave her 15,500 mph.

As she worked the problem, Jason did the figures in his head. He was beaming with pride when he finished. She'd nailed it, and as he watched her across the table, he found himself reveling in the feeling of normal life returning.

"Ahem!" Heather said and stared at the backgammon board.

"Oh, sorry," Jason said, scrambling to make his first move.

"Did you find any clues yet?" Heather said, switching subjects.

"Clues?"

"When's Mommy coming home?"

Jason finished his move and met her eyes, trying to

project confidence despite his own worries and doubts. "I don't know yet, honey, but people are working on it, a lot of people, and she will be soon."

"She's not going to miss Christmas, right?" Now Heather sounded like the little girl she still was.

"I hope not, honey," Jason said, struggling to keep his voice steady as inside pins pricked at his heart. "I want her back, too. Just as much as you."

Heather made another move, advancing quickly.

"I mean, she promised we'd see the parade this year live in person," Heather said. The Hollywood Christmas Parade had been a family tradition around the TV since Heather was an infant, and Heather and Laura especially always got giddy snuggling up to watch it together. It could be sixty or seventy out and they'd have hot chocolate, candy canes, Christmas cookies, and a warm blanket to cuddle under. While at first Laura almost had to drag him kicking and screaming to join them, now Jason found himself a willing participant, amused and delighted by their childlike joy.

"I promise," Jason said. "No matter what." He reached for his iPad on the bedside table and made a quick reminder to check logistics. It was still a month away, but that time would pass quickly and who knew how far ahead one had to plan.

"Grandma said the police have leads," Heather said.

"Leads? Well, they know who attacked us," Jason said.

"So they can find Mommy," Heather said confidently.

Jason hesitated as he finished his next move and Heather focused on the board. He and Laura had long ago promised never to lie to their daughter. Oh they'd entertained her with Santa, the Easter Bunny, and the Tooth Fairy, dodging her innocent but telling inquiries, but they drew the line at flat out lies. They saw no purpose in it, and their daughter was too smart. Her trust in them was essential for all she'd need them to guide her through many tough decisions earlier than most kids her age would have to face them. Laura's parents probably would prefer he use more tact, but they weren't here, and he was the parent.

"They searched and they questioned the men, but they don't know where Mommy is," Jason finally said as Heather made another move. "They think maybe someone else took her while I was distracted."

Heather's lips pursed as her shoulders sank. "What if they don't find her?"

Jason took a breath, fighting to keep the tears he felt at the tips of his eyes from flowing. He reached across the table to cup her cheek with his palm, his eyes on hers. "Listen to me, baby. We're going to get her back. No matter what it takes. I'll never give up."

Heather locked eyes with him, her own brown eyes so like her mother's. The sadness clouded them for a bit and then she smiled, putting her hand over his. "Me either. Never."

"Good," Jason said, heat flushing through him as his unconditional love swelled within. He fought the urge to push the board aside, wrap her in his arms, and hold her.

"Now stop stalling and move," Heather said, nodding toward the board.

Jason laughed.

They finished the game in thirty-five minutes, Heather handily winning, and were about to start another when Roger and Susan returned.

"Well, dear, it's almost time to head home," Susan said

sweetly to her granddaughter.

Heather groaned. "But visiting hours are 'til nine-thirty!"

"You have homework, right?" Susan said, shooting her one of those 'don't test me' looks grandmas and moms are experts at.

Heather sighed. "Yeah, yeah."

Jason shot her a mock scolding look. "Hey, school is your first priority right now. You focus and you do the work, okay? I'll worry about the rest."

Heather nodded. "I know."

"Promise?"

Heather wouldn't meet his eyes until he reached down and began tickling her, then she giggled and squirmed away. "I promise, I promise."

He toyed with the idea of telling her he'd be home the next afternoon when she got out of school, but decided he'd rather surprise her and held his tongue. Instead, he pushed the rolling table aside and sat forward. "Now give me a hug."

Heather scooted up and hugged him, Jason wincing a bit when she bumped against his ribs as she wiggled. He kissed her and they both whispered, "I love you," then Roger picked Heather up and set her on the floor.

"I'll see you soon, sweetheart," Jason said, suddenly choking up at saying 'goodbye' to his other great love.

Susan nodded and grabbed Heather's hand, leading her out.

"Thanks for bringing her," Jason managed before they were gone.

"I hear you're going to the park tomorrow with the detectives," Roger said.

"Yes," Jason confirmed.

"Okay, I'll meet you there," Roger said and was out the door after his wife and granddaughter. Jason would rather he didn't but it was a battle he knew better than to start.

Jason noticed they'd left the backgammon board and started to call after them, but then decided it might have been intentional. He and Heather would probably play again in a couple nights before he went home. So he began putting the pieces away before settling back in his bed and waited for his nighttime meds.

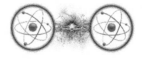

JIMMY BURNETTE SAT on the edge of his king bed at The Westin Pasadena and made the call. Even though he knew in his heart no good would probably come of it, it was his duty. He'd sworn an oath. And it had been his duty for over twenty-five years now, though he'd rarely been called upon to perform it. Almost no one he spent any significant time with knew it. To them, he was a hero, astronaut, legendary pilot, father, or grandfather. Maybe their boss. But the top secret part remained just that. And it was a pain in the ass.

The voice that answered was especially gravelly and sounded tired. "Yeah?"

Well, he'd done it, so Jimmy resigned himself to what followed. The mission was important. He'd believed in it twenty-five years ago, and he believed in it now. "He's suspicious," he began, knowing the man at the other end would know the context.

"Tell me."

"His lab people from Caltech found residue of minerals that are associated with Shortcut jumps and one is uncommon on Earth as well," Jimmy said. "The detectives told us they're certain the gang isn't responsible for abducting Laura, so Jason is working on a theory it was someone else, someone with capabilities beyond what most people know about. It's just a matter of time before he makes the connection."

"They'll think he's crazy."

"A card short of a full deck, yeah. But he's a desperate man and he's smart, and he's determined to try anything and believe anything that will get his wife back." Jimmy couldn't help wondering about Jason's sanity himself but then the man was famous for ideas that pushed the envelope, and his beloved wife was missing. If anything, he suspected it was only temporary insanity borne of desperation.

"When are you taking him to the park?"

"Tomorrow."

"Who will be there?"

"Me, two detectives, a couple crime scene people, and a couple people from his lab." He might as well volunteer it. The boss would have asked. Even if the information was mostly insignificant.

"Okay. Do your best to keep him from telling them everything. It will just complicate things unnecessarily."

"He knows it sounds crazy," Jimmy said, chuckling. "I doubt he's going to just blab it to anyone he doesn't really trust just yet."

"Good. Containment is key. We have to have time to

work our angles."

"He's convinced Laura is still alive." And Jimmy sensed Jason was right.

"So am I."

"He'll be devastated if she isn't." *And so will the whole world*, Jimmy thought but kept the sentiment to himself.

The man sighed. "Well, in usual circumstances we could almost guarantee it, but we both know this is far from usual."

"Agreed. Maybe his hope will be rewarded."

"Keep me informed," the man replied coldly. From his perspective, Jimmy knew, there'd be advantages either way.

"You got it, brother," Jimmy said and the line clicked off, so he hung up and laid back on the bed. Okay, he'd done his duty. He could live with that. His whole life had been spent following orders, honoring commitments. Now he just hoped he could help Jason find his wife before they had to activate. He couldn't help liking the guy. His determination and work ethic was inspiring. Either way, he had a job to do, and he'd follow orders. Because when it came down to it, the mission was paramount, and Jimmy was definitely on a mission. He knew what was expected. And what wasn't.

Above all else, the boss had zero tolerance for failure and losses. At all costs, no matter what, they had to win.

CHAPTER 9

THE NEXT MORNING, Jason awoke to an email from Peter about Laura's smartphone.

Jason,

Our examination of the GPS data on Laura's iPhone has produced the following data:

- The cell phone arrived at the park and walked around (10 satellites strong consistent signal)
- The cell phone blacked out (0 satellites) either due to signal loss or interference
- The GPS log showed five "bizarre" data points over the course of one second (4 satellites very weak). These placed her in the Pacific Ocean, the Atlantic Ocean, and the Caribbean, and twice in Mexico City.
- The cell phone blacked out (0 satellites) for approximately 10 seconds.
- The cell phone location showed the park again (10 strong satellites).

Drawing conclusions preliminarily, something happened to either block the iPhone or cause signal loss of some kind. But I would interpret the bizarre data points as resulting from confusion that forced the iPhone to attempt to approximate location, but getting jumbled results due to the interference.

Determining what that interference was will be difficult.

Meteorological data and astronomers reported a Moonbow that night, and the full Moon was low in the sky. Given the rain, this may account for the flash of light you report seeing but would not account for the jumbled cell data.

Based upon the two hits in Mexico City, the most likely assumption would be that Laura was located there. However, unless she was physically picked up and whooshed there on some kind of super-supersonic jet to the Pacific Ocean in less than a second, it's impossible. GPS data doesn't lie, but we'll continue to sort through it all and attempt to find answers.

I am enclosing the raw data for your perusal. It could just be a software glitch and a few other things. Let me know if you come up with any ideas.

Regards,
Peter Edtz, Ph.D.

Jason stared at the data for a long time. It truly was a jumble that made no sense, Peter was right. GPS satellites work like lighthouses, all they do is broadcast their position and current time. To find someone's location history, you need their phone, which receives the GPS data and then computes its location. Modern consumer GPS's updated as fast as three times a second and had an accuracy of five meters. Because of her employment with NASA in government service, Laura's smartphone's GPS was faster (five times per second) and more accurate (one meter on Earth). So what had happened to Laura and her phone to cause it to become confused, generating jumbled data? Data that placed her in locations impossible distances apart within seconds of each other?

Frowning and frustrated, he stared and stared at the raw data for what seemed like forever. When he got back from the park, he'd have to run calculations; attempt to make sense of it somehow. There had to be a reason, some logic he could determine.

Jan knocked on the door and entered, smiling. "You ready for your big adventure?"

Jason set his iPad to sleep and nodded. "Can't wait."

Jan noted Jason's packed suitcase resting on the dresser nearby. "I see the nurse's aid got you packed,"Jan said. "We're gonna miss you around here."

"You think? I'm not sure about Holly," Jason joked. "She was kinda mean last night."

"That's 'cause you're her favorite," Jan said with a wink. "Her most of all." Jason climbed out of bed and grabbed the shirt and slacks he'd hung in the closet the night before, slipping into the bathroom to get ready. He didn't even need the crutches this time. The bathroom wasn't a long walk and he took it slow, but still it felt great yet again to be acting normal, and by the time he emerged from the bathroom, dressed, his hair combed, he was smiling ear to ear.

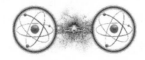

AT ARROYO PARK, despite Jason's protests, one of the bodyguards Jimmy had assigned—who resembled Popeye with all his muscles—grabbed Jason by the arm and helped him up onto his feet outside the car. Jason took a deep breath, soaking in the warm sunlight and cool breeze. Despite the L.A. smog, the air smelled rather pleasant today, pollen from the flowers and trees masking the usual smells of exhaust and urban decay.

Jimmy's men watched him a bit as he started walking toward where Jimmy, Roger, and the two detectives were waiting. "I got this, guys, really," Jason assured them as he reached the group, but they stayed close by just in case.

A minute later, Peter and his forensics teams joined them from a nearby van.

The blue sky overhead was filled with bright white clouds, with little sign of the usual smoggy clouds that typically layered the region. Jason took it as an encouraging and optimistic gift from God or the celestial powers. He smiled as the group gathered around him. His limbs felt light and his chest light as heat radiated throughout his body. It was good to be actually doing something to actively help find his wife.

"Why don't you walk us through that night, Dr. Maxx?" Detective Connelly suggested.

Jason led them around the park as he and Laura had traversed it that night. As they went, he described the increasing intensity of the rain and how they'd headed toward where they parked, then led them across the lawn in the direction he'd indicated as the others followed, the detectives continuing to make notes on iPads.

Jason stopped beside the walnut tree. For a moment, he pictured Laura standing there and he could almost smell the tantalizing scent of her perfume and feel the warmth of her presence. "We sheltered here for a bit, hoping the rain would let up, and when it did, we headed across this grass and heard one of them comment about us being in love."

"Do you remember exactly what he said?" Connelly asked.

"Something like 'Awww look, they're in love' then something Spanish," Jason said as he started walking again. "We heard the others laughing then but didn't see them 'til we came around these two trees." He wove through the large trees, the others following. "From the matching jackets and bandanas, I figured they were a gang, so we walked faster, steering to the left a bit, and that's when I ran into the big one, Bene about here."

Jason came to an abrupt stop and motioned. "The others were gathered over there." He pictured them as he said it and felt a sudden burst of anger rising within. How dare they attack innocent people like that? How dare they threaten him and his wife? And now she was missing! Had they taken her? Killed her? Did they intend to kill him? A tinge of fear added to the anger as his mind raced and he stared at the spot they'd been gathered for what seemed like a long time, until…

"So then words were exchanged and such and they attacked?" Coben said, jarring Jason back to the present.

"Well, the others were taunting, saying I was mocking him, egging him on," Jason said, the encounter playing back like a movie through his head. "And I tried to get away but they fanned out to block me. Somehow Laura slipped through and made her way over to that tree." He acted it out as he described it, wincing at the sharp blows and hearing the cursing and accusations all over again.

Coben nodded. "That's where our CS guys found the cell, badge, and purse."

"Right," Jason agreed, turning in a slow circle as he relived it in his mind. "And there was the glint of a knife, maybe a gun, and the men closed in around me. And then they were kicking and punching me, and I lost sight of

Laura. She transformed into a black shadowy form for a minute and then just disappeared. But they kept pounding me. I wondered where she was. Then the blinding flash of light."

"Flashing light from where?" Connelly asked, looking around for possible sources.

"Everywhere," Jason said, lost in his memories, then he shook out of it and looked around himself. Other than a few street lights on poles, there was nothing obvious that could have made the flashes, and based on their position he was certain even a burst from one of the street lamps or multiple of them wouldn't have the same effect. "All around. And it scared them. They were muttering about cops, running—that kind of thing."

"Did they keep beating you?" Jimmy asked.

"Yeah, they let up a bit but hadn't stopped, then I was looking for Laura and they did stop, and I passed out." Jason looked at the faces watching him with concern. "That's really all I remember. Pretty much what I told you at the hospital."

"As I recall, the officers found you about here?" Connelly said and pointed.

"I have no memory of it, of course," Jason said, wishing he did. He'd hoped revisiting the park would bring back memories, but it hadn't. Maybe then he'd know what had happened to his wife.

Connelly nodded. "It's good to nail down the locations, your movement and such."

Peter's team was already at work over by the tree gathering evidence. While Peter had invented or improved almost every one of the spectrometers and other gadgets they used, he was visibly uncomfortable working outside, away from his climate-controlled lab. As his team of field technicians methodically scanned the crime scene for evidence, it was clear that the collection effort was being led by Roy Zeeman. Roy was a former explosive ordinance technician who left seventy-five percent of his hearing and ninety percent of his patience in Afghanistan. He was also a legendary field technician at JPL, who didn't appreciate "propeller-head" interference from his Ph.D. coworkers.

Roy was scanning the ground with a metal box about the size of a child's lunch box. Earlier Peter had called it an "FLS, a forensic laser system." It was originally developed by an Army research program to search and characterize buried explosives by looking for trace amounts of residue nearby. While it was developed for finding bombs, different lasers could be used to highlight anything that emitted light: textiles, geological minerals, and body fluids at crime scenes. Everyone saw its applications to law enforcement, but it was too expensive, costing a municipality the equivalent of about three police cars. At that cost, most crime scene units could only dream of owning an FLS. Even the detectives watched with interest as the team worked. The only one who didn't look impressed was Roger, who was scowling impatiently off to one side.

"That looks like a pretty impressive laser and camera system," Coben said.

"Starman is actually three detection systems and three high power pulsed systems that talk to each other through artificial intelligence," Jason explained, switching to scientist mode as Roy swept the laser spot from side to side as a false color image updated on the monitor. The system kept switching laser outputs from ultraviolet to blue to red until a consistent fluorescence image appeared on the screen.

"The lasers alternate until the imager detects a mineral, a

material like wood, or plastic," Roy added. On the screen, Jason saw a multi-colored display of light splotches—green, blue, yellow, and violet. The different intensities of the wavelengths of emitted light from the minerals formed a spectrum of colors that appeared much like a fingerprint.

Roy motioned to Jason, "Hey boss, I have something here. I am gonna let the system move on to Raman." Roy quickly set up a small tripod and pointed the laser back at the spot on the ground. "OK, everyone who wants to keep their eyes intact move back three paces." With that terse warning, even as the others were stepping away, Roy pressed a red button on top of the lunchbox-sized FLS. The laser's broad beam focused down to a pencil thin beam at the base of the tripod.

"With the extra power, we can get the Raman spectrum of the material and *that* is the true fingerprint we need," Roy said with some pride. He pointed out the different materials he had located and identified with the forensic laser system, muttering as he read the indicator showing various materials being found: "alluvium deposit" ... "caution tape"... "dog urine"... "Wait, huh? Peter! Peter!"

Peter turned and his eyes widened as he read the readings off the FLS. Peter turned excitedly toward Jason, almost tripping over equipment on the ground as he did. "We found something here that isn't in the spectrometer's database."

"How is that good news?" asked Roger as he approached the group.

"It's interesting because it's unusual," replied Jason.

Roy jumped in. "OK, propeller-heads, stand back and let me do my job. We still have Step Three." With that, he pressed another button and the laser focused further into a tiny spot on the ground. The ground began to arc like a spark plug ignition. "Last step, laser ionization breakdown spectroscopy. We will see the elements present, and if we are lucky, we will get some molecular lines for isotope analysis."

Roger looked at him like he was speaking Russian, but the others stared at the small screen as the neural net analysis did its work—flashing numbers and figures as it tried to sort out the fluorescence, Raman, and ionization data.

"We found evidence of the same materials we discovered on the badge, purse, and cell phone casing: Niobium, copper, nickel, tridymite, and potassium," Peter explained.

"Which means?" Jimmy asked.

"We'll have to take samples back to the lab and analyze the spectra more carefully," Peter continued even as another of the team approached from behind him. "Compounds and ratios can be determined from even very small sample amounts. We can identify the minerals present, amounts, and other factors. Even how they interacted, if they did, at this location."

"We have a small inconsistency in the data," Roy said. "The fluorescence and Raman data looks great, but some of the molecular ionization peaks are in the wrong places. We're definitely gonna need to go and measure some lab spectra. The isotope ratios are screwed up."

"How can that possibly be?" asked Jason, frowning.

"I know," said Roy, "those isotope ratios are always the same all over the globe."

Jason's eyes widened. Could that mean that the evidence wasn't from Earth? They'd think he was crazy if he brought that up now. He'd best wait for the lab results. After all, there was always the chance it was just an instrument error or a calibration issue.

"Jesus. We're living *Star Trek*," Coben said, shaking his head. It was clear he and Connelly were totally lost by all the equipment and science talk.

Jimmy grinned. "Gotta love the future, boys."

"We're also detecting a lot of radiation," Tasha, a young woman from Peter's team jumped in. At that, the two detectives and Roger took a step back, looking concerned

"What kind of radiation?" Jason asked calmly. Radiation could be found in all kinds of places, especially in a big metropolis like Los Angeles. It wasn't necessarily dangerous, though the mention of radiation usually evoked such thoughts in most civilians.

"Alpha," Tasha said.

"Which means?" Jimmy asked again.

"The kind you'd see coming from smoke detectors or pacemakers," Tasha finished.

"A smoke detector?" Coben said, his brow creased. "The nearest building is way over there past the trees on the other side of the street. It makes no sense."

Roger exhaled, pinching his lips together as he spoke through clenched teeth, "Laura didn't have a pacemaker. Minerals, some unknown material, radiation... How does any of this help us find my daughter?"

"We don't know yet," Peter admitted. "But it's evidence, and there are various conclusions we might draw from what we find and any interaction as well as the levels of the compounds. Everything from how she was taken to who took her, where they're from, where they've been, weapons or materials they used. All kinds of things."

Roger just shook his head, snapping, "It sounds like

babble to me. We should be out there searching, talking to those gang people again..."

"Mr. Raimey, we've about explored all the avenues at this point," Connelly said. "We need something new to go on. If this will help us, then let's give it a chance. Anything new this turns up is more than we know right now."

"Roger, I know it feels like we're just reviewing the same old evidence and story," Jason said, nodding with resignation. He couldn't get the smartphone data numbers out of his head. They scrolled through his mind like they were on a screen. He'd been doing basic calculations on them even as they toured the park, trying to find some clue there. He met his father-in-law's eyes with focused intensity. "She's out there, Roger. I can just sense it. And I won't give up. We will find out who or what took her and bring her home."

"Who or what?" Roger repeated with a smirk, his lips pressed into a fine line. "You say that as if we don't already know! Some damn gang hoodlums is who. We know that. We just have to make them confess."

"We really don't think they have her," Coben said. "We've interviewed them multiple times, talked to their girlfriends and neighbors, searched their homes and hangouts. There's just no evidence of your daughter being with them."

"They seem genuinely baffled at the idea of kidnapping her," Connelly added.

Roger scoffed, arms folded across his chest. "They're lying, for fuck's sake. I mean, who else was here? You've heard Jason's description multiple times."

"What if it was someone else?" Jason said, feeling surprisingly calm at the moment as his mind continued racing through all the various pieces and the questions they raised. Then it struck him. What if the bizarre smartphone data pointed to some central location all the points related to? He had to get back to his iPad and get to work.

"Like who?!" Roger demanded, his voice dripping with disgust.

"There are lots of possibilities," Jason continued. "But some evidence suggests it might even be someone we've never encountered. Someone with technology that's really advanced—"

Jimmy stepped forward to interrupt, "There's no evidence of that."

But Roger plowed on. "Now you sound like you're talking goddamn space aliens or some shit."

"We're getting off track," Jimmy interjected.

"Anything's possible," Jason said, immediately regretting it. He didn't have anything close to the kind of proof he'd need for these people to take such ideas seriously, so he didn't blame them for doubting him. "It could just be someone we have no connection to or knowledge of, but who knows about me and Shortcut. In a few hours, when we've analyzed the data, we'll know more. A day or two, even more than that."

Roger's mouth twisted as if he'd swallowed sewage or vomit. "You're crazy. Completely losing it," he said and marched off back toward their vehicles.

Jason's mind continued rerunning the smartphone data and his question about a central location. As a scientist, he was trained not to eliminate any possibility or question without data to back it up. At the moment, he kept asking what did all those locations have in common besides the obvious?

Jimmy and Peter appeared to be thoughtfully considering what he'd said, but the two detectives looked skeptical. Surely they were used to unknown factors in such cases. But then the idea of space aliens would strike most people as crazy talk.

"We hope this stirs up something useful," was all Connelly said. Coben held his tongue.

Jason opened his mouth to explain, but Peter nodded to the detectives. "Can you show us approximately where the purse, badge, and cell phone were lying?" he asked.

"You bet," Coben said, and he and Peter headed for the tree where Peter's team was at work as Jason stayed behind and watched with Jimmy and his escorts, thankful to Peter for saving him.

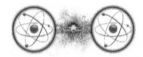

THE WHOLE WAY back home as the bodyguards drove them to the house near Caltech he'd bought with Laura, Jason's mind kept replaying the moment Laura disappeared—her form fading to a black shadowy outline, and then the flash of light. He'd only ever encountered that exact phenomenon in Shortcuts, but how was it possible someone else not only had that technology but in a more advanced form?

After greeting his in-laws and putting his suitcase in his room, Jason went to work on the GPS data. First, he examined the random data points looking for commonality. There was no distinct pattern to them, so he decided to start with the satellites closest to the data points.

A fluttering feeling filled his chest as he set his jaw and ignored everything around him, concentrating with the same hyper focus he always employed when launching into challenging mathematics. He opened up Google maps on his iPad and marked each pinged location with pins, then pulled up records of orbital positions for all the satellites over the United States the night Laura was kidnapped. With thirty-one GPS satellites operating, only twelve at most would be overhead at one time. Feeling an acute sense of purpose, he opened the raw data file of NMEA data—so called because the National Marine Electronics Association defined the communication standard that is used by GPS devices today. The data was a set of numbers starting with $GPGGA,090000.00,3406.73515750,N,11810.48462152,W,1,0 5,2.87,160.00,M,-21.3213,M,,*60. The coordinates section told Jason that Laura's phone was at the park that night right after they had parked.

To start, he imported the NMEA data into Google Universe, an upgraded version of Google Earth that included data for every known object in space. It was a virtual reality planetarium that could recreate the entire known universe from anywhere at any time. Next he moved in Google Universe to a view of the park and started playing the animation that would follow the GPS data from the night of Laura's kidnapping. His mind relived that night in flashes of memories as he watched the orange marker representing Laura's smartphone meander around the park. He double checked Peter's findings by counting the satellites overhead, which appeared as large red circles slowly drifting across the sky verifying that there had been ten satellites overhead that night. Pausing when the GPS did in front of the park sign, he decided to verify the calculations and data the GPS generated. On the chance Peter's theory about a glitch was correct, instead of trusting the algorithm, he pulled up the raw data and set about recreating the phone's calculations himself using spherical trigonometry.

Watching it in real time, he didn't notice the marker behaving strangely at all. But, when he rewound and slowed down the playback, he noticed that the marker did indeed disappear for a fraction of a second.

He wondered where the false GPS coordinates were. Pausing, he quickly plugged in the first random raw datapoint, knowing that it would take him somewhere over the Atlantic Ocean. When he moved the virtual reality world to that location, Jason stood on the virtual ocean and saw water in every direction with the GPS satellites hovering above. Next he moved the VR world to Mexico City. There were two data points several miles apart. He calculated how far apart they were—4.8 miles—then noticed that the signal strength was slightly stronger in Mexico City than the other locations. That left him wondering if any of the satellites and locations were connected.

Flipping through Google Universe's menus, Jason toggled a setting that displayed three numbers next to each satellite overhead: altitude, azimuth, and distance. *Why is it never easy?* Tools like Google Universe were built for astronomers, not mathematicians. The data was in a topocentric coordinate system, which worked perfectly when a person was on the ground looking up at the sky to see the satellites but didn't work here because the locations jumped from the Arroyo Seco Park to Mexico, seconds apart. So he had to deal with two different topocentric coordinate systems: one for Pasadena, one for Mexico City. Thus he needed to convert from observer-centered topocentric coordinates to an Earth-centered equatorial system so all the coordinates were in the same system from which he could build a mathematical model.

First he needed the satellite's altitude, the angle measured upwards from the horizon. An angle of 0° would be on the horizon and 90° would be directly overhead (which astronomers call the "zenith"). He glanced at the altitude for one of the satellites and wrote it down as $a = 35°$.

Next, he needed the satellite's azimuth, which is measured clockwise around the observer's horizon from north. So an object due north has an azimuth of 0°, one due east 90°, south 180° and west 270°. He recorded the satellite's azimuth as $A = 108°$, which meant that this particular satellite was in the southeast part of the sky.

The next piece was the latitude of the city, Pasadena: $\phi = 34.15° N$.

Then Local Sidereal Time which was measured by the rotation of the Earth, with respect to the stars (rather than relative to the Sun). One sidereal day was basically equivalent to the time taken for the Earth to rotate once with respect to the stars and lasts approximately 23 hours, 56 minutes. He wrote this down as $LST = 23^h 47^m 23^s = 356.85°$.

All these data points would be used to calculate the new coordinates in the Earth-centered coordinate system. The first parameter necessary was the declination, which he determined using the law of sines. Declination was the angular distance of a point north or south of the celestial equator. First, he had to measure the trigonometric function equal to the ratio of the side adjacent to an acute angle (in a right-angled triangle) to the hypotenuse, called the cosine. He took the inverse sine of both sides: $\delta = (sin\ sin\ (a)\ sin\ sin\ (\phi) + cos\ cos\ (a)\ cos\ cos\ (\phi)\ cos\ cos\ (A)\ ) = 6.46°$.

Now that he knew the declination, he calculated the right ascension—the angular distance of a particular point measured eastward along the celestial equator from the sun at the March equinox to the point above the Earth in question. From the law of sines: $sin\ sin\ (15(LST - RA)) = -\frac{sinsin\ (A)\ coscos\ (a)}{coscos\ (\delta)}$. Knowing this, he then solved for the right ascension: $RA = \ = 355.95° = 23^h\ 43^m\ 9^s$.

These steps had to be repeated for each of the ten satellites and then each of the GPS locations he wanted to verify. Once he had all the locations and GPS satellites in the same reference frame, he began populating the mathematical model with metadata from the GPS logs; other data besides the actual location data, such as the precision of each data point and the signal strength of each satellite. Usually, populating a mathematical model was a task he left to his Caltech students, but Jason wanted to ensure that every single point of data was accurate. It was no surprise when he noticed that the mysterious data points had terrible precision and much weaker signals than the GPS locations themselves. After an hour or so, the model was complete, and he could start investigating: drawing lines between satellites and locations, projecting the motions of the spacecrafts, and looking at the problem from every angle. And the entire time he focused on his work, he completely forgot about the stress and emotional turmoil that had been his constant since he'd awoken in the hospital bed.

He played with the model for several hours, toggling different features on and off. Eventually he grew frustrated that he hadn't found any geographic correlations on Earth with the model, but he was still suspicious of those two locations in Mexico City. So he went back inside Google Universe. While he stared at the GPS satellite with the strongest signal he noticed that the Moon was almost directly behind it. He fast forwarded a fraction of a second to the other time when her phone thought it was in Mexico City;

from that location, the satellite was blocking the Moon too. In fact, his model showed that all of the data points formed a direct path with their closest satellite and the Moon.

That's when it clicked. His mathematical model and the calculated GPS locations were inconclusive, not because of noise like Peter thought, but because Laura's smartphone had been in space! The bizarre data results came from the smartphone trying to compensate for unusual data resulting from locations not on its Earth-bound grid. The GPS receiver wouldn't know how to process the incoming data within its existing, programmed parameters, and would go into an undefined state, making a best guess in order to provide coordinates. But the resulting instability created several data points that jumped across the globe as the software indecisively flipped between various locations.

Charting the results formed an irregular pyramid with lines tracing from the "fake locations" on the ground through the closest satellite, converging on the Moon every time, which would logically indicate Laura's actual location was probably somewhere near the Moon. But the Moon? How could she get from the park to the Moon in seconds? Who had that capability? How was she transported?

Then it hit him. *She had no suit! What if she'd been exposed to space?! She'd be dead is what.* That thought brought all the emotions surging back. What would he do without her? How would he tell Heather? Susan and Roger would blame him. For a moment, his mind slipped totally off his work as he struggled with the pain of his loss and fears again.

Then, taking a deep breath, he shook it off. She wasn't dead. He just felt it. He couldn't waste his time thinking like that, so he went back to work. Just to be sure, he double checked his math, but his faith in numbers proved well founded as usual. It wasn't wrong. Laura had been taken into space and at least passed the Moon. And all that had happened in less than a second from the time she'd disappeared at the park. Who on Earth had the capability to do that?

No one. No one does.

His mind flashed back again to Laura's disappearance. The shadowy outline. The flash of light. They'd run computer simulations of *Maxx-One*, over and over a thousand times before the mission, simulating each Shortcut. And every time the spaceship went into a Shortcut, the computer simulated what the ship Shortcutting would look like in space if an observer was actually there to see it: *Maxx-One* fading to a black shadowy outline and then a flash of light as it reached speeds upwards of ten thousand times the speed of light (6.7 trillion miles per hour). He pictured Laura, then *Maxx-One*, and it all backed up his earlier conclusion: Laura's disappearance was exactly like a Shortcut.

Could someone have Shortcut Laura to space? It was the only explanation that made sense of all the evidence and data. Laura—a human being Shortcut. How could that work without a spherical spacecraft surrounding her? And if her phone had been with her far enough to register the location, how did it wind up back at the park?

The rest of the day, he couldn't get it out of his mind. It was his first thought after waking from each nap and accompanied every step and effort he made during physical therapy. *Laura was in space.*

Now he had to prove it well enough to convince the others.

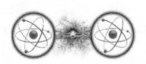

TO SURPRISE HEATHER, he answered the door when she returned from school that afternoon. She let out a yelp and skipped into his arms, and for a moment he held her tight, enjoying the comfort of her childlike embrace. That night, they went to an Armenian restaurant Heather had discovered with her grandparents while Jason was in the hospital and decided was her new favorite. They came home full and with lots of leftovers. Afterward, they stayed up late and tried their best not to bring up Laura, but ultimately failed. Heather was way beyond her young years in just about everything, so when it did come up, they discovered she shared Jason's unwavering faith that Laura was alive, despite others' warnings to the contrary. They made a secret pact to be strong for her and each other. Then Jason read Heather a favorite childhood story her mother had always read to her, kissed her good night, and left her to dreamland.

The next morning, Jason awoke to a new memo from Peter Edtz.

From: Peter Edtz

To: Jason Maxx

Sample A: Niobium 23.3%, Copper 54.2% Nickel 14.8% Tridymite 2.6% and Potassium 5.1%

Sample B Niobium 23.7%, Copper 53.5% Nickel 15.1% Tridymite 2.1% and Potassium 5.6%

Sample C: Niobium 22.9%, Copper 53.9% Nickel 15.4% Tridymite 1.7% and Potassium 6.1%

Oddly, the potassium isotope ratios still don't match those that we usually see on Earth. They're actually closer to what we've measured from lunar rocks.

Jason stopped reading and called Jack, Li, and Peter at Caltech. Three hours later, they'd all convened in Jason's lab. With Jason's iPad projected on the LCD smartscreen, they reworked the figures and tested them in Matlab, a programming language and numerical environment built for scientists and engineers; they then ran them through dedicated calculating computers at Caltech. All four men talked back and forth, discussing and suggesting as fast as they could work.

A few hours later, they all stopped and looked at Jason.

"Your wife is on the Moon," Jack said, confirming Jason's own conclusions.

"So I'm not crazy?" Jason said, feeling immense relief at finally having someone else repeat what he'd been thinking, and knowing it had come from their own examination of the data points and facts, not any suggestion by him.

"That's what the data indicates," Peter said. "We've rechecked your calculations and your process multiple times and come up with the same conclusion. Laura is in space or was."

Jason closed his eyes and sighed, feeling release as a certain amount of the tension he'd been carrying around started to fade. "I just wanted to hear someone else say it."

"Convincing the police and NASA suits may be more challenging," Li admitted.

"We also need to explain how her phone registered a location in space when it was still at the park," Jack said.

Jason nodded. "Yes, that is quite the mystery and I admit to being flummoxed by it at the moment."

"So we'll do some work on that angle," Peter said.

Jason smiled his thanks. "We need more data," he said, confident and excited to be back in his element. Lying in a hospital and talking to detectives was not his world but math and science were. And doing math and science had done more to help him feel better than anything else he'd experienced since the attack. "What else do we have?"

"You've got everything I have so far," Peter admitted.

"What about Clay and Ye?" Li asked. Clay Karshe and his wife Ye Meun were meteorologists and the world's foremost experts on tornados. But Jason had brought them on board his Caltech team because their expertise in meteorology was essential to planning for various potential issues Shortcut spacecraft might encounter. "We sent them the samples from the park and the rest of the data to check for any indicators and do some investigating."

"Can we get them over here?" Jason asked, unaware they were away at Harvard giving a lecture and seminar for the week.

In five minutes, Clay and Ye had joined them via Zoom. Ye Meun was one of the most intelligent and driven women Jason had ever seen, tall and lithe, her yellow brown skin and silky, long black hair the perfect counter to her shiny green eyes and stunning smile. Clay Karshe, her husband, was a decade older, short, chubby, and big boned with black hair and a matching beard and skin so pale it was blinding in the sun. Their devotion to each other was only outmatched by their amazing collaborative abilities. If any couple could be said to finish each other's sentences and read each other's minds, it was Ye and Clay. Jason had never seen the like of it. Clay was quieter and reserved, usually only opening his mouth when what he had to say was important and significant. Ye was the outspoken, extroverted one and had a great sense of humor and play that she employed even as she worked and interacted with friends and her husband.

As they came on the screen, Jason and Peter began filling

them in on their discoveries with the GPS data and other evidence, and finally Jason's theory about the Shortcut and Laura. But before they could finish, Clay interrupted.

"A Shortcut! That's unbelievable," he said. "That means our puzzling discoveries make sense after all. We'd been debating and reviewing, trying to come up with alternative answers and conclusions. But if Laura was kidnapped with a Shortcut—"

"—it all comes together," Ye finished, smiling broadly with a laugh. "Thank God."

"Are you guys fans of science fiction?" Clay asked.

"I've read it, but I prefer nonfiction," Jason admitted.

"Peter has one hell of a collection of pulps," Jack said, his enthusiasm apparent. "We've often borrowed them to read classic stories. So yes, Li and I are."

"Good, because what we're about to tell you will sound like one of those stories," Ye said.

"Yeah, it's a whopper," Clay agreed.

"But it's the only theory that explains all the evidence and circumstances," Ye added.

"Stop teasing us," Jason said. "What's your theory?"

"The rain wasn't natural, it was artificially made," Clay said.

"Though, maybe not human made," Ye added, exchanging a look with her husband.

"Right," Clay said. "So we detected trace amounts of potassium iodide in the soil along with unusual levels of plain old salt."

"Salt?" Jason said.

"Yep, just like you might use on your steak," Ye replied. "Weird, huh?"

Jason was still skeptical as he stated the obvious question. "Isn't salt common in soil?"

"Well, the soil in the park does have naturally occurring salt,"Ye continued, "but the numbers felt higher than usual, so we decided to look at weather data of the salt in the air that night, which we found was abnormally high."

"But Pasadena is near the coast. How do you know that wasn't just salt from ocean spray?"

"Because ocean spray is in the air typically less than five micrograms per cubic meter," Clay replied. "Pasadena, as you know, is well landlocked, too. We looked at the historical airborne salinity levels and found that they were off the charts, over a trillion times higher on the night she was kidnapped. Levels that high would be enough to cause it to spontaneously rain without forming any clouds, which is what you saw that night."

"So, if there was lots of excess salt in the air that night, where did it come from?" asked Jason, remembering how the rain had tasted when it got in his mouth.

"What if the optical system used to kidnap Laura was made out of salt?" Clay asked.

"We wanted to use salt for the optics on Maxx-One because of its low absorption rate—it allows high-power ultraviolet, visible, and infrared light to pass through it—but we couldn't because it is also hygroscopic and degrades when exposed to water," Peter said, reminding them all.

Jason nodded. Of course. He couldn't believe that fact had slipped his mind.

"But if you didn't expect to encounter water where you

were going, or thought you could avoid it," Ye said.

Clay shot his wife a warning look and held up a finger as if to say 'hang on.' "Ye's getting ahead of ourselves. What if the rain was caused by your mode of transportation and thus was unpredictable because you hadn't anticipated the problem."

"Like say aliens in a spaceship," Ye said.

"Aliens?" Li said. "Extraterrestrials?" He and Jack exchanged disbelieving looks with Jason. Only unlike the cops and Roger, they all knew better than to dismiss it out of hand.

"Told ya," Ye said. "Right out of science fiction, only it's not."

"We think the rain was caused by water degrading the ship's salt optics," Clay continued. "The salt caused the surrounding water vapor to condense and rain on the park when they descended."

"A spaceship? We didn't see any flying craft when we were there that night," Jason said, spinning through the memories in his mind once again.

"Doesn't mean it wasn't there," Clay said. "For one thing, it would explain the radiation. The ship has to have some power source, right?"

"If whoever took Laura has the technological skill and knowledge to shortcut her from the park, as you suspect and as the evidence implies," Ye continued, "it doesn't seem far-fetched for them to have the capability to create a spaceship, one with nuclear power, and maybe that spaceship can cloak itself like the *Maxx-One*."

"If their technology is similar to the *Maxx-One*, then that also explains the potassium iodide," Peter said. "We use it to make the electrolyte in the laser cells."

Clay chimed in, "Which would explain why we found trace amounts on Laura's belongings—purse, ID, cell—as well as spread around the park itself."

"And let's posit that their spacecraft doesn't have adaptive optics," Ye said. "They didn't expect to need them, because they're unfamiliar with our atmosphere. So in order to fire their lasers through the atmosphere, they have to come closer to Earth, and, the closer they come, the more rain it causes, thus causing further complications, since their lasers' cells would struggle with the same water issues as ours."

"Come to think of it, that also explains the precipitation data for that night," continued Ye. "It got stronger in jumps until it was a full-blown rainstorm and then the rain just stopped."

"Which must have been when the alien ship left after they completed the Shortcut," Clay added. "They'd probably have to be pretty close to the living creature to capture it in a Shortcut."

"And so they came down over the park and caused the rain, which complicated the Shortcut," Li said, nodding and looking impressed. "This is quite amazing stuff."

"No one will believe it," Jason muttered.

"Maybe not, but who on Earth has the ability to kidnap someone with a Shortcut?" Ye said. "If it exists, a ship like this didn't just come from a short distance, it probably traveled thousands, maybe millions of miles."

"Which would require a shit ton of laser power," Clay added.

"Right," Ye agreed.

Jason took a deep breath. "The detectives and NASA administrators are gonna struggle with this one." They had to gather as much data as possible to back it up, if they wanted to convince the skeptics.

"Probably," Ye agreed, "but there's more."

"What if they were after you?" Clay jumped in, looking at Jason.

"Me?" Jason locked eyes with Clay, startled. For some reason, he'd never thought of it, and the possibility raised all sorts of new questions and emotions in him.

"Well, yeah, why take Laura? If they have some interest in Shortcuts, it makes more sense they'd be after you," Clay said.

"What if the rain was falling so hard that they couldn't grab you?" Ye asked. "Since Laura had the umbrella and was sheltered under the tree, she wasn't wet, so they grabbed her. It might have been they wanted you both, but if you'd been dry with Laura, they'd have taken you, too."

"What's to keep them from trying again?" Jason said and everyone stopped and looked at him. He was right, though he'd gotten there ahead of them this time. And along with pain and loss and fear for his wife, he now was feeling fear for himself as well. Who could be after him? And what would they do to him if they found him?

"You were probably safe in the hospital," Ye said. "These buildings have all kinds of equipment, radiation generators, thick walls, and so on that might cause them difficulty. Plus, we have no idea if they could Shortcut someone through a wall or only from out in the open. That might be an issue, too."

"Right, but we think you should be careful," Clay said.

"Because they may try again."

Jack and Li had their cell phones out and were already dialing as Jason let the warning sink in. Who would come and save them both if whoever took Laura got him, too? Especially if she was out in space somewhere? At that moment, he was thankful he'd never been prone to panic, because his mind was racing a mile a minute and his body had tensed involuntarily so much he had to breathe and purposefully relax to avoid aggravating his still healing body.

Before they left, Jason handed Peter a bag he'd brought from the house. "Let's test these clothes for the compounds you found and any radiation. I was wearing them at the park."

For best accuracy, the resulting data needed to run through computers overnight, so Jason went home without having definite answers.

And that night, he hardly slept at all.

CHAPTER 10

IN A NEWLY REMODELED conference room on the second floor of his Caltech lab the next afternoon, Jason took the detectives, Jack, Li, Jimmy, Roger, and Phil Cline—via Zoom from Houston—through all the evidence he and his team had uncovered and laid out their theory of the crime. All but Phil were seated around a large conference table made of dark wood with matching padded chairs, and Jason was laying out various diagrams and documents via shared PowerPoint. Most of the others seemed to patiently and thoughtfully consider the science as it was presented, but throughout the presentation, Roger Raimey looked noticeably uncomfortable, shifting frequently in his chair, scowling and frowning, and generally pursing his lips in disgust. When they'd finished, he exploded.

"You have got to be kidding me! You actually expect us to believe this crap?" he said, practically jumping out of his chair.

"Roger, we're following the evidence, as incredible as it sounds," Jason said, scanning the other faces in the room for their reactions. Jack and Li were convinced like Jason, of course. Jimmy watched with thoughtful interest while the detectives looked pretty skeptical and Phil Cline was just shaking his head.

"You're talking nonsense fairy tales," Roger said and glared at him, then whirled toward the detectives. "Is anyone here going to actually make a serious effort to find my daughter?"

"I can assure you we have been taking it very seriously, Mr. Raimey," Connelly said, leaning back in his chair.

"And yet we're here listening to this bullshit!" Roger said, arms crossed as he paced along the wall. "The man thinks my daughter is in space because of some crazy readings on a phone that wasn't even with her but left behind where she was taken."

"Roger!" Jason snapped. "You're here because you're Laura's father, but if you can't control your temper and let us work, you should go home!" He knew Roger was no scientist, but he was growing frustrated with his negativity and refusal to get with the program.

"You're in no position to tell me what to do!" Roger replied.

Detective Cobden turned and locked eyes with Roger. "Mr. Raimey, Jason is right. We have a job to do and you're getting in the way."

"Your job is to investigate a crime, not listen to bullsh—"

"Our job," Connelly snapped, "is to consider all possible evidence in pursuit of the truth. We're trying to do that here."

Roger glanced around the room. Everyone was staring at him with irritation. He growled and his shoulders sank as he leaned back in his chair, head down.

"We don't know that the phone wasn't with her and somehow returned to where she was taken," Jason continued. "Scientific data doesn't lie. Not even if the questions and conclusions it points to seem far-fetched or hard to believe."

"And you also don't know that it wasn't just scrambled by whatever tech they used to abduct her," Connelly jumped in. "Or something else."

"Roger's not wrong," Coben said, elbows on the table as he rubbed an eye with his fist. "This is one crazy theory."

"And yet, the science points us to its truth," Jason replied, again feeling absolute conviction. "Science doesn't lie, and we follow the science!"

"We didn't want to believe it either at first," Jack agreed more calmly, as always the picture of calm professionalism. "But there's so much evidence now."

"We need to ready a rescue mission as soon as possible," Jason added, leaning forward in his chair as he slapped the table with his palm. They'd already wasted enough time. These men would come around. The important thing now was to be prepared so they could rescue Laura as soon as her actual location could be ascertained.

"Putting aside the issues with the phone and the believability of the entire scenario, do you have any idea how much that will cost?" Phil asked. "A rescue mission will require a much larger craft than we have presently available and ready, and building a new craft takes months."

"I'll make it happen," Jason said. He mentally started running down a list of assignments to give his department heads, calls to make to vendors, and a rough timeline.

"Even if you manage that miracle somehow, there's the issue of funding," Phil continued. Though he was relaxed in the chair, his face and eyes looked strained.

"I'll fund it myself, if I have to," Jason said. Now he

thought of friends and others he could reach out to. It would take a lot of money, but he'd earned the respect of the right people, and given the circumstances and the scientific evidence, they'd support him. He was sure of it.

"With what? You've been successful but not millions of dollars' worth," Phil said.

"I have friends," Jason said. He mentally made a note to check with Elon Musk and Richard Branson about the size and readiness of any craft they had in the pipeline that might be adaptable under emergency circumstances. He'd spoken with them and others when Laura disappeared and they called with best wishes, so they were aware of the situation and had expressed a willingness to offer whatever support they could. Laura's life could depend on it.

"Come on, Jason," Phil said. "I get that you're under a lot of stress. And I know how much Laura means to you, but if I took this to the funding committee in Washington, they'd demand my resignation, then laugh me out of the room."

"Which is what we should be doing," Roger said. "You need mental help, Jason. It's time we got you evaluated."

"Roger, please," Jimmy said.

"Oh, don't tell me you're buying this?" Roger said, whirling on Jimmy and shaking his head.

"I'm very thoughtfully considering everything they've said," Jimmy replied. "But I'm not yelling. That solves nothing."

"It certainly makes me feel better," Roger said and went back to pacing again.

"We know how it sounds, Phil," Li said, shifting in his chair with nervous excitement as he had been the whole meeting.

"It's unbelievable," Jason added. "I admit it. But what if it's true? I want my wife back. I need her. Heather needs a mother, and I'm not going to give up on her." The thing was Jason could feel Laura somehow. It wasn't that they shared some weird psychic connection necessarily, just that they had become so much like one through their love and partnership that they really did know how each other thought and felt, even when they were apart. And right now he could feel her longing for him and Heather—feel her love and concern and their shared passion. She was alive somewhere. He just knew in his heart.

"Forget the aliens theory, maybe there's someone on Earth who developed capabilities beyond what we know about," Jack said.

"As scary as that is," Li admitted. "The data supports Laura being somewhere out in space."

"We don't even know if she's still alive," Coben said.

Jason winced like someone had shot him. Just the thought of it stabbed at his heart like a blade. She couldn't be dead. She wasn't. He refused to believe that no matter what the detectives thought, but if he lost their support, what had to be done would be that much harder.

"I'm sorry, Dr. Maxx, but you need to be realistic," Coben said. "Your wife has been gone for almost two months."

"I can *feel her*," Jason said. "She's alive out there."

"Your psychic feelings aside," Connelly said, exchanging a skeptical look with his partner. "There's really very little to go on."

"Maybe not the kind of evidence you're used to following," Jason agreed, his words coming out faster as his passion and determination rose within. "But we're scientists.

Besides, what purpose is there in taking her if they were just going to kill her? They could have murdered her at the park. They had to want something." It made no sense to go through all the trouble of shortcutting, cloaking a flying ship, and abducting Laura just to kill her elsewhere. Why work so hard just to murder someone where no one can see with nothing gained?

Coben took a deep breath. "Crimes like this—they can be senseless. Sometimes criminals just do things on impulse. Yes, most kidnappings involve ransoms, but not all abductions. She could be raped or assaulted—" He stopped as Jason looked away, eyes sad at the thought.

"These are people whose technology and abilities go far beyond common criminals," Jason said. "The effort alone hints at a motive far greater than cheap thrills or impulse."

"And there's been no sign of her body," Li added.

"But also no ransom demand," Coben said. "We just don't know."

"She'd never give up on me until she knew," Jason said as he leaned forward in his chair again, his face close to the camera. "And I won't either!" When those on the other end winced, Jason stopped and leaned away. He knew that if the situation were reversed, Laura would be pushing just as hard and having the same conversation with these men. Roger might be less angry, but he'd be just as convinced she was wasting time.

"I admire that. I really do," Connelly said. "But space is really outside our jurisdiction."

"Not to mention training," Coben muttered.

The two detectives exchanged a look, then Connelly cleared his throat. "Dr. Maxx, I know you're confident you're thinking clearly about this, but concussions can do crazy things to a person's memory."

"You think I'm making it up?" Jason exclaimed, clenching his jaw. "I can play through the entire event like a movie in my head. You haven't found any viable explanations. I'm giving you one."

"Viable is a matter of opinion," Coben snapped. "What you're suggesting is pretty far out."

Connelly shot his partner a calming look, and his eyes met Jason's with far more sympathy. "We're just trying to make sense of it, find answers, find Laura—"

"So what—she's dead somewhere, buried? She's still out there hidden all this time right under our noses?" Jason's speech was rushed and his hands splayed at his side, then relaxed again.

"We've seen a lot of abductions where that was exactly the case," Coben said, brow furrowed.

"Not Laura," Jason insisted.

"How can you be sure? We know the Estradas Buenos were there that night," Connelly said. "It seems more likely—"

"Laura was fifty feet away under a tree," Jason replied. "You yourselves told me you believed Bene Rodriguez, and now the evidence points to something else, however unlikely I may seem."

"Witnesses lie, and sometimes they are very convincing," Connelly said. "We've been fooled before."

"You just said that your job is to consider all the evidence," Jason replied. "The science supports this theory." Jason turned to Phil on the Zoom screen. The detectives couldn't help much even if they wanted to, and he knew they'd never stop trying to find an explanation that made sense to them. It was what they always did, but this was way outside their knowledge and skills. "We have to do this ourselves. You love Laura. You've known her longer than I have. If there's any chance—"

Phil nodded, his voice still calm despite any doubts. "I'd never give up on her, Jason. Of course not. But what you're asking is just too much."

"Somebody call that X-Files guy, maybe he can help," Roger said with a sneer.

Jason ignored him and locked eyes with Phil. "What's it gonna take to convince you?" Jason demanded.

Phil sighed, lost in thought. "If we actually had some proof she was alive—"

Jason nodded. "Okay, so we'll keep working. But in the meantime, if there are aliens out there, and if they are after me, they'll be back. And that puts us all in danger."

"We can up your security for a while," Jimmy suggested. "Take you and Heather somewhere no one can find you."

"But then how will I do my work?" Jason said. "I might as well just give up like Roger and the detectives here. *I can't do that.*" He glared back at Roger, who continued wearing a hole in the carpet along one wall.

"There's just not enough, Jason," Phil said. "I'm sorry."

Jason slammed his palm on the table again and stood, nostrils flaring. "I'll do it with or without you. Whatever it takes."

"I wish you the best of luck, truly," Phil said and Roger snorted.

Jason locked eyes with Jack and Li, his intensity and determination apparent to all.

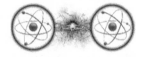

JASON SET A meeting of his entire staff for the following morning, inviting department heads from JPL as well, and Jack and Li. Jack arranged for him to use the auditorium in the Cahill Building where Jason's lab was located. At ten-thirty, Jason stepped to a podium to address the waiting crowd of about one hundred people associated with the Shortcut program and related areas. Scanning their faces he recognized Peter Edtz, Clay Karshe, Ye Meun and several others. Jack, Li, and Purva sat on chairs behind and to his left on the platform.

For half an hour, Jason repeated the research into Laura's disappearance that Peter's team had assembled along with the theory Jason, Jack, Li, and Peter had devised. Then, pausing for dramatic effect, he said, "From now on, for the next eight weeks to however long it takes, your number one goal, everything you work on, will be related to successfully launching a rescue mission to bring Laura Maxx back. The challenge is extraordinary, but so are the circumstances. To succeed, we will all have to push ourselves beyond expectations, defy limitations, and work harder than we ever have before. But I've run the numbers as have others on this platform. We believe this team is the only team in the world right now who could pull it off, and we want you to prove it. You will have our full support and every resource necessary to do so. And I thank you in advance for your dedication to this task."

With that he stepped back and scanned the faces again as

they processed all he'd just imparted with great passion and conviction. The room was a cornucopia of colognes, perfumes, sweat, chemical smells, and more, reflecting both the personal and professional habits of those assembled within. There was scattered applause but most of them looked stunned, their minds racing to not only understand but imagine how they could accomplish the immense challenge he'd just given him. Then hands went up.

"Yes," Jason pointed to an Asian scientist from JPL.

"How can we rescue her if we don't know where she is?" the woman asked as others mumbled agreement around them.

"We'll work the problem," Jason said. "Just like we'll work every other angle of the problems that will no doubt arrive in our journey to successfully meet this challenge." He pointed to another, a kid whose long, braided hair and pimply face made him look more like he belonged in high school than at Caltech.

"The cell phone. How do we know that's not just interference or some glitch that caused jumbled data in the park," he said.

"The answers to both these questions are part of the challenge," Jason said. "But believe me, they are foremost on our minds. We believe that when we have those answers, we will need to be ready to launch a rescue attempt immediately. We cannot wait until we have them to start preparing." Jason pointed to another woman, older, with graying hair. He recognized her as a professor of astrophysics who worked two floors down from his lab, but her name escaped him.

"NASA has agreed to all this?" she asked, brow furrowing.

"We're working on NASA," Jason said. Jack stepped forward and joined him at the podium and Jason gladly stepped back, ceding it to him for the moment.

"We know the questions," Jack said. "We've asked them all ourselves time and time again. And we know the uncertainties are reason for doubt, but we also know no scientific breakthroughs would have ever been possible without scientists overcoming their doubts and attempting the impossible. We're asking you to do that again here."

He stopped and scanned the room himself, smiling confidently as if he had complete faith in all the people—his people—and what they were capable of. Within moments the air of uncertainty and doubt that had permeated the room began to fade. Whereas Jason Maxx was a newcomer, Jack Matthews was a man all of them admired and believed in. If he supported this, they would do their best, putting aside any doubts.

After a moment, Jack smiled at Jason and then turned back, nodding to those assembled. "All right, expect your marching orders imminently. Reports on all this research have been sent to your inboxes already along with summaries of your expected focus in helping this project succeed. The rest will be addressed specifically by one of us"—he motioned to his colleagues on the stage— "in the next day or two, I promise. Now, let's get to work!"

With that, the room broke into noisy chatter and thumping of chairs as people rose and many headed for the exits, others lingering in small groups, but all discussing what they'd just been told. Jason, Jack, Li, and Purva remained together on the stage and watched them go.

"Don't worry, Jason," Purva said, patting his arm. "Our people are the best. They won't let you down." And from her smile, Jason knew she really meant it.

"I'm counting on it," Jason said.

"And they'll enjoy it, too," Li said with a chuckle. "There's not a one amongst us, no matter what their doubts, who doesn't love a challenge."

"And kicking its ass," Peter Edtz added as he joined them. They all laughed.

"I think ass kicking is very much on the agenda for this one, my friends," Jason joked as he finally relaxed, and they laughed again, then headed off the platform together to resume their work.

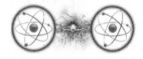

FOR THE NEXT few weeks, Jason poured himself into the science with renewed vigor. He not only had his management responsibilities to catch up on but the review of all his employees' work, and he spent extra time reviewing all the work they'd done investigating Laura's disappearance, wanting to make sure nothing had been missed or even miscalculated. They'd nailed it. He couldn't have done better himself. He came home every night for dinner with Heather and to help her with homework, then tuck her in before returning to the office. He also suffered ongoing pain in his chest wall from the rib fractures and regular shortness of breath. He had to use a device called an incentive spirometer multiple times a day to help keep his lungs from collapsing until they'd fully healed. Atelectasis, the docs called it. If he didn't expand his lungs as much as possible, frequently, he would have atelectasis and be prone to infection or pneumonia. Made of plastic and about the size of a small notebook, it had a mouthpiece that looked like a vacuum tube. When Jason inhaled, the suction moved a disc up inside a clear cylinder. The deeper he breathed, the higher the piston rose. Numbers on the cylinder indicated how much air he took in each time, and there was also a gauge that verified he was inhaling at the right pace.

Jason met with designers to review and revise plans for refitting the larger spacecraft his team had designed for long distance missions. The rescue mission, he felt, should plan for a crew of at least eight, so he asked for ten berths to ensure everyone—including Laura—would have a seat on the way back. He reviewed the specs for some weapons and defensive materials. Making the ship fast was the top priority, but the unknowns involved prompted Jack and Li to insist that some protective measures be taken. For that, he also consulted with Jimmy, whose military and NASA experience gave him special knowledge in the topic. Revised spacecraft designs were suggested and approved with prototypes rushed into production with a deadline of two weeks minimum until they were ready for testing. Finally, he began considering crew recruitment, which would be made more difficult if Phil Cline continued refusing to throw NASA's support behind the project. Finding qualified, experienced people in the private sector was possible but difficult, and few of those with experience in both the military and actual spaceflight would be available. He'd have limited time for training his team, so it weighed heavily on him as he considered his limited choices.

He walked in the door at one a.m. one night and headed immediately to his bedroom, when he heard Heather's voice. She sounded as if she were crying and Susan spoke, trying to comfort her.

Setting the shoulder bag carrying his laptop and iPad at

the entrance to the hallway, Jason turned the opposite direction from the master bedroom and headed down the hall toward Heather's room.

"Why did they take her?" he heard his daughter ask, her worry apparent from her cracking voice.

"I don't know, sweetie," Susan said.

"But who are they, Grandma?"

"I don't know that either, dear," Susan said, sounding close to tears herself.

"What do they want with my mommy? I just want her back safe," Heather said then.

Jason stepped in the doorway and saw Susan sitting on the edge of Heather's bed, wrapping his daughter in her embrace as tears flowed down both of their cheeks. "I know, baby. I know." Worry, sympathy, and sadness flooded his senses, his chest tightening. He wanted to wrap his daughter in his arms as well and reassure her, tell her he just knew Laura was out there and that they'd find her again.

Tears formed at the corner of his eyes as Roger came rushing in and asked, "What happened?"

"She misses her mother," Susan explained.

And then Roger was gently stroking Heather's hair as Susan held her, both of them whispering words of comfort to her.

Jason's heart ached as he fought the urge to rush over and take Heather in his arms. Susan almost had her calmed down, and he feared seeing him might just upset her more at the moment. But as he watched, he winced, hurting for his poor daughter—an innocent victim in all this—and wishing none of it had ever happened.

Jason had been amazed the first time he'd walked into his daughter's room after returning from the hospital. Susan had made a miracle. It was set up almost exactly like her room in Houston had been—from furniture placement to art, even the bookshelf placement of Heather's stuffed toys—Jason felt he might as well have been standing in Texas. It was perfect, exactly what Heather needed to ease the transition, and Jason had such gratitude to her grandmother for making that happen when her parents weren't able to.

Susan rocked her granddaughter for five minutes or so until Heather slowly drifted off, then laid her gently back down, positioning her comfortably and tucking her in beneath the covers before standing and turning to see Jason watching. She put a finger to her lips, signaling him to be quiet, and silently crossed the room, leading him outside and pulling the door shut behind them. Roger sat on the edge of the bed and stayed with Heather, watching her sleep.

"How often?" he asked.

"It's been happening more and more," Susan said. "It was just once in a while at first, but now it's almost every night."

Jason sighed. "How does she know Laura might have been abducted? She should never have been told."

"I agree," Susan said, her face turning stern. "But with you and Roger constantly arguing about it, she couldn't help but overhear. Which she did. And she's quite upset."

"Damn it," Jason said and leaned back against the wall, his shoulders sinking. He should have been more careful, but Roger was constantly badgering him about what was going on, and Jason was so worn out, he hadn't thought about it.

"She feels like she's lost her family, Jason," Susan said. "You missed the parade, a promise Laura and you both made. Her mother's gone. You're barely here. It's a lot for a ten-year-old to deal with."

The Hollywood Christmas Parade had been just after Thanksgiving and Jason hadn't come home from the hospital until two days after. He'd tried to explain to Heather and apologized profusely. Her grandparents had even offered to take her, but she'd insisted on waiting. "I want to do it with mommy," she'd said. And so Jason had broken a promise he'd sworn to keep. It tore him up just remembering. "I come home every night," Jason said, knowing it was a weak, hollow reply, but he didn't know what else to say. Suddenly, his own guilt was overwhelming. But he had to find Laura, he couldn't just stop looking. It was as much for Heather as himself, wasn't it?

"With your mind clearly elsewhere," Susan said. "Yes, you do your best, I know. And I know it's hard, but she needs more," Susan said. "It's been traumatic for her, and you were in the hospital a long time."

Jason nodded. "I'm sorry, Susan. I'm just so focused on Laura right now."

Susan reached out, softly squeezing his forearm. "I understand and appreciate it. We all want her back. But find some time for your daughter. She needs you too."

Jason's eyes met hers. She was genuinely concerned about all of them. "I will, Susan. I promise."

Susan nodded and released his arm then turned stern again. "And stop letting Roger bait you. You both are being stubborn jackasses about this. The women of this family are tired of it."

Jason looked somberly into her eyes. "Did you tell that to him?"

Susan nodded. "You bet I did, and I will again."

"How'd he take it?"

Susan chuckled. "Even Roger knows not to argue with me on certain things."

"I'm glad you're here," Jason said, smiling, and reached up to clasp her shoulder. It was the closest he'd felt to one of Laura's parents in months, and it was a good feeling. "I don't think I could make it through this without you."

Susan smiled back, a sad smile lacking her usual warmth, then turned, pulled free of his touch and headed down the hall toward the guest room. Jason listened outside Heather's room for a few minutes, making sure she was still sleeping, then retrieved his briefcase and headed into his own room to get some sleep.

TWO DAYS LATER, Jason sat in a courtroom at the Pasadena Courthouse off East Walnut and North Euclid, in downtown Pasadena. The third-floor courtroom was large and looked like something right out of a Hollywood movie with its imposing judge's bench, jury box, and walled off pews for spectators—all made of matching wood stained the same dark color. The city prosecutor walked Jason through the assault at the park as the gang members, including Bene and his friends, sat facing him at a defense table with their assortment of public defenders. Detectives Coben and Connelly waited outside in case they were called upon again to testify. The prosecutor emphasized Jason's reputation and the importance of his work as well as the extent of his hospital stay and the fact that months later he remained active in physical therapy and suffered lingering symptoms of pain and discomfort. Altogether, it made Jason feel like he was on an episode of Law and Order or L.A. Law. It was rather surreal.

When the prosecutor finished, the defense attorneys took their turn questioning Jason, but his story was solid and remained consistent, despite their onslaught. The prosecutor's smile when they'd finished assured Jason it hadn't done them much good.

After he was dismissed as a witness and the court adjourned for a break, the two detectives met him outside in the hallway.

"How long will they get?" Jason asked, wondering about the men's sentences.

"A few years at most, I'd expect," Connelly said. "Bene most likely a bit more than his friends because he was the leader and initiated the incident. But don't worry about it. They won't bother you again. We'll make sure of it."

Jason grunted. "I hadn't even thought of that. Mere curiosity." Instead his thoughts turned again to the idea that someone else might be looking for him to do him harm, and he found himself wondering again who it might be.

Coben and Connelly nodded then exchanged a look, hesitating a bit, as if they had something on their minds they wanted to say but were unsure or dreading it.

"It's been three months since the attack, and we've gotten nowhere searching for Laura," Coben said with a sigh. "Unfortunately, with nothing new to go on, there's not much we can do. We've got other cases to work and there's only so much time we can devote to a case without movement."

"You're closing the case?" Jason said.

Connelly shook his head. "Not at all. We wouldn't do

that. It'll remain an open case file, of course, and we'll check into it regularly, especially if there are any new developments, but we just aren't going to be able to work it as actively as we have been."

From the ways they dodged meeting his eyes and their sad expressions, Jason could tell they felt bad about it, and despite the frustration surging inside, he extended his hand and shook first with Coben, then Connelly, saying, "Well, thank you. I appreciate all your dedication to this, truly. And I'm glad those men won't be attacking anyone else for a while at least."

"We're sorry we couldn't do more," Coben said. "But if you hear anything, call us right away."

Jason nodded. Apparently it was all up to him now. "Of course," he replied, then turned and headed for the elevator. The two detectives followed.

"We're very sorry for your loss, Dr. Maxx," Connelly said. "We hope you can find peace at some point."

"Are you telling me to give up?" Jason asked.

"No," Coben said. "Just be realistic. In the majority of cases where there's no trail—"

"I know the stats," Jason said as he stopped beside the elevator and waited for it to arrive. Coben reached forward and pressed the down button for him. "When it's time to move on, I will do what I need to. But I'm going to do it with Laura back. I really believe that."

Connelly and Coben nodded. "Good luck," they both said without much conviction as the elevator dinged and its doors whooshed open.

Jason stepped inside and turned back, smiling. "Thank you, gentlemen." Inside, he wanted to yell at them but he knew it wouldn't do any good. The answers needed were beyond their experience and expertise, and they had other cases they saw as more viable and easily solved.

Popeye, whose real name was Cal Shoemaker, and his partner Reggie Anderson met Jason at the base of the elevator. "We brought the car around," Reggie said.

"Thanks," Jason said and followed them.

It wasn't until he'd settled into the car that he felt the breath go out of him and his shoulders sank. *Where are you, baby?* He cried out silently, sending his thoughts to Laura wherever she was. *I'll never stop. I'm going to find you but I need your help. Send me something, some sign, some clue. Please, baby.* There was a pinching in his chest and his eyes were gummy. His throat felt scratchy all of a sudden and he took a deep breath, fighting off the swelling emotions.

It was the first time he'd allowed himself to even consider the possibility she might be gone for good, and even as that sunk in, bringing with it an enveloping sense of dread and sadness, he was already shaking it off. *No!* He couldn't go there. He couldn't give up. He couldn't even entertain such ideas. He had to stay focused. He was all she had. Fine. He would find Laura himself. He had to.

It wasn't until a few blocks later that he registered the black SUV two cars back and how it remained with them at every turn and lane change, the whole way back toward Caltech. He watched it execute a few moves and felt a tightening in his chest as he leaned forward and asked, "Are we being followed?"

Cal and Reggie exchanged a look.

"Did you notice something?" Cal asked.

"That black SUV back there seems to have stayed with us

since the courthouse," Jason said. "Seems unusual, doesn't it?" He'd noticed clicking on his phone line a few more times since he first heard it at the hospital and the other day he'd picked up the phone and heard muffled voices before he even dialed, but when he spoke, asking if anyone was there, they'd stopped, silent, as if they'd never been there.

Cal and Reggie immediately checked their mirrors and exchanged another glance. "Don't think it's the aliens, Doc," Reggie said. "I doubt they'd use SUVs."

"Okay, but why would someone else be following us?" Jason asked.

"Reporters?" Cal suggested.

Jason's fingers were cold and his stomach rolled as he shivered a bit. "Is someone spying on me?" He just had an uneasy feeling, and enough was enough.

"Why would they do that?" Reggie asked.

"I don't know, but can we ditch them just in case?"

"Hang on," Cal said and pushed the accelerator. Jason was forced back in his seat a bit, the seatbelt steadying him as Cal sped up and executed a quick series of turns and lane changes, doubling back a couple times, in an effort to lose the SUV. It was an impressive effort. Not a single tire or brake squealed and he managed it without cutting anyone off or seeming to take any real risks. In the end, Jason saw no further sign of the SUV and relaxed as their speed evened out to normal again and they entered the Caltech campus headed for the Cahill.

But as they pulled into the parking lot and headed for the handicap slot next to the door, Jason spotted the SUV parked in a space a few cars down, waiting.

"Isn't that them?" he demanded.

Cal and Reggie shook their heads. "There are lots of black SUVs, Doc," Reggie said.

"Pretty sure we lost them," Cal agreed.

But as soon as the car stopped, Jason was up and hurrying rapidly toward the SUV before they could react.

Reaching it with the two men hurrying to catch up, Jason pounded on the back window with the flat of his palm. "Who are you? What do you want?" he yelled.

"Doc, calm down," Reggie said, as the bodyguards reached him.

"This isn't very smart if they are following," Cal added.

Jason pounded again. "Come on. We saw you. Get out and explain yourself."

The front doors on the SUV opened and two men in dark suits with neatly trimmed hair stepped out and walked slowly back toward where they were standing as Cal and Reggie quickly put themselves in front of Jason.

"Stop hitting my car, asshole," the driver said, frowning.

"Stop following me!" Jason snapped back. "I memorized your plate. I know it was you."

"We don't even know who you are," said the passenger.

"I saw you. And don't think I won't report this," Jason said, glaring at them. "You leave me and my family alone, whoever you are."

The men continued to stare back as Reggie and Cal ran interference.

"Doc, let it go. Inside," Reggie urged as he and Cal took hold of Jason's arms, one on each side.

"I'm going," Jason said, and pulled free, stopping to glare

one more time at the two SUV men before storming off toward the building, the bodyguards following. His breaths were heavier and faster now, his footfalls slapping the pavement.

As Jason beeped them in with his pass and approached the elevator, Cal said, "Doc, that wasn't very smart. If they were following and dangerous, you put yourself right where they wanted you."

"You guys are supposed to protect me and you weren't doing anything," Jason snapped back. "Someone had to let them know we're onto them."

Cal sighed. "Our job is to protect you. Not beat up someone who may or may not follow you for unknown reasons."

"It was the same plate. I memorized it," Jason said. "Doesn't that concern you?"

"Yes and no," Reggie said. "It depends. It could be a coincidence. They made no threatening moves. Maybe they had business here."

Jason shook his head. "I didn't like their attitudes or their glares," he said.

Reggie chuckled. "I don't think they liked yours either. In the future, Doc, please let us do our jobs. It's safer. And we have training you don't."

Jason grunted, his heart racing so much his lungs strained to catch a breath. "But you weren't there and I had to act."

As the elevator opened, he stepped inside and hit the button for the third floor immediately. Reggie and Cal had to scramble to catch the closing doors and climb aboard as Jason leaned against the wall, ignoring them. He knew the detectives, Phil Cline, and Jimmy thought he was paranoid, maybe even crazy, just like Roger did. His theories of aliens and abduction by Shortcut were hard to believe, he could admit, but that didn't mean he was going crazy. Evidence was starting to mount. And in this case, he'd seen the SUV. He was certain it was the same plate. So why were Cal and Reggie, the men assigned to protect him, acting so casual and unconcerned about it? Why did it seem they had no concerns about a threat to his safety? He was absolutely certain he was being watched, and he was determined to find out who it was and what they wanted and make it stop—whether Jimmy and his men helped him or not. Jason Maxx would not cower in fear. Let them deal with it.

CHAPTER 11

JIMMY BURNETTE ARRIVED in Phil Cline's office at NASA right on time for the scheduled meeting of department heads who worked on Shortcut projects at nine-thirty a.m., Friday, December fifteenth. The weather in Houston was a pleasant fifty degrees, hardly Christmasy despite the many decorations, signs, and even blaring music to the contrary all around town. The office, in an administration building at Johnson Space Center, clearly belonged to a busy man. Stacks of paperwork in various configurations covered the desk, a counter that ran behind it, as well as the tops of three four-drawer file cabinets sitting adjacent to each other. There was also a pile of books, mostly research, but including a novel or two—Jimmy recognized *The Martian* by Andy Weir among the titles—and a few bound reports or theses by students and faculty as well. The walls were covered with white boards, charts, star maps, and even a map of Johnson Space Center—all of which contained either markings or numerous pins and post-its with various notations on them. Phil Cline himself wore a dress shirt and tie, the knot loosened at the neck along with the shirt's top buttons and the sleeves rolled up on each arm.

As Jimmy and several others came through the door, Phil greeted Jimmy with a handshake before they both moved around the room shaking hands: Dr. Paula Kim, Propulsion

Lab, Dr. Stacey Crowder, Aerodynamics, Dr. Karl Louis, Flight School, and several others. Then they all grabbed coffee, adding sugar and cream as desired from a coffee setup on a counter along one wall, then took their seats around the large round table occupying one end of Phil's office.

Phil began, "This is an informal meeting to bring everyone up to speed with the status of the Shortcut Project at present."

"I thought the Project was on hold while Dr. Maxx chases after his crazy rescue scheme," Dr. Kim fired off right away, then sipped the sugary concoction she'd made of her coffee. Jimmy watched this with hidden disgust. How anyone could do that to perfectly good Colombian finest was criminal as far as he was concerned. And though he knew his charms could work their magic on almost any female, Kim had the personality of a hitching post, and the scowl to match. *I've seen livelier corpses,* he thought.

Phil sighed. "In essence, yes. Though we've been asked to offer support."

"I take it you've declined," Dr. Louis said. "Why?"

"That's fairly obvious," Dr. Crowder said, sipping her own coffee which was light sugar and light cream—not as bad as Kim's but still not ideal for the purist Jimmy, who preferred his straight up black. Crowder also bore the scent of a flowery, sweet perfume Jimmy couldn't name. It reminded him, though, of something his granddaughter might wear, not a fragrance for adults, and he fought the urge to roll his eyes. When Crowder had first come to NASA, she'd been a real hottie and they'd once had a steamy night or two in astronaut quarters, but be liked his paramours young, and he barely recognized the woman he'd once found so alluring. "No clear destination, no definitive idea what the mission will entail or where it's going…"

"Yes, to both those," Phil said. "And more importantly, no clear idea what it will cost, which as you all know, is not the way we can afford to operate while maintaining fiscal accountability and congressional buy-in. We have to have a fairly solid end game in mind to fund any project these days." Phil's own coffee was heavily creamed but without sugar. Not the way Jimmy would ever do it, but understandable given the NASA administrator's softness of character and mind.

Jimmy cleared his throat. "The fact is Laura Raimey Maxx is missing and possibly in danger," he said. "Though we have had no definitive proof she's still alive, there are signs that point to the possibility."

"But none solid enough we can risk the resources," Phil said.

"Right," Jimmy agreed. "Fair enough. The bigger concern for Mister Cline, I believe, is Dr. Maxx's mental state. He's been showing a lot of paranoia about being spied on, not just by aliens but someone else. There'd been an incident just the other day with his bodyguards and an SUV he believed was following them as he returned from the courthouse to Caltech."

"What kind of incident?" Dr. Louis asked.

"A minor confrontation," Jimmy said dismissively.

"He's convinced himself of the truth of many things he just can't prove definitively," Phil said, far more gravely, his creased forehead and facial expression demonstrating his concern. "And they are the types of things that make a man sound mentally questionable, to say the least."

"Space aliens, spying," Jimmy began listing them. "Not to mention his insistence that we go rescue his wife when we know neither where she is nor if she's alive." Several of those around the table scoffed.

"Exactly," Phil said. "But he's got his whole Caltech team and several vendors fully engaged in attempting to rush a rescue mission through to full preparation."

"Won't that take years?" Kim asked.

"Months for sure," Jimmy said. "Maybe longer. His determination is admirable and his people are very loyal."

"Even if they can pull off a miracle, crewing and launching it is something they have no facilities for," Phil said.

"And so they need us?" Crowder said.

"In essence, yes," Phil agreed.

"Good luck," Kim snorted as she downed the last sip of what she called coffee and got up to pour herself another cup.

"His latest whim is carrying around this German device called a DMG," Jimmy said, smiling. "Supposed to prevent aliens from being able to snatch him like they took Laura. Disrupt their lasers or some such."

"DMG, short for Dark Matter Generator," said another attendee, also a coffee assassin, whom Jimmy recognized as belonging to NASA's astrophysics team. "In the same way polariton laser energy is used to entangle particles, the DMG uses dark energy to disentangle particles; our team modified it to allow Shortcut lasers to pass through walls by turning photons into axions and then back into photons."

Jimmy nodded, acknowledging the scientific gobbledygook and went on, "Anyway this DMG can supposedly disrupt the aliens' lasers, causing them to pass through Jason and instead affect objects nearby. So in effect, if they did Shortcut Laura, they won't be able to take him the same way."

The scientist smiled. "If he was right, it's pretty smart as a defense."

"Or completely looney," Kim said, rolling her eyes. Her attitude toward Jason hadn't improved one iota since their confrontation after the Maxx-One mission months before.

"Whatever the case, we're not able to give him our support right now, so things will be slowing down, but I still wanted you all to keep me abreast of any new developments we might pass along," Phil said, this time less the skeptic and more the concerned friend.

"So we're going to help him, even if we don't join him?" Crowder said.

Phil leaned forward, his gaze intense as he met her eyes. "The fact that I don't believe our agency can go along with his present scheme doesn't change how I feel about Laura Raimey. She's one of our own. And if she's in danger, there's nothing I wouldn't do to help her, do you understand?" His eyes scanned the faces around the table one by one considering their reactions. "We're still offering Jason our protection for now, and we're still going to offer him any new data we uncover in our own Shortcut Project work, despite any concerns we may have about either his state of mind or his mission."

After a moment, they all nodded or mumbled and grunted in consent.

"So if you haven't already, I'd like you to fill me in and

then I'd like formal reports in my inbox as soon as possible," Phil said. "Paula, we'll start with you, okay?"

Phil leaned back in his chair then and nodded to Kim, who dryly launched into the latest update on her team's work as Jimmy got up to pour himself another cup of straight up coffee. This could be a long meeting.

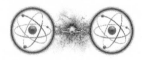

THAT MORNING, PETER Edtz brought Jason a new report on Laura's smartphone.

"RTG," Peter said as he walked into the office and tossed a printed-out report on Jason's desk. "Those radioactive particles that turned up? 238Pu." Jason had noted the mention of it on one of the reports from the Arroyo Seco park search.

"A radioactive plutonium isotope," Jason said, searching his memory as he flipped through Peter's latest report. Was it some kind of nuclear reactor?

Peter nodded. "Yes. Radioisotope Thermoelectric Generator." It was the politically correct term for a nuclear power source that can supply power to a spacecraft for hundreds of years. "Like NASA used on some early probes, such as the two Voyagers, Cassini, and Curiosity." "So it's primitive technology?" Jason asked. "That wouldn't fit the profile of our aliens."

"I don't know about primitive," Peter said. "We still use it sometimes because it's proven, it works, and it can be managed safely. We did find some medical radioisotopes on her badge, but we found no trace of 238Pu. None on her purse either, yet it's all over the smartphone."

"Which means the smartphone was exposed to something the other two weren't," Jason ascertained.

Peter nodded. "Exactly. As if maybe it went somewhere the others didn't."

"Like a spaceship," Jason said, sitting forward and smiling. "We can prove this?"

"The 238Pu part, yes," Peter said. "Definitively. The spaceship remains speculative, of course."

"But it's kinda hard to explain," Jason said.

"Granted," Peter said. "I also sent techs back to measure the area around the tree under which Laura was sheltering and no indicators of 238Pu there either."

"So it's likely the exposure was not on that location," Jason said.

"Well, yes, but given the length of time since the attack, of course, results are open to various questions," Peter said.

"But it's something definitive and it's new. Those are helpful."

Peter smiled. "Yes, they are."

"Excellent," Jason said, smiling and feeling encouraged. Anything new and definitive was a sign of progress. "Thank you." And he dove into reading the report as Peter sat and watched, a satisfied look on his face.

TWO DAYS LATER, Jason met Jack, Li, and Purva at The Athenaeum, the private club on the Caltech campus, for lunch. They ate in a private dining room down the hall from the Hayman Lounge, which occupied the club's southwest corner on the main floor. Built in 1930 to promote social, cultural, and intellectual exchange, The Athenaeum's members included Caltech faculty, trustees, alumni, staff, and select grad students. It had hosted such luminaries as Albert Einstein, Robert Millikan, and more. Jason's first time there had been years ago when he came to visit Jack and Li but now he was a member, and it was a bit awe-inspiring to feel a part of such a legendary place.

The club's Greek-inspired exterior was white stucco with clay tiles on the roof. The Hayman Room had tannish peach walls with a bar along one end surrounded by square tables with tan chairs where diners ate, drank, studied, and more. It accepted guests there for formal business or those returning from a challenging time on the tennis court. Jack and Li had reserved a private room because the agenda of their working lunch was to discuss details of Shortcut and a rescue mission for Laura. Around them, the air was filled with the smell of sweat, food, and people—perfumes, lotions, clothes, and more—as glasses and silverware clanked and voices rising and falling in conversation drifted down the hall through the open door to their room.

After a waitress had taken their orders and served them water, tea, and coffee, they were left alone and Li began.

"There's no easy way to say this, Jason," Li began his shoulders sagging as he met Jason's eyes, "but NASA passed again on funding the rescue mission. The new information on radiation found on Laura's phone just wasn't definitive enough."

Jason exhaled, shaking his head in disgust. "Well, I cannot believe they've turned their backs on us, but we'll just have to proceed without them."

Jack and Li exchanged a look, then Jack said, "And that's what we're here to discuss. We've done some budget projections and, unfortunately, with no clear idea of the destination or length for the mission, the numbers are daunting."

"We just don't see any way we can do this without major funding," Li said. "And without those specifics locked down, getting funders to jump aboard has proven challenging."

"I'm not just going to give up," Jason said, his voice rising with his frustration. "What would you do if it was Purva out there?"

Purva reached over and squeezed Jason's hand as her soft eyes met his. "We believe in you."

"Yes," Jack agreed. "We do."

"But in this case, I'm afraid it's not enough," Li added. "Without more funding, you'd be asking us to bankrupt our funding for everything we are working on. We can't afford to do that. Nor to keep diverting personnel off other projects indefinitely in the meantime. I'm sorry."

"So what are you saying? You're out?" Jason demanded, his voice just below a yell now.

"No, but we may have to slow down and wait for funding," Jack said, shifting uncomfortably in his chair. He clearly hated delivering the message.

"And we know that's the last thing you want to hear," Purva said gently, her hand still resting gently atop Jason's.

Letting Purva's hand slip away, Jason sat back in his chair, trying to gather himself, then spoke more softly, "Do you know what it's like knowing the woman you love may be out there somewhere and just wanting her back all these months?"

"There are no words," Purva said with true empathy.

"We don't know really," Li added, his face pained. "We haven't been there, and we feel terrible about this, but there are realities we have to face."

Jason nodded, leaning forward in the chair, his elbows on the table. "You know I wouldn't want you to sacrifice everything you've worked for. Neither would Laura. And I know how it all sounds, but I'm not crazy, so let me review the evidence again. See if there were any mistakes. Rerun the tests myself, do the math…"

"Our people are good, Jason," Jack said confidently. "They did their jobs with excellence. You won't find anything they didn't."

"Then why won't the government believe us?" Jason said, sitting back in defeat. There had to be something he could do. Laura needed him.

"It's pretty far-fetched evidence and all, Jason," Purva said, but her voice wasn't skeptical, instead it carried a passion and emotion filled with concern. "We're behind you. We're convinced, but some people just need more."

"So, what are my options?" Jason asked, almost pleading. There was a tightness in his chest and his mouth was so dry he kept drinking from his glass between words just to get them out. He felt a pressure in his temple—a headache coming on. He'd do whatever it took. He'd just have to start talking to potential funders and working that much harder. The fact that he was sure he was on the verge of a breakthrough with the Shortcut theory that would make Shortcuts more efficient over longer distances and also more cost effective would have to help. How could it not? "I'll go to Houston myself and beg, if I have to," he finally added.

Purva reached over and squeezed his hand again, her pained eyes filled with sympathy.

"We're not sure it would do much good at this point," Jack said as he sighed. "If we thought it would, we'd go with you."

"Absolutely," Li agreed, nodding adamantly. They paused a moment as the waitress returned and filled up their glasses from a pitcher.

"I know that if she could, Laura would contact us," Jason said after he'd had another drink from his refilled water. "Let us know she's okay."

"We think she would, too," Purva said.

"And it would make a huge difference," Li said sincerely. "But until she does…"

Jason looked away. He knew the rest. They needed something tangible, some reason to hope. Some sign a rescue was warranted, that it might actually get Laura back. Scientific data and theories were too much cold speculation and too little warm, human factor.

God, baby, please. Let us know you're out there. I wanna come get you, but we need your help. He pleaded to the heavens again, hoping beyond hope it would matter somehow yet beginning to doubt. Had he really lost the love of his life? What would he tell Heather? How would they recover?

"Look," Jack said. "We're prepared to give you as much as we can. You can keep working, of course, but some of the building and the actual launching of a mission will just have to wait right now."

Jason nodded again. "I understand."

The waitress arrived with their food, and they paused as

she set it out before them, checking to see if they needed anything before disappearing again. Jason barely noticed the plate of chicken marsala in red wine sauce and glazed red potatoes she left in front of him. As the others ate, they tried to engage him, but Jason barely responded, eating in silence as his mind raced for solutions, but only found more problems.

Never had he felt so hopeless. So alone. He knew their words were sincere. They'd believe in and support him, but without the funding, what did it matter? He couldn't help Laura, bring her home. He might as well be standing still. And Jason couldn't remember the last time he'd actually felt this way.

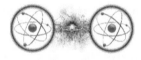

BECAUSE HEATHER'S SCHOOL had a teacher in-service day, she'd been out, so Roger and Susan had taken her to Disneyland. That night at dinner, Heather told Jason all about the rides, shows, and people watching, complete with pictures she'd taken just for him. Afterward, because she had no immediate homework, they watched an episode of her favorite TV show, *Young Sheldon*, during which Heather fell asleep, laying across his lap. She barely stirred when he carried her upstairs and tucked her in bed, so he kissed her goodnight and left her there, returning to the kitchen to find Roger, and Susan looking stern-faced as if they'd been engaged in some sort of serious discussion.

"She's exhausted," Jason commented, smiling. "Thanks for taking her. She clearly had a great time." The kitchen still smelled of the delicious lasagna Susan had made for dinner from the family recipe—the same recipe Laura always used.

Just smelling it reminded him of her and eating it had been like having Laura back for a moment. Heat radiated through his chest just smelling it again as his tongue watered at the memory.

"Whenever she wasn't crying, she did," Roger snapped.

"What?" Jason asked, surprised. Susan lifted a coffee pot she'd just prepared and offered him a cup. He nodded and she poured a mug, sliding it across the counter as he sat on a stool facing them. "What do you mean?"

"She talked the whole time about how much she wished you and Laura were there to see this, ride this ride, see this show, those people," Susan explained. "And several times she just cried because she missed you both so much. It was the saddest thing I've ever seen. They call it 'the happiest place on Earth,' but you wouldn't have known it."

"She sure took a lot of pictures for someone so miserable," Jason said, struggling to believe it. Heather had been so bubbly when she talked about it, so filled with excitement and joy. How could she have been miserable?

"She's putting on an act for you, Jason," Roger said. "That is not the same girl we spent the day with at Disneyland. Trust me. She's torn up inside."

Jason looked away. "I know it's hard for her." He kicked himself for not being more aware and sensitive to Heather's feelings. He was her father. He should have seen this himself.

"Her schoolwork's suffering too," Susan said. "Her teacher sent home a note today. Heather's grades have dropped. Her scores on tests and homework are way down."

"Can I see it?" Jason asked and Susan slid a note on official academy stationary across the counter. Jason paused and read it. It was exactly as she had said. "Maybe I should get her a tutor."

"I work with her," Susan protested.

"A tutor's not going to make a damn difference," Roger snapped, scowling.

Susan put a hand on his arm and calmed him with a look, then turned to Jason again. "We want you to consider letting us take her back to Houston for a while, to be with her old friends, her old school," she said tenderly. "She can stay with us. Just 'til things get settled. Her whole life has been disrupted coming here in the first place, and now she's off to such a rocky start. She's having a hard time making friends, fitting in. How can she when she feels so alone and isolated? She can't talk about her mom's kidnapping at school because it's this big mystery that scares the other kids. A couple moms wouldn't let their daughters come over for playdates because they didn't want them to be around 'our situation,' I was told." Susan shook her head. "It just breaks my heart."

Jason sipped his coffee slowly as his heart sank and tried to gather the emotions rushing through him. On the one hand, he felt anger threatening to rise and bite back with resentment. On the other, they loved Heather and he felt their concern and caring for her and for him. He had to stay calm, think this through. An emotional reaction with Laura's parents was never a good idea. Besides, he was just learning all this. He needed time to process. "I had no idea."

"Susan didn't want to tell you," Roger said.

"You've got so much to worry about already," Susan said. "But after today...how could I not?" Susan turned away and pulled a tissue from a Kleenex box, dabbing at her eyes.

"No, I'm so glad you did, really," Jason said. "I need to

know. She's my baby." He choked up a bit—the anger fading into guilt and sadness—and hid it behind another deep draw from the mug.

"Christmas is almost here, and don't kid yourself," Roger said. "That kid knows her mother isn't going to make it home for it. And it's killing her."

"It's killing me, Roger," Jason said, almost pleading. "I'm doing everything I can."

Susan locked eyes with him—soft, filled with compassion and nodded. "We know that. We really do. We just think she'd benefit from some kind of sense of normalcy again, you know? She had that in Houston, but she's never had the chance to find that here. So maybe for a while, that would be better for her."

Jason nodded, then put his face in his hands. "Yeah, I hear you. But I've lost my wife, Susan. I don't want to lose my daughter too. I need her. Need her close."

"Just think about it, please," Susan said. "Promise me you'll do that."

Jason took a deep breath and nodded again as he looked up at them. "Of course. You know how much I love her."

Susan smiled. "So do we, dear. So do we."

Jason smiled back but it was forced, then stood and headed for his den as he fought to conceal the tears that started rolling down his cheeks. Inside, part of him feared they were right, but seeing Heather every day helped keep him going, believing, pressing forward no matter what.

He closed the door to the den and sunk into the chair behind his desk, face in his hands again. *God, what a nightmare this is for poor Heather.* He couldn't blame her at all. He was so busy trying to find solutions, it was easy to keep it together, not dwell on it. But Heather didn't have that. They'd ripped her away from her home and friends and taken her far away to a new school, just to have her mother abducted and taken away, and her father put in the hospital, injured. When had she ever had time to find a life here? He ached for his daughter, his stomach rumbling, as his throat thickened. He felt slight nausea, like a stomach bug. *It's all my fault. It's all because of me.*

Only he was doing everything he could, and now NASA and funding seemed determined to keep him from that as well.

HALF AN HOUR LATER, he opened his laptop and logged into Caltech's secure network with his credentials, throwing himself into his work refining the Shortcut formula. Knowing it was possible to take Shortcuts using nonspherical objects, Jason had been removing spherical assumptions and replacing them with arbitrary geometries with the goal that retrofitting any spacecraft with laser cells might make Shortcutting possible. Knowing that the rescue mission would require a bigger craft, his team modeled the latest Maxx design after SpaceX's *Dragon 2*, adding space for an increased crew complement and room for defensive and offensive weapons capabilities, if deemed necessary. Since the meeting with Jack, Li, and Purva, he'd also been making inquiries with Elon Musk, Richard Branson and others about projects in development that might be borrowed and employed in a rescue mission. Preliminary talks had not revealed anything deemed viable but he had feelers out to the Chinese and Russians as well and was awaiting a response.

In the meantime, he'd also been working on improving the craft's solar collection efficiency, laser power, and lens control to increase shortcut distances as well as improving the calculations themselves for better accuracy that would make the longer distances safe. The side benefit of this was improved location predictions. Some of his staff, inspired by the alien craft, had suggested perhaps returning to the idea of using salt optics, but, at present, the extent of design modifications required and cost made it impossible.

That night, he made a breakthrough on polariton efficiency of the lasers that he hoped would make longer distance shortcuts more efficient. Finishing his calculations, he wrote up a report and sent it to the lab personnel responsible for engine development, then went upstairs and immediately fell asleep.

The next morning, he delayed going into the office so he could take Heather to school personally. Cal drove with Reggie sitting in the front passenger side while Jason rode with Heather in the back. When they got to the school, the sun shone bright overhead as he walked her to her classroom.

"I love you, Daddy," she said as they stopped outside the door and kissed and hugged.

"I love you, too, honey," Jason said, releasing her. "You have a great day, okay?"

That's when it happened. He had just put his hand on the DMG he wore attached to his belt when it started vibrating and a bright light flashed somewhere nearby. He stumbled, feeling as if the floor had been yanked from under him like a carpet, as if something was trying to lift him right off his feet but failing.

The aliens were trying to abduct him *right now*!

He caught himself against the wall and steadied himself, then saw Heather's terrified face as she watched him from the classroom doorway. He had to protect her. Had to get away from her so she didn't get taken instead.

"Daddy?!" she cried out.

"Baby, go inside. Now. Hurry!" he urged, almost yelling. She ran toward him, but he pushed her away. "Go! Please!"

She hesitated a moment but he motioned intensely again, and she finally turned and disappeared into the classroom.

Then he ran.

As he ran, he turned back and saw a trashcan near where he'd been standing turn into a black shadow, flash brightly, and then disappear. He actually laughed. Bet that would surprise them. As he dashed, he felt the DMG vibrating again; this time he didn't turn back.

Looking down at the battery level on the DMG, he saw that it was below ten percent. If the aliens tried a fourth time, he wouldn't have enough power left to deflect the Shortcut.

He ducked outside and found the sun gone, replaced by rain. Although winded and struggling to breathe, he didn't stop again until he got to the car and leaned against it, catching his breath. His chest and lungs hurt for the first time in a week from the intense activity.

"What happened?" Reggie asked with obvious alarm as Jason opened the door.

"I'm pretty sure the aliens just made a second attempt," Jason said, climbing in. "Drive! Now!" He motioned urgently.

"They tried to abduct you?!" Cal said, swinging into action as he pulled the car away and sped up, headed for the street.

"What's going on?" Reggie said, eyes darting around outside as he frowned and his hand came to rest on the shoulder holster under his jacket.

Within a block, Cal shut off the wipers. The rain was gone and the sun was shining brightly again. On the way to Caltech, after he'd called Heather to reassure her he was okay, Jason told them.

CHAPTER 12

C AL AND REGGIE rushed Jason immediately into a shielded magnetics testing lab in the basement of the Cahill on Caltech's campus and called for Jimmy, the detectives, Jack and Li to join them. The lab was a white-walled, sterile environment with open spaces and a few tables pushed back against the walls, but where they waited was an observation booth which looked a bit like a control booth, with computers, file cabinets, and an intercom into the main testing areas. Jason sat in a rolling chair beside a counter overlooking the main lab's floor and turned around to face Cal and Reggie as they waited in silence.

For the next few minutes, with his heart pounding and adrenaline pumping, Jason felt almost like he was on trial as they fired off question after question. Within thirty minutes, the others began arriving and the once sterile room heated up from all the bodies, filling with the smell of after shave and sweat.

"Slow down, everyone," Jason finally said, taking a deep breath to calm himself. The crowd surrounding him might as well be statues from all the tension in the air. He was fine and decided to take charge of the situation. "I'm okay. The DMG did its job."

"Just tell us what happened, son," Jimmy said.

"I walked Heather to her class and then I felt this pull on me, and a tingling sensation, and I knew it was happening," Jason said. "So I told her to get in her classroom away from me and I ran. The last thing I saw was a trash can disappearing, so I think they'll find that a poor substitute, but I'm safe. Can we all calm down now?"

"We're glad you're safe," Li said.

"Heather's probably a mess," Jason said. "I need to check on her."

"Purva is calling," Jack said as Jason saw Purva picking up a phone across the room. "But we need to keep you here until we're sure it's safe."

"They failed," Jason said. "They know I can foil their lasers. I doubt they'll try again any time soon." He pointed to the DMG on his belt. "As long as I have this, I'm fine."

"That was a smart idea, Doc," Jimmy said.

"It doesn't hurt having a wife who's a laser expert," Jason said and smiled.

"We should probably come up with a protocol in case they try again, just to be extra safe," Jack suggested. At that moment, Detectives Connelly and Coben arrived to join them,

"Because no one took me seriously when I said they would?" Jason replied, shaking his head. "I was ready. You weren't. Maybe I'm not so crazy after all." He decided not to admit that he'd been tempted to turn off the DMG and let them abduct him so he could get to his wife and try to work from there to get her back home. What had stopped him in the end was Heather—he couldn't let her lose both parents—and the realization that if the aliens were not well-intentioned, he might be unable to rescue Laura or set things right in their custody. In the end, he'd only entertained the thought for a few seconds while he ran.

"No one said you were crazy," Detective Connelly said but his arms were crossed as he leaned against the wall nearby.

"I know," Jason said, locking eyes with him. "You were all too polite. But we all know you were damn well thinking it. Don't treat me like an idiot."

Coben grunted then raised his hands in surrender. "Fair enough. Can you blame us?"

"Not really," Jason said with a shrug. "This kind of thing is outside the realm of normal experience, I get that."

"All right, well, we need some details for our report," Connelly said, straddling a chair, his iPad at the ready. "So let's go over your movements from the time you left the car please."

Jason chuckled. "Okay, fine."

He ran them through it, interrupted several times by various questions from Coben, Connelly, and Jimmy. They took copious notes, as usual, on their iPads, and then discussed various scenarios for keeping him safer, none of which Jason felt would make much of a difference if the aliens really wanted him and upped their technology on the next attempt.

"Really, the safest thing is to stay indoors," Li added.

"I was indoors for this attempt," Jason reminded him.

"Right, but that classroom was not far from the door and on the first floor, so probably the least shielded by walls and infrastructure of any place in the building," Jack said.

Jason shook his head. "Look, I gotta keep working. My

house has less shielding than any school. I'll just keep wearing the DMG. It's the best defense we've got. The rest of it isn't going to be worth a damn if they really want me."

The others exchanged looks that basically admitted they knew he was right and were out of ideas.

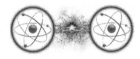

WITHIN AN HOUR, Purva called to report Susan and Roger had picked Heather up and taken her home, so Jason insisted on going to see her. Jimmy, Cal, and Reggie argued against it, but finally realized he wouldn't back down and insisted on accompanying him.

As soon as he walked through the front door, Heather threw her sobbing form into his arms. "Daddy! I was so scared."

"I know, baby," he said as he nestled his face in her hair. "I'm sorry."

"What happened? Was it the aliens?"

"I think so, sweetie, but I'm safe," Jason said. "I'm here."

"Why are they doing this?" Each word came out between sobs and her face was red and shiny with tears as she looked into his eyes for answers. "Is it your work, daddy? Can we go back to Texas? No one bothered us there?"

Jason observed Susan and Roger exchanging a look as they stood watching from across the room, and he felt a pain like a knife jab in the back of his throat. "Honey, I need to be here to work so I can help find mommy, but I'm safe. I protected myself with this." He put his hand on the DMG and leaned back so Heather could see it and their eyes met.

"Their lasers don't work when I have this. That's why I wanted you away from me. So you were safe. Because it can only protect one of us at a time."

Heather cocked her head in thought and sniffled. "Would they take me to Mommy, Daddy?"

"Honey, I couldn't stand to lose you both," Jason said. "And I'll never give up trying to find Mommy and bring her home."

Heather smiled, through tears. "I love you, Daddy."

"Oh baby, I love you, too," he said as his own tears flowed and he held her again, reveling in the warmth for a few moments.

Then Heather pulled away and locked eyes with him again, wiping at her runny nose with an arm. "Daddy, is Mommy okay? How do you know?"

"I can feel her, baby," Jason said then put Heather's hand on his chest near his heart. "I can feel her here. I love her so much that I just know."

Susan and Roger frowned behind her but Jason ignored them and looked into his daughter's eyes. "I believe, Heather. Do you?"

Heather's eyes showed complete trust and reliance on her father's words and she nodded as she leaned forward and hugged him again. "Yes, Daddy. I believe."

After a few more minutes, he calmed her down and Susan took her into the kitchen for some food, while Jason stayed behind to talk with Roger, Jimmy, and the bodyguards.

"She belongs in Houston," Roger snapped. "She feels safer there."

Jason sighed, then looked at his scowling father-in-law. "I

heard what she said, Roger." He sat on the edge of the couch. "And I'm starting to think so too."

Roger and Susan looked surprised, but he met their eyes and held them.

"Why don't we go there for Christmas and let her have some time with her old friends?" he continued. "Then I'll decide what's best for all of us."

Roger's chin jutted as he grunted, then nodded and turned, heading off toward the kitchen.

"We can protect you wherever you decide you need to be," Jimmy said.

"I need to be where I can work," Jason said. Security was the least of his concerns. "But I have to take care of my daughter, too. And she needs to get away for a bit. Having the holidays in a familiar place will help her right now."

Jimmy nodded. "I understand. Michele and the family are there, and I was fixin' to pay them a visit anyway, so I'll be there as well. We'll make sure no one bothers you. Whatever it takes." He put a hand on Jason's shoulder and squeezed.

"You and I both know if they really want me, they'll find a way," Jason said with no emotion. He felt weighed down, as if all the energy had been sucked from his body. He still believed what he'd said: Laura was out there and he had to save her. But right now, he couldn't even find the energy to hope. Instead, he just nodded again, resigned.

"Do you need anything?" Reggie asked.

Jason shook his head and slid off the arm down into the couch. After a few moments, they left him to take up their posts, and he was alone.

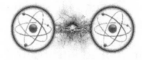

THEY FLEW TO Houston two days later. Susan and Roger were amazing. They poured on the energy, getting the decorations up, and making their house look like it always had at Christmas, as if it had been the plan all along to be there. Heather spent time with an endless stream of friends. At first, Susan insisted they come to the house to play with her, but eventually, when Jimmy showed up to pick up his granddaughter, he talked them into letting Heather go out and take a sleigh ride in the park, even visit Santa's village and the mall. Each time, Heather came back bouncing and happy. She was like the daughter Jason hadn't seen since they'd left Texas, and finally he had to admit Heather seemed happier in Houston than she'd ever had in Pasadena.

As was tradition, Roger's neighbors had a caroling party and rented a school bus, and the whole family went along, stopping at various houses to serenade happy faces with traditional carols by candlelight. Heather cuddled against Jason's arm, helping hold the candle as he held the lyric sheet, and she sang with great gusto, reminding him of her mother. Jason did his best to sing along too, but his mind was elsewhere, weighed down by the decisions he faced and worry about Laura. Could he really live without his daughter nearby when having her was such a comfort, such a source of inspiration and hope? Part of him knew his resistance to the idea was as much about not wanting to cede Roger and Susan any victory in their effort to take charge of his family's lives. But on the other hand, Heather was a new girl since they'd come back, and it filled him with happiness and peace just to see that. How could he deny her the joy of being with old friends in a familiar place when their life in

California was such chaos and would remain so until he got Laura back home?

After the caroling, they all went back to the neighbor's house for Christmas cookies, candy canes, eggnog, punch, and light sandwiches, chatting about life, school, work—everyday, regular things. As he sipped apple cinnamon punch and munched on sugar cookies, Jason was distinctly aware how normal everyone else's life seemed compared to his own and how relieved Heather seemed at being in a normal world again, a world she'd always known. And his heart broke at the idea of taking her away from that. He had no choice. This was where she belonged, at least for the moment.

The day after they'd arrived in Houston, Roger and Jason had put aside their anger with each other and rushed around buying Christmas presents to make sure Heather had the same kind of Christmas she was used to. A few had been brought from California, including some Laura had bought throughout the year, as was her habit. But they wanted Heather to have a full stocking under the tree Christmas morning, so they bought everything from clothes to toys, even a new laptop. Roger got her a bike. Jason didn't bother to point out it wouldn't be easy to transport back to California. He figured if she stayed, she'd use it at her grandparents. She had another in Pasadena that had arrived with the movers.

On Christmas Eve, per tradition, they attended services at the Southern Baptist church Roger and Susan had attended for years. It was a candlelight service with a short homily and many carols. Jason actually felt surprisingly uplifted and encouraged by the experience, but perhaps it was the love and warmth the congregation showed each other. Whatever likes, dislikes, rivalries or issues might be hiding beneath the surface of every day had been left behind for this one night. Peace on Earth was more than a cliché for them. They were one body, one family, and nothing would interfere with the joy of their celebration together.

On Christmas morning, Heather woke early, like any normal kid, and soon they were immersed in the joy of watching her revel in handing them each presents with their names on the tags then joyfully opening hers, delighting in each one. The smell of peppermint and warm cinnamon tea filled his nose, accompanied by pine tar from the tree and the sound of crinkling paper and laughter. Like many a parent, he found himself immediately transported back through all the Christmases before with his little girl, reliving the joy, the amazement, the wonder of parents watching the magic of Christmas unfolding for their child. The emotions overran him like a wave—humility, happiness, guilt, fear, and then enormous gratitude. Altogether, it was the most conventional moment Jason had experienced with his daughter since he could remember, and it sealed the deal. Heather deserved convention, normalcy. Not a life of fear and sadness. For better or worse, she would stay in Houston with her grandparents while Jason worked on rescuing Laura. It would be hard for him, hard for her, but it was what she needed, and right now, putting her needs first was what Laura would want. And Jason wanted it, too.

Like most families, after opening presents, the family convened around the dining room table for a feast: turkey, cranberry sauce—both jellied and regular—hot homemade rolls and bread, stuffing, mashed potatoes and gravy, green bean casserole and more. The sweetness of jam, the tart sweetness of cranberry sauce, the warm savor of gravy and melted butter—every bite was a delight. Jason couldn't remember that last time he'd felt so stuffed and so satisfied at the same time. The food warmed his body and the family time warmed his soul. Despite missing Laura the whole time, despite his struggles with her parents, they became one family, united that day, and it had a healing power that was exactly what Jason needed as much as Heather.

That night, Jason got a call from Jack and Peter back at Caltech in his lab. He took it in Roger's den.

"You're working on Christmas Day?" he asked, both surprised and touched.

"Well, not all of us have families," Peter said.

"My kids are with their mother," Jack said. "So why not do something useful? Besides, Peter told me they were close to a breakthrough with your revised formula and we wanted to work it through. There were several team members who felt the same. We don't want to let you down."

Jason felt a surge of emotions from guilt to joy. His throat grew thick even as his chest radiated with heat and he found himself smiling ear-to-ear. He was struggling to come up with a response, when Peter saved him the trouble.

"The new laser prototype was finished Wednesday, the night you left," Peter said. Jason had gotten a memo. "So we've been running tests ever since. And the test craft is ready, too. It was just waiting for final touches, which we finished last night."

"That's amazing," Jason said.

"Well, we couldn't have done it without those tweaks to the formula and calculations you sent over just before you left town," Peter said. "They changed everything."

"Well, I'm starting to realize I'm just a small part of a larger team, but thank you," Jason said, truly excited. Even though he'd been working with teams for the past two years at NASA and now Caltech, Jason had grown so used to being a loner in the years before that he still found it hard to truly trust and rely on other people. It had always been easier to push on himself, fully confident that he knew his work better than anyone. But Peter, Jack, Li, and their teams had been really stepping up for him and challenging his reluctance.

"Jason, how'd you like to be part of a test while you're in Houston?" Jack said.

"A test?" Jason asked, leaning back in Roger's executive chair.

"I'll send Li and Purva," Jack said. "They volunteered. We'll send the test craft from here to Houston then on to Cape Canaveral, which is where Peter is going as soon as we get off this call and make arrangements. Li will bring the specs."

For a moment, Jason considered insisting he review it all personally before they involved NASA, but then he hadn't been leading the way this time. Peter and Li had. And he was starting to realize his people were more than competent without him second guessing them every time. Perhaps he should give them the chance. "Okay. I'll call Phil and arrange everything with NASA," Jason volunteered. "Their people are just as invested. And Johnson and Kennedy are slowed down for the holidays."

"Sounds great," Jack agreed.

"NASA might want a big show," Jason added, picturing a gaggle of press and mob of space aficionados, "but with the mission being kept secret at the moment, we should downplay its significance. That plus holiday travel should keep the attention and crowd to a minimum—a few employees and their families—just to avoid rumors and questions."

Jack smiled. "Phil's getting quite a Christmas present."

"This one's a present for all of us," Jason replied, feeling excited at the prospect of taking any action that moved them that much closer to making a real rescue mission possible.

"Well, we'll just have to wait a few days to unwrap it," Peter said. "Expect some videos and reports shortly in your email."

"Okay, then let me call Phil Cline and see if I can get the ball rolling," Jason said, surprised and pleased with the unexpected development. It made his day after all the discouragement he'd been experiencing.

"And Merry Christmas!" Jack said cheerfully.

"Yes, Merry Christmas," Peter added.

"To you as well," Jason said with great enthusiasm. "Thank you."

After the line went dead, Jason danced a jig around Roger's office before picking up the phone and dialing Phil.

THE FOLLOWING FRIDAY, December 30th, Jason took Heather with him down to Johnson Space Center. The Raimeys, having shown no interest, stayed at home. There, he met Purva and Phil Cline, who drove him in Phil's official car to the chosen test site deep inside the complex on an open field. Jason recognized several faces amongst the small crowd who'd gathered to watch, including Li, who was leading a team in setting up a large circle marked with wire flags, while others huddled around a safe distance away, some in lawn and folding chairs, others on blankets like they'd come for a picnic.

Phil parked at the curb and the three of them got out and walked across the field toward the circle. It was a clear day with a few clouds, the sky above a lustrous light blue. The air carried faint scents of citrus and sage, probably from the well-tended flowerbeds that beautified the space center's campus at various points. The sun bore down on the field almost like a spotlight marking an important place. It reflected brightly off the center of the circle where a parabolic reflector—basically, a roundish set of interlocking mirrors suspending the test ship with cables like a ball hovering over an empty bowl—lay on the ground to focus energy. This was to collect solar energy that could then be channeled into the Shortcut test craft to send it on its way to Kennedy Space Center at Cape Canaveral.

"Thanks for letting us use the space centers today," Jason said as they walked.

Phil smiled and nodded, his hands in his pockets to keep warm. "Always nice when we can have a show for our families over the holidays. It gets pretty quiet unless someone wants to watch boring readouts or hear occasional computer talk from a rover or probe."

"The ISS might be more interesting," Purva interjected.

"Indeed, but except for facilitating calls to families, we only bother them if we need to so they can have the holidays off, too," Phil said.

At safe points around the circle, television cameras were set up on tripods and crewed by two people. There was also a PA system with large speakers set up and focused on the safe areas where the observers had gathered. As he passed some of his NASA friends and their spouses or families, including Bob Cooper, Matt D'Aunno, and Leti Najera from

Mission Control, Jason took his eyes off the solar concentrator to mumble greetings and shake hands briefly. It was a small group compared to what it might have been, but still larger than Jason had hoped for, but he felt relief at the clear cultivation Phil had done with the guest list. Most were employees and their families with some support role to the project's future or past.

When they were almost to the edge of the circle, Li stepped out to meet them. He was beaming as he shook Jason's hand firmly and said, "'I find the great thing in this world is not so much where we stand, as in what direction we are moving', Oliver Wendell Holmes, Sr. in *The Autocrat of the Breakfast Table*. Welcome to a giant step forward for the Shortcut Program. Jason, would you like to fill Phil in?"

"No, this is your show. By all means, go ahead," Jason said and motioned to the crowd. He was too excited to watch Heather's and Phil's reactions and see the results for himself and stepped back closer to them, waiting on Li.

Li excused himself and hurried back over and gave a few more instructions to his team, then returned to lead Purva, Phil, Jason, and Heather to a small command center viewing stand to the east of the Dish Stirling—a location a safe distance back but with the best view. It contained several small monitors, two keyboards, three joysticks, cables, and various controls, and hanging over it on poles and a frame was a large video monitor aimed for the observers to view. Similar screens were also located on either side, forty feet from the circle as well.

"As you can see, we are in video conference over Skype with our teams at Caltech and Kennedy Space Center," Li explained, pointing to where Peter and Jack appeared on monitors, talking with their own teams at the other locations. His voice took on a narrator's tone—official, authoritative, confident.

Li positioned himself at the center of the command tent, in front of a microphone on a short stand, flipped some switches and nodded to his team. As he spoke, his voice went out over a loudspeaker so the whole crowd in attendance could hear his explanations. "Welcome to today's demonstration of the Shortcut Theory developed by Dr. Jason Maxx in association with NASA and the California Institute of Technology," Li said, looking primarily at Phil. "Our latest goal is to develop the ability to Shortcut from Earth directly to space to avoid the need for rockets. We're not quite there yet, but we've made the first step by improving both the accuracy over long distances of our navigation and efficiency of the laser's energy usage. In the near future, the spacecraft will have an adaptive optics system to counteract the turbulence in the atmosphere in real time, allowing Shortcuts over longer distances—theoretically up to 700 miles or 1000 kilometers through the air." With the edge of space only 62 miles above sea level, Jason knew this was overkill, but was exactly the kind of capability needed to avoid reliance on NASA or someone else for launches in the future. For now, however, they'd still need a boost to safely exit the atmosphere. Shortcuts would be done once the spacecraft entered space. But as a demonstration, today they'd be shortcutting within Earth's atmosphere, a good precursor to the tests in space that would come.

"Right now, the distances are less than half that, but still much further than Maxx-One would have been capable of," Li added. "The solar concentrator, which in this case is similar to a Dish Stirling, charges the ship more quickly and pulls in energy more efficiently than the lenses could on their own. This increased light-collection efficiency was unnecessary in space-based tests, where the sunlight is stronger. Today, we're going to attempt the first test flight with the new navigation upgrade and a nonspherical spacecraft. As a precursor to tests done in space, we'll be working entirely within the Earth's atmosphere today, giving you as observers the first, best opportunity to witness this great new technology in action." The crowd applauded and Li paused a moment to allow it to die down.

Then he continued, "Now, since our lasers require line-of-sight to work, and you can't see Houston from Pasadena, we are using El Paso as a midpoint. The ship will Shortcut to midair over El Paso, charge directly from the sun, which will be straight overhead and in optimum charging position at this time of day, and then Shortcut again to our location here at Johnson."

Li stopped and motioned to the solar concentrator. "The solar collector will then recharge it and send it out quickly again to somewhere over the Gulf of Mexico near Gulf Shores, Alabama. There, once again in midair, it will recharge from the sun and make one final jump to Kennedy Space Center."

The locations had been chosen because each was an exact midpoint. El Paso between LAX and IAH (George Bush Intercontinental Houston Airport), a 1376 mile (2214 kilometer) flight. And the Gulf of Mexico stop midway along the 853 mile (1373 kilometer) path from Houston to Kennedy.

"We've drawn the circle to demonstrate the improved accuracy of our positioning system, which now generates positions in a much more refined area," Li explained. "There is a similar setup at Kennedy as well, where Peter Edtz is supervising the team."

He paused and smiled at Jason. "Shall we get this show rolling?"

Jason extended a hand, palm up toward him. "By all means." Then he leaned over to Heather and said, "Keep watching that mirror in the middle of the circle, baby. That's where all cool stuff will happen."

"'kay," Heather said, sounding excited. Jason chuckled watching her brow crease as she focused more intently on the solar collector. She looked just like her mother when Laura was deep in thought. His thoughts went to his beloved then and he closed his eyes, saying a silent prayer and sending her love and greetings with his spirit as he did. While he was capable of narrating the launch, he knew Li was in a far better, more focused frame of mind. In addition to all the physical and emotional turmoil he'd experienced the past few months, the test had come about so quickly—with Li, Jack, and Peter managing the planning—that Jason felt a bit out of touch, and, in any case, he always had to fight the urge to hold his breath every time a test launch occurred. He'd barely remembered to breathe in NASA Mission Control, and he'd had Laura to remind him.

Li motioned to his team who finished checking readings on various equipment, then cleared themselves from the circle to safe observation points. When they were ready, he continued, "What you should expect to see is a bright flash and then the appearance of our spacecraft at the center of the solar concentrator. It will then charge momentarily and disappear again. If you look closely during the charging process, you may notice the spacecraft appear as a black shadow for just a few seconds before it disappears. This is all standard to the Shortcut, quantum entanglement process."

Li flipped a switch and keyed the mic again. "Okay, Peter, are you all ready at Kennedy?"

Peter's voice came back and they saw him in the video monitor on the command console in front of them. He bore a confident smile, his shirt and tie a contrast to the usual casual dress he wore in the lab. "Ready when you are, Li."

Li flipped another switch. "Jack. We're all ready at both sites. Launch as able."

Jack appeared on the other monitor and smiled. "All right. We're ready here, too. Let's do it."

As the process began, Li continued narrating every step as it happened in real time over closed circuit TV as well as PA systems at all three sites. There was no glamor to observing flight tests, especially in this open field. And everything seemed to move at a snail's pace while you waited. It was nowhere near as exciting or thrilling at the moment than it appeared in movies or on TV. "Right now, you are watching the laser charge. The lenses that surround the spacecraft have been optimized to collect and harness the power of solar light, like a magnifying glass focusing light on an ant. You may notice that the spacecraft appears black. This is because it is absorbing nearly one hundred percent of the light that hits it, so there is no light left over to bounce back into your eyes or these television cameras.

"Once the laser is charged, we can't fire it just yet because the air in our atmosphere causes a problem for laser beams: it likes to bend them. To fix this problem, a test beam is fired from the spacecraft."

On the large screens, the test craft faintly flashed repeatedly. An odd shaped lump with lights like something out of an Asimov or Heinlein novel.

"This test beam is used to determine how 'windy' it is up there," Li continued. "The spacecraft's advanced computers then observe how the shape of the test beam changes and programs the lenses to counteract those changes. Additionally, the laser shield will create a light sphere of sorts around the spacecraft so that it will act like a singular particle for the actual jumps. Once it has done enough tests, the computer gives us a thumbs up and the laser shield activates. Then the main laser is ready to fire in—"

Other voices of controllers from Caltech and Kennedy joined him and they counted down together, "Five... four... three... two... one..." Then, things got more exciting.

There was a big flash and the test spacecraft disappeared from the screens as the observers collectively gasped and clapped, some breaking into amazed chatter at what they'd witnessed.

"And it disappears," Li confirmed. "Our test craft, the *Mini-Maxx*, is on its way."

The video monitors now cut to a view of the sunny, blue sky over El Paso, Texas. Moments later, the *Mini-Maxx* test craft appeared overhead in the sky as a small, dark object, spinning crazily—almost as if it was out of control. Jason hadn't seen a spacecraft this large exhibit this behavior before outside of his simulations, so he was actually excited to see it in person. This test was unmanned, but watching it like this, Jason thought of the astronauts, amazed they could ride through something so traumatic and still keep the focus to do their jobs. His body felt hard as a rock from tension and he forced himself to take a long breath.

"If you're joining us from UTEP today," Li said with a mischievous glint in his eyes, "we'd like to remind you not to stare into the sun without those special sunglasses. As you can see, the spacecraft appears to be a small black object over El Paso. Over in Juarez perhaps some of your neighbors are calling Fox Mulder right about now."

A few in the crowd chuckled and called out snarky comments.

Li continued, "This is totally normal and part of the Shortcut process; the spacecraft is recharging in preparation for the second leg of its journey to Houston, Texas."

After a few moments, the *Mini-Maxx* disappeared with another flash the same as they'd seen before.

"And now it's on its way to us here at Johnson Space Center," Li narrated. "When the test craft arrives at Houston, it will sit right in the center of the solar concentrator in that circle you see in front of us here. We managed to prevent it from shooting off, but it will still have some angular momentum left over, so don't be surprised if when it arrives it is spinning like crazy inside of the solar collector."

The observers around Jason and Heather gasped with amazement as the *Mini-Maxx* test craft suddenly appeared right in front of them atop the solar collector's mirrored surface at the center of the circle, spinning crazily again. They heard a scraping sound and soft screeching of metal against glass every time it shifted as it turned.

"Oh, there it is!" Heather called out as the *Mini-Maxx* arrived, pointing excitedly and nudging her father.

Jason laughed, breathing easily again and feeling a warm buzz at how the test was succeeding. They'd done it. Shortcut was working exactly as they'd planned. It was one thing to imagine it in theory, but to see it live and in person always thrilled and amazed him. "I see it, sweetie. Isn't it cool?"

"So cool!" she agreed and hugged his arm as he leaned down and kissed the top of her head, wishing Laura could be with them to witness it.

"Welcome to Houston, *Mini-Maxx*," Li said over the applause and chatter. "Even though it looks like it's out of control, the spacecraft is behaving exactly as I predicted. Before it can make its next jump, the test craft will have to slow down and despin so that the whole process can start again."

Yes, they weren't done. There were two more stages. Jason returned his focus to the screens as the spacecraft slowed and steadied, lights on the command center panel lit up indicating the recharging process was complete. Indicators out along the solar collector lit up to match them. Most were yellow or white but there were a few of varied colors like blue, red, orange, or green.

"Okay," Li said. "She's ready. Those of you along the coast of the Gulf of Mexico, prepare yourselves for the next Shortcut in—"

Jason's mind became a blur, Li's voice fading into the background, as he continued watching the screens, his daughter beside him. Two minutes later,, the video monitors cut to a view of the sunny, blue sky over the ocean near Gulf Shores, Alabama as the *Mini-Maxx* appeared, spinning crazily in the sky, almost a small dot at the distance from which the cameras were shooting. Jason hoped the observers had brought binoculars along for better views.

They repeated the whole process again, waiting while the craft recharged, then another countdown, followed by a flash, and its disappearance as *Maxx-One* made the trip to its final destination.

Finally, Kennedy Space Center appeared on the screen, a large, now abandoned shuttle launch platform centered in the background off in the distance. Up close, the area was a flat, grassy field with a similar circle to the one on the ground in front of them in Houston.

"Expecting arrival momentarily," Peter's voice rang out.

Then *Mini-Maxx* appeared with a flash and settled onto the field, spinning crazily as it had in Houston.

"Success!"

Thunderous applause broke out on all three sites and carried over the speakers. It was momentarily deafening through the PA, and Jason grinned ear-to ear along with Heather, Li, and Purva. The entire exercise had taken less than eight minutes from start to finish, but it clearly made up for the long wait before it had begun.

"That was awesome!" Heather shouted, trying to be heard over the crowd.

"Yes, it was," Purva agreed and tousled her hair.

Jason turned to Phil Cline. "What did you think?"

Phil grinned. "Heather got it right. That was awesome. You really made some progress."

"Now we just need a way to get out there and go get Laura," Jason said.

Phil's grin faltered. "We still don't know where she is or where to look. How far we'd need to travel. There's so many unknowns."

The lightness Jason had been experiencing at the test's success faded a bit under Phil's skepticism. He'd hoped it might make an impression but inside he'd feared it wouldn't be enough, and he'd been right. Phil was still the cautious administrator he'd always been. They both turned as a car pulled to a stop nearby and an Asian woman stepped out and hurried toward them, waving an iPad. She ran straight for Phil.

"What's going on, Glenda?" Phil asked as the woman stepped up beside him and paused to catch her breath.

"We've been working on cleanup. Going through some of the noise and extra messages on the DSN this week," she said, speaking quickly as she almost bounced on her feet.

The DSN, short for Deep Space Network, consisted of antenna sites in California, Spain, and Australia each 120 degrees of longitude apart to ensure full coverage of the Earth that NASA used to monitor space probes like the two *Voyagers*. It had been in use since the late 1970s and was underfunded, so much of the equipment was very old and required a lot more labor to maintain and monitor.

She handed him the iPad. "A message came through from *Voyager 1*."

"Wait. I thought comms went down over a month ago on *Voyager 1*," Phil asked, looking surprised as he started reading the iPad.

"They did, but we got a message today. And usually it's just ASCII data and numbers. This one had words," Glenda said. "We thought you'd want to see it right away."

Reading over Phil's shoulder, Jason saw the raw message on the screen. He hadn't seen ASCII format for a long time, but there it was—in the old communications style of 70s and 80s computers:

18, 361, 1.4485, -0.33698, 39.2099, W5XPM. Jason, I am well. Never traveled this far. A place with no name. Carry it through. Come get me. I believe in you. I love you. GTG.

"What's this number?" Phil asked with a puzzled look as he pointed to the screen and the last numbers before the message: W5XPM.

Jason read the screen over his shoulder and his breath caught in his throat. THUMP! He could hardly believe his eyes. *Holy shit!* "That's Laura's Ham radio ID."

"Mommy?" Heather said hopefully as she pushed in, trying to see the screen.

"What?" Phil said, shocked.

"She used Ham radio to communicate with schoolchildren on Earth during her last two space shuttle missions," Jason quickly replied.

"It's a message from Laura Maxx, Mr. Cline," Glenda said, grinning. "When we saw that, we pinged the spacecraft but got no response." She pointed to the first line of numbers, and added, "But the message is from today and the coordinates are out near Mars."

"Holy shit," Phil whispered, then remembered Heather. "I'm sorry."

"No, it's okay," Jason said, so stunned he could barely speak. He'd believed it, yes. Hoped it. Imagined it. But to hear it now out loud. For real. He felt like he was floating again, his body suddenly light and a sudden buzzing in his limbs as adrenaline spiked. Jason and Phil exchanged a look. Laura was in space. And now, they knew where to find her. How else could it come from *Voyager 1?* What else could the message mean?

"What's the message say?" Heather asked eagerly.

"Jason, I am safe. Never traveled this far. A place with no name. Come get me. I believe in you. I love you. GTG," Glenda read aloud as Jason's heart sang along with every word. He couldn't stop smiling, and he had to stop himself from jumping out of his chair. "What's that last part—GTG?"

"Got to go," Heather said immediately. Jason almost laughed. Laura and Heather used the phrase so often in texts, they'd started using it as shorthand at home in speech. "GTG," one of them would say. Only, unknown to Heather,

Jason and Laura never used GTG between themselves in that context. Instead, when they used it, they always meant it to say "Good to go," a kind of shorthand that had come out of encouraging and supporting each other, a subtle cheerleading that couples did for each other. In that moment it clicked. *It's really her.* He had no doubt about it. *Laura's alive! We can actually get her back!* He read the words again and it all clicked. She was telling him to come get her, in fact.

"It's text speak," Heather said, grinning.

Jason and Purva whooped and hugged, then Li joined them.

"What's going on?" Jason heard Jack ask over the small video screen.

"Laura sent a message," Purva quickly said. "She's okay!"

Jack's and Peter's whoops echoed from the screens now as Jason hugged Heather and then Purva and Li each took a turn. Then she turned and practically tackled Phil, hugging him tight. Jason fought the urge to shout to the whole world.

"What's that middle part about," Glenda asked, "'a place with no name? Carry it through? Come get me'?"

"Obviously, she doesn't know where she is," Phil said. "Can't identify it."

"Something she said to me when she needed me to come and do something important with her—a kind of personal code," Jason said. "She's telling me to work the problem, and that I need to come in person to get her." But inside, Jason knew there was more to it than that. It was a reference to a song with personal meaning to them both—U2's "Where The Streets Have No Name." He just had to figure out why she'd made that reference. As Heather let go and Phil breathed again, Jason met his eyes. "Well?"

Phil nodded as Heather, Jason, and the others locked their eager eyes on his. "This changes everything, doesn't it?"

"Is that a yes, Phil?" Li teased.

Phil chuckled, shifting nervously under the pressure of their probing stares. "You heard the lady. Let's go get her."

Jason and the others whooped again and started dancing around and soon Phil and Glenda joined them. Laura was alive and well and they had her location. All they had to do was go get her and bring her home. Jason couldn't remember the last time he'd felt such unmitigated joy. Aliens be damned, he'd bring his beloved back.

It wasn't until he got home that night that reality set in. He was a *mathematician*, not an astronaut. And here he was planning to lead a mission into space to rescue Laura against unknown forces? The math he could handle, but this?! They'd thought the alien theory was crazy but this was the real insanity! For the first time, fear of losing his wife, never seeing Laura again, was replaced by something else: fear he wasn't up to the task. There were a million reasons he needed to go, that they'd need his skills on the mission. But when it mattered most, when force and strength, not math were what counted—would he have what it takes? Jason fell asleep with a new resolve. He had to be ready for anything. No matter what. Nothing could stop him from going to get back the love of his life. He would do whatever it took.

CHAPTER 13

O N JANUARY FIRST, Jason arrived at Phil Cline's NASA office just after nine a.m. to meet about moving forward with a rescue mission. Phil spent a few moments reviewing through the memos Jason had sent over the past two days about retrofitting spacecraft already in development and mission parameters, then leaned back in his chair. Jason wondered if the test results and Laura's message had sent Phil back to long hours the past few days. He looked tired and stressed, despite having supposedly spent most of the holiday away from the office. Jason himself had never felt so energized. Ever since they'd gotten her message, Jason had had a singular focus: getting Laura home as soon as possible, driven by a renewed empowerment and faith that she was out there waiting, alive.

"It will be *Orion 6*," Phil said, referring to the sixth *Orion* spacecraft off the line. Consisting of three components—a command module manufactured by Lockheed Martin, a service module made by the European Space Agency, and an additional deep space habitat for longer distance missions— all of Orion's component parts were designed to be as generic as possible, so that the spacecraft could be easily upgraded as new technologies become available. While the first five Orions were designed for four to six crewmembers, *Orion 6* was the first of a new line designed for up to ten.

Unlike the space shuttle, *Orion* capsules were designed to be launched with the aid of a larger rocket, with the crewed compartment returning to Earth via splashdown much like the Apollo missions of the 1970s.

"So here's where we are," Phil said, "The innards are done, but the cabin has not been assembled, so there's room for adding the components needed for Shortcut within the weight allowance. The building of the exterior was to start later this month, so we'll push that ahead as far as we can and begin incorporating Shortcut technology into the design."

Jason nodded, pleased. It sounded easy but would actually be quite complex, as it would require a complete redirection of certain areas of the design, particularly related to the craft's exterior.

"There will be some pushback from the Textron folks and the Spanish and Italian teams, of course," Phil said, referring to the teams responsible for the design of the optical solar reflectors and other key elements of the modified *Orion's* exterior design. "But this is a unique case with a special mission parameter, so they'll go along." They both knew with NASA calling the shots and controlling much of the budget, the teams would have little choice, but Phil liked keeping good relations with his vendors as they were vital to NASA's success, so he'd handle it diplomatically.

"I'd be happy to talk with them if you think it would help," Jason said.

"Everybody will be talking with everybody by the time this is done," Phil said, seeming to ponder his words—his mind running over the various aspects of preparing a mission, "but initially, the big issue is the timing. I'm just not sure how fast we can rush this. We'll know more once I have a few conference calls with the key players." NASA had lost too many astronauts in its lifetime to risk lives with anything but the utmost preparation. What Jason was asking them to do was a challenge to a system of checks and balances they'd put in place over multiple decades just to ensure the utmost safety for their astronauts. Launching a speedy rescue mission created challenges that would test them on many levels. Once NASA had approved the design specs, things could move fairly quickly.

"My people can step up as needed," Jason said. "Especially when it comes to the Shortcut components. Laura's alive out there. We have to do whatever it takes."

"You know I will do that," Phil said, testily. "Laura means a lot to me, too. We all want her back. But I need you to be realistic. Speeding the process is going to take several weeks' planning. There's no way around that. So let's set up some conference calls with all the key people to discuss how we'll coordinate, okay?"

Jason exhaled, then said, "Okay. I'll be back in Pasadena late tomorrow and start getting everyone assigned and on task. Just say when."

Phil leaned back in his chair again as the tension eased from his face and body. "First thing, I need your people to get with the Pegasus team about refitting their module for Shortcut so we can test the new lasers in space. It launches in three weeks and will be dropping supplies at the ISS, then heading to Mars to place a satellite in orbit. Is that feasible?"

"We'll make it happen," Jason said, knowing his people would find a way.

"There's one more consideration you need to accept," Phil said, looking somber.

Jason braced himself for more bad news and nodded. "Which is?"

Phil's eyes met Jason's again. "We've been operating under an assumption that you're going on this mission, and Laura's message, plus their attempt to kidnap you, does indicate these aliens want you there—"

"Of course, I'm going!" Jason interrupted, frowning.

Phil raised a finger to stop him. "But you still have to be declared flight ready by one of the NASA flight surgeons first." Jason started to protest again but Phil raised his voice and continued over him, "Because the health issues of space flight are very real. If we don't take them seriously, you could arrive there catatonic, in no condition to participate in any mission, let alone help Laura."

"I'm going!" Jason insisted, his chest tightening as his teeth clenched from fighting to control a sudden burst of anger rising within.

"You might be more of a burden than a help to your crew, so we will do this the right way," Phil added.

Jason opened his mouth to protest again but then remembered all the things Laura had told him about dietary issues, muscle atrophy, and the various physical challenges of space travel. As much as he hated hearing it, Phil wasn't just blowing smoke on this. There were genuine concerns, especially given Jason's recovery from the hospital. So instead, he nodded. "Okay."

"Good," Phil said. "Then let's talk about mission parameters and crew."

For the next forty-five minutes, they went over Jason's memos in detail.

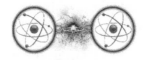

THE NEXT DAY, Jason had breakfast with Heather and the Raimeys and then spent the morning ice skating with her at Discovery Green across from the Convention Center, making a few more memories before saying goodbye. The air was crisp and cool and smelled surprisingly fresh given the urban sprawl surrounding them, but the sun was shining and the sky clear. The rink was set up behind the Anheuser-Busch stage and Cemex Terrace along the park's major lake, Kinder Lake. Children and families raced around them, laughing, dancing, playing. Nearby on sidewalks that surrounded the lake, people walked dogs, played Frisbee or tossed footballs, even sat on blankets. Leaving Heather made him sad every time he thought of it, so instead he enjoyed her skating circles around him, taking his hand and leading him along, then circling again, excitedly. They pointed out other people, dogs, and other sights to each other as they went, just a father and daughter delighting in time together.

When they got back to the Raimeys a couple hours later, Roger had Jason's bags already loaded in the car.

"We better get headed that way," Roger said, meaning the airport.

Jason nodded and knelt to hug Heather on the driveway.

"I wish you didn't have to go," she said as he squeezed her tight and held her, once again inhaling the sweet scent of her bubblegum shampoo and trying to memorize it.

"Me too, baby," he said, then pulled away enough to kiss her.

"I'll miss you soooo much," she said sadly.

"I'll miss you more," Jason said, his voice cracking a bit as he tried not to choke up.

Then she looked him dead in the eyes, looking so much like her mother and said, "I believe in you."

He pulled her into a tight embrace again, hiding the tears that flowed down his cheeks. "Me too, baby girl."

"Bring mama home," she said.

Then he kissed her again and let her go, standing. She held his hand a moment then ran to Susan.

"Are you sure you don't want us to come along?" Susan asked.

"Roger's just going to drop me off," Jason said. "Heather has school tomorrow, so let her enjoy her last day off."

"I love you, Daddy," Heather called again as Roger got into his Mercedes on the driver's side and Jason opened the passenger door.

"I love you, too," Jason said and then climbed in and shut the door before he could tear up again. As Roger backed out of the driveway, Heather and Susan waved and Jason waved back, and Jason felt an overwhelming mix of longing and sadness as he looked at his daughter's face. Heather was smiling, but he knew she was emotional just like him. He hated leaving her so much, but it was the only way to get her mother home to her. *The next time I see you we'll be a family again*, he swore to himself and her, and then Roger turned down the street away from them.

It had been Jason's goal from the moment Heather was born to cultivate the kind of parent-child relationship with her he'd never had with his father, only his mother. A physicist by passion, professor by necessity, Lucas Maxx had always felt more at home alone in his lab pursuing his various projects than dealing with other people, and that discomfort seemed to extend even to his own son, though somehow not his wife, Elizabeth. The rare times Jason remembered experiencing warmth from his father always revolved around his mother. She was the family cheerleader, the confidant, and the support to them both. She'd taught Jason the importance of service to others and the honor of seeking to dedicate one's life's pursuits to the betterment of humankind. For his father, success in his own projects was promoting the better good by advancing physics.

"That should be more than satisfying enough for humanity," he always insisted then scoffed when he listened to young Jason and Elizabeth as they contemplated how mathematics or the sciences might actually be used to solve the world's great problems: hunger, poverty, world peace, and more. "All pipe dreams! What good are they?" he'd said time and again.

His father's skepticism just left Jason wanting to prove him wrong. A man who found so little joy in living and the love of his family was hardly inspiring in the face of his mother's opposite outlook filled with joy and hopeful longing. And that his father's response to Jason's own accomplishments so often turned into criticism and minimization of his successes only added fuel to the fire. Publicly, he held his head high, refusing to give Lucas Maxx the satisfaction of seeing the pain it caused, but privately, he frequently lamented to his mother about it.

"Why can't he once be proud of me for something?" Jason had asked.

"He's proud of you in his own way," Elizabeth Maxx had assured her son. "His generation just isn't good at showing it."

Secretly, Jason suspected his father resented that his son's intelligence and accomplishments had so quickly surpassed his own, but he knew better than to say it. His mother had kept a steady truce between them until cancer took her when Jason was fifteen. A few months later, he'd left home for early admission to MIT. After that, he only saw his father on holidays or special occasions, and they'd remained fairly distant and uncomfortable with each other until the elder Maxx's death in 2011 from a heart attack.

He remembered his father's skepticism in the early days of Shortcut whenever his son had told him about it. He could only imagine his reaction at what Jason was trying to accomplish now. "Pipe dreams!" "Insanity!" His mother would have believed, though. She'd never lost faith in either of them. Jason never wanted Heather to feel about him the way he had about his father. He'd sworn to always encourage and celebrate her accomplishments, to spend time with her and enjoy doing it, and make sure she always knew how proud of and loved she was by her father. To ensure it, he and Laura had always made sure their work travels didn't take them away from her for very long at a stretch. A few days as a couple, and individually for only a few weeks at a time, and then only when necessary.

He knew for certain he was leaving her now out of necessity, yet somehow watching her out the window as Roger drove away, an inner voice still accused him of failing her in some way, leaving her when she needed him most. *I'll be back as soon as I can, baby*, he reminded himself, then he shook it off with a grunt and got busy on his iPad working on plans and specs for the work required by the rescue mission ahead.

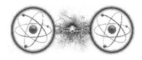

AS SOON AS he arrived in Pasadena, Jason went straight to Caltech and hit the ground running. Jack had set up a bunch of meetings with his key team leaders and immediately began discussing and breaking down each team's assignments and needs in order to fulfill their responsibilities and make the rescue mission a success.

They made a list of adjustments needed to refit the *Orion 6* spacecraft for a Shortcut enabled rescue:

1. Electronic controls needed to be installed in the cockpit for Q-switch and lens control, requiring physical room inside the ship for circuit boards, power supplies, and control panels.

2. Communications protocols must be implemented to enable the Orion's onboard computers to interface with the Shortcut computers and share location data and system vitals: Are the cells overheating? Is there enough power? Is the laser fully charged? etc.

3. The exterior of the *Orion 6* had to be coated with laser cells, including mirrors, active lasers, isolators, and Fresnel lenses—all the elements enabling Shortcuts to occur.

4. Additional wiring would be needed to connect the laser components on the outside to the electronics inside, including ship's computers and controls, which would mean boring holes in the outside of the ship and installing ducts through which to run the wires.

These adjustments would then mean they could omit the thermal protection coating because the Shortcut laser cells would handle the necessary heating and cooling functions. This would have to be carefully negotiated so funding could be rerouted to make the refitting as cost effective as possible. Government contractors hated giving up funding, thus Phil's warning about pushback being likely. Jack and Li agreed to coordinate negotiations with Phil and the other NASA administrators so Jason could focus his energy on supervising the build. Peter Edtz was in charge of the laser team. David Leland and Sarah Ruth would head up the communications team from creating and installing protocols to wiring and ducts. John Allison was in charge of the cockpit controls team.

With these duties assigned, Jason met with each team lead about design parameters and adjusting them according to the *Orion* blueprints he'd brought from NASA. Then he sent them off to inform their teams and get to work, requesting each to send him budget and timeline updates within twenty-four hours.

While Jason was busy coordinating his team, Jack and Li interfaced with NASA about the ongoing negotiations and set up meetings in Houston with NASA and contractors. They also arranged for the JPL communications team to monitor the Deep Space Network frequencies used for *Voyager 1* and *Voyager 2* to ensure any further messages from Laura could be brought to Jason's attention as soon as they arrived. Jason began checking in with them daily to see if any more messages had arrived. He also sent a message of his own just in case, encouraging Laura, letting her know Heather was fine, and telling her they were preparing a rescue. He ended each message with "I believe in you, my love. Jason." The words had taken on new meaning since the *Voyager* message and Heather's use of them. Because they didn't just believe in him, they believed he'd do whatever it took to make things right and protect his family. Knowing that would carry him through, no matter how tired, stressful, or frustrating the roadblocks he might encounter in trying to get Laura home.

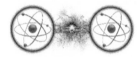

FOR THE NEXT two weeks, Jason slept at the lab, spending his days in meetings or encouraging and helping his teams. At night, he personally verified all the math his team did by hand to ensure its accuracy and signed off on all reports and designs submitted before forwarding them to NASA or vendors. He also went to Houston for a few days for meetings with Phil and personnel there, whatever was needed.

Most of this time, he forgot all about his injuries, but occasionally, when he had a long walk or steep climb, he'd have to stop and rest from shortness of breath before continuing on. It was more an annoyance than anything else, sort of like a ship's anchor slowing him down. But Lynn, the physical therapist he still saw three days a week, assured him it would pass eventually as he got back into better condition, and so he pressed on without complaint.

"Keep working," she said with the passion of a true believer. "Your lungs have improved a lot, whether you realize it or not."

"Absolutely," Jason said, wanting to believe with the same passion but struggling to convince himself. Recovery always seemed to drag on. In some ways he felt very much back to normal, but then he'd have to stop and catch his breath going up stairs or talking across campus, and he was reminded his physical fitness was anything but 100 percent.

At least his lungs improving was good news. Having Lynn come to him allowed him that much more time to keep working. He had a mission and a singular focus: bringing Laura home, and nothing would deter him. He knew he couldn't fight it. He had to get better if he was to lead a mission in space. Whatever it took.

JIMMY AND HIS Black Ops team gathered around a long wooden conference table on the dark, shadowy fourth floor of a nondescript, modern, black, steel and glass building in Arlington at ten-thirty a.m. that Thursday. The man who had called the meeting, Lawrence Rohner, was part of a Top Secret Black Ops project known only by the code name "Project V." It was so secret that only a few people outside the participants even knew the code name. Jimmy had been recruited in the 90s after his first two space missions. When he'd first heard the project's objectives, Jimmy had thought Rohner was out of his mind. But somehow the man had convinced him to give it two years, and so Jimmy had, and during those two years he'd seen things that not only erased his doubts but scared the shit out of him. If the American public knew what he knew, they'd be scared, too. Project V had changed Jimmy's world and outlook forever and now it was so woven into the fabric of his life, he just took for granted he'd always be part of it.

Rohner was an ex-CIA administrator whose project was a standalone, meaning although he had credentials and a reputation, he was officially retired with no status. Only when he called in powers given him by a top secret presidential order could he act. And if and when that day came, Jimmy would be ready to answer the call. It didn't matter what it involved; what Project V was created to combat was that dangerous, that important, *that* scary.

Rohner was already seated at the head of the table, waiting as they arrived. For a man, he was of below average height, barely over five feet, and his green eyes bore an intensity that matched the intensity of his mission. His sandy hair was now mostly grayed and kept short and neatly groomed, despite a growing bald circle at its center. His clothes were top dollar—a three-piece designer suit, shirt, and silk power tie, all subtle colors, with shined leather shoes that reflected the dim lighting of the room, and Jimmy's nose caught the hint of the musky old school cologne Rohner always wore. It was the only sign of age in a man of power who otherwise seemed as ageless as he seemed invincible.

Rohner nodded as Jimmy entered and motioned him to the only open seat at the table two chairs down from himself on the right side near where a video projector sat at the center of the table, its lens pointed at two large LED screens suspended on the wall at the end opposite Rohner . Seated around the table were a few familiar faces and a few strangers. Jimmy nodded to the others present as he passed and took his place, settling into the chair as an aide stood and offered him soda, coffee, tea, or anything else he asked for. Jimmy ordered sweet tea. He needed the energy.

Rohner cleared his throat right after and looked around, meeting their faces one-by-one before he said, "All right, welcome, my friends. As you surely suspect, we have a situation, and the time has come to act."

For the next half hour, Rohner filled them in on the Jason Maxx situation and the mission, quoting Jimmy's reports and even using PowerPoint to display a few images and documents. The gist: he'd wanted to stay out of it and not risk exposing Project V and all its secrets, but Maxx was a star mathematician with technology to revolutionize space travel and aliens had taken his wife. Maxx wanted her back and had convinced NASA to launch a rescue mission. Project V had to be a part of it. and Jimmy was already in place.

Rohner turned to a man Jimmy recognized, Lieutenant Colonel Vincent Capobianco, a dark haired, dark complected man of unknown background, who had so many medals he almost needed a second uniform to carry them. This guy was the baddest of the badasses, and his toned muscles reflected it. Afghanistan, Russia, Iraq twice—he'd seen them all and more. Jimmy would never know about any more than anyone else. If there was a top secret, dangerous op, Capobianco had been in on it and probably led a team. "You will have a team of seven, including yourself. The rest of the rescue crew will be composed of Maxx and Jimmy, the pilot. Take one of your men as copilot, as one will be needed. The other spot will be left for Laura Raimey."

Capobianco raised a brow and looked at the boss. "NASA will approve?"

"They don't know about us yet," Rohner said, then looked at Jimmy. "But they will be educated soon enough." Jimmy nodded in confirmation.

"What vehicle are we taking?" asked Capobianco's top lieutenant, Major Martin Killan—the whitest of the white boys, Ivy League educated, ex-Navy Seal, poster boy-type. He'd come up just as Jimmy was finishing his last tour and headed for NASA, but he'd reportedly been with Capobianco since very early on. He was the only other man on the squad of Rohner's muscle led by Capobianco whose name Jimmy knew.

"Ours," Rohner said and Jimmy looked at him with surprise. Rohner smiled a smile that hinted at power and menace—his lips pressed together in a thin curve, no teeth showing through. "Arrangements are being made. They will have little choice. They can't possibly have a ship ready on their own in any reasonable time frame. They just haven't realized it yet, but when they do, you're to offer our ship, Jimmy."

"They are planning to use Maxx's technology, the Shortcut system," Jimmy said.

"Our ship can be refitted just as easily and cost effectively as theirs, maybe more so," Rohner said. "It's already built and ready, and it has improvements we have made that they don't even know about."

"What about the weapons and the comm systems?" Capobianco asked. "All that is top secret."

"Select personnel only will be allowed to participate and know about that," Rohner said, waving a hand as if to dismiss any concerns. "It will be carefully controlled."

Capobianco grunted. "I don't see how. This Shortcut system sounds complicated. Refitting an entire ship will take a large team if you want to do it quickly."

Rohner smiled the same menacing smile. "It'll be handled, Vincent. Trust me."

Capobianco raised his hands in surrender but his eyes said he still harbored sincere doubts.

"Our men will be ready," Killan said. "Will we train with NASA?"

"For appearances, yes," Rohner said. "Though you will begin training here, of course."

"Assault and extraction?" Capobianco asked.

"Whatever's necessary," Rohner said.

"Maxx will object," Jimmy said. "He believes negotiation should be the first course."

Capobianco sneered, "Of course he does. He'll be easily dealt with."

"He will be included in all the training," Rohner said. "And he will consider himself the leader, even though Jimmy will go on the books as the official mission commander."

Jimmy nodded. "He will have to be prepped to accept the idea. That will take time." Then Capobianco and Rohner exchanged another look that gave Jimmy the eerie feeling there was more going on he didn't know about. It made him wonder if his status as "official commander" was just words.

"So we start early," Rohner said with a shrug. "As soon as they accept the ship. But I leave that part to you as you are the one who has the relationship. He's either on board or he stays home."

"That he'll never allow," Jimmy said with a hint of warning in his voice. He didn't want to be the one to try and tell Jason that. In fact, he'd hate to see it happen. Jason of all people deserved to go.

"Like he has a choice," Capobianco said. It was sotto voce but coming from him held such an implied threat that Jimmy involuntarily shuddered. Yes, he would definitely make sure he kept Jason as far from Capobianco as he could for as long as possible.

Rohner leaned back in his chair and clicked his teeth. "Okay, so if we all understand that, let's talk about mission objectives."

The meeting went on half a day and would be one Jimmy would never forget. He heard things that day that he wished he hadn't, and he suspected subtext he was unaware of that he sensed was even more disturbing. But he was in the thick of it and had no way to remove himself. He had to see it through, and dedication to duty had been the hallmark of his life, so as always, he'd obey orders and fulfill his duty. No matter what. That's what he'd trained for and committed to his entire career, and his reputation had been built on it.

CHAPTER 14

A WEEK LATER, Jason went back to Johnson Space Center Mission Control in Houston for the launch of the Shortcut-equipped *Vision* spacecraft that would carry supplies to the ISS and then the satellite on to Mars. He was greeted by many familiar faces from the *Maxx-One* launch, although CAPCOM for this launch was Stacey Crowder.

Once again, Jason joined Phil at an observation station near the back as the controllers did the work, taking the rocket through the stages of launch. On the large screen at the front of the room, Jason saw the rocket on the launch pad. This time, unlike the last, Jason felt far more at ease there, although he did subconsciously feel a sudden urge to hold his breath when the ship's giant engines hummed to life, and he remembered to keep breathing steadily throughout.

"We have main engine start," Leti Najera said from Propulsion as steam rose from below the heating engines to envelope the lower part of the rocket.

"Now at fifteen seconds and counting," said Bob Cooper from Communications. "... fourteen... thirteen... twelve... eleven... ten..."

"The prevalve has been opened," Najera said.

"… nine… eight… seven… six… five… four… three… two… one."

"We have ignition," Najera said. Flames appeared at the base of the rocket and they felt a distant rumble from the powerful engines.

"And liftoff of *Vision 2*," Crowder said immediately after.

"Liftoff is approximately forty-six minutes, thirty seconds past the hour," Najera said.

"Roll in five seconds," Cooper reported.

On screen, the rocket twisted to an azimuth of 100.6 degrees as it continued to rise at 30,000 miles per hour, growing smaller and smaller against the blue sky on the screen.

"Mark, fifty seconds," Cooper said.

"Plot looks real good here," Jamal Ammar said from Nav. "We are approximately twenty-nine miles downrange at fifteen miles in altitude."

"All systems go for staging," Crowder said.

The rocket entered the atmosphere shortly thereafter and disappeared from the view on the screen. Around two minutes in, the first stage dropped off and the second stage thrust was initiated. In another two minutes, the final stage separated, leaving the command module containing supplies for the International Space Station and the satellite. Five minutes later, *Vision 2* came into range of the International Space Station as it began maneuvering toward its docking point.

The view switched to external cameras on the ISS, and Jason watched as the command module came into view and fired its boosters to adjust position and speed as it approached the space station. Time moved in slow motion as *Vision 2* used boosters to turn and then slowly drift back toward the ISS dock, locking into position. Onboard the ISS, astronauts reported the successful docking and then retrieved the supply shipment from the command module's cargo bay, before clearing it for separation.

Less than ten minutes after it docked with the ISS, *Vision 2* separated again and resumed its journey out into space.

"That completes Stage One," Cooper reported as everyone smiled around him, the mood in the room one of confidence.

Phil Cline clapped Jason on the back.

"Commencing Shortcut in three minutes," Najera said.

"Here we go," Phil said.

So far, everything couldn't have gone smoother. The upgraded lasers worked. They'd already proved it with *Mini-Maxx*. It was just a matter of moments until Phil would have the confirmation he needed to fully support a rescue mission. Considering how much depended upon it, not least of which his hopes for getting to Laura as soon as possible, Jason felt a surprising lack of tension. It would work. He just knew that with confidence. They'd done everything right, and it would work because it mattered so much. Their objective was too important.

"Leaving exosphere in twenty seconds," Cooper reported, then began counting down.

The ISS operates in the thermosphere, the upper region of the atmosphere where the air molecules are so far apart that the most of it is formally considered outer space. Because there is very little air to block light from the sun, spacecraft that traverse the thermosphere experience drastic changes in temperature that can range from 32°F at night to over 3,000°F during peak solar activity. Above the thermosphere is the exosphere, the uppermost region of Earth's atmosphere, which gradually fades into the vacuum of space. The ISS cameras followed it as it propelled off into the distance, becoming a small dot, and then the screens switched back to cameras on the *Vision 2* that showed a large Earth gradually getting smaller.

"... five... four... three... two... one," Cooper finished.

"Initiating Shortcut in ten seconds," Najera said.

"Coordinates locked and confirmed," Ammar reported.

"... nine... eight... seven... six... five... four... three... two... one," Cooper counted.

"Shortcut one initiating," Najera said.

Jason held his breath, fists clenched. *Come on, baby, show your stuff.*

"AO System Failure, wavefront reconstruction error," Matt D'Aunno reported from Flight.

Jason stiffened and leaned forward. It should have worked.

"Reinitiating for second attempt in five," Najera said as she hit buttons to fire the Adaptive Optics system's test laser for another attempt.

"Coordinates reconfirmed," Ammar said.

"... four... three... two... one," Cooper said.

"Shortcut one initiating," Najera said again.

Vision 2 would be transitioning into its jump instantly, but again, Jason heard:

"Adaptive Optics System Failure," Matt D'Aunno said.

"Abort!" Crowder called out. THUMP!

Still calm and focused, Jason stood and called out, "Wait! Something must be blocking the lasers. Can we check for debris or some objects in its trajectory?"

"We checked last week; the Space Surveillance Network showed us in the clear," Crowder said, then to her controllers, said: "Return module for recovery."

"Initiating orbital sequence for emergency reentry," D'Aunno said.

"But we should try again," Jason said. "It will work." But his surefire confidence went unheeded as the controllers continued about their duties.

Phil put a hand on his arm and pulled him back down into the chair. "There's a limited window for recovery. Satellites are expensive. We will investigate and try again."

Vision 2 would turn back and orbit the Earth a few times before attempting reentry to allow time for recovery ships to be moved into position.

"But how long will that take?" Jason demanded.

"As long as it takes to be sure we've diagnosed the problem," Phil said. "I'm sorry."

"Shit," Jason said under his breath and leaned back in his seat, deflated. He'd been so sure. Felt it in his gut. How could his confidence have been so misplaced? "It should have worked."

"We'll do a thorough investigation," Phil said from beside him. "This is why tests like this are so important."

Jason stayed silent. There was nothing flashing through his head worth saying. This was not a good sign. Phil could delay the rescue mission by months now, depending upon how long a second test would take to organize. Meanwhile, Laura would be out there waiting, hoping, wondering.

Jason stood and marched out of mission control. There was nothing more for him to do but call his people and get them investigating as quickly as possible. NASA would do its own investigation, of course, but Jason wanted his own people to verify every finding.

The new lasers failed! He couldn't believe it. In his mind, his father's old criticisms echoed over and over as a memory of the scent of the Old Spice the man had worn haunted his nose. "Your goals are too big, Jason. Science is about the real world, not some fantasy land from you and your mother's day dreams! Stick to what's possible and forget the rest." How many times had his father shot him down with those same words or fired them off in response to his son's missteps or failures? Enough that Jason could still hear them in the man's voice decades later.

His fingers fumbled as he dialed Jack's number at Caltech, a tightening sensation filling his chest. *We're coming, my love. I swear it.* But he knew Laura wouldn't hear him.

THE NEXT AFTERNOON, he met with a specialist in space medicine at NASA for his first flight readiness evaluation. Tall, thin, with long blonde hair and blue eyes, Dr. Diane Dyson was a spitting image of the seasoned professional she was. Thankfully, because her office was at Johnson Space Center, not a hospital, it lacked the hospital's antiseptic, industrial clean smell, instead smelling of air fresheners, perfumes, and the scattered floral arrangements that decorated the waiting room. The caveat was the waiting room and everything else looked like a 1960s bunker, because it basically was, cinder block walls and all. Still, it was a refreshing change after so many months spent at Huntington.

"Your PT's right," the doctor said. "You've got a long way to go. In fact, ordinarily having had a pneumothorax period would disqualify you for space flight just because of the increased likelihood it could happen again. So I have serious reservations about you going to space at all, let alone on a tense, stressful mission."

"I have to go," Jason said, his voice rising in irritation as she knelt to examine his ankle.

She raised a finger to stop him, confident and steady. "But I have been instructed that you must be ready and able to fly at all costs. So I'm going to do everything I can to get you ready."

Jason relaxed. Good. They weren't going to try and stop him.

"Your lungs are still at ninety-eight percent and your deconditioning will be a real issue," she said. "We're talking about a high stress environment in zero gravity for much of the flight, not to mention issues of diet and water and required sedentary positioning for many hours, then an immediate jump into high physical activity as you actuate a rescue. You stand a good chance of breathing trouble. Not to mention fainting. And God forbid you receive a heavy blow to the chest, collapse a lung again, and die up there."

She paused for a moment, checking her notes, then continued, "That aside, our biggest concern is cardiovascular deconditioning. Ordinarily, astronauts need to be fit enough to run several miles a day as a matter of course. I doubt you could do one very quickly. Let alone multiple."

She was very matter-of-fact about it all to the point that Jason wondered if she'd been read into the importance of the mission—what Jason had at stake. He couldn't argue. Although he'd once kept himself in prime condition as an athlete, in the last few years his focus had shifted and he'd slacked off, running a mile in the morning four days a week and skipping his workout altogether. He got some exercise from playing with Heather, walking around Johnson Space Center and Caltech, etc., but he knew that even before the attack, he'd been out of shape, so it wasn't hard to believe the weeks of bedrest had made it worse.

"We'll run a Tilt Test," she continued, "but I think orthostatic stress is also going to be a big issue. You're fortunate this isn't the usual mission. Ordinarily astronauts do a lot of physical exercise in space during long duration missions, but this really isn't a long-duration mission. You'll have short exposures to microgravity and the usual concerns about fluid redistribution and Space Adaptation Syndrome, which we'll discuss later. Right now, we need to get you on a heavy exercise program and revise your physical therapy accordingly. We'll need countermeasures for the orthostatic stresses as well, so I'll work on that." She checked her iPad again. "Lynn Nelson is your PT?"

"Yes," he confirmed.

"Okay, I'll give her a call," Dr. Dyson said. "You need to make time to work hard and get into better shape. This will be the bulk of your readiness training for flight and you'd better take it seriously. I can only do so much to make you ready. The rest is on you. Trust me, when I say you don't want to fail your part. Sure misery awaits, not to mention the risk of far more serious consequences." She stopped and looked sternly at him a moment until he nodded.

"I understand. I'll do what it takes. I promise."

She smiled. "Good. Because from what I understand, Laura needs you. That should be quite the motivation. How long since you've had breakfast?"

"About three hours," Jason said, puzzled.

"Okay, let's go downstairs for that Tilt Test then," she said and stood, moving toward the door.

She led him downstairs to a room with the words "Cardiology Lab" on the door and took him inside. The room was white walled with a counter and rolling computer desk and chair. A technician was waiting for them, a tall black woman, standing next to a metal table with black straps sitting atop a wheeled stand at the center of the room.

"This is Phylicia," Dr. Dyson said. "She's going to take you through the test."

"Okay," Jason agreed as Phylicia extended her hand and he caught a hint of roses from her perfume.

"Phylicia, this is Dr. Jason Maxx," Dr. Dyson said.

Phylicia's grasp was firm and strong as she shook his hand. "How you doin'? We'll take good care of you."

"I'll discuss your results after," Dyson said. "Just come back up to my office." And then she disappeared out the door.

"Okay, have you done this before?" Phylicia asked.

Jason shook his head.

"Okay, just take off your shirt, then lie on the table and let me strap you in while I explain," she said.

Jason did as he was told.

The goal of the tilt-table test was to show how your body responds when it changes positions. Jason started lying on his back on the table with straps across his waist and knees to help him stay in position. Phylicia put an IV in his arm and attached small discs with wires to his chest that ran to an electrocardiograph on the computer table next to a laptop. "To track your heartbeat," she explained. She also put a cuff around his wrist to measure his blood pressure during the test. "This will monitor your blood pressure and we want it at heart level, so we put it here," she explained as she did.

"I want you to breathe normally," she said. "Don't tense up. You are going to feel lightheaded at some point. You might faint. That's okay. It's what we're testing for. No shifting around. Don't move your legs. And no talking please."

When he was ready and had given verbal confirmation that he was, Phylicia tilted the table to thirty degrees, all the time watching his reactions. Then she checked his blood pressure and heart rate and noted them on the laptop. She left him in this position for about five minutes and then tilted him more to a sixty-degree angle, then checked his blood pressure and heart rate again. After about ten minutes, she tilted him up to eighty-five degrees. This time, he started feeling a tingling and grew light headed.

"You okay, Jason?" he heard her ask.

He took a deep breath as he started to recover then nodded. "Yes. A bit woozy there for a moment." But after five minutes, Jason started feeling nauseated and his vision blurred and then went dim as he passed out.

When he woke up again, he was lying prone again with Phylicia at the computer table monitoring his heart rate and blood pressure. "You back with the living, Jason?" She asked and stood to come over and examine him.

Jason shook off the haziness and groaned. "Yeah. What

happened?"

"You passed out. Not unusual with people we test who have been deconditioned like you have. I'm gonna have you rest for a bit before you go, okay?"

"You got your readings?" he asked eagerly, his mind starting to panic.

"Oh yeah, I got the good stuff all right," she said and smiled as Jason relaxed again.

After about half an hour, she removed the IV and undid the straps then told him to sit up. "Okay. Dr. Dyson will go over your results. You did good." She smiled. He wondered how often she said that to someone who'd passed out on her table.

Back in her office, Dr. Dyson said his results were positive, confirmed reduced tolerance and orthostatic stress, and reminded him just how important his physical conditioning program was. Counter measures would only be so effective.

Jason left feeling discouraged but challenged. He was going to space. Laura was waiting. He wouldn't let physical issues stand in the way. He'd work hard and do whatever Lynn and the Dr. told him to get in the best shape he could.

Because he had to fly. There was no plan B.

"I KNOW HOW disappointed you are," Jack said as soon as Jason explained over the phone what had happened with the satellite test. "But we'll find out what caused it and make sure it never happens again."

"Check for reports of downed satellites, meteors—"

"We're on it, Jason," Jack said. "But you know the DOD tracks anything larger than two centimeters. So it would have been on the Space Surveillance Network report."

Jason sighed. "Well, something had to have blocked it."

"It's certainly most likely from our perspective," Jack said, "but NASA will be looking at malfunctions, programming issues, and every other possibility. If we want to get ahead of it, we have to do the same. So I'll get our people on it and sending you daily reports."

"Thanks," Jason said. As frustrated as he was, he knew Jack would do everything right. He trusted him completely.

"What did the Dr. say?" Jack asked, his voice switching from business to friendly concern.

"I don't want to talk about it," Jason said.

"That bad?"

"Let's just say I have a lot of working out ahead of me," Jason said. "So many obstacles trying to hold me back on this one."

"Well, that's the story of your life, isn't it? Bucking the odds? Chasing the impossible?" Jack said.

Jason knew the very existence of Shortcut proved it. He'd defied all the naysayers and obstacles to make that a reality. Sometimes he thought his marriage to Laura was another example. Who'd have thought a math geek like him could get a superstar astronaut and pilot like her? "Aren't you on my side?" he teased.

"Always," Jack said. "You're not in this alone."

"Sometimes a man just wants to whine and wallow and

be supported," Jason added and they both laughed. Jason extended his hand and they shook. He felt lucky to have such friends.

"We don't have time for that," Jack said with a mock stern look. "Get back on it and do what you do: kick ass and defy odds. Laura needs you."

Jason said a quick thanks and headed to NASA's administrative offices to meet with Phil Cline. Phil had called and asked Jason to stop by after his medical appointment and Jason expected he wouldn't like what the administrator had to tell him. So he walked, leaving his rental car parked beside Building 30, which housed mission control. Building 1 housing the Administrative offices was about half a mile to the southeast. Jason made it there in ten minutes, enjoying the fresh air, and immediately regretted it. His ankle felt like it was on fire. But he clenched his teeth, sucked it up, and made his way inside to Phil's office.

Brenda, the secretary, greeted him with a warm smile and ushered him into the office where Phil was waiting. As soon as Jason sat down across the desk from him, Phil said, "I know you're discouraged, but I want you to know I made this investigation our highest priority. They will work as fast as they can."

"I have my people on it, too," Jason said, waiting for the bad news.

Phil nodded. "Good. We also have another rocket available in three weeks to give the satellite another try. Once we can confirm the coordinates from *Voyager* are accurate, we can fund a rescue effort with full government support."

Jason actually felt better. He smiled. "Thank you. That is good news."

Phil shuffled some papers on his desk and leaned back in his chair. "I'm afraid I have other news that you won't like."

Jason took a deep breath and braced himself, involuntarily reaching down to rub his sore ankle. "What's that?" he finally said as he straightened in his chair again.

"We've run into some unexpected supply issues with the build of the *Orion 6*," Phil said. "It may slow us down for several weeks or longer."

"What?!" Jason leaned forward so fast, Phil started, as if he expected him to jump right out of the chair.

"I was just as surprised as you are," Phil quickly added, his eyes avoiding Jason's. "And I expressed my displeasure. But it's an issue beyond our control and that of any of our vendors, I'm afraid. We are looking for alternative sources, but the contracts are pretty complicated. In these circumstances, we don't have a lot of room to step outside them."

"Jesus Christ, Phil!" Jason snapped as he felt his nails digging into his thighs. "Laura is out there needing help! This is ridiculous!"

"This is the reality of government supply chains sometimes, Jason," Phil said. "When we have issues, they rarely come at convenient times and that's particularly the case here."

"Fix it, Phil," Jason demanded. "I really don't give a shit about the excuses or the contracts. I want Laura back, so you fix it."

"We have a little time while we investigate," Phil said, rubbing absently at his arm. "Hopefully by then we'll have resolved the issue, one way or the other. In any case, Dr. Dyson already emailed her assessment. You have some things to work on anyway before you're cleared. That will take time."

Jason hadn't expected the report to make it to Phil so fast.

"I'm on it and I'll be ready," Jason said, collecting himself after the deflation that came with the quick arrival of his Dr.'s report, and then leaned forward. "What would you do if it was your wife, Phil? No one's keeping me off this mission. No one. You just find a way to get that ship ready, or I'm going to start talking to the press. Maybe some pressure in the right places—"

Phil cleared his throat and cut him off. "Jason, I know you've had a frustrating week, but going off half-cocked to the media is never a good idea. I'm doing everything I can."

"Oh fuck yeah! You're all Mr. Helpful and Positive over there," Jason said, his anger showing again. "Actually, it feels like you are doing everything you can to get in my way." He stood and marched toward the door before turning back. "And frankly, I'm goddamn sick of it. I am going for Laura. With or without your help. I *will* find a way. And if you make yourself an obstacle, you can damn well believe I'll be telling everyone."

"For God's sake, Jason," Phil said, wincing as if he'd been struck. "Sit down. I'm on your side."

"You're gonna have to prove it," Jason said. "'Cause I've had enough!"

Then he yanked open the door, marched past Brenda, and headed for the door. He didn't even notice his lungs complaining as he power walked back to his car and headed for the Raimeys.

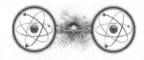

JASON KNEW HE wasn't being fair with Phil Cline. His anger wasn't really about Phil or NASA. It was about his insecurities over the mission and having what it takes to get the job done. Phil was just a handy scapegoat—a target for his own inner turmoil. It wasn't Phil's fault that problems kept arising. He just wished the administrator was as good at suggesting solutions as he was at explaining problems. It had taken long enough to get to the point they could affect a rescue. Any further delay felt like torture. Laura was counting on them.

After their contentious meeting, he started back to the Raimey's, then turned around, deciding he couldn't face Heather or his in-laws at the moment. Instead, he called and told Susan he had late meetings, apologizing, and headed for The Woodlands, a major planned community north of downtown, the place he and Laura had gone for their first date. That night in August almost twenty years back, they'd eaten a romantic dinner at Grotto Ristorante, an Italian place just off Market Street and enjoyed delicious pasta and wine, each ordering different selections so they could share. Then they'd driven twenty minutes north and gone for a romantic water taxi ride along The Woodlands Waterway which was lined with wide, lighted sidewalks along both sides and was popular for people watching, strolls, and sitting to chat on one of the thirty art benches spread out over the half mile long course.

Jason and Laura had chatted like young lovers all night, until they got on that water taxi. Then Laura had snuggled up to him, leaning her back against his chest, head on his shoulder and cuddling in the gentle night air as they enjoyed the ambience. They'd dreamed together about the future, talking about kids, family, and what their hopes and desires were. To their amazement, they'd discovered they both wanted much the same life, and that had cemented things. They'd already nurtured a strong attraction and growing friendship, but knowing their life goals and dreams were so compatible, they both decided then and there this was the person they wanted to pursue life with, though neither told the other 'til several months later.

"Which would you want—boy or girl?" Laura had asked at one point.

"For a child?" Jason had responded; the question had been unexpected.

"No, for a dog," Laura teased and laughed.

"I hadn't thought about it," Jason said. "I just want them healthy. Both have their appeal."

Laura laughed again. "I actually found something you haven't done the math on?"

Jason grinned. "Well, girls are more expensive by my calculations. Just from the shopping standpoint—"

Laura had punched his thigh but then smiled and looked at him. "So, a girl who hates shopping then?"

"Is that possible? Like with genetic manipulation or something?" Jason had joked back.

"Well, look who can be a typical male after all," Laura fired back, grinning.

"I don't want to be predictable," Jason said. "Random numbers and chaos theory are personal favorites of mine."

Now, as he walked along The Waterway all alone remembering that moment, Laura's beautiful eyes and smile remained as clear in his mind as if he were right there, reliving every minute of that taxi ride. He could almost smell the scent of her hair and the memories comforted him. He realized chaos was what he was trying so hard to avoid at the moment. It was the source of his greatest frustrations.

On another date, as they walked the downtown trails next to Buffalo Bayou, Laura had asked him why he found chaos theory so fascinating, when he seemed to order his life so meticulously in other ways.

"Well, what I'm trying to create in my Shortcut theory is managed chaos, really," Jason had explained then. "The underlying patterns, repetition, and even self-organization are not really chaotic at all. Even within the chaos we find organizational systems. Road traffic, weather, climate—they all have systems to them, maybe starting points or theories that dissolve under the randomness of nature or unknown factors like human beings. Traffic roads and signs and signals are all planned in great detail to anticipate and manage certain expectations, but all it takes is one crazy driver to throw the whole thing off and create huge traffic jams that take hours to correct. Bad weather does that, too. From hurricanes and tornadoes to climate change impact. Subtle changes in various factors can produce unpredictable results later on that defy any expected system or pattern. It's fascinating because it provides unending points for study and examination. And yet underneath, discernible patterns and repetition always resemble things we've seen before elsewhere." He'd pointed to a stunning vista they'd just encountered beside the trail.

"It's so beautiful," Laura said. "Like a painting."

"Yes, with seeming organization in parts yet random chaos in others," Jason pointed out. "Groups of like flowers—roses there, autumn sage over here, and day-lilies across the way. Trees and shrubs, even rocks, are bunched together yet their placement on the overall vista is much more random. Patterns. Chaos in action. And mathematics is ultimately about the study of patterns."

Laura had stopped and enjoyed the view with him for a moment, each of them pointing out favorite features: flowers, trees, birds, even the way the sun hit certain rocks or bushes and created unique shadows, some with familiar shapes, others a mystery. "Chaos again," Laura said and chuckled. And he'd felt such a surge of warm fuzziness discussing that with her. She understood in a way no woman before ever had. And she accepted it without question—as if saying if it came with him, then it fascinated her too.

Jason widened his eyes and shook. "We can't escape it! Oh no!"

Laura had punched his arm then and ran ahead, forcing him to chase her, following the sound of her laughter.

Later, after he'd caught up and they'd slowed to a walk again, she'd said, "You know, organizing chaos sounds a lot like what parents and teachers do every day. My dad does that with his players. Without a good coach, a whole team can just fall apart."

"Exactly," Jason said. "And sometimes in spite of a good coach."

Laura had laughed then, too. "Oh God, don't ever say that to Roger. He'll rant your ear off for hours."

"You know, everybody thinks it's the biggest, most obvious things that change the world," Jason said. "The nuclear bombs, the mass shootings, the Earthquakes or hurricanes, population migrations, or outbreaks of disease. But chaos theory says the small things matter more. A butterfly moving its wings that somehow causes torrential rain to wipe away villages or storms across the world. The amazing thing is that chaotic systems don't always stay chaotic. Sometimes they reorganize themselves spontaneously into an orderly structure."

"Hmmm," Laura had said, leaning against his arm as she took his hand. "Like emotions in human beings, perhaps?"

He'd looked into her eyes and they'd both smiled. It certainly was what had happened with his feelings about Laura then and his feelings for her now, he thought as he remembered. When they'd met, his feelings had been all over the place, but now, they were much clearer, focused, and much more intense. Sometimes he thought emotions couldn't reach their full potential until a person settled into them. Then, when you could understand and identify them, that was when they were felt most deeply and had the most potential impact.

He marveled at how his hands felt cold with dread while his chest filled with warmth at the thought of his love for her. His stomach was rolling, his mouth filled with sourness, and yet his pulse was pounding and he couldn't stop smiling. Emotional chaos in action. And yet his feelings for Laura had never been more clear. No matter what chaos threw at him, he was going to rescue his wife. Going to carry it through. Love would win no matter what. Because some people waited a lifetime for a love like theirs and never found it.

"The whole thing," he'd explained to her then, "is just part of a bigger puzzle I hope to one day solve."

"Which is?" she'd asked.

"At its core, I hope to create a source of universal energy, a way to even the playing field somehow, so all nations—

poor and rich—can use a source they have in abundance to meet their energy needs and stop fighting over fossil fuels," he said. "Then they could carry it through and turn their energy and resources to things like feeding their people, eliminating poverty, fixing infrastructure—things that would improve quality of life for everyone." Internally, he'd imagined his father scoffing as he said it. More daydreams from fantasy land.

"It's noble," Laura admitted. "But it sounds a bit like one of those cliché beauty pageant answers like 'world peace.' Vague enough to hold possibilities and hope for anyone who hears it but also vague enough to hide the fact it's seemingly impossible at the same time."

"Math convinces me anything is possible with the right formula, despite the chaos," he'd said. "Fuck chaos." And he'd really believed that then, and even more so now.

At that moment, they'd come to the parking lot again where a car stereo was blaring U2's "Where The Streets Have No Name," a song Jason had always loved.

"I wanna feel sunlight on my face," Bono was singing. "I see that dust cloud disappear without a trace."

Jason and Laura started singing along at the same time, "I wanna take shelter from the poison rain. Where the streets have no name, oh oh. Where the streets have no name..."

He'd looked at her with surprise and pleasure and she'd started laughing. "Fuck chaos," she said. From that moment on, the song had taken on a new meaning to them. It had become the comfort anthem that saw them through any difficult circumstances or challenges. One they went back to again and again. A song that had forever created a special bond and understanding between them of a shared desire to do something that would make a real difference in the world and change it forever. An understanding they both thought of every time they heard that song that was just their own.

All of a sudden, Jason snapped out the reverie. *A place with no name. Carry it through,* Laura's message had said. She was referring to the song and the conversation before they'd connected over it. But what was she trying to tell him? Something about solving a larger problem? Changing the world? It had to be. He just had to figure out what.

"Fuck chaos," he said then as he turned back toward where he'd parked the car. He was tired, so he'd go get some sleep, but tomorrow, when he flew back to Pasadena, somehow, some way he'd make solutions to the supply problem, to prove the new lasers reliable, and to speed up preparation of the ship and mission. He'd do it because he had to. He'd do it because he doubted anyone else would.

He'd do it because from one solution would come the other: understanding the riddle of Laura's message.

CHAPTER 15

"IT'S CALLED THE X-39B OTV—Orbital Test Vehicle," Jimmy said as he faced Jason and Phil the next morning in Phil's NASA office. Jason received Jimmy's call on his cell just as Heather left with Roger for school. Jimmy asked him to come to NASA for a meeting at Phil Cline's office at nine-thirty a.m. His flight for Pasadena wasn't leaving until two p.m., so reluctantly, he'd agreed. He'd never heard of the X-39B, so his immediate reaction was *why am I here wasting my time when I need to be solving problems to rescue Laura?* It took him a moment to digest the conversation.

"The Air Force vehicle?" Phil asked, puzzled. "I thought that was remote controlled."

"That's the X-38B," Jimmy said. "The X-39B is bigger and designed for piloted flight."

"The Air Force is volunteering a top secret, armed military spacecraft for the Shortcut rescue mission.?" Phil said, looking completely surprised. "What's the catch?"

"The Air Force has armed spacecraft now?" Jason asked, shifting impatiently in his chair. He thought he knew every spacecraft NASA had ever flown, but the X-30 series was new to him. Jimmy and Phil exchanged a look, then Phil said, "It's been around for a couple of decades. The original idea was an experimental test program for a reliable, reusable, unmanned spacecraft with top secret weaponry. At least that was the rumor."

"It's true," Jimmy said. "And just by telling you that, I have to read you into a lot of stuff you won't be allowed to share with anyone."

Jason felt a rolling in his stomach and shifted uneasily in his chair, his limbs suddenly weak. "What's this have to do with us? Why are we here?"

Jimmy leaned back in his chair opposite Jason, smiling. Both sat facing the desk with Phil ensconced behind it in his usual chair. "Simple, Doc. You need a spacecraft ready to go fast. We have one and we're offering it to you."

Phil was right. This was far too expensive of a technology to risk revealing it to civilians without really unique and special circumstances and something to gain. Why was Jimmy, the Chief Security Officer for NASA, offering them a top secret armed Air Force vehicle? And what did he or whoever he worked for besides NASA want in exchange?

"You've been part of this for months," Jason said, "Why is this the first we're hearing of it?"

"Powers that be finally decided to get involved," Jimmy said. "Bureaucracy is slow as snails."

Jason found it hard to believe that the government had suddenly experienced a sense of empathy and generosity.

"What are the conditions?" Phil asked, his surprise replaced by a focused administrator's demeanor.

"I'm the mission commander, plus a co-pilot and team of six I select," Jimmy said as if he'd expected the question.

Phil jumped in, "We can't just send a rescue mission

against aliens who have shown a propensity for violently abducted a U.S. citizen without them being prepared to respond with appropriate force."

Images of bullet ridden aliens and spacecraft filled Jason's head, diving him a headache. It was his worst nightmare and he hated the idea immediately. "By launching an intergalactic war?" Jason snapped, shaking his head. He had expected they'd want to be ready to take Laura back by force if necessary. But this sounded like Rambo or Seal Team 6 level stuff. And it scared him. Inside, adrenaline pumped and he gulped down a breath before adding, "So what? We fly up there to where Voyager's location is and storm their ship, take Laura, and then come home?" Jason asked, imagining a very unpleasant encounter with aliens who'd just blow them all away instantly with high tech, high powered weapons they'd never imagined.

"We go in, secure the location, find Laura," Jimmy said, still shockingly relaxed and calm despite the subject matter, "and bring her out safe. If the aliens don't interfere, we leave them be. Violence only if necessary and provoked."

Jason took a deep breath, shifting in his chair again. The walls were closing in. Was the air lighter in here somehow? Of course it had occurred to him that the aliens were hostile, but if Laura was okay and unharmed, going in weapons first seemed like a stupid approach. Especially when there might be a shit ton more aliens waiting out there with better, bigger weapons.

"You are free to say no and wait however long it takes NASA to get you another ship and whatever crew you can find," Jimmy said with growing impatience. "But this team is the best we can get. Guaranteed to pull this off with minimal damage and injury. I can't be confident of that with just anyone."

"And what if they wind up starting a war with aliens so powerful we don't stand a chance?" Jason asked.

Jimmy took a deep breath, then leaned over and pulled two files from a shoulder bag on the floor beside his chair, holding one out for Jason even as he slid the other across the desk to Phil. "This is not our first visit from these new... 'friends,' I'll call them," he said. "And we don't think that's very likely."

Jason opened the folder and flipped through. It contained pictures of alien technology, a partial alien ship, and various sites where supposed encounters or visits took place. The words 'Project V – Top Secret' were at the top of every page. Most pages also had whole paragraphs and scattered sentences that were blacked out and unreadable. "You've seen what they can do with their technology," Jason said. "It's clearly far ahead of anything we have. How can you be sure?"

Jimmy locked eyes with him. "Because we've never experienced violence from them before."

Jason tried to wrap his mind around it as his heart raced and heat flushed through him. Jimmy had known about alien encounters the whole time and yet they'd treated Jason like he was crazy when he suggested the possibility? Fucking spooks and their secrets! Jimmy could have told him when they were alone any number of times, reassured him he wasn't so out there. Instead, he'd held it close to the vest. What else was he keeping secret that might help the mission? Could he be trusted at all? Jason narrowed his eyes and stared at Jimmy a moment, then took a deep breath and finally managed to ask, "Out of how many encounters? Under what circumstances?"

"Three, we think," Jimmy said, unperturbed. "We know

they've been here. We have the images, but no one was there to confront them."

"So you don't know?" Jason said. "You can't know."

"Do you really think we'd have a spacecraft standing by and ready for just this kind of scenario if we hadn't studied extensively those we aimed to engage?" Jimmy asked with a gleam in his eye as his gaze met Jason's and he leaned back in his chair.

Jason shut the folder and sighed while Phil continued reading through his. "Who knows? I've seen plenty of stupid decisions made by the military. The second Iraq war was sure a great plan, wasn't it?"

Jimmy's smug smile returned. "Well, we've had our failures, as have you. But then we're in a position to help ensure Laura comes home, and we're confident you can refit it with Shortcut technology in a month or less and be ready to go. Who else can offer you that?"

Jimmy just stared at Jason while it sank in.

Jason pressed his lips together and narrowed his eyes, his head aching with something like the initial phase of brain freeze, a broiling stomach adding to the sharp pain in his head. He felt a bit like he imagined a deer would feel in a forest filled with hunters during prime deer season—although it wasn't so much fear as just feeling cornered, his mind searching for a way out. He exhaled quickly and it came out as a snort. "What if I decide to wait on NASA?"

Jimmy shrugged. "Your call, pal, but my understanding is we have supply chain issues that could delay you for months, not to mention the latest Shortcut laser issue."

"You're willing to go even without the lasers passing a test?" Phil said, his body rigid, lips pursed as he closed the folder and set it on his desk.

"We both know another test is imminent," Jimmy said. "You have several rockets waiting in the wings to use for it. And rescuing one of our own is not going to wait. What we're offering is a ship and crew ready to go as soon as the test resolves the issues."

"We don't even know if Jason will be flight-ready in time for that," Phil said.

"You can't go without me," Jason objected, leaning forward quickly and shooting Phil an annoyed look. "I'm the one who understands Shortcut—"

"We've read all the papers, studied the mission transcripts and briefs," Jimmy said with the wave of a hand. "Pretty sure we can figure her out, Doc. But I've read Dr. Dyson's assessment. You'll train with my men, and we'll make you ready, or you'll stay behind."

Jason stared at Jimmy a minute, but they both knew that as much as he hated the idea of armed confrontation with aliens, he'd do what it took to make sure he was aboard the rescue ship. Someone had to be there to mediate the worst-case impulses of those men and ensure Laura came home alive. Jason gritted his teeth and breathed slowly, steeling himself. "I'll be ready." It was a statement of fact, with no hesitation.

"You want us to launch an armed space mission against unknown alien aggressors and keep it top secret?" Phil said, shaking his head as he rubbed at his brow. "What about the President or Congress? NASA doesn't have the authority to declare war."

"Nope, which is why you and I are going to talk to the president as soon as possible," Jimmy said. "But we're not going to declare war. That would bring too many people in the loop and create unnecessary complications. Besides, we do hope to resolve this peacefully. We just want to be prepared for the worst."

"This is crazy," Jason said, shaking his head.

Jimmy chuckled. "Crazier than your insistence on aliens for months with no proof? It is what it is now that we have evidence, and so we have to take appropriate measures, don't we?"

Jason leaned back in his chair and rested his hands on his thighs to avoid clenching them. There was no more point arguing. He had to do what he could to make the best of it. The people in charge could just go around them if they refused, and it was the fastest way to affect a rescue and save Laura. Maybe he could at least convince the team that diplomacy first was the best approach.

Jason looked at Jimmy. "When do we leave?"

WHILE PHIL AND Jimmy jetted off to Washington, D,C. the next morning, Jason headed to CalTech to continue working. Within ten minutes after he'd arrived at his office, Peter Edtz was standing in his doorway. "We think you're right," he said. "Some object blocked the lasers."

Jason sat up excitedly and motioned to a chair opposite him and Peter sat. "Fill me in."

"We analyzed the error message and believe that the adaptive optics system failed to generate a stable laser guide star," Peter said. The Shortcut laser used a guide star as part of its adaptive optics system, like those used on telescopes.

This system was necessary to counteract refraction, which bends light, and is the same optical effect that makes stars twinkle and mirages appear in the desert. Sometimes, natural stars were employed by telescopes for this purpose, but the Shortcut system manufactured its own artificial star at the destination, a "guide star." Basically, a laser shone through the atmosphere to create the guide star, the light from which was reflected by components in the atmosphere back to a wavefront sensor on the spacecraft. This detector would sense distortions in the guide star and send the data to the Shortcut computer, which would reconstruct the wavefront. Once the flight path between the spaceship and its destination had been determined, the laser could then be programmed to "unbend" any distortions. This increased the range of the spacecraft and enabled it to take Shortcuts within Earth's atmosphere.

"We think that the wavefront reconstruction error was caused by an unstable guide star," Peter continued. "It could have been a software issue, but no errors occurred in our recent lab tests, though. The same was true when we tested it again in the tank." Since it was not always practical to test the adaptive optics system outside, a water tank was sometimes employed to simulate turbulence. "But when we left the tank open and out overnight, a test the next morning generated the same error message we saw during the *Vision 2* test. Debris had contaminated the water in the tank and was interfering with the lasers."

Jason felt an adrenaline rush and leaned forward in his chair. So far, the results seemed to align with his theory. "So I was right?"

"There's more," Peter said, "But we don't have confirmation officially."

"Confirmation of?" Jason waved his arm anxiously for

Peter to elaborate.

"Your theory possibly," Peter went on. "A few astronomers in Chile reported an explosion in space the night of last December 23rd, and they attribute it to a satellite being destroyed. Possibly by some kind of top secret ASAT test." ASAT stood for anti-satellite weapons. "We're trying to get verification, but obviously if it's secret, this will be difficult. Still, we have Phil making inquiries through official channels to the Chilean government as well as Brazil's, Argentina's and a few others."

"So the satellite explodes and debris floats into the path of Shortcut's lasers," Jason extrapolated. "I knew there had to be something."

Peter nodded. "And since it was top secret, the DOD and the Space Surveillance Network aren't admitting it exists."

Jason leaned back, grinning. He suddenly felt taller and stronger, more ready to face the world than ever. "Do you have this written up yet?"

"I will by this afternoon," Peter said, smiling back. "And then it's just waiting for confirmation."

"Write it up and send what you have to me, Jack, Li, and Phil Cline at NASA, okay?" Jason said as he rose and extended his hand. "This is great work, Peter. Thank everyone for me."

Peter stood and shook Jason's hand. "Will do."

As Peter turned toward the door, Jason licked his lips—his mouth suddenly dry—and said, "I have a question for you on another topic."

Peter turned around and smiled. "Sure thing. Ask away."

"How fast could your team install another Shortcut

system in a backup spacecraft if we needed it?"

Peter frowned. "It was a major ordeal just to find one spacecraft. Where would we get a backup?"

"Just answer the question," Jason replied. "If we had one, how fast? And how long to make the parts you need?"

"Well, we made duplicates of everything, so we have the parts," Peter said, still looking confused. "If we faced that scenario, probably a week or so. Especially if it's a civilian craft that doesn't require us to adapt and work around military hardware and armor." He shot Jason a quizzical look. "Why?"

"Just wanted to know in case we need it," Jason said. "Important to have contingencies."

Peter smiled. "One of the reasons we like working with you is we don't have to remind you of that. Do you need me to work up something more specific?"

Jason shook his head. "No, just thinking aloud. Do me a favor and keep this between us for now, okay?"

"Sure thing, boss," Peter chirped and then hurried off.

Within two hours, Peter and a small team left Caltech for the Space Launch Complex 6 near Vandenberg Air Force Base on the California coast, the home of the X-39B spacecraft to supervise its refitting and prep for the rescue mission. Jimmy and Jason had decided to do the refit with just select people from Jason's team and Project V techs to preserve secrecy and better control and speed up the process. All parts and supplies would be shipped directly to Vandenberg. Meanwhile, Jack and Li would take over supervising the teams investigating the latest Shortcut laser issue during the satellite launch.

That afternoon, Jason met Lynn at the Braun Athletic

Center on Caltech's campus to start the physical conditioning prescribed by Dr. Dyson at NASA for his astronaut training. They started with some stretching exercises, after which Lynn checked his ankle, then they launched into a routine that was fairly standard for astronauts: push-ups for 15 seconds, 15 seconds' rest, squats for 15 seconds, 15 seconds' rest, pull-ups for 45 seconds, 15 seconds' rest, and repeat. Jason made it through the push-ups, but on the pull-ups, he grew short of breath and nauseous and had to roll over and vomit on the floor.

Afterward, Lynn handed him a towel to clean up. "Well, you've got some work to do, right?"

Jason coughed as he wiped off his mouth and spat into the towel, trying to get rid of any residue. "Yeah."

Her eyes met his. "Are you sure you're up for this?"

"Laura needs me. I have to be."

She nodded. "Okay, then let's get back to work."

For the next two weeks, every day, they repeated it, until he not only made it through the workout but could spend thirty minutes on the treadmill on pace for an eighteen minute mile. Jason pushed through exhaustion and frustration with Lynn's gentle prodding, refusing to give up as his mind alternated between imagining holding Laura again and worst case scenarios about the mission and why he had to be along.

After a particularly good session, Lynn had a proud look on her face. "Well, you're getting there. So tomorrow, we'll try the jogging trail and see how you do, okay?"

He grunted, standing straight with his shoulders back. "Bring it on."

On his way back to the office, Jason got an email from Phil

that they had scheduled the second test run for the satellite for two weeks from the following Wednesday aboard another Delta IV rocket. This was tentative based on the satellite investigation proving their theory about the foreign satellite. Holes in NASA's schedule were few and had to be filled weeks out, so Phil was rolling the dice, but Jason took it as a sign his old friend was being optimistic and supportive. NASA and a team from Jason's lab at Caltech had refitted the satellite with software that would constantly monitor the *Voyager* dish's S and X-band radio frequency communication, thus allowing it to locate *Voyager 1* and confirm its active coordinates during the flight when it came in range. They'd also equipped the satellite with a higher-level relay system than the original that would enable it to send data and communications to Earth at much faster speeds throughout its mission, even when charging for Shortcuts. This would allow NASA and Jason's team to monitor the spacecraft's journey during Shortcuts for the first time and over long distances in close to real time for the rest of its travels.

If all went well, they'd not only prove the readiness of the new Shortcut laser system but put a satellite in orbit around Mars and confirm *Voyager 1's* location and the destination for their rescue mission at the same time. Jason decided his frustrating days were fading into the past as hope swelled again within him.

CHAPTER 16

WITH THE PRESIDENT having signed off on the rescue mission, the following week, Jason flew to Houston to begin his formal astronaut training. Because of his role on the flight and his familiarity with the Shortcut system and its controls, his training program did not include training on those systems, but he did begin with computer-based training on the ship's systems. He learned how to operate them and to address basic malfunctions. He spent most of his time alone in a cube or working solo with a trainer. Each day he also worked with a NASA physical therapist doing stretching exercises followed by his usual routine of push-ups.. After that they ran together as far as he could on NASA's eight-mile jogging trail. At first, he barely made it half a mile at a steady pace before he was too winded and had to stop, but each day, he got slowly better as his lung regained strength and healed from its injury.

He didn't meet his fellow astronauts until ten days in, when he arrived at the ship mockups—partial recreations of various areas of the ship. These were used for training in onboard systems and habitability. The first morning there, Jason worked with Jimmy and the co-pilot, Major Martin Killan, practicing meal preparation, equipment stowage, and trash management. That afternoon, they learned to use cameras and then joined their fellow crew of five men and one woman to try on their flight suits and practice walking around in them. Based on the pumpkin orange ACES (Advanced Crew Escape Suits) used by space shuttle astronauts, the suits were military grade made of Kevlar fabric with embedded armor. But their color was light gray, not orange, in order to blend in better with their environment. The helmets, though removable, fit like one piece with a double visor—the outer part providing extra protection against sunbursts and heavy exposure to sunlight and other cosmic rays, while the inner visor remained transparent. Both visors were made of special bullet proof material. The military team and Jimmy quickly adjusted and were moving around comfortably in them, due to previous experience wearing them. Jason struggled, getting more easily winded and moving awkwardly. He told himself his ankle and recovery was responsible for his own poor performance, but in truth he knew he'd have to work that much harder to get in shape for the mission.

That afternoon, he completed his first mile on the jogging track and celebrated with the NASA PT, Scott.

"Real progress, buddy," Scott said as they high fived. "I'm impressed. Each day makes it easier for you on the mission. So keep it up." Scott started walking away from the track, but Jason stayed put.

"Where you going? You're not giving up are ya?" Jason grinned and put his hands on his hips in faux challenge as Scott stopped and turned back. "Let's go again, wimp," he teased.

"How about tomorrow?" Scott replied with a smile. "Then we'll try to add a quarter mile to it and see how it goes."

"Deal," Jason said and extended his hand. They shook

and then Scott put an arm around his shoulders as they walked off together.

The next day at mockups, Jimmy and Jason put on full suits and drilled on emergency procedures for doing inspections or repairs on the Shortcut lasers and mirrors in case it became necessary, working first on inside controls and then simulating a spacewalk outside in full gravity. They practiced repairing or replacing mirrors, tuning up lasers, and other possible maintenance, running each several times.

Being surrounded by the military team members, all with the short haircuts and well-toned bodies typical of military special forces soldiers, Jason felt decidedly uncomfortable. They all spoke using military phrasing and responded to instructions with short answers, speaking loudly to be heard. Their familiarity and comradery with each other was obvious and Jimmy, being ex-Seal, fit right in. Jason felt like the oddball outsider. The soldiers even had nicknames for each other, and they used them so often Jason had trouble remembering their real names. But if he used the nicknames, he got funny looks, as if he hadn't earned it yet. It was a bit like going back to high school or junior high again.

"YOU'VE MADE REAL progress in a little under a month," Dr. Dyson said with little emotion as she looked over his stats in her office the next week. "But I'm still concerned that if the alien ship has gravity, the minute you arrive and start to move you'll faint due to blood pooling in your legs."

"I assume they have gravity, but we don't know," Jason said.

She nodded. "Right, so there are two scenarios.

Weightless, in which case you might struggle with nausea and space adaptation sickness or gravity. So there's an anti-grave suit Scott's going to set you up with and get you trained in to help. That and fluid loading to increase your intravascular volume and decrease the likelihood of orthostasis."

"Okay," Jason said. He was willing to do whatever would help.

"I'm also putting you on these," she said, pulling two pill bottles from a drawer and setting them on the desk. "Midodrine will increase peripheral vascular stiffness. Basically, toughen up your blood vessels and prevent fainting. For adaptation issues, let's use scopolamine. Dexedrine is another possibility, but we'll send some along in case and see how you do."

Jason took the bottles and read the labels. Scopolamine was a nasal spray.

"The instructions are there," she said. "You'll need more midodrine before the mission, so I'll make sure you have it. Scopolamine and dexedrine you take when needed. Understand?"

Jason put the bottles in his pocket. "Yes, ma'am." He'd do whatever was necessary. No way he was missing this mission.

"I've okayed your participation in the Reduced Gravity Program, or as our astronauts call it: 'the vomit comet'," she said. "It'll give you a chance to experience microgravity and its effects before you go. But take it easy. You've made remarkable strides, but you're not fully there and probably won't be even during the mission. We're also going to get you on the 20G centrifuge tomorrow; see how that goes."

"The centrifuge?"

He got the answer the next day when he met Dr. Dyson, Scott, and a tech at building 29 the next day and entered a room containing what looked like a giant wire frame propeller with three cabs. It was fifty-eight feet in diameter and filled the entire room with an observation booth at one end that looked in through a reinforced glass window.

The tech explained, "She's been updated, but we used the first version to train astronauts in the sixties. She can produce forces up to twenty times that of Earth's gravity. Usually the mass of the payload sets the limit that can be obtained on any test. Since your flight won't carry all that much, we've kept them fairly light for you. You'll start in the cab on the right, and I'll help you strap in and adjust the seat."

"We're going to start you out at one and then move up in increments, depending upon how you do," Dr. Dyson added. "You should be prepared to experience the graying of your vision, tunnel vision, and you'll probably faint."

"Don't worry," Scott added with a pat on Jason's back, "Happens to everyone."

"I've kinda become an expert at that by now," Jason joked. They politely laughed.

"Keeping a sense of humor is good," the tech said. "You ready to give her a whirl?"

"Literally," Jason said and followed her to the cab at the right end of the centrifuge and waited as she made a few adjustments to the seat then indicated for him to climb in. He was wearing a blue jumpsuit with the NASA logo and his last name stitched across the upper pocket above his heart. Facing the seat was a control panel with a few buttons, a speaker, and some LEDs.

"Okay," the tech said and Jason saw over her shoulder as Dr. Dyson and Scott entered the observation booth and settled into chairs. "Let's get you strapped in." She handed him each strap and he slid his arms through them and then she strapped in his knees as well. When she stood again, she made adjustments to the straps. "You comfortable?"

THUMP! "Does it matter?"

She laughed. "Well, yes. We do want you to at least start that way. We don't want them too loose though. We want you safe."

"I feel pretty snug," he replied. THUMP!

"Good," she said, making some final adjustments, then stood back a bit and examined him. "Okay, I think you're ready. Good luck." With that, she disappeared and reappeared a few minutes later in the observation booth.

Jason uttered a quick silent prayer, bracing himself both mentally and physically. He had to do well here. He had to prove himself. Anything less might force NASA to declare him unfit for the mission, and time was running out to change their minds. Despite the pounding in his chest and ears, he focused on breathing normally—long, deep breaths—then he heard the whine of hydraulics as the system fired up as Dr. Dyson's voice came over the microphone.

"Okay, Jason, this is it. Sit back and relax as much as you can. Don't try to talk. Just give us a thumbs up for 'yes' if you need to and shake your head for 'no.'"

"If you're able," Scott added.

As soon as the machine started up and began spinning, he realized how comical it was for her to say that. As the spinning increased, he was pushed back hard against the seat and found himself wondering how anyone would try to talk under such circumstances. The skin on his face and hands seemed to stretch like a Stretch Armstrong doll, though he couldn't visually confirm it. He just rested where gravity had put him and focused on his breathing. THUMP! THUMP!

"Okay," the tech said over the speaker after a few more minutes, "we're at two and looking good. Feeling okay?"

Jason made a thumbs up as he saw the numbers on the cab control panel's LED rising.

"Let's try three," she said, and he felt the spinning increasing again.

THUMP! THUMP! THUMP! He did pretty well until they hit four. That's when he lost color vision and saw only grays. Then his chest tightened and his vision narrowed—tunnel vision, Dyson had called it. He worked harder to control his breathing and tensed his legs, bearing down before nausea set in and he blacked out.

WHEN HE WOKE up ten minutes later, Dr. Dyson, Scott, and the tech were there waiting. He was lying on a table, his heart no longer pounding, his breaths normal. His body had a few aches and some stiffness but his head felt fine.

"You did good, buddy," Scott said cheerfully.

"Better than I expected actually," Dr. Dyson said and smiled, a rare show of emotion. "But there's stuff we can work on. The centrifuge gives us an idea of your preparedness and spending time here will help you prepare to better handle the experience of your flight. The equipment we discussed will help with countermeasures to make things easier as well. Scott and some others will take you through that and help you learn to use it, okay?"

"We'll wait 'til tomorrow though," Scott added.

Jason nodded. "That was…fun."

They laughed. "We get that a lot," the tech added.

"Come on," Scott said, offering a hand as Jason tried to stand. "Let's walk it off. Then maybe a five-mile run?"

Jason laughed this time, shaking his head as Scott helped him off the table. He felt queasy, like having a flu of sorts, and ached everywhere, his limbs a bit wobbly. Scott leaned against him for support.

That Friday, they went up in the Navy C-9, a twin-jet variation of the McDonnell Douglas DC-9 that NASA had pulled out of semi-retirement for reduced gravity training. At present, the Zero Gravity Corporation had been contracted to do the astronaut's Reduced Gravity Program, but with the secrecy of this special mission, NASA wanted to limit exposure to outsiders, so the old "vomit comet" was brought back into service just for Jason and his crew.

The crew sat in eight of the twenty seats in the back of the plane, their instructors taking up four more. There was a huge area at the front left open and ready for practicing moving around in low gravity or for testing equipment. The walls were all thickly padded and had only a few small round windows. As they fastened their seatbelts for the climb to altitude, one of the instructors explained that the plane would perform parabolic maneuvers like roller-coaster rides over the Gulf of Mexico, adjusting them so the crew could experience seventeen percent of Earth's gravity, similar to the Moon.

Once the plane reached altitude, skirting the edge of the atmosphere, they unstrapped and moved forward. Soon, they found themselves weightless for about twenty seconds at a time. At first, Jason marveled at the sensation, some of the soldiers making braggadocio comments or taunting each other. As the only zero g virgin among them, Jason earned the distinction of being the first member of his crew to vomit, though by the end of the day, he was not the last. In fact, Jimmy was the only one who made it through unscathed. He was also the only one who'd been in space. The weightless maneuvers continued over thirty-five times, and they began practicing spinning and stopping, moving from place to place, traversing the area, and other skills they'd need in the weightless environment of space. Despite some nausea at first, Jason found it a lot of fun, and he even engaged in a bit of teasing and play with his fellow crew members. It wound up being the first time he felt accepted by them, at least for the moment.

THE NEXT DAY, Scott and a trainer named Kao Lin, an ex-mission specialist, fitted Jason for an anti-grav bodysuit and took him through the basics. Kao's name sounded Asian but instead he was a short, long-haired hippie geek with peach fuzz facial hair and both ears pierced. He didn't have the stereotypical clean-cut NASA astronaut image for sure.

The anti-grav suit was an experimental suit designed by Dr. Dyson. It was form fitting like a full body suit and had rapid inflating bladders around the legs and across the abdomen. Jason could inflate and deflate them as needed.

"Basically," Kao explained, "the air bladder inflates around your legs and abdomen." He reached down and pushed a button that caused the suit to begin inflating. "This will keep fluid from redistributing into the lower body during gravitational stress."

"That will help not only with movement, but to avoid passing out," Scott added as Kao Lin made some adjustments to the suit.

"No passing out is good," Jason said. Scott smiled.

Kao hit a button and the suit deflated. "Why don't you give it a try?"

Once they had Jason comfortable with activating and moving in the suit, they moved on.

"Now, let's work on some AGSM," Scott said. "Anti Gravity Straining Maneuvers."

"These will prevent G-LOC," Kao added, "during which you can fall and injure yourself, float into someone else's equipment. Lots of fun scenarios."

"Basically, loss of consciousness," Scott said. "Your suit should increase your tolerance by two-and-a-half to three Gs, give or take."

"And reduce your muscle fatigue fifty percent," Kao added.

"Yes," Scott said. "So there are two components to AGSM: breathing and isometric contraction."

"In English," Kao said and smiled at Scott, "you'll wanna practice rapid exhaling every three seconds to maintain your oxygen content and decrease the carbon dioxide in your blood. It also relieves pressure in your chest and helps the heart refill with deoxygenated blood."

Jason grasped the basics and watched as Scott and Kao simultaneously demonstrated the technique.

Jason practiced with them for a few minutes until he had a good grasp on the idea.

Then Kao said, "Okay, so isometric contraction is because when your muscles contract, blood vessels constrict and have less room for blood. This increases chest pressure and takes blood away from the muscles, which can cause hypoxia, impaired function, and unconsciousness."

Scott jumped in again, "So what you do is learn to flex your legs and abdomen."

Again, Scott and Kao demonstrated the technique a few times together, then had Jason practice with them.

"Now let's try them together," Kao suggested.

So they did again and worked on it for another twenty minutes or so, with each of them observing and making suggestions as they did to help Jason master the technique.

"Now your body will fire up adrenaline to counter," Kao said, "But it tends to take six to nine seconds, by which time most people have passed out. AGSM helps you stay conscious long enough for the adrenaline to work, so practice that a lot, until it's second nature.

"Okay," Jason agreed.

"At first, you'll probably get exhausted a lot," Scott said. "So start with short intervals because it's anaerobic. With practice though, you should increase your capacity and muscle strength."

"Make sure you keep your carb stores up," Kao added. "Plenty of carbs means plenty of energy."

"You got it?" Scott asked.

"I think so," Jason said.

"It's okay, 'cause we'll start practicing every session," Scott said and shook hands with Kao.

"Now let's talk fluid loading," Kao said. Then he explained that once they'd been in space and weightless, the astronauts would need to fluid load about an hour before any potential exposure to a gravity field to increase their blood volume and decrease the chance of fainting, disorientation, or passing out. They'd drink one liter of water and take six salt tablets each. Sometimes, nausea was a side effect, but the alternative was worse.

The salt tablets and water would be plentiful on board the ship. He just needed to remember the procedure, so Scott promised to review it with him a few times before launch. And to top it off, as he walked away, Jason felt no lingering side effects, a sure sign to his mind that all the effort was paying off.

THE MOST CHALLENGING training of all came on Saturday morning, when they arrived at the Neutral Buoyancy Lab's water tank. Used to simulate the zero-g condition experienced by crew members during space flight. The crew got in the tank, again in full suits with helmets, Jason using his anti-grav suit as well, and ran through spacewalking procedures. While the others had extensively practiced already, they only wanted Jason there to learn one maneuver—moving between the X-39B and an alien spacecraft, on the chance that happened in zero g. In fact, no one had any idea what conditions to expect when they arrived where they were going.

They started on a mockup beside the tank in a nearby room. The crew lined up in a formation as per the instructions of the military team leader, a gruff man named Colonel Vincent Capobianco, and rehearsed climbing out of a recreation of the X-39B hatch and along ladders toward another ship and then entering through an airlock at the other end. One by one, in a trail, they moved as quickly as they could, each one following the others, and watching each other's backs and the area around them. They'd be re-running the same thing with weapons and using explosives to breach the hatch later. First outside a tank and then inside. The speed and tension of the exercise really got his adrenaline going. To be successful, they had to make their way out the hatch, across the ladders, and into a formation outside the enemy ship's hatch in breach position as quickly as possible with no errors. Jason struggled the first few times, stumbling. And after an hour at it, his muscles ached, slowing him down. But after a break, Capobianco insisted he try it again.

Capobianco rode them like a drill sergeant until they got it right. By the time they did, Jason was so exhausted, he didn't know where he'd found the strength to do it over and over so many times, but he felt great satisfaction at having gotten it right. He wouldn't be the one holding the team back, despite what he was sure they all suspected.

At the end of the day, Jimmy sat down with Jason, Martin Killan, and Capobianco in a an antiseptic, white walled meeting room with large bay windows overlooking NASA's campus, drinking coffee, sodas, and water as they relaxed their aching muscles. They all smelled of sweat and adrenaline, their hair mussed, their movements slower from tired muscles.

"You tired, civilian?" Capobianco asked sharply, staring

at Jason with an intensity that wasn't quite anger but wasn't pleasure either. He had dark hair and dark skin and spoke with a confidence that what he said would be heard and obeyed, typical of officers, and from his build, Jason knew he'd never want to cross the man.

"That was quite a workout," Jason admitted.

"You did great," Jimmy said sincerely and smiled.

Capobianco shot him a stern look. "You may have noticed we are a unit. My squad has been together fifteen years, most of us. Hostage rescue and infiltration are our specialties. We have never failed a mission."

"Well, it went well, I thought," Jason said, genuinely impressed.

This time the Colonel frowned. "What the fuck do you know? You're just some goddamn brainiac who spends his day writing figures on a blackboard. We're fixin' to be in the real shit up there. We don't know what we might find. What the ship is like. The layout. How many enemies to expect. Their weaponry. You think we can just waltz in there and take your wife back like we're going to some goddamn church picnic, don't ya, Doc?"

"No." Jason shook his head. "I'm not sure what to expect. But I'm open to trying diplomacy before we resort to violence, if that's what you mean."

"Fuck diplomacy. Diplomacy is how your wife dies."

Jason sighed, his face tightening as his limbs felt twitchy, but he kept control. "I don't think it has to be that way."

"We've seen it happen hundreds of times," Capobianco said.

"Well, that's why you're going along," Jason replied,

locking eyes with him. "To make sure it doesn't."

"You're goddamn right," Capobianco said. "So don't you forget it. You do what we say when we say, go where we say, and you let us do our jobs—you get your wife back. You get in our way, someone dies, and it might be you, your wife, one of my men. You get my men killed, I may take you out myself." He growled the last part and leaned forward, glaring at Jason.

Jimmy reached over and put a hand on the Colonel's arm. "Easy there, bubba. We're all on the same side here."

"I'll be ready to do what it takes," Jason snapped back right after.

"You better be," Capobianco said, still glaring.

"Except no one has ever experienced this scenario," Jason replied, "so you may have done hundreds of rescue operations where diplomacy didn't work, but no one has ever had a personal encounter with an alien before. So in reality, no one knows what to expect."

"We *got this*," Capobianco said and guffawed. "You don't understand shit. And I warn you, you better learn quick. You will not fuck this mission. I will not allow it."

"You do know I'm the reason we're going on this mission?" Jason snapped, losing it and glaring back, his heart pounding as he planted his palms flat on the table and leaned forward.

"You do know we're the assholes that will keep you alive and make sure you come back?!" Capobianco yelled back, imitating Jason move for move and leaning forward to glare across the table.

Jason couldn't help it. He laughed. It was like two kids sparring on the playground. Jason relaxed and slid back into his chair. As intimidating as Capobianco was on the surface, Jason found himself surprisingly confident. He had his own areas of expertise and the mission's success depended on those as well, no matter what the Colonel thought. "Colonel, I understand, and I'm here to train and learn what I need to. You want to go back and work all night, let's go." He stopped smiling and leaned forward again without leaving his chair. "But I'm going on this mission, and I'm the one who makes sure *you* come back safe with Shortcut. Don't forget that either."

The two stared at each other a moment before Jason stood and headed for the door.

Jimmy hurried after him. "Jason, where ya going? We need to talk strategy."

"That asshole's gonna do whatever he wants, no matter what I say," Jason said, whirling to face him in the corridor. "This isn't going to work."

Jimmy smiled. "Son, we don't know what we're walking into. If they want us dead, they could try to kill us all the minute we walk off our ship. Hell, they might just blow us outta the sky before we ever get there."

"Laura said they want me there," Jason said. "I'm pretty sure they want to talk to me. So why would they do that? "If they wanted us dead, why not kill me at the park? Why take Laura and lure us out? It makes no sense."

Jason took a deep breath and forced a smile. "I get the unknowns here. I get the need for caution and even potential force. But going in aggressive and warlike is the wrong approach. They have not hurt Laura after months. They made a concerted effort to abduct me and her both but not harm us. And they seem to have the technology to do it if they wanted. We should find out what they want; why they did this. That won't happen with bullets. That happens with diplomacy."

"Well, like it or not, this is the crew the president approved," Jimmy said. "You have to work with them to get Laura back"

"If he's gonna treat me like the enemy, this isn't going to work," Jason finally said.

"The Colonel's tough," Jimmy said. "Hard to impress. But he's the best. I'd follow him anywhere. You prove your merit, he'll give you respect. But right now, this is the proving ground. Like boot camp. Don't expect him to lighten up 'til he's seen how you handle yourself. I promise you, when the shit hits the fan, if it does, there's no one else you want out front guarding your ass...or Laura."

Jason shrugged. "I hope so. Believe me, I do."

Jimmy clapped him on the back. "Goddamn you're a downer, Doc. Go home and get some rest already. We need you in positive spirits tomorrow, okay? We're just gettin' started." He grinned. "Oh-eight-hundred, Doc," Jimmy said. "You're on mission time now."

"Right," Jason said and shook their hands before heading for the door as he pulled up the Uber app on his smartphone.

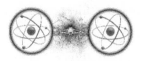

THAT NIGHT, AFTER tucking in Heather and saying his good nights to the Raimeys, Jason went to his room, picked up the phone, and dialed a number he'd had to track down, nervously awaiting the person he hoped and expected would answer.

"This is Elon," the familiar voice said.

"Elon, this is Jason Maxx."

"Jason, I saw the footage of that test you ran at NASA last month. Holy shit! When can I get me some of that Shortcut technology for my rockets?" Musk laughed.

"Well, actually, let me tell you why I'm calling,"Jason said. "Do you still have that launch set for next month?"

"We have three coming up," Musk said. "*Starship 30* on the 25th, a payload ship. And two manned missions, *Starship 19* and *Starship 24*, brother. Very exciting stuff!"

Then Jason began explaining what he wanted, and when he finished said, "This could jeopardize your relationships with the government, so I know it's a lot to ask."

"You let me worry about that, Jason. If my wife was stuck out there, there's nothing I wouldn't do to bring her home safe," Musk said with utmost sincerity. "After word gets out SpaceX helped rescue a national hero they'll have a hard time coming down too harshly, and with our contracts and history, they need us. Besides, you know the old saying, 'It's easier to apologize than ask for permission. Just tell me what you need."

"I'll have a guy from my team call you tomorrow first thing," Jason promised. "Elon, really, I don't know how to thank you."

"Can I keep the Shortcut tech when the ship comes back?" Musk joked then, before Jason could answer, added, "We'll work that out later. Just have him call this number. Whatever you need."

"His name is Peter Edtz," Jason said as they hung up, his voice cracking from the overwhelming emotions he was feeling. What he had just set in motion could cost him a lot—

Federal criminal charges, friendships, his relationship with NASA, maybe even his position with CalTech. None of that mattered compared to getting Laura back safe. And after what he'd seen of Jimmy and Capobianco's team, he just knew in his gut there was another, better way. He had to try. Too much was at stake.

After taking a moment to gather himself, he called Peter Edtz. "Sorry to call so late."

"Forget about it," Peter said. "What's going on?"

Jason explained. "So call him at that number and find out what you need and he needs."

"So you're not just talking theory? You really want to do this?"

"I'm still deciding," Jason lied, knowing he'd already made up his mind, but he needed to hear how that discussion went before he actually put things in motion. "I want to have it ready if we need it," he added.

"Okay, I'll let you know how it goes," Peter said.

It took Jason nearly two hours to fall asleep after he hung up, his mind racing through so many possibilities and questions as he lay there. But he finally managed, and he dreamed of Laura.

CHAPTER 17

A WEEK LATER, Jason rose early and ran a mile, as he'd been doing daily since he'd hit that mark on the NASA course. He'd progressed from a twenty-minute mile to twelve minutes in a month of hard work but he was determined to cut it more. He'd discussed it with Scott, wanting to run longer, but Scott felt it better to just concentrate on increasing his time at the shorter distance rather than trying for longer runs, so he'd stuck to the mile limit.

When he arrived back at the Raimeys', where he was staying, Heather was waiting for him on Roger's perfectly groomed lawn. He looked at his watch, puzzled: six a.m. His daughter had never been an early riser.

"What are you doing up, sweetie?" he asked.

"I miss Alice," she said sadly, her eyes missing their usual sparkle.

"I know, baby," Jason said as he strode across the lawn toward her. "Want me to have her come?"

Heather shook her head. "Not 'til mama's home. It's too hard. Alice is with her family and says she's having fun." Heather ran to hug him. "I need some help practicing my derivatives and integrals. Can you help me?"

Jason had been coming home so exhausted, he'd often just eaten quickly and gone straight to bed. Consequently, he knew Heather was both frustrated and sad at the loss of time with him. But this was his workout time and precious preparation for a physically draining day. He thought for a moment, then said, "Well, I still need to work out. Wanna help me with my push-ups?"

"Sure," she said with a giggle, her mood cheering a bit.

"Okay, let me get in position, then you climb on," he said. Jason led her to the center of a flat, grassy area and lay face down. Heather climbed on his back. He began doing push-ups with her weighing him down, and as he did, he fed her equations. "What is the integral with respect to 'x' of 'x' times cosine of 'x' from negative pi to pi

$$\int_{-[?]}^{\pi} (x)dx$$

?"

"That's too easy. Cosine times 'x' is an odd function with limits that are symmetric across the origin; that makes the integral zero," she replied, and he did a pushup.

"What's the derivative of sine times cosine?"

"Well, if I use the product rule that makes... cosine squared... minus sine squared," she answered and he did another.

"How about the integral with respect to 'x' of 'x' squared times cosine of 'x' from zero to pi—

$$\int_{0}^{\pi} x^2 \cos\cos{(x)}dx$$

?"

"Tricky. You're mean, Daddy. Why are you making me integrate by parts? Oh, wait, the first term is just zero and the second term is... negative two pi..." she said. Pushup.

They ran through a dozen more, and then she said, "Daddy, what happens to me if you don't come back?"

The question took him totally by surprise. "What, babe?"

"From rescuing Mommy," she said. "What if something bad happens and you don't come back?"

He stopped doing push-ups and she climbed off so he could roll over to face her. He sat up as she knelt beside him. "Nothing bad's gonna happen. I promise."

"How can you be sure?"

They had sworn they'd never lie to her, but Jason had never been more tempted. He thought a moment, then said, "Whoever took Momma kept her alive all this time. If they meant us harm, why would they do that?"

Heather shrugged.

"I think it's because they don't want to hurt us, they want something else," he said.

"What?"

"That's what I'm going out there to find out," he said.

She sighed. "But isn't it dangerous?"

Jason closed his eyes and nodded. "Yes. Space travel always is." He looked her square in the eye and added, "Good people are going with me to help make sure I'm safe and that we both come back."

"You promise you'll come back?" she asked.

Jason grabbed her and pulled her to him in an embrace. "With all my heart, baby. With all my heart." Her hair smelled of strawberries and her breath of chocolate milk. Her grandma was spoiling her. But they always ate breakfast together so he knew she was still hungry.

She hugged him back then pulled away and smiled. "Okay, because the teacher said next semester's math is even harder, and these integrals exhaust me."

Jason laughed and tousled her hair. "I hope when Mommy's back, hard integrals are all we ever have to worry about again."

Heather crinkled her nose. "Ugh. You're all sweaty and stinky. You need a bath."

Jason laughed again. "You're right. You go take yours first. I have to finish working out, then we'll eat breakfast together, okay? I'll make some pancakes."

Heather bounced to her feet. "Oooo, the bunny kind?"

"Whatever you want." He held up his hand with his index and middle fingers crossed and Heather laughed.

"Can you make equation pancakes?"

Jason made a face. "Last time that was a disaster, remember?"

She giggled and nodded as Jason got back into position to resume his push-ups.

"What function am I approximating now?" he asked.

"Sine!"

"Actually, more like cosine. I didn't start at the bottom," he said.

She rolled her eyes then turned and hurried into the house.

Jason watched her go and then went back to more push-ups. *God, I love you, girl,* he thought, his muscles warm and buzzing. And the equation big enough to demonstrate it was one he knew he'd never write.

AS JASON GOT ready for bed, his phone rang. It was Peter Edtz.

"It's done," Peter said. "We can do it in five or six days, I think, and we can start tomorrow. We have to go to the desert. And we won't have time to do the same amount of preflight testing—"

"I know," Jason said, feeling a tightening in his muscles as his stomach fluttered. "I have no choice but to risk it."

"Elon said they can launch within 24 hours' notice," Peter said. "But they launch from South Texas and you'll be at Vandenberg."

"Elon has a private plane he can fly me on that can leave from Vandenberg," Jason said.

"They'll try to stop you," Peter warned and cleared his throat.

"Hopefully I can sneak out in the middle of the night," Jason said, "and by the time they realize where we are, it will be too late."

"Do you want me there?" Peter asked.

"I can't ask any of you to risk anything further," Jason said.

"If it gets Laura back, I'll face whatever I have to," Peter said. "I'll meet you in South Texas."

Jason felt immediate relief knowing Peter would have his back. "You're a good friend, Peter. Truly a blessing you came along and joined my team."

"You know we have to warn Jack and Li," Peter said warily.

"Yeah, we'll do that in a day or two," Jason said, stomach fluttering again. "As soon as you're back."

"Okay, I'll organize a small team," Peter said. "Elon's offered his plane. It can fly out of Pasadena. Keep us more under the radar."

"Good idea," Jason said, realizing how much both men were sacrificing for him. "Thank you."

"Whatever it takes," Peter said and hung up.

Elon Musk had become too involved in politics for Jason's taste. There was little benefit to scientists, especially in math and space travel, of being too vocally political. The Twitter incident, in particular, had alienated large numbers of influential people, but Elon was also the type of guy who was there for his friends. And he wasn't afraid to defy authority and take risks. To save Laura, Jason needed someone with those qualities. So he'd called his old friend and his friend had come through. This wasn't about PR. It was about saving the woman he loved, the mother of his daughter, the woman he needed more than air. There was no turning back now. All Jason could do was push forward and trust his instincts, hoping everything went as he'd prayed and planned for.

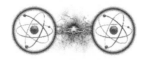

AFTER JASON DROPPED Heather at school and headed for Johnson Space Center, his phone rang. It was Li, calling on Skype. He hit a button and Li's face appeared on the dash.

"Morning," Li said.

"What's new?" Jason asked, knowing Li wasn't calling for idle chit chat.

"Did you happen to see what *Aviation Week* posted yesterday?" Li asked.

"I prefer waiting for the print version."

Li laughed. "Well, listen to this." He began reading as Jason reached over and turned off the car radio. "We've been looking for events that might have affected *Maxx-One*'s flight somehow." He started reading: "U.S. intelligence agencies believe Argentina performed a successful anti-satellite (ASAT) weapons test at more than five hundred miles altitude December 23rd, destroying a Brazilian satellite using a kinetic kill vehicle launched aboard a ballistic missile… Details emerging from sources indicate that the Brazilian Jobim A37 spy satellite launched in 2014 was attacked by an ASAT system launched from the Complejo Argentino de Acceso Al Espacio (Argentine Space Access Complex). The attack is believed to have occurred as the satellite flew at an altitude of 530 miles at a location four degrees west of Punta Indio in the Buenos Aires province. Intelligence agencies report the test is believed to have occurred around one-thirty a.m. that day…"

"Holy shit. This is confirmed?" Jason asked as he turned onto Saturn Lane, less than a quarter mile from NASA.

"Unofficially, yes," Li said. "The Argentinians and Brazilians aren't exactly forthcoming, but the US National Security Council released an official statement today confirming the event described in the article."

"So I was right?"

"Based on the satellite's known orbit trajectory, the estimated payload of the Argentinian ASAT, and the angle of the supposed attack, it could have put debris right in the path of our lasers four days later on December 27th," Li said. "So we smashed up some satellite parts from an old model and tested their effects on the laser beams."

"Adaptive Optics System Failure," they said together and grinned.

"Yep," Li confirmed. "A report's sitting in Phil Cline's email this morning."

Jason whooped and had to slow his car when in his excitement his foot hit the accelerator, almost causing him to ram the rear of a minivan in front of him. "He better okay the second test now."

"We'll get on him as soon as he gets to the office," Li said with a grin. His eyes and voice confirmed he was as excited as Jason was about it.

"I'm almost there; I can go in person," Jason said as he flipped his left turn signal on and turned into Johnson Space Center, using the main gate off Saturn Lane.

Li shook his head. "You've yelled at him enough. Let the rest of us have some fun, will ya?"

They both chuckled.

"Poor Phil," Li said. "Administrators get all the fun. Ask Jack."

They both laughed loudly this time.

"Thanks, Li," Jason said, then the call disconnected. They'd done it. They'd proved his theory. He was so excited he parked his car a mile from that morning's training destination and ran there, making it in under ten minutes.

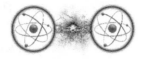

AT 0800 HOURS, the crew convened outside a newly remodeled office building on the west side of Johnson Space Center for what Jimmy dubbed breach and infiltration training—basically, a practice run of the strategy they'd use to enter the alien ship, secure Laura, and bring her out.

It started with Capobianco going over the approach on a white board he set up on an easel in the parking lot. A breacher would breach the door either by opening it with a knob or button or using his shotgun or an explosive charge. The first soldier would then enter and move left into position one, the corner just left of the door. The second soldier would move to position four, the corner right of the door. The third soldier would move to position three, the corner opposite four, and the fourth to position two, the corner opposite position one. Then the last guy would come in and if the room was secured, move to the next door and act as guard as the breacher moved in. Then they'd repeat it again. The rear guard would remain back in the corridor to guard their exit with Jason until told it was either safe to enter or until they headed back to the ship.

Jimmy acted as rear guard, also handling communications for the team.

After running through it on the board to make sure everyone knew their positions—Jason had a feeling that was mostly for himself and Jimmy—Capobianco ordered them to check their gear then went around and inspected each one personally. He spent extra time examining Jason and Jimmy. The soldiers wore special combat equipped spacesuits that enabled carrying of grenades, ammunition, and other ordinance on them within easy reach. They also each carried sidearms in holsters sewn high up on the back right shoulders of their suits, within quick reach as backup weapons. All had extra ear pieces and assault comms—a crypto comm system that was much more secure than that of standard spacecraft. Jason had no experience or training, so he remained weaponless throughout. After Capobianco spent a few minutes scolding Jason for various deficiencies with his suit—the tank suits were not the same design and this was his first time in the special combat suit—the Colonel then helped DeMarco into a backpack carrying the extra suit they'd bring along for Laura, if needed. Once that was ready, it was go time.

"All right, let's do this," Capobianco said. "Squad to ready positions!"

Everyone scrambled into formation with Capobianco in lead, followed by the others, then Jimmy and Jason.

"Ready?" Capobianco called out.

"Hoooahhh" was the collective reply.

Capobianco raised a hand in preparation to signal. When he lowered it, a few seconds later, they all moved in almost at a run.

The next hour went by like a whirlwind, with the team executing the maneuver through the entire building, room by room, until they'd cleared and secured each one. Dummies had been set up at desks and in chairs, leaning against walls, and other various positions. These were either dispatched with simunitions or otherwise rendered harmless—knocked out, handcuffed using wrist and ankle ties, or disabled with shots to the knees—except for three designated hostages. Each hostage required them to secure the person then lead them back out safely the way they'd come. Once they'd successfully exited, they reformed and started again.

For the soldiers, even Jimmy, it was like clockwork. Jason found himself a bit overwhelmed, even stumbling or hurrying to get clear at times as others rushed past or around him. But soon, he got the hang and began anticipating each move, getting into the groove. Once it was over, two and a half hours after they'd started, they assembled again in the parking lot to assess their work. Killan had remained an observer, timing them and making notes on an iPad that Capobianco now reviewed.

After offering feedback on a few issues he'd seen, Capobianco said, "Okay, lunch until fourteen hundred, then we do it all again, switching up. Dismissed."

The soldiers began scrambling off, headed to either the cafeteria nearby or cars. Jimmy lagged behind and moved to face Jason.

"You did good for a first timer," Jimmy said.

"It went so quickly," Jason said. "I had to think hard, learn to anticipate." The truth was, the entire exercise had made Jason increasingly uncomfortable. Violence was something he abhorred, and he'd never imagined himself caught up in such a scenario and didn't want to. His hope was this was all for naught, that the encounter with whoever had taken Laura wouldn't necessitate any use of force.

"You started getting the hang of it there at the end," Jimmy said. "This is why we practice, and we'll do it again this afternoon and twice in the tank as well. By the last time, you'll be an old pro."

Jason grunted. "I doubt it." But he appreciated him saying it. "What happens if the aliens outnumber us?"

"Then you get to sit back and watch how the pros do it, son," Jimmy said and smiled. "These guys have faced that dozens of times. You'll be amazed." Jason realized Jimmy might be right. If saving Laura came down to fighting, they needed to prepare. But actually doing it was so vivid and startling. It left him unsettled. "I doubt I'll ever get used to it."

"You managed just fine. Let's eat." Jimmy smiled and motioned toward the cafeteria. Jason joined him, limping slightly on his ankle, which was still a bit sore from the day before and had gotten a workout.

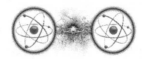

THE NEXT AFTERNOON, Jason was back in Mission Control for the second attempt at launching the Mars satellite and testing Shortcut's new laser system. All the same faces and players were present, but this time Jimmy Burnette joined him in place of Phil Cline, who was in Washington, D.C. meeting with a Congressional committee. They sat at a console in the back of the room, Jason tense and quiet. So much depended upon success this time.

Once again, Bob Cooper counted down from the communications station, "… nine… eight… seven… six… five… four… three… two… one."

"Shortcut one initiating," Leti Najera said from Propulsion.

Jason held his breath and closed his eyes, waiting.

"Shortcut completed successfully," Matt D'Aunno reported from Flight as cheers erupted around the room. Jason breathed again, opening his eyes to see D'Aunno and the other grinning ear to ear.

"Reinitiating for second attempt in five," Najera said as she checked readings on her console and turned to give CAPCOM Stacey Crowder a thumbs up.

"Coordinates reconfirmed," Jamal Ammar said from Navigation.

And so it went for the next two hours as *Vision 3* made her way to Mars, this time with no stop at the ISS to drop supplies.

When it was over, Jimmy slapped Jason on the back with his usual jocularity. "That was fun. I haven't watched a launch in ages. Congratulations."

"Thanks," Jason said, maintaining his cool despite his rising excitement.

"You know you can celebrate if you want, right?" Jimmy said as they stepped out into the parking lot. He motioned around. The parking lot was full, but of cars, not people. No one was watching.

Jason jumped up and screamed, then landed again and high fived Jimmy, who chuckled.

"Professionally done, son," he said and they walked together to Jimmy's car and headed to the NBL for an underwater run-through of the infiltration maneuver they'd run at the empty building the day before.

It was two days before data came back confirming the satellite had located *Voyager 1's* signal. Phil, back from D.C., invited Jason to his office to review it.

"The coordinates haven't changed much," Phil said, handing Jason a readout. "It looks like the ship is circling or maintaining a purposeful position at least."

"So, we know where we're going," Jason said as he read the data.

Phil nodded. "Yes, provided they still have *Voyager 1* on board. It's all we have to go on."

Jason watched him, waiting for more. Phil shifted in his seat and finally surrendered.

"Okay, the X-39B refit will be finished in twelve days," he said. "We can launch five days after. Really, there's just one thing left to do."

Jason mentally ran through his internal checklist and came up blank, his eyebrows furrowing and his head tilting slightly as he looked at the NASA director, fearing another delay. "What's that?"

Phil grinned. "Name the ship. It's a tradition here, Jason. Go check with your crew." He laughed.

Jason stiffened and offered an exaggerated salute. "Yes, sir." Then hurried out and headed to rejoin the training review.

"WELL, WE'RE HERE," Li said with a wide grin. "What's the big news?"

They'd convened in Jack's office at Caltech—Jason, Peter Edtz, Jack, and Li. With Peter's team having completed the installation of the Shortcut tech on *Starship 30* the day before, Jason felt it was time to let Li and Jack in on the plan. So far he'd kept them out of it to protect them, but to pull it off, he needed their support, so he'd called a meeting.

"I won't be going to rescue Laura aboard the X-39B,"

Jason said.

Jack's and Li's demeanors immediately changed, Jack biting his lip as Li's eyebrows drew together and he sat forward in his chair.

"What happened? Is it your health?" Li asked.

"What did the Doctor say?" Jack asked.

Jason shook his head. "No, it's not that. I've become more and more concerned with the attitude exhibited by crew leadership toward how to execute this mission."

"Jimmy Burnett?" Li asked, shooting Jack a look.

"Yes, but more Vincent Capobianco, the Seal team leader assigned to lead the assault squad," Jason replied.

"Assault squad?" Jack's brow furrowed as he reached up to rub an eyebrow. "They're preparing for all scenarios, even worst case, but they're not there to assault unless they have to—"

"That's what they claim, but I just don't believe them," Jason said. "The whole thing doesn't feel right, and it's been made clear that I am along for the ride, with no real authority. I don't trust that these men have Laura's and her captors' best interests at heart."

"We don't even know who's taken her," Li said. "Maybe they are right to be wary?"

"It goes beyond that," Jason said. "I suspect the plan is to shoot first and talk later. Maybe even capture an alien or whoever's out there, without even trying diplomacy."

"Surely they will do whatever's best for getting you all back here safely," Jack said.

"I no longer have confidence in that," Jason said.

"So you're just not going?" Jack asked, face blanching.

Jason and Peter exchanged a look before he responded, "I've made other plans."

"We've worked hard for months to make this happen," Li said as he absentmindedly twisted his wedding ring on his index finger. "It's our one shot."

"Not anymore," Jason said. "I called Elon and he's loaning us *Starship 30*. As of yesterday, it's fully outfitted with Shortcut tech and ready to launch by next week."

"Wait? You've run all this by Phil and NASA and this is the first we're hearing of it?" Jack said, his neck bending forward as he looked down at his desk. "I can't believe they signed off—"

"They don't even know about it," Jason said. "And they won't until I'm well under way."

"What?!" Jack exclaimed.

"You can't be serious," Li echoed.

"You and I know this is out of Phil's hands," Jack said. "And I have to protect Laura."

"What happens to her when they find out and come after you in a military ship with concerns you're a traitor or renegade?" Li asked.

"The X-39B is set to launch from Vandenberg," Jason said. "Elon will fly me to South Texas for the launch. By the time they realize where I am, it will be too late."

"But they could still try and follow in the X-39B," Jack said, brow wrinkling. "They know the coordinates."

Peter and Jason exchanged another look. "We're taking steps to ensure that won't happen," Jason said.

"My God! You've involved Peter in this?" Jack said with a pained gaze as he rubbed his hand against his pant leg. "Do you know how this could damage Caltech's relationship with NASA?"

"That's why I left you out of it," Jason said. "To protect you."

"I volunteered," Peter added quickly.

Jason shook his head. "Peter followed orders. This is on me."

"So you installed it with your team?" Jack asked, looking at Peter.

"A few key people, yes, but only the minimum," Peter said.

"And as far as they're concerned, this was to enable testing in a different environment with Elon's flight," Jason said.

"These are smart people," Li said, his lips pressed into a fine line. "Surely they know something's going on."

"I told them Jason wanted to see how Shortcut functions on different spacecraft. They'll keep their mouths shut," Peter said.

"And they'd believe he's not so focused on the rescue mission, he has time to plan outside tests and experiments?" Li said, shaking his head.

"And Elon has relationships with the government too," Jack said, his face tight. "He could be just as much in trouble as the university—"

"He said he'd stop at nothing if it was his wife," Jason said. "He'll handle the government. They have years of history and contracts, and they need each other."

"Jesus. This is insane," Jack said. "You know we'll support whatever gets Laura back safely, but this is going to cause an uproar. There will be consequences."

"Which is why this meeting never took place," Jason said. "It's on me. I don't want you involved. All I want is, privately at least, your support."

Jack and Li leaned back in their chairs, shoulders sinking as it all sunk in.

"We can't protect you," Jack said, eyes narrowing as his shoulders sank.

"Not asking you to," Jason said.

After a moment, Li and Jack exchanged a look, then Li nodded. "We're with you. God help us all."

Jason grunted. "Thank you."

They shook hands all around before Jack pulled out a bottle of Scotch. "This calls for a drink."

THAT NIGHT, JASON'S smartphone rang just as he reached up to flip out the light for bed. It was Jack.

"There's another message," he said right away.

Jason squinted as he flipped on a light and sat up on the bed. "What? From Laura?"

"Yes." He started reading, "18, 361, 1.4485, -0.33698, 39.2099, W5XPM. Jason, got your messages. Miss U2. Been treated well. So much to show you. No names. Hurry. I believe in you. I love you. GTG."

There it was. U2 again. And the no names reference—

streets with no names. *So much to show you?* Now, he knew for sure she was trying to clue him in to something related to their conversation that day at Buffalo Bayou. But what? Solving hunger or poverty? It had to be something big for sure.

"I think we should reply," Jason said.

"We can try, but I'd keep it brief," Jack said. "Not sure the limitations."

"I'll send it over in the morning," Jason said. "Thanks." And then laid down, his mind racing through possibilities until he finally fell asleep.

In the morning, Jimmy and Phil rushed to greet him as he entered the Administration Building from the parking lot.

"We don't think replying is the right move," Phil said right away, looking grave.

"What? Why?" Jason asked.

"We can't risk endangering the mission by tipping them off," Jimmy said.

"You're assuming they're reading the messages," Jason said.

"We have no way of knowing," Phil said. "But I'm sure you've heard of Stockholm Syndrome. If Laura's under their influence or they have a way to intercept the messages, the whole mission could be threatened. We need you to hold off sending her any information about when we launch or the mission itself, just to be safe."

Laura was trying to tell him something. Resisting the urge to communicate so they could dialogue more was hard, but he understood their point. He wouldn't do anything to endanger Laura.

Jason stared at them a moment then nodded. "I just wanted to let her know we're coming, to reassure her."

"She'll find that out soon enough," Jimmy said. Jason acquiesced with a nod and Jimmy smiled his famous all-charm smile. "We knew you'd understand."

Jason turned, practicing his AGSM breathing as he marched back toward his car. He wished he hadn't bothered coming there and hoped maybe Laura would get one more message through before the launch. *What are you trying to tell me, baby? Come on.*

TWO DAYS LATER, with the planned launch ten days away, Jason did his final run on the Centrifuge. This time he made it up to 5Gs before he passed out. Jason was proud of himself. Scott congratulated him as well. It was a sign of positive progress, even if he secretly wished he could have blown them out of the water with a score higher than 10Gs. Then again, no one besides experienced fighter pilots could last much past 8 or 9Gs usually, so he'd proven himself. Still, a man could have goals.

After that he went in to meet with Dr. Dyson again for a final pre-flight review.

"5Gs? Nice. The meds and anti-grav suit seem to be helping, plus the AGSM exercises, and Scott says you're almost up to two 10 minute miles a day on the track," she said, actually looking pleased. "You've certainly acquitted yourself as a man of dedication, if nothing else. Your wife will be proud."

"Thank you."

She set two pill bottles on the desk and pushed them across to him. "More midodrine and some dexedrine just in case. Remember, they all take twenty to thirty minutes to be in full effect, so don't wait too long to take them. Anticipate. Beyond that, are you comfortable with all the countermeasures? Do you have any issues or questions we need to discuss?"

He shook his head. "Not really. I appreciate *your* working so hard to help me make this happen."

"To be honest," she said as their eyes met, "I didn't think you could do it. It's why I may have seemed reserved at first. I didn't want to risk getting either of our hopes up. But I can say I've never had anyone work harder to be ready. You earned it, Doctor." Her eyes softened from their usual intensity and her voice filled with sincerity. "I hope you enjoy the trip. I have a feeling it will be a challenge, but then you seem to thrive on challenges, so good luck." She stood and extended her hand.

Standing, he shook it. "Thank you."

"I'll be in Mission Control to check in throughout the flight," she said. "So go kick some ass up there."

"Yes, ma'am." He took the pills and headed out, feeling almost as if he could fly there without a spacecraft.

"DID WE HAVE to do this at three a.m.?" Jimmy groused, shivering a bit as he slid into a chair across from Rohner in the first class lounge at George Bush Intercontinental Airport. The lounge's regular hours were six a.m. to ten p.m. He didn't question how Rohner had arranged access.

"You wanted to be sure no one from NASA knew about our meeting," Rohner said coldly. "The chances at this hour seemed pretty good. Did you control the message?"

"We warned him off," Jimmy said, yawning and rubbing his arms to warm them up. "Brenda will notify me if any come up. He's used to leading, not following, but it's his injuries still limiting him, he's manageable."

"Good."

Rohner leaned forward and passed Jimmy a dossier.

Jimmy had to step out of his chair to grab it. He opened it and read quickly, skimming. "Capture or kill?"

"We want to examine one of them up close," Rohner replied. "If we can. The most important thing is to gain control of the ship and secure their technology."

"This could escalate the situation greatly," Jimmy said. "I thought the priority was the hostage."

"You of all people know we have greater concerns," Rohner replied.

Jimmy did know, but that didn't make him any more comfortable with the revised orders. He knew better than to protest, though. "Capobianco knows?" He knew the answer but wanted to confirm.

"Of course."

Jimmy sighed. "Is that all?"

Rohner gave a slight nod.

Jimmy stood and grunted, taking the dossier with him as he headed for the door.

"Be safe up there, Colonel," Rohner said.

Jimmy offered a quick wave and left. All the way home in

the car, worst case scenarios played out in his head. He'd always obeyed orders, but that didn't mean he never questioned them. And these orders raised tons of questions. He wasn't sure he agreed with them. He definitely didn't like them. Especially not the feeling he'd had since the team first met that Rohner and Capobianco hadn't read him in on everything.

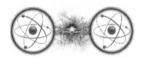

TWO NIGHTS LATER, a Thursday, Jason gathered at the Raimey's for dinner with Susan, Roger, Heather, Jack, Li, Purva, and Peter Edtz. The launch was Saturday morning in California. He and the crew departed early the next morning for preflight quarantine. They'd chosen the name *Carpathia II*, after the ship that rescued survivors from *The Titanic*. Only this *Carpathia* would never make the rescue.

As they finished a delicious main course of Susan's lasagna with white wine, garlicky roasted broccoli, and tomato salad with red onion, dill, and feta cheese, Jack raised his glass in toast. "To the *Carpathia II!*" he said cheerfully. Jason had kept his plans from the Raimeys and Heather, so everyone else played along.

The others raised their glasses and said, "*Carpathia II!*" Even Heather joined in with a glass of grape juice, though she had tried to argue for wine despite Susan's vetoes.

"Godspeed," Li said.

"Thank you all," Jason said, emotionally. "This wouldn't have happened without you. I can't say that enough." And he meant it. Mathematicians spent so many hours alone in rooms working on their formulas and theories that it was easy to forget how much they needed others, especially in applied mathematics, to help prove their theories. Jason knew he wouldn't be there ready to launch a rescue mission without so many people, but most especially his core circle. They'd picked up the slack when he was discouraged and injured. They'd urged him on when obstacles arose in his path. They'd kept the faith even when his tunnel vision and belief seemed misguided or even crazy. He could count on any of them to help work any problems, go to bat with NASA or vendors, or just stand up in support by his side as he did with no need to ask. If he'd learned anything through this crisis, it was that a man couldn't survive without good, faithful friends, and learning that had just made him love them more. His father had been wrong. He'd made a better world with the help of his friends. And he wasn't done. He'd never faced adversity like this before, and his friends were the ones helping him to face and overcome it if he could. He'd die trying.

"You're lucky no quarantine like the usual," Purva said. "At NASA, you probably wouldn't be having such a fine last meal."

"'Last meal,'" Peter teased, "Let's hope not."

"Hear, hear!" They all raised their glasses again. All were relatively cheery, except Roger who remained subdued and brooding.

"May your journey be swift and peaceful," Peter added.

"Hear, hear!"

Jason hoped for that last one most of all. Capobianco and his team seemed far too eager for a violent encounter. Jason just wanted to find Laura, talk with her captors, and leave each other in peace. He knew it might be impossible, but he'd pray for a miracle anyway.

After an hour or so, they shook hands—Purva hugging him—then Li and Jack hugged him too, a rare occurrence that had even Purva looking curious.

"You be careful," Jack said, clearing his throat.

"Godspeed," Li said with a stiff neck, and then before anyone asked questions, they were gone, leaving him alone with the Raimeys and Heather.

"Heather, it's time for bed," Susan said.

Heather's face fell and she whined, "But I want to spend time with Daddy."

"I've gotta get to bed, too," Jason said as she hugged him. "Early launch. How about you sleep in my room tonight?"

Heather brightened. "Really?" Her parents had discouraged her from sleeping with them since she was five or six, but tonight, Jason had no problem making an exception.

"Sure. Go on up and get your pj's on, okay?" he kissed her head.

"On it!" she said and hurried up the stairs.

Jason stood alone facing Susan and Roger.

Susan quickly hugged him. "Just bring our baby home, okay?"

Jason hugged her back, and she stayed there a moment. "I won't come home without her."

Then Susan pulled away, hand on his cheek and smiled at him a moment before heading up the stairs after Heather.

Roger stood there brooding a moment, then extended his hand.

"I know you think this is crazy—"

"You're a fine man," Roger interrupted. "I haven't said that enough."

"Or ever," Jason blurted.

Roger grunted. "Fair enough. Well, I've thought it. And I may not believe in aliens, but I believe in you, so please, bring Laura back to us." He choked up a bit as he said his daughter's name, but extended his hand.

They shook firmly, and then Roger turned and disappeared into his den.

Jason watched him go a moment, amazed, then turned and headed upstairs to join Heather for his last night on Earth before becoming an astronaut. He'd never imagined that dream would become a reality, and he was nervous, excited, and happy all at the same time. Mostly, he couldn't wait to see Laura, and his heart warmed, eyes moistening, as he thought of her. *I've missed you, baby. I'm coming.*

Before heading to bed, he called Phil Cline at home. "I've been pretty hard on you. Too hard. I'm sorry."

"I deserved some of it," Phil said. "No one likes an administrator. I didn't either, before I became one. It's okay. Go bring Laura back."

"I will."

A few minutes later as Jason tucked Heather in, she whispered, "I love you, Daddy. Please come back to me."

"I promise," he said and choked up. "I love you, too."

Heather hugged him and then lay down. As soon as he'd settled beside her, she fell asleep with her head on his shoulder. He softly stroked her hair, his mind filling with memories of his life with Laura, Heather, and Shortcut. Their lives together had been quite an adventure, and the mission was the culmination of all of it. As his vision blurred from sleepiness, he whispered a last prayer, "Lord, keep us safe and bring us home."

That night he dreamed of dancing with his wife again.

CHAPTER 18

JASON AWOKE AT 03:00 in the Air Force Hotel at Vandenberg Air Force Base, near Lompoc, California. *THUMP! THUMP!* His heart was pounding and his stomach churned a bit. It was the day before the scheduled launch of *Carpathia II*, and Jason was to meet Elon's plane on the runway at 05:15. It was time to shower and get ready.

As he stood, he felt a sudden urge for water and drank an entire bottle quickly in a few gulps. He'd packed the night before, so he'd be ready to move quickly. He took a shower and spent a few minutes shaving and brushing his hair, then called an Uber. Though the crew would get up early the next day for the launch, most were either sleeping in or spending their last free moments on free activities, so he hoped no one would be around the prelaunch ready building when he stopped by.

Arriving around 05:00, he felt like he was in a bit of a daze as he keyed the code he'd been given into the keypad lock and hurried inside. *THUMP! THUMP!* He headed to the astronaut ready room to retrieve his anti-grav suit and helmet, which he carried out and put in the trunk of the Uber, before instructing the driver to take him to Runway 6.

The driver shot him a suspicious look but didn't ask any questions, and as they drove away, Jason saw no signs of anyone having observed them. The driver was no doubt used to dealing with passengers with security clearances. Jason took a deep breath and settled back in the seat. His plan was going like clockwork. *THUMP! THUMP!* He might actually pull this off. For just a moment, he felt like some kind of spy or operative on a mission.

THE BURNER CELL rang at 05:15 as Jimmy was lying in bed debating whether to get up and run. It was his last day before the mission, and usually he'd spent such opportunities in quarantine. This was a rare chance to have a little fun, so the night before he'd entertained the idea of a sunrise run in the early morning breeze along the nearby beach. Only, when the 04:35 alarm had gone off, he'd just wanted to roll back over and sleep more.

"Yeah?" he said as he clicked to answer and held the phone to his ear.

"Any idea what our man is doing putting his anti-grave suit into an Uber this morning?" a familiar voice asked. It took him a moment to register that it was Reg, one of the men he'd assigned to protect Jason. Their security duties had been downgraded since he'd been spending so much time at NASA, but they were still around, keeping an eye on Jason under orders from Rohner.

"What?" Jimmy reached over and flipped on the lamp on the bedside stand, eyes squinting as they adjusted to the light and he sat up. "Who's doing what?"

"Jason Maxx arrived at the prelaunch building at 05:00 and just emerged with his anti-grav suit and helmet," Reg said. "The driver helped him put it into the trunk, and we're following them."

"Yes!" Jimmy said as he scrambled out of bed and groaned. His scalp prickled as he tried to shake off sleep. It was too damn early for this shit. Or maybe he was just getting old. "Keep following! I'm on my way."

THE UBER DRIVER pulled up to the Lear Jet and Jason found Tony Pantazis, the pilot for *Starship 30* waiting. They'd meet secretly the day before to discuss the mission and would spend the flight prepping at Musk's suggestion. Like NASA, crews usually spent weeks together training and prepping, but this was a special circumstance. Pantazis would handle the flying and Jason would handle Shortcut and assist. Pantazis had been up three times on previous *Starship* missions.

"My best man," Musk called him. "He'll get you through this."

After talking with him twice by conference call and in person the previous day, Jason had every confidence that was the case and relaxed as soon as he saw him—anxiety changing to excitement. This was really happening.

"You ready?" Pantazis asked as the Uber driver opened the trunk and helped Jason retrieve his anti-grav suit and helmet.

Jason smiled, feeling a lightness in his chest. "Absolutely."

Pantazis slapped him on the shoulder as the plane's pilot appeared from the other side of the jet where he'd been doing preflight checks, and they headed toward him and the waiting ramp.

That was when Jason saw the black Mercedes speeding across the tarmac toward them. *THUMP! THUMP!* "Are we expecting someone else?" he asked as they reached the ramp and a puzzled Pantazis turned to look.

Tires squealed as the Mercedes slammed to a stop a few yards away and Jason recognized Cal and Reg, the two bodyguards Jimmy had assigned to him, as they climbed out and raced toward them.

Pantazis stepped forward and raised his hand, palm out. "Gentlemen, this area is for authorized personnel only."

"We're authorized,"Cal said and the two men pushed right past him, headed for Jason.

"Stop right there!" Reg ordered.

"Where ya going, Dr. Maxx?" Cal asked.

"To talk to a friend," Jason said, not willing to tell them anything. His mouth was suddenly dry again. Pantazis' eyes narrowed and locked on the men as if he was considering what to do.

Guns appeared in the two men's hands. *THUMP! THUMP!* "We can't let you do that," Cal said.

"What are you doing?" Pantazis demanded.

Jason's knees weakened as the men grabbed his arms.

"You need to come with us," Reg said.

"I can't do that," Jason said, trying to pull free, but their grips were strong, and he was already aching from where their fingers were curled around his upper arms.

Jason saw a flash of movement in the corner of his eye as

Pantazis sprung forward.

"Let him go," Pantazis said and tried to pull Reg off him.

Suddenly, they were wrestling with each other, grunting and cursing, and then Jason heard a loud retort. A gunshot? Pantazis grunted and was falling, and Jason saw a red pool forming.

"My God, what did you do?!" Musk's pilot exclaimed.

"We'll shoot you, too, if you try and interfere," Cal snapped.

Another sedan appeared and raced toward them, pulling to a stop beside the Mercedes, and Jimmy Burnette climbed out, hurrying toward them.

"Stop!" he ordered his men. "What did you do?"

"He tried to interfere," Reg said.

"So you shot him?" Jimmy snapped. "I told you to watch him. You were supposed to wait for me."

"He was getting on a plane to leave," Reg replied, glaring.

Jimmy motioned harshly toward the men and their guns. "Put those away and wait in the car."

"We have orders from Mister Rohner," Cal replied.

"You work for me, too, remember? Go!" Jimmy ordered and pointed toward the Mercedes.

The men glared at him a moment, and then their hands slipped off Jason as the guns disappeared and they turned, striding off toward their waiting car.

Jimmy and Jason turned to where Musk's pilot was examining Pantazis' prone form on the tarmac.

"Is he breathing?" Jason asked.

The pilot looked up and shook his head. "He's gone."

Jason fought the urge to curse. He'd never intended to get anyone killed. Then it dawned on him—he'd lost his pilot. His whole plan was going up in smoke.

"Where were you going, Doc?" Jimmy asked.

"It's Caltech business," Jason lied. "I'll be back tonight for the launch."

Jimmy shot him a look. He wasn't buying it. "Bullshit." Their eyes locked a moment as they stared at each other in silence, then Jimmy went on, "You've got some other ship or something, don't you? This is Musk's plane, isn't it?"

"I told you—" Jason said, wrinkling his nose as he looked over to see Reg and Cal glaring at them from the Mercedes, then Reg was talking on the phone.

"Let me help you, Doc," Jimmy said, his face surprisingly sincere. "You need a pilot, and someone to look out for you. I work for NASA. You can trust me."

"Why should I?" Jason snapped, his body rigid as he licked his lips.

"Because from day one, I've wanted what you want—Laura back safe," Jimmy said.

His face looked totally sincere. But he was a government man and former military. Jason didn't think he could trust him.

"You want it so bad you'd risk your career?" Jason shot him a skeptical look. "Because if you help me, I'm pretty sure that's over," Jason said, not adding that he suspected NASA wasn't Jimmy's only employer.

"That's my problem, not yours," Jimmy said.

They stared at each other a moment more before Jason asked, "Are you armed? Give me your weapon and your phone." He held out his palm, a knot forming in his stomach.

"We can stand here arguing and give time for the men Cal and Reg surely called for"—Jimmy glanced over at the glaring Cal and Reg still watching from the Mercedes. Sure enough, Reg had his cell phone in his hand—"to show up or we can talk on the plane."

"Phone and gun," Jason repeated sternly.

Jimmy sighed and reached into his pocket, handing Jason his cell phone. Then he reached behind his back and pulled an automatic pistol from a holster attached to his belt. He handed that to Jason, too.

Jason accepted the gun and motioned toward the plane. "You can ride along until we stop for fuel." He shot the pilot a look, and the pilot nodded in understanding.

"What about Tony?" he asked with a final glance at Pantazis' still form.

Jimmy motioned toward his men. "They'll see to it."

The pilot took one more look over at Cal and Reg then turned and led the way up the stairs onto the plane, and Jason glanced back to see Cal and Reg reacting with alarm as Reg lifted his cell phone again.

Once they'd settled on the plane and the pilot had retracted the ramp and sealed the door, Jason handed him Jimmy's gun and cell. "Lock these in the cockpit."

The pilot nodded and disappeared behind a door as Jason followed Jimmy to the first row of double seats.

"You don't need to stop for fuel on a two hour flight to Texas," Jimmy said knowingly as they fastened their seatbelts.

"We might want to drop you off," Jason snapped. "How can I be sure you can even fly *Starship 30*?"

"A hundred bucks says the cockpit looks like every rocket I've ever flown," Jimmy said. "A few minutes to orient myself and I'll be off and running. I can fly anything with wings, Doc."

Servos whined and the plane's engines hummed to life.

"And that's even if I trust you," Jason replied.

"I told you," Jimmy said, "I understand how you feel about Capobianco and his team. I want Laura back safe. I don't want violence. But if you're gonna do this, someone should be along who can act if things get dicey."

The truth was, Jimmy had been sincerely working hard to find Laura and get her back. Jason had never doubted that. And though he knew Capobianco and his team and had obviously worked with them before, Jimmy got the feeling he didn't share their attitude toward violence or toward Jason himself. With Pantazis gone, he might need a pilot. Musk had security. He'd just proceed with caution and if they had to, Jimmy could be contained until *Starship 30* was safely en route.

"I'm in charge," Jason said. "You don't even show a weapon unless I say so."

"Fine," Jimmy said immediately. "I read ya loud and clear."

"And I'm keeping your phone," Jason said. "SpaceX security will be watching you until we take off."

"I have no doubt of it," Jimmy said. "You know they'll come after us."

Jason smiled. "They can try."

Jimmy's brow furrowed. "You know something I don't, don't you? Been planning this for how long?"

"Long enough," Jason said. "Now let's talk about the mission."

"Okay, Doc." Jimmy raised his hands in surrender. "What's the plan?"

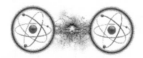

JASON CALLED ELON to let him know about Tony, and Elon promised to meet them when they landed.

Two and a half hours later, he waited as they stepped off the stairs. Jason pulled him aside as two SpaceX security men led Jimmy into a hangar. A warm Texas wind blew past from the Gulf, the slight smell of salty sea teasing Jason's nose. The facility was smaller than Vandenberg, but the runways looked new. It was all very impressive.

"We should get another pilot," Jason said, resigned.

"I wish I had one," Musk said. "But we didn't plan for this. His co-pilot left yesterday to train with another crew."

"What if Jimmy can't handle it?"

"My people will go over it, but the controls are pretty standard," Musk said. "Given his flight hours, I doubt he'll have any trouble." He took a deep breath and locked eyes with Jason. "The real question is do you want to risk it or wait?"

"If I wait, they'll do it their way," Jason said. "I have to do this now."

Musk nodded. "We can make sure he has no weapons aboard."

"No," Jason said, shaking his head. "I want a weapon, but I want it locked up and only I know the combination."

"Okay," Musk agreed.

Once he was sure he trusted Jimmy, he'd give him the gun just in case, Jason decided, still hoping they'd never need it.

"I'm sorry about Tony."

Musk sighed, putting a hand on Jason's shoulder as he reflected a moment. "We all are. He was a good man, but it's not your fault. Let's get Laura back. I'll make sure the family knows he was a hero."

Jason nodded. "What now?"

Musk turned and led Jason toward the same hangar Jimmy and the security men had disappeared into moments before. "Preflight prep," Musk said. "Usual stuff for you, but Jimmy won't get much time to relax before you go."

Jason shrugged. "He's a pro. He can take it."

Musk chuckled and led Jason inside.

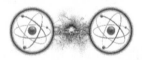

THE NEXT MORNING at 5:45 a.m., Jason found himself strapped in next to Jimmy in the cockpit of the enormous *Starship 30 rocket*, facing straight up and awaiting launch. Now, here he was an actual astronaut launching into space! Despite all he'd read, the personal accounts he'd heard from Laura and other astronauts, and watching videos, the entire experience was truly awesome beyond words."… nine… eight… seven… six…" a SpaceX communications controller counted down.

With a thunder from below, the Raptor engines of the enormous *Starship 30* lit and the entire spacecraft rattled and shuddered like a skyscraper in an earthquake. Flames began shooting down, though neither Jason nor his crew could see them, except on monitors. The entire vehicle swayed, space almost bending before his eyes. It was frightening and exciting at the same time, so beyond anything he'd imagined.

"…five… four… three… two… one," the countdown continued.

An adrenaline rush paled by comparison. The spacecraft lifted off and it was like someone had given him a giant kick in the back, pressing him hard against the seat as he faced upward as the rocket rose. With the vibrations and rumbling engines, he felt one with the ship as he watched the launch pad disappear out the window. The pounding exhaust shook the ship constantly, and within seconds, they were going one hundred miles per hour straight up. The acceleration was just brutal, the vibrations so high he clenched his teeth for fear of chipping or knocking them out. He hadn't expected it to be so rough and imagined the rocket vibrating back and forth like a tuning fork. With each second he felt himself pushed back harder and harder against his seat as the ship rattled and vibrated.

"We have liftoff of *Starship 30*," the comm controller called out to cheers in the background behind her.

At forty-five seconds, they were propelled faster than the speed of sound and the rocket bounced from turbulence as it shouldered its way through pockets of air. Jason heard the spine-tingling scream of the slipstream clearly through the cabin walls. It was the sound of immense power unleashed in barely controlled fury.

While the vibrations and scream of the slipstream faded to inaudible levels, he began to feel a bit like someone was pouring sand over him, such was the pressure pushing him against his seat, and it was getting harder to breathe. At first he thought he'd accidentally activated the anti-grav suit and panicked a bit because there was no way to move and reverse it, but then he remembered their trainers warning them about this sensation during training. The spacecraft was now accelerating at 3Gs and it felt almost as if two people were standing on his chest and wouldn't get off. He found himself praying that the machine would hold together for the final minute as Jimmy or Killan—he wasn't sure who, but their voice was distorted and shaky—ticked off the final mach numbers: "Mach 22... 23... 24..." and finally, "Mach 25."

It lasted for another six minutes, almost seven—the official time was supposed to be six-forty, he knew—and then suddenly they were weightless, leaving Jason dizzy and disoriented from his sense of time and space. Loose debris floated up from beneath the seat and hovered around him. He caught a brief glimpse of the blue-green planet out a side window—a giant 3D globe, only all too real: Earth, home.

"Visors up," Jimmy instructed and they all raised both visors, allowing them to communicate directly rather than relying on the radio comm units attached to the white head suits each wore underneath.

They had six minutes to reach the first Shortcut launch point and exit the exosphere and this part of the journey was fairly turbulence free despite the spacecraft braking from its 3G acceleration. The rest of the crew waited as Jimmy and Jason ran through a pre-Shortcut checklist of all the essential systems.

"Life support?" Jimmy said.

"Nominal," Jason replied, using the term he'd heard astronauts use in flight.

"Guidance."

"Nominal."

They were almost to the Shortcut and Jason thought of all the times he'd watched it from the outside, the debriefings with Dominick Creed and Matthew Wayne where they'd described the sensations, and then of the park, when he'd watched his wife disappear: shadows, a bright flash. He couldn't wait to see what it was like for himself. He was finally getting to experience for himself the results of all his hard work.

"Shortcut," Jimmy said.

"Preparing to power up, readings nominal," Jason replied.

"Commencing Shortcut in three minutes," The SpaceX Propulsion station controller said.

"Here we go," Jason muttered. Unlike the rocket engines, Jason expected to feel nothing as Shortcut's laser system powered up. It wouldn't be until the jump, and that he expected it to be quite dramatic. *Okay, baby, this is your chance. Do the job I designed you for.* So much was riding on it.

"Leaving exosphere in twenty seconds," the comm controller reported, then began counting down.

"Laser Shield activating," Jason said. Outside *Starship 30,* Jason imagined the lasers creating a temporary light sphere around the spacecraft now, as it would before every jump.

On a small screen mounted above his head on the fuselage, he watched the Earth receding slowly, and then the screen switched back to the dark star field ahead of the ship.

"Initiating Shortcut in ten seconds," Propulsion said.

This was it. The moment of truth at last.

"Coordinates locked and confirmed," SpaceX Navigation reported.

"… nine… eight… seven… six… five… four… three… two… one," Comms counted down.

"Shortcut one initiating," Propulsion said.

Jason held his breath involuntarily, concentrating all his senses on absorbing everything so he could document it later. There was a light vibration around them and then his vision grayed and everything around him turned to shadows as a bright light flashed outside. Then he was thrown back against his seat, the ship spinning. It had happened so fast, his senses had only registered bits and pieces of the full experience.

"Shortcut One successful," the Comms controller said, since neither man aboard *Starship 30* could speak in the moment as the ship spun at incredible speeds.

"Brakes initiated," Propulsion reported. "Shortcut Two commencing in ten seconds."

For forty-five minutes, they jumped over and over via Shortcut, headed for the coordinates out by Mars they'd gotten from *Voyager 1*. Thanks to the upgraded systems, the journey to Mars only took half the number of jumps that the *Maxx-One* had taken during its lunar mission nine months before. It was an unforgettable experience. In that time, he'd had plenty of chances to register the various sensations and think them through. By the end, his senses were overwhelmed and he felt exhausted from concentrating.

After the tenth and final jump, the ship stopped spinning and slowed, settling almost to a stop in deep space. The dot now appearing in their monitors, and growing larger by the minute, was Mars, not Earth—red, orange, glorious—as Jason reported, "Destination reached. We're here."

"Yes, we are, but where's *Voyager?*" Jimmy asked, checking readings on the controls and then glancing through the front windows and panning the space around them.

"No sign of her," Jason agreed. He leaned over and looked out the round side window closest to his seat, seeing nothing but vast blackness and stars. There was a constant beeping of equipment all around and flashing lights, LEDS, or readouts caught his eye as he panned the cabin.

"Nada on radar either," Jimmy confirmed. "They sent us two messages from those coordinates. Are we sure we're at the right spot?"

"Equipment like this doesn't make mistakes," Jason said.

"We're at the right spot, Doc," Jimmy said. "They're just not here."

Jason felt his throat closing. "Where are they? Why would they move?"

"Maybe it was a trick to lure us out here," Jimmy said. "Give us false hope."

"Jason? Is that you?" It was Laura's voice in Jason's ear, and from his reaction, he could tell Jimmy heard it too.

"Where's that coming from?" Jimmy asked. "Not through comms."

"It has to be," Jason said, puzzled.

"Jason? Honey?" Laura's voice said again.

"I'm here, babe. It's me," Jason replied out loud.

He could almost hear her smile. "I've missed you. Hang on," she said.

"What does that mean?" Jimmy asked. Then the windows of the ship went dark, as if someone had suddenly thrown a blanket over the entire ship. A light flashed and Jimmy and Jason were thrown back against their seats. Something with incredible pull was pulling them quickly off the coordinates. They hung there, pressed back tight against the nearest seat or surface, unable to move, as alarms blared around them. Yet Jason couldn't see anyone else or even turn his head. And it was total silence, like a vacuum of sound. Not a scream or a moan or a thump to be heard. What was this?

"What's happening?" he tried to say but it came out: "Whaaaaaaaaaaaaassssssssssssss hhhhaaaaaaaaahhhhhhhpppppppppeeeeeeeeeennnnnnnnnnnnniiiiiiiiii iinnnnnngggggg?" and echoed over and over.

Then the ship was jolted as the RRCS kicked in trying to slow the ship. There was a whine as servos strained and more alarms beeped, but the ship kept moving, ignoring all that, until it finally stopped, and they were thrown forward in their seats a bit. Both caught their breath and looked out the front window, which was filled with a bright surface—a wall, maybe, or the side of a ship. Beside him, Jimmy just stared, transfixed. "It looks like some kind of ship."

What they could see of the ship had geometric dimensions Jason's mind couldn't categorize or identify. It was larger than the Starship and a space shuttle, about the size of a 747 perhaps, with no discernable wings, windows or openings of any kind and the hull material had a color and texture he had never seen.

"No ship I've ever seen the likes of," Jason replied.

"You're here," Laura's voice said. "Welcome!"

"We're moving toward it," Jimmy said, scanning the dashboard and looking a little surprised. "Firing boosters, but we can't stop moving toward it."

Jason saw out the window that their ship was rotating into position toward what looked like a portal on the side of the alien ship, angling and turning as if preparing to dock. "It's ok, let it happen," he said.

"Can't stop 'em, so might as well get ready," Jimmy said. "Get those straps off, Doc, and be ready. Visors down. And I need my gun."

"What if they are peaceful?" Jason asked, hesitating. "They've kept Laura safe all this time…"

"And what if she was the bait in a trap?" Jimmy countered. "I understand your feelings, but better to be over prepared than overwhelmed."

Jason sighed. "We're about to meet extraterrestrials. I figure no matter what we'll be overwhelmed." The thing is Jimmy was right. Jason knew nothing about guns. It made sense to have someone who did just in case. Since he'd come along to Texas, he'd been on best behavior. No attempts of any kind to thwart SpaceX security. No arguing. He seemed to be on the same page as promised. Jason decided to trust him and motioned. "It's in a lockbox by the door. The code is 7-7-6-5." Musk had handled and briefed him privately just before launch.

Jason slipped his visor down and moved toward the door behind Jimmy, who located the lock box on the wall beside the door and typed in the code, retrieving his pistol.

"Okay, now I feel ready," Jimmy said as he secured the

weapon in the side pocket of his SpaceX jumpsuit, then, seeing Jason's look, added, "Just in case."

As they stood by the door, there was a thump and grinding, the squeak of metal on metal, and the ships were lined up hatch to hatch. They stood there, tense, ready to spring into action as a small tunnel extended from the alien ship and connected with a vacuum seal to the outside of their hatch. It was really only a few inches at most, but it would preserve the air.

Seconds later, the hatch warning lights lit up and a klaxon sounded as a computer voice warned: "Airlock doors opening. Impending atmosphere breach!" Standard procedure whenever a hatch was to open in space. Then the hatch opened with a hydraulic whoosh, simultaneously with the portal on the alien ship. Jimmy stood and led the way cautiously, Jason following.

As soon as they'd cleared the tunnel, they floated down, their feet landing on the decks of the alien spacecraft as artificial gravity took over. The alien decks felt just like their own—though they were shinier and looked almost ceramic, instead of metal. But the surface wasn't slick and they had no trouble staying on their feet as they crept forward.

Then with a WHOOSH! the hatch slid up so fast it left them stunned, and it was like having sand dumped over their heads and a sudden surge of gravity weighed them down like magnets to the deck. Jason's stomach turned as nausea set in, but he couldn't move to activate the anti-grav suit or his medicine. Then he realized he still had his helmet so what was the point?

Something hit them like a blast of air or sound, bowling them over like living pins, and they were falling.

The last thing Jason remembered was his feet leaving the

deck and floating up as his body leaned back and then there was blackness.

CHAPTER 19

JASON AWOKE ATOP a transparent table—or was it a bed—surrounded by white walls covered floor to ceiling in large flat screen monitors. *Where am I?* The wall surfaces looked ceramic almost, just like the deck where they'd entered the alien ship. He was out of his helmet but still in his suit, yet breathing was no issue. He turned his head and couldn't see the helmet. Where had it gone? Had he broken it when he fell? Nearby monitors flickered to life, playing scenes from his life: his speech at the Lightspeed Conference, the launch of *Maxx-One*, several Shortcut tests with *Mini-Maxx*, including some from odd angles he didn't remember from any of his own team's recordings. There were static scenes too: newspaper clippings, journal articles with his byline, personal photos of himself, Laura, his family and team, photos taken unknown to him as he walked across Caltech's campus or Johnson Space Center, of astronaut training, even from in college when he was fifteen years old. *How did they get all this?*

He sat up, rubbing his eyes and face, then looked around. The room was round and there were more monitors on tables like the one he'd been laying on but there was no sign of his crew or Laura. Jimmy was nowhere in sight. He was alone. The whole room was like This Is Your Life for a modern age—his image everywhere. It was like the high-tech equivalent to dying and watching your life flash before your eyes.

"Jason!" He heard his beloved before he saw her, but suddenly she was there, rushing toward him as a tide of emotions swept over him. She'd never looked more beautiful. She was almost glowing. He slid off the table and stood on the floor as they embraced, his entire body a jumble of warm fuzzy lightness and joy. They kissed then held each other, out of breath with passion, amazement, relief. Laura was as beautiful as the day he'd met her. He realized he'd forgotten that somehow in the comfort of routine, but seeing her again after so long brought it all back. She wore no perfume, yet the sweet scent of her was overpowering and triggered a flood of memories from their life together: their first kiss, that day at Buffalo Bayou, their wedding day, the birth of their daughter, Laura going into space, the launch of *Maxx-One*.

"I missed you every day," Jason whispered as he held her tight for the first time in months.

"I missed you every hour," she echoed, phrases they used to say to each other often when they'd first fallen in love and had to spend time apart. "I knew you'd come," she said and smiled. "I never stopped believing."

"Are you okay? They didn't hurt you?" he asked as he pulled away and looked her over.

"I'm fine," she said. "But you—you were hurt, Althon showed me. In the hospital?"

Jason nodded. "I had a pneumothorax and a concussion. I was in a light coma for two weeks but back on my feet in two more and working hard to find you."

"Oh, darling," she said, momentarily sad, concerned,

worried.

"I'm okay now, babe." He reached up and took her hand off his shoulder, squeezing it in his.

She leaned down to kiss the top of his head.

"Where's Jimmy?" Jason asked.

"He's safe," Laura said. "Althon is keeping an eye on him."

"I can't wait to meet him." He motioned to the monitors. "What is all this?"

"*This* is so much more than what it seems, my love," Laura replied, the look in her eyes so confident and serious it surprised him. "You understood my messages? He sent back my cell phone also to help you along."

Jason nodded. "Yes. You referred to our song, U2. Carrying it through."

She nodded back with a delighted laugh. "Yes. Yes."

"But there must be something more I'm missing," he added.

She took his hand leading him across the room, causing a tingling sensation that reminded him of the first time they'd held hands years before. "Let me show you."

After a few seconds, he realized she was pulling him right toward a wall with no opening, only she wasn't slowing as it drew near, and then just as they got there and he feared she'd crash into it, an opening appeared as if from thin air—a doorway of sorts—and she led him through into a larger room filled with tables and objects. He recognized *Voyager 1* right away just inside the door, and surrounding it were devices of all shapes and sizes, none of them familiar. Some were huge and sat directly on the floor, others were elevated on transparent, glass-like tables.

"What is all this?" Jason asked.

"This is Wonderland, babe," Laura said and smiled.

"THEY'RE ON *STARSHIP 30!*" Rohner's aide shouted as he raced into Mission Control at Vandenberg where Phil Clines and a very angry Rohner were waiting with a few controllers, along with Colonel Steven Carter, the newly appointed commanding officer of Vandenberg Air Force Base.

"Then we'll go after them!" Rohner shouted and whirled toward Carter and Phil. "How soon can we launch?"

Phil shrugged. "A few hours. We'll have to call everyone back."

"They've got an hour!" Rohner snapped, a vein bulging from his forehead so much Phil expected it might burst at any moment. Rohner was short but impeccably dressed with intense green eyes and graying hair groomed to conceal a growing bald spot. Phil had met his type before—the kind of wealthy, powerful men who expected everyone to snap to and do their bidding. No time for politeness or semantics. When they talked, people better take action.

"Some of them may need a little longer," Carter said, "but we'll do our best." Rohner glared at him as Carter turned and began motioning and calling instructions to the controllers, who went to work on phones and computers.

The man was angry, he understood it, but there were practical concerns, so Phil tried his best to explain. "We've never had a crew member go missing the day before a launch," Phil said. "Scrubbing the launch is the only protocol we have. It's not like postponing or holding. People assume we're going to try again another day. Not all of them live on base."

"Do I look like I care?" Rohner snapped as he held out his hand and the aide handed him an iPad, which Rohner began reading. "So that son of a bitch Burnette is with him, just as we suspected. Can we track them?"

"Ordinarily, they're broadcasting it like an event every time so that would be easy," the aide said, "but this was silent and unscheduled."

"I thought *Starship 30* was due to launch this week?" Carter observed.

"Yes, but they obviously changed its mission and plan," the aide said.

"Get that asshole Musk on the phone. Now!" Rohner ordered. "And I want the X-39B in the air in an hour."

"We'll get her up as fast as we can, but with just Major Killan left to pilot, we may need to get another pilot," the aide said.

"Figure it out, fast!" Rohner shouted and the aide nodded, hurrying off.

Phil just moved away. No sense arguing with a man like that. How the hell had he gotten involved in this anyway? Phil was tempted to call the President and ask but that would only make more trouble. And more trouble was the last thing he needed at the moment. So opting not to do anything that might raise his blood pressure, he went to work and ignored the man. That was something everyone at NASA had long ago learned how to do.

LAURA PULLED JASON toward one of the machines near the center of the room. It had a circular enclosure in the middle with large, dark, chute-like openings on each end— presumably one for input and one for output. He'd never seen anything like it. And next to it was a round bin of sorts containing various pieces and parts, some organic like food scraps, others more like building materials. A strange odor emanated from the bin. It reminded him almost of garbage.

"What is this—garbage?" he asked.

"Basically, yes," she said, pushing him eagerly toward the bin.

Jason scooped up as much as his hands could carry and carried it across to where the machine was as Laura reached down and slid her hand along the side, producing a vibration and humming sound from the machine. Jason assumed she'd turned it on. He stepped over beside it, and fed the items carefully into the nearest opening, since no guidance was given on which to use. The machine rumbled, crunched, and chugged, and then a jar-like transparent vial appeared at the other end with lightning-like energy bolts dancing around inside.

"This power vial could fulfill the current energy consumption of the United States for over forty years," Laura said proudly as she picked it up without fear and offered it to him.

He took it, fearing a shock but instead the surface was smooth. It felt like metal but was transparent like glass.

"Do you remember you told me you dreamed of creating

a source of universal energy, a way to even the playing field?" Laura said, prompting his memory again of that day at Buffalo Bayou.

"Yes," Jason said. "Of course. My beauty queen moment."

Laura laughed. "World peace, changing the world. This is that moment. This is that solution."

She pointed to the vial, and Jason nodded along, wanting to understand, but his mind was trying to grasp the deeper meaning, let it all sink in.

Registering his confusion, she continued, "What if anyone could make energy from garbage —any matter waste— energy as powerful as nuclear fusion, enough to power every city, every vehicle, every need?"

"This machine?" Jason asked, looking at the device again.

"Yes," Laura grinned. "Energy is mass times the speed of light squared."

"E equals em cee squared?" he repeated. "Einstein? Mass energy equivalence?"

"That's what this machine does," Laura continued. "Only using anything. Even garbage and waste. It takes matter and converts the energy in it to a usable form. Imagine cleaning our environment, eliminating pollution and landfills, replacing fossil fuels, and lowering our carbon footprint all with one machine, a machine anyone could probably afford and use. Can you imagine the possibilities?"

Jason smiled back, amazed, trying to wrap his mind around the implications. The clues in her *Voyager* messages came into full clarity. The U2 song pointed him to his desire to solve hunger and poverty with math, to make a real difference someday—it had led him to this moment. This was his chance. Their chance. Math could feed the hungry and clothe the poor—indirectly, but make it possible at least. It was unbelievable.

She continued, "No more fighting over fossil fuels, poor and rich nations now becoming equals with the same supply of mass to convert into energy…"

Jason continued the thought, "It could transform economies and industry…"

"Eliminate poverty and hunger by freeing up funds to invest in real solutions," Laura added.

"Funds for infrastructure to improve quality of life, housing," Jason said.

"Yes!" Laura said, leaning her head against his shoulder, her voice filled with excitement and joy. "So many possibilities with one new technology! Imagine how it could transform our world in just a decade or two if we had less to fight about and compete over with each other and could focus instead on solving universal problems that plague all of us."

"It's amazing," Jason said and put his hands on her shoulders, pulling her to him as they swung around, almost dancing at the joy of it. He could hardly believe they stood on the cusp of actually doing it, all thanks to the benevolence of some aliens from another world who'd somehow found them, watched them, and come alone. What would his father say if he were here to see it?

Then he realized his father would hardly be the only skeptic. Changing humankind's hearts, minds, and attitudes would be another huge hurdle, but this would be an immense leap toward the possibility—one hard to deny. Jason was still trying to wrap his mind around how everything came together. Benevolent or not, the aliens had harmed his family: taking his wife, his daughter, scaring them with the fear of losing her, leaving them stressed and wondering if she'd ever return; just the pain of not knowing. The kind thoughts from earlier faded behind frustration and anger. "What does this have to do with abducting you? Taking you far away and keeping you all these months?"

"Everything," Laura said and cupped his cheek in her hand. Then she shocked him. "They need our help, and I was in no hurry to leave after I discovered why he was here. When you realize all I've gained, you'll understand." Their eyes locked a moment as she soaked in his anger, frustration, and fear, not dismissing but accepting it as valid, expected, legitimate. After a minute, she continued, "I'll let Althon explain. I can't wait for you to meet him." She grabbed his hand, guiding him across the room again.

"If they wanted to talk to me, why didn't they just do it?" Jason asked, his frustration obvious. He'd been through so much trying to get here and save her and she had wanted to stay? "Why all the subterfuge? Do you know what I've been through trying to get here to rescue you?"

"Of course I do," Laura said as she pulled him to her, arms around his waist as their eyes met. "And I feared for you after what happened during my shuttle flight all those years ago."

"I didn't go crazy," Jason said. "I didn't lose it. I had Heather to think of. But saving you, finding you, it was my only goal and mission."

Laura smiled and kissed him. "And I knew it would be, my love. I knew I'd see you again as soon as possible. Which is why I determined to use my time here to learn everything I could to help us both." She motioned to the room around her again and continued leading him toward the far wall. "I was skeptical too at first, but think about it. An alien coming down to Earth is a huge risk. He couldn't risk others interfering. This is too important. He's an emissary. He came by himself. Please let him explain."

Jason smiled. "Of course I will."

JIMMY AWAKENED IN a plain white room that had no smell and was utterly silent. No disinfectant. No industrial cleaners. No beeping machines. And was the transparent surface he was lying on a table or a bed? It wasn't a hospital. So where the hell was he? And what was with the floor to ceiling flat screens? The last thing he remembered was being aboard *Starship 30* and seeing the alien ship.

He looked around. Jason was nowhere in sight. "Jason?" he called out as he slung his legs over the side and sat up. Wherever he was, it was odd. Like no place he'd seen before. The walls were pure white, almost ceramic. Just like... He checked his watch. They'd launched three hours ago. Not much time to rescue them and get them back to Earth, so that meant... He was on the alien ship!

"Jason!" he called again and reached down toward the pocket of his flight suit where he'd put the pistol. He thought about Rohner, who was surely furious at them both and no doubt ranting to whomever was in hearing range. He was not someone easy to reason with. He'd see this as a betrayal, regardless of Jimmy's intent. And Jimmy wasn't sure it wasn't. He'd come on the mission. That was his duty. He just hadn't done it Rohner's way. Whether or not that was a mistake, time would tell. First, he had to find Jason and Laura and assess the situation. He looked around for a door but there was nothing like that. Just solid walls and flat screens all around him. There wasn't even another transparent table, so where had they taken Jason?

After a few moments, he started rapping his fist on the walls, listening for a hollow sound on the other side. There had to be a hidden door. He just had to find it.

After a few moments of no luck, Jimmy called out again, "Jason, I'm trying to find you, but there's no door here."

As if that had been a cue, suddenly there was a vibration and an opening appeared in one of the walls. Jimmy peered through. Some kind of corridor of the same ceramic-like construction as the room. He sighed. It didn't look dangerous. "Might as well follow it," he mumbled to himself.

He stepped into the narrow passage and followed it, then, after thinking about it, reached down and drew the pistol. Who knew what he might encounter? Jason and Laura might already be dead or subdued. He had to be ready.

The passageway had three sharp turns separated by straight paths, and he traversed each with caution but determination, until another opening appeared at the far end and he saw Jason and Laura standing together, smiling.

"Jason! Thank God you're safe!" Jimmy called as he went through the opening. "And you found Laura."

"We're fine, Jimmy," Jason said, seeing the pistol, as Jimmy stepped forward.

"Where are the aliens?" Jimmy asked and then alarms blared and the lights flashed and suddenly glass-like walls appeared around Jimmy, boxing him in—like some kind of transparent cage.

"All this is unnecessary," Laura said, raising her palms to

signal Jimmy to stop. "He's not a threat."

"He? There's only one?" Jimmy asked and from his reaction Jason wondered if Laura had made a big mistake.

"I am here," the alien's voice said in everyone's ear. " I mean you no harm."

"He can see us?" Jimmy asked.

"Yes, so you need to calm down and listen to what he has to say," Laura insisted, looking at Jimmy, her eyes pleading. "You've known me a long time, Jimmy. Believe me. Things are not what they seem."

Jimmy locked eyes with her and saw something. He lowered the pistol and slipped it back into his jumpsuit. "It's okay, Althon," Laura called.

Lines of light appeared in a wall a few feet down the corridor as an opening appeared to reveal a figure walking upright like a man. It was about six feet tall, but had no discernible facial features: no eyes, lips, nose, ears, or mouth. It also had no hair anywhere, though it did appear to have appendages that functioned as legs and arms, but they were disproportionate to those of humans: the legs shorter, the arms longer. It halted in the opening and examined them.

They all just froze, staring at it in awe. Jimmy felt numb, pure amazement. It was something he'd never expected to see and certainly nothing like he'd ever imagined it would be. His mind raced a mile a minute as he struggled to reconcile his spinning thoughts and emotions and focus again on the moment at hand.

"I am unarmed," Althon said at last but nothing moved where his face should be.

Laura smiled at the alien then looked at Jimmy. "Promise him you won't hurt him."

Jimmy's eyes locked on hers. There was something there. "I promise," he said. Immediately, the alarms silenced and the invisible walls disappeared. Now they were all standing together in a triangle.

Jimmy walked over toward Althon, examining him. "Why are you here?" Jimmy began as he stared face to face at the alien.

"There are many among my people who fear the dangers humans present to the intergalactic community," Althon began with sincerity Jimmy couldn't deny. "Some of them would have come here with intent to capture or destroy the threat without taking the time to understand it. But others of us, those I represent, believe humans have much potential to contribute to the future and deserve a chance. Laura described me as an 'emissary,' and that is perhaps the best term for the role I have chosen. I came here because of Jason's work and a desire to ask his assistance. In exchange, I came to offer technology and knowledge that might assist them to become ready to participate in an intergalactic community."

"Become ready how?" Jimmy interrupted, eyeing the alien suspiciously despite being impressed by his words so far. What was the catch? "By sabotaging the *Maxx-One?* Kidnapping our citizens?"

"I did not sabotage the *Maxx-One*, but I do know what happened," Althon said.

"You took Laura," Jimmy fired back.

Althon responded with no visible change. "I needed to get Jason's attention. And I only kidnapped Laura by mistake. It was Jason I wanted to talk with."

"Then why keep her for months? Why not send her

back?" Jimmy demanded.

"That was her choice," Althon said and Jimmy's mouth opened, his eyes widening as he spun to look at Laura. She nodded in confirmation.

"What does this have to do with helping us 'become ready'?" Jimmy asked.

"I can help you become ready by solving some of the longstanding problems that are contributing to the violent tendencies many humans demonstrate in dealing with one another or use to acquire things they lack," Althon said, his voice remaining as calm and soothing as it had throughout. "Solving these problems might, as Jason says, 'even the playing field' and perhaps eliminate the need for so much violent confrontation in ways that will better prepare you to interact with, trade with, and live alongside those of us who make up the intergalactic community at large. At least, that is my hope."

"You have examples of this technology on this ship you can show us?" Jimmy asked.

Althon offered what appeared to be a nod. "Of course. It is all here." He motioned across the room behind Jason and Laura where tables were filled with various scientific-like objects. They were standing inside the alien equivalent of a future technology museum: machines and gadgets everywhere of all shapes and sizes. The only object Jimmy recognized was *Voyager 1* standing off in a corner.

"So that's how you sent those messages," Jimmy said to Laura, amazed and puzzled at the same time.

She nodded. "Althon had taken it apart, examining it, but he helped me put it back together, and I got the power supply working. He didn't know I was sending messages until I finally told him though."

"*Voyager*'s systems are so primitive a form, none of my instruments detected it," the alien admitted.

"The probe is very old," Laura told him.

Althon continued, "Demonstrations are possible. Allow me to show you myself, and perhaps you will see with your own eyes what I have come to offer you."

"Laura and I have seen it," Jason said. "The capabilities and possibilities are truly astounding. And it is very much technology that can change our world for the better in several ways."

Althon's face took on a pinkish glow—the essence of a smile perhaps? "Thank you, my friend."

"What's the catch?" Jimmy asked.

The alien's face faded back to neutral. "I do not understand."

"He's asking what you want in exchange," Laura said.

Althon brightened again. "I need your help, or Jason's specifically."

"With what?" Jimmy asked.

Althon motioned toward a corridor that jutted off a few feet away. "Let me show you. Just down there."

Jimmy nodded. "Okay, let's go."

Althon led them toward the corridor he'd indicated. As they reached the far end of the corridor, an opening appeared in the wall and Althon walked on through. Jimmy, Jason, and Laura followed.

THE NARROW PASSAGEWAY had lots of right angle turns, but Althon led on and the others followed. Sometimes it would appear they'd come to a dead end, but Althon just kept moving, confidently ahead and, at the last minute, an opening would appear revealing another passage, so on they went.

After passing through three or four such magical doorways, they wound up in a large, cavernous room filled with humming and whirring devices. There were several dishes with translucent surfaces in rows aimed upward toward what appeared to be a giant contact lens that made up the entire ceiling. It all looked familiar to Jason, and Laura grinned as he took it in.

Althon stood there a moment as they absorbed it, then said, "My ship is disabled."

"Disabled how?" Jimmy asked.

"I was attacked," Althon replied.

"Attacked by who?" Jason said, feeling alarmed. Was someone out there after Althon who might pose a danger?

"I am an emissary, as I told you," Althon went on, "but not everyone among my people believes in sharing our technology with others amongst the stars. My mission was discovered by one such group who sent a scout ship to disable my craft."

"You own people did this?" Jimmy asked, his body stiffening as he blinked rapidly.

Jason felt his heartbeat racing again. What had they

walked into? They needed to get to safety. A people with such powerful tech must have incredible weapons.

"Yes, and I'm afraid when they disabled my ship, they also disabled yours," Althon said.

"We're stuck here?" Jimmy said, looking ready to run back to *Starship 30*.

"No," Laura said, shaking her head. "*Maxx-One.*"

"What?" Jason said as he and Jimmy both shot her confused looks.

Laura motioned to the lens overhead. "Jason, this is Shortcut. The optics—" she motioned overhead then turned toward the translucent panels—"tunable Fresnel lenses."

Jason suddenly realized why everything looked familiar. This entire room was a giant Shortcut device. The adaptive optics, power systems, and cooling hardware were obvious, but he couldn't spot any wiring or computer controllers. The walls were lined with the intricate cooling systems that looked like a fine mesh of interconnecting plates and pipes that he assumed were filled with microchannels flowing with coolant just like the *Maxx-One*. There was one section that was opened-up and surrounded by hand tools. *Laura must have fabricated the tools she needed.* Peering inside the maintenance hole, Jason saw the familiar sphere of mirrors, one inside another, that would direct the light where it needed to go and he suddenly realized the entire ship was a sphere of sorts, with those odd geometric edges he'd caught glimpses of from the cockpit of *Starship 30*. This entire ship was a Shortcut device.

"But if your Shortcut is broken, how did you get Laura here?" Jason finally asked as he gathered his senses. He had a sudden urge to examine everything. Learn all about it. This was genuinely amazing. And somehow minds different from his own had come up with the very same concept he had only millions of miles away.

"They have two," Laura said.

"This Shortcut is for moving the ship," Althon explained. "A smaller device we have is used to transport items and crew. It is in a different location and was not affected by the attack."

"So what does any of this have to do with why we're here?" Jimmy asked, sighing. He was clearly growing impatient.

"I need your help to fix it, Jason," Althon said.

"We've been working on the lasers since I got here," Laura said. "And the things I've learned to advance my own work...I don't know where to begin." Her face had lit up as she spoke, her eyes sparkling, her voice almost a hum and she was moving constantly as if she could barely contain herself.

"I am not an engineer or scientist," Althon went on. "I am a diplomat. I do not know how to fix it."

"Jason, he needs your expertise," Laura added.

"But won't those who attacked you come back?" Jason asked.

"The scout ship called for a larger craft," Althon said. "They are looking for me now. I was able to use the ship's engines to move it to this location. It is not where they found me, so they must search. But the solar system is large, and my ship small. They have not yet found me, and if we can fix it, maybe I can leave before they do."

"But surely you have radar or something to detect your

own ships," Jimmy said.

"I have blocked it, and restricted all communications," Althon said.

Laura interjected, "After I told Althon about how I was using *Voyager* to communicate with you, he and I timed the transmissions so that we would transmit to Earth and then move the ship to prevent the other aliens from finding us. That helped slow them down by sending them on wild goose chases after a phantom *Voyager* probe. They have not been searching long but this ship can't travel far until it's repaired."

"So if we can fix it, you can escape," Jason said.

Laura nodded. "Help him, Jason."

"And what do we get in return?" Jimmy asked.

"Technology to help you, as I said," Althon replied.

"But what if they find us before it's fixed?" Jason asked.

"You can escape," Althon said. "I can protect you."

"We need to get out of here," Jimmy said, shaking his head.

"We can't just leave him here, stranded," Laura said.

"If their scientific technology is this amazing, imagine what their weapons will be like," Jimmy said, rocking back and forth on his feet. "We don't want to risk getting mixed up in some kind of alien conflict."

"We won't," Laura said.

"How can you be sure?" Jimmy demanded.

"Because he's moving the ship, constantly," Laura said. "It's slower than Shortcut, but it's not staying in one place. In half a day, he can circle a planet, so he keeps moving the ship to new locations."

"So there's a risk he'll run right into them," Jimmy said.

"I am monitoring their activities," Althon said. "But I am not transmitting signals that would allow them to trace me."

"He's being stealthy," Laura explained. "They aren't. They have no reason to be. The last we checked, they were out past Uranus. So we have moved in closer to Earth."

"It still sounds like a big risk," Jimmy said.

"Jimmy, if he can provide the tech he's promised, we have to help him," Laura said. "And he can. I've seen it."

Jason nodded. "I want to see this Shortcut. So much here could advance my work by decades."

"Imagine what we could accomplish," Laura said.

"Where do we start?" Jason asked, looking at Althon.

"So no matter what I said, we're staying," Jimmy said, his shoulders sinking.

"Yes," Jason and Laura said simultaneously.

"What do you need my help with?" Jason asked Althon.

"Come. Let me show you."

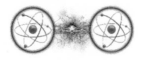

AS JASON AND Althon went to work, Laura took Jimmy aside.

"It's going to be okay, Jimmy. Trust me," she said. "Come, let me show you the technology." And she grabbed his arm and led him reluctantly back through the passages they'd taken to reach the Shortcut room as Jason and Althon got lost in technical talk Jimmy didn't understand.

"We shouldn't leave them," he said.

"They'll be fine," Laura said. "We'd just be in the way. Althon will not harm us."

And Jimmy finally realized he had little choice, so surrendered, following Laura back to the technology museum room.

CHAPTER 20

JIMMY'S RELUCTANCE DIDN'T surprise Laura. She'd had to reckon with her own fears months ago, when she'd first arrived on Althon's ship. But she'd had time to get to know not just the alien but his ship and its contents. And she'd come by her faith in him through hours of study and experimentation. She firmly believed Althon's arrival would become one of the most important events in human history.

"What are we doing back here?" Jimmy asked.

"I want to show you something," Laura said, motioning to the tables around them. "Althon has collected useful technology from across the galaxy, And he's offering to share with us. Come here." She led him to a circular machine shaped almost like a miniature septic tank with large chute-like openings at each end. Jimmy had never seen anything like it. An odd smelling bin sat on the floor next to it.

Laura reached down and slid her hard along the side of the machine again until it hummed to life. Then had Jimmy feed material that looked like garbage into the machine through one of the openings. It rumbled, crunched, and chugged for several moments before a jar-like vial clattered out the opposite end from where he'd fed the material. Energy bolts like miniature lightning strikes danced around inside.

"Welcome to the new century," Laura said as she stood straight and smiled. "That's enough energy to power the entire U.S. for forty years."

"Jesus," Jimmy said, not wanting to believe it.

"You can pick it up. It's totally safe," Laura encouraged him.

Jimmy reached down, hesitating a moment, then touched the vial, deciding not to pick it up. "How?"

"The oldest equation in the book," Laura said confidently. "E equals em cee squared. Matter into energy."

"How do we know it works? Or that it's even safe?" Jimmy asked.

"I've been here long enough to get to know Althon well," Laura said, her eyes filled with sincerity as they met his. "He's never said anything that didn't prove true."

"Well, it didn't blow us up yet," Jimmy said, reaching down to pick up the vial. He held it up closer to his face and examined it. "This is revolutionary. What else?"

"We could spend hours," Laura said.

Laura led him around the room demonstrating various items and explaining them. Finally, when they came to a machine that was not much bigger than a vacuum cleaner, she took the vial Jimmy had produced and inserted it into a slot on the side. The machine rumbled for a few seconds and then spit back out an empty vial. "It stores the energy from the vials."

"How much can this hold?" Jimmy asked.

"Five million vials," Laura said without hesitation.

"Five million?! Holy shit!" Jimmy said, his breaths stalling as he suddenly forgot everything, overwhelmed with a rising giddiness. This was astounding, if it was true. World changing!

"And he's offering it to us," Laura said. "Imagine what will happen once our engineers and scientists break it down and begin recreating it. No more power shortages anywhere on Earth. Forever."

"It's incredible," Jimmy admitted, and she could tell he was still absorbing it, trying to understand and accept all that it meant.

"Wanna see a few more?" Laura asked, grinning ear to ear.

Jimmy smiled. "Why not?"

JASON AND ALTHON spent the first two hours of working together just talking through the components of the alien ship's giant Shortcut system. For Jason, it was absolutely amazing to see his own ideas recreated by someone else, especially aliens from a distant world. And while some aspects of the design varied from those his team had settled on, all the same pieces and principles were being employed in the alien's Shortcut system as that Jason's team had built, and that realization was like a huge affirmation that made him feel proud. He'd created something amazing, and he'd done it right. In a sense, it was like scientists recreating his experiments and theories to prove them correct—a process every scientist was familiar with—it's how science is done. The difference here was it had been done completely in isolation, with neither party having any knowledge of the other...until now. To Jason, that just made it all the more amazing.

As it turned out, Althon knew very little about the mechanics of his ship's Shortcut system. He knew its purpose and how to use it for navigation but little about the technology and components it was constructed of. So they started out identifying the various parts and components. Althon knew what some of them were but not all, so Jason spent a lot of time examining each component and its design in detail, comparing it to his own design to try and identify its function. Because of the sheer size of the Shortcut device and its intention for heavy use, there were many more parts than in Jason's own but other key parts were conspicuously missing. He also spent time looking not only for how each part or component varied from those of his team's system but how the design ideas might be employed or borrowed to improve his system. He made copious notes on his iPad as they went, identifying each component as best he could and at least its approximation to similar components on his own device, and when they got to the power supply and the reaction control system—which Althon called the "positioning apparatus"—Jason was not surprised to find the damage to Althon's ship was the same as that to *Maxx-One.* RCS capacitors and the power supplies had been disabled with the power supply displaying similar marks and emanating a faint odor of melted metal and plastic.

"Can you repair it?" Althon asked. "I am not an engineer."

"Neither am I," Jason said, "but I think we can find a way to fix it." Jason was no engineer either, of course, but he had assembled Shortcut models and demos from various parts—especially when he was first developing the theory and design—and thus became intimately familiar with their inner workings. As a result, he was fairly certain he could diagnose the issues and find a solution—provided replacements were available.

And so the pair set to work identifying the problem areas and possible solutions. As it turned out, the alien ship had the equivalent of 3D printers with schematics for all the ship's parts, but since Althon had not known exactly where the damage was affecting the system—he and Laura had spent hours searching to no avail—he had not been able to make use of them. With Jason's help identifying the specific parts in need of replacement, Althon was able to finally employ his ship's technology to make replacements. The process took a few more hours during which Jason made numerous schematics and notes about various features of the alien Shortcut he wanted to consider adapting to improve his own.

It turned out Althon's equivalent of hands struggled to deal with anything as small as the capacitors.

"I do not have the right tools," the alien explained.

Jason sifted through the tools Laura had 3D-printed. Some of them looked like they had been inspired by alien technology, but all the basics were there too. He cracked a smile when he noticed that she'd exactly replicated the color of her favorite pliers. He finally selected a long tong-like clasping rod and a twisty tool with a handle and long curly rod similar to a screwdriver and began fiddling with them until he had the capacitors in place. Eight of thirty-two were damaged. Fortunately, they fit into pre-molded slots with built-in claps at the corners. He used the tong-like tool to place and hold them then used the end of the curled rod on the twisty tool to manipulate the clamps into place.

After they'd replaced the capacitors and were starting on the power supplies, Jason asked, "Did they not train you in ship repair before sending you on this journey? That seems very unwise given the distances you are traveling."

"I know how to repair the ship, but Shortcut is special," Althon said. "Not all ships have it, and those that do call experts or go to repair facilities for help when it malfunctions."

"So why not call one yourself?" Jason asked.

"Because then the people who would stop my mission might come, might find me first, and interfere."

"It seems pretty risky to come so far alone," Jason said. "Surely there are others who support your mission. Why not recruit them?"

Althon seemed thoughtful for a moment. "I tried for many years to convince others to join me. No one would come. My uncle gave me this ship when he went on to the next life phase."

Jason began examining the space where the power supplies were. "The next life phase? He died?"

"I believe that is how you say it."

"I do not see how these power supplies are attached," Jason said. He'd gotten on his back and examined it from every angle possible. There were no screws or bolts or brackets visible.

Althon got on his back beside Jason and pointed to two metal slats that formed a box framing each power supply. "This." The alien reached up with two appendages Jason assumed to be the equivalent of arms and somehow stretched the tips to grab hold of two sides of the box, almost like claws, sliding, pulling, and shuffling until it came apart into two pieces in the shape of Ls. "I did not know how these things worked either until I studied the guides."

"The guides? You used manuals?" Jason asked.

"Repair data on the ship," Althon said. "Before I departed, I found these for most of the parts, but Shortcut is restricted and I did not have access when I prepared the ship."

Jason couldn't imagine having the courage to set off alone in a ship you barely understood for the far reaches of space. So many things could go wrong, leaving you stranded. "You were very brave to come alone," Jason said as Althon handed him the L-shaped pieces and he examined them. They were a bit like puzzle pieces with oddly formed notches that appeared to slide together and hold them in place as one piece.

"Others of my mind would say foolish, but my mission is important," Althon replied.

"You didn't fear they'd come after you?" Jason asked as he reached up and carefully pulled the power supply away from the wall.

"The scout ship had to call for help. They could not capture me alone, and it took much time for another ship to come. Also, I am very good at hiding. I move around a lot." Althon handed him the new 3D printed replacement and he slid it into place, then struggled to figure out the connections. After a few minutes, he discovered a similar design to the L pieces with slots that fit together around them and was able to attach them appropriately, using color-coded markings on the slots to determine which piece attached where.

"How do we plug this guy in to power it up?"

Althon paused, perhaps confused by Jason's question. He responded by waving an appendage, causing the power supply to come online and wirelessly provide power to some of the nearby equipment.

Jason raised an eyebrow. "Impressive. There's one thing I don't understand," Jason said, pausing to look up at Althon. "Why disable *Maxx-One*? Did they mistake it for yours?"

"No," Althon said, "but humans were not known to possess this technology, so the scout assumed you had obtained it from me. In that case, he wanted to disrupt you."

"Disrupt? If he didn't want us to have it, why not destroy it?"

"Our government has strict rules about interference with other space faring species," Althon said. "He is allowed to disable while he reports and awaits further instructions, but he cannot destroy without authorization. He had much more freedom to damage my ship."

"So governments are the same throughout the galaxy," Jason observed.

"Perhaps this is why people throughout the galaxy dislike their governments,"Althon said. They both laughed.

Getting back to work, Jason repeated the process and began replacing the second damaged power supply.

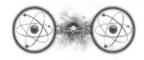

ROHNER WAS SCREAMING again, his face so red Phil totally expected his face to explode. He couldn't wait to get away from him. It had taken them six hours, during which Phil was surprised Rohner didn't spontaneously combust, but they'd gotten a backup pilot and Capobianco's team aboard *Carpathia II* and were doing the launch countdown when things went to shit.

"Running Shortcut system test," Major Martin Killan reported from the cockpit.

"Shortcut system test initiated," his new copilot, Lieutenant Cynthia DeMarco echoed.

Then there was cursing and rapid fire chatter.

"What's happening?" Killan asked

"The Shortcut system is giving an error message," DeMarco replied.

"Wait. What now?" Killan said, sounding more alarmed.

"Our computer systems are down," DeMarco replied.

"Get them back up! Right now!' Killan said.

"What the fuck is going on?" Capobianco asked over the radio from the passenger compartment behind him.

"We're not sure," Killan said.

"Well fix it and get us in the air!" Capobianco barked.

"Sir—"

And then the comms went silent.

"*Carpathia II* this is mission control," said Bob Cooper at Comms, "please acknowledge?"

"What the fuck is going on?" Rohner demanded.

"Some kind of technical glitch," replied Dr. Stacey Crowder who was serving as CAPCOM.

"Glitch?! What glitch?!" Rohner exclaimed.

"*Carpathia II*, this is mission control," Cooper repeated, "please acknowledge?"

"Comms appear to be down," Crowder said.

"I want that bird in the air!" Rohner demanded.

"They're running checks now, sir," Leti Najera said from Propulsion.

Phil looked around the room as alerts started lighting up monitors at the computing stations and several others. Something was seriously wrong with their spacecraft.

"Fuck checks! Somebody find out what is going on right now!" Rohner replied.

Phil had had enough. "Sit down and let them do their jobs, Mister Rohner," he yelled. "You'll know when we know."

Rohner recoiled but sat down, Phil presumed because no one dared yell at the man and he was shocked. But he knew it wouldn't take long for the government man to recover and be back to his old self.

Phil hurried down the aisle of monitors to CAPCOM's station and leaned over closer to Crowder, whispering, "Get an electrical crew out to that launch pad and standing by as soon as we can reach the crew, in case they're needed."

Crowder nodded. "Already in the works."

"*Carpathia II*, this is mission control," Cooper repeated again, "please acknowledge?"

Still no response. And two hours later, they pulled Capobianco's crew. Something had gone majorly wrong with *Carpathia II* and there would be no launch until it was repaired.

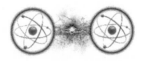

AFTER THE SECOND power supply had been successfully replaced, Jason used a digital multimeter he'd retrieved from

Starship 30's tools to test the functionality of diodes as well as the current and voltage. Everything seemed optimum from his limited experience and pressing a hand against the outer surface revealed no unusual heat emanation. He showed the readings to Althon, who also seemed satisfied, and then both got to their feet.

"Is that it?" Jason asked.

"I will go check," Althon said and disappeared through a mystery hole, presumably to the cockpit or control room to check various readings

As the final power supply finished coming online, various auxiliary systems began powering up too. "Are we good?" Jason hollered down the hole. Althon popped back out and telepathically turned one of the room's walls into a gigantic screen. "I don't know yet. Let me pull up the data manual on diagnostics."

While waiting for Althon to read through the manual and run the diagnostic tests, Jason sat down dazed. He'd taken in so much new information today: from his first launch, to seeing Laura again, to meeting an alien, and then discovering that aliens already use Shortcut. It was a lot, but he needed his head in the game. Jason watched as Althon sped through technical information on the large screen. The alien language didn't appear to read left, right, up, or down; instead the text was animated in concentric circles that grew starting from a central point and expanding outward in all directions. "The preprogrammed routine of diagnostic tests are running now," Althon explained. "When they're done—"

Loud beeps sounded from the console and flashing highlighted text that reminded Jason of warning messages appeared. "What's the matter?"

"The system is giving me errors," Althon said.

"What kind of errors?" Jason asked, leaning forward. "Can you translate?"

"Math isn't my specialty," Althon said.

This was his element. "What kind of math, do you know?"

"It is internal, to make everything work together," Althon explained pointing to the screen.

It took a moment of Jason staring at the concentric circles filling the screen before his eyes focused and he saw the equations. They weren't in the same math language he was used to, but at least the structure looked familiar; he recognized fractions and integrals, but all the symbols were unusual. He searched his mind for the equations that he'd used throughout his applied mathematics career and translated the alien equations into more familiar Greek, English, and Arabic symbols on his iPad. He was astonished how similar it all was to the math he had studied back home. Math really was a fundamental language of the universe. Emerging from the complexity of it all, he shared his findings with Althon, "It looks like there is a problem with the laser calibration," he said.

"Yes, that is one way of interpreting what the warning means," Althon said. "Difficult to translate."

"Laura fixed the lasers, right?"

"Yes, she did much repair on them, both here and in other places," Althon admitted.

"We need to run a more exhaustive test on that subsystem," Jason suggested. "Can you do that?"

Althon thought a moment then what passed for his fingers began flipping through the screen—menus popped up, text scrolled. "I think so, yes. I will try."

Jason wondered if he, Laura, and Jimmy would make it home. What kind of chaos was going on back on Earth? What if the other aliens found them? There's no way Jimmy's handgun would be enough firepower in that scenario. "It's too bad your universal translator can't translate this for me."

"I might be able to translate parts," Althon said as Jason noticed more circles, equations, and other text cycling on and off the screen in rapid, unusual patterns. Then the machine beeped. "Let me see if I can translate these results."

Althon flipped through more menus and scrolled again and a few minutes later, Jason was looking at a report in English. "I don't know how accurate it will be with math and technical data."

Jason leaned forward and began reading. "Let's see." Some sentences had jumbled syntax, but he could make sense of them in context. He read to the bottom, then asked, "Please scroll." Althon complied, and Jason went on reading. Back on Earth, Jason was the world-expert on Shortcut laser calibration routines. He had devised the mathematical models used to set up each part of the laser system to come together and pull off the alignment needed for a successful Shortcut. Eventually, piece by piece he made sense of it and realized what was the problem. "It looks like part of the laser calibration code got wiped out when the power supplies went offline. Possibly scrambled."

"Oh no," Althon said. "Can we fix it?"

"A new calibration routine would have to be written," Jason said. "And I don't know your programming language. Not sure how the universal translator might handle all this."

"Will you try?" Althon's voice was almost like a whimper.

"Of course," Jason said. "Can you show me how to use

this?" He motioned to the screen.

Althon gave short instructions, demonstrating each move, and Jason began fiddling with the data. At various points, he stopped to perform mathematical calculations to determine the proper alignment and control that would be needed then typed those in and wrote code around it. The scale of Althon's ship made the whole problem much more challenging, but he and Althon figured out a way to pair his iPad with the ship's computer then command the vast computational power of the ship using the iPad and run mathematical simulations that would have taken multiple human lifetimes to run on that fastest supercomputer back on Earth.

"This may take a while," Jason said.

"I can go nowhere until it's fixed," Althon said.

And they went back to work.

"SIR, THE TECHNICIANS say it's probably some sort of virus," Rohner's aide reported after the team he'd sent had gone over the X-39B to examine the issues keeping the spacecraft grounded. "The system is just locked down. They can't do anything with it."

"Well, tell them to fix it now!" Rohner ordered.

"They said it could take hours or days," the aide reported, then winced in anticipation of his reaction.

Rohner whirled and threw a coffee mug across mission control where it disintegrated into pieces of clay and liquid against a nearby wall. "Fucking Jason Maxx! I don't care what it takes! Tell them to get that bird in the air!"

"Yes, sir," the aide hurried off and Rohner noticed Phil Cline and the rest of his team had slipped out, leaving him alone in the room to stew. So stew he did.

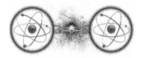

IT TOOK ALMOST four hours of back and forth tweaking and adjusting and testing to get code that seemed workable. When they'd finished the sequence and Jason ran it through the computer to test it, more error messages popped up, so Jason made more tweaks—Althon helping translate it as best he could—and they tried again. After four tries, the warning signs went away.

Jason grinned. "I think we've got it."

"It's a miracle! You have saved me!" the alien exclaimed, almost happily.

Jason chuckled. "Just let me clean up the math a little bit to make sure," he said and started tweaking the English version on his iPad. As he finished each section, Althon ran it through the translator then made tweaks of his own and inserted it into the proper place in his Shortcut computer's code.

After a few minutes, Jimmy and Laura came to check on their progress.

"Please tell me you're done," Jimmy said in his Oklahoma drawl. "I think Laura has run out of places to show me on this ship."

Jason looked up and grinned.

"You're done?" Laura asked, reading his face.

"That should be right. We just have to test it," Jason said, with a satisfied smile.

"All those months trying to bring Jason here and keeping Laura for a few hours' repair?" Jimmy joked.

Althon nodded. "I shall go try it with the main control room navigation system." Then, with a flash, he disappeared, leaving the three humans alone.

"The damage to his ship's Shortcut system was a lot more extensive than the damage to *Maxx-One*," Jason said. "Laura was able to help him with the lasers, and other parts he could fix on his own, but certain parts were Shortcut specific. The entire calibration system Shortcut uses to track stars and navigate was malfunctioning. Whatever the scout ship did, they scrambled the software. I had to reprogram the math by hand."

"He needed math? Then good thing we came to rescue you," Jimmy said, grinning at Laura.

"You saved his life," Laura said. "He could have been stranded alone."

"*We* saved his life," Jimmy said, and Laura reached over to squeeze his hand.

"You're telling me he left his home world and traveled all this way without knowing how to fix his ship if he ran into trouble?" Jimmy said. "That's crazy."

"Or brave," Jason added.

"His mission is very important to him," Laura said. "He is very dedicated."

"He told me this system does not break often," Jason examined the system's controls, wondering how to turn it on. They had tested it offline, but to really know if it worked, they needed to try it. The question was, could they perform a Shortcut with *Starship 30* docked? He could at least initiate the system and ask for calculations.

"But he had to know some enemies might come after him who could damage it," Jimmy said.

"To scramble the system like that—it's not a minor attack," Jason said. "Imagine if our enemies had technology like that." Jason shuddered at the thought, and Jimmy looked equally discomforted.

"This is new," Laura said. "He said he knew such technology existed, but did not know anyone outside the government possessed it."

"I did not discover humans had Shortcut until I came to investigate reports that they might be a species worthy to join the intergalactic community—my mission's goal," Althon said, his voice sounding like he was right next to them despite the fact he was still somewhere else. "But once I discovered it, I needed time to assess and determine how they would use such advanced technology. Laura did much to convince me you are ready and can be trusted."

"Well, some of us," Laura said.

"Are the people who came after you from the government?" Jimmy asked.

"No, another faction," Althon said.

"Did it work, Althon?" Jason asked as he finished examining the controls.

"The readings are normal here," Althon said. "And I just ran calculations with no trouble. Thank you."

"Good," Jason said. "So I think if we flip this and this—"

"No wait!" Althon appeared behind them as Jason flipped

switches on the control panel and the Shortcut system hummed to life.

Althon glided forward and quickly shut it off again.

"What's the matter?" Laura asked.

"My people can track me two ways," Althon said. "By signature of the Shortcut system and engines, and by frequency. To detect the signatures, they must be within certain proximity—a planet or two. But frequencies travel much further."

"Your Shortcut system works on frequencies?" Jason asked, puzzled.

"No, but because of commonality and the risk of collision, our Shortcut systems are attached to radio frequencies to transmit locations where we jump so that other ships don't attempt the same coordinates and collide," Althon explained.

"So when Jason turned on the Shortcut system, the frequency started broadcasting again," Laura said, realizing the danger.

"Maybe it was not on long enough for them to detect it," Althon said, and Jason hoped he was right.

But then an alarm started blaring.

"What is it?" Jimmy asked.

"They've found me," Althon said. "I can move again, but they might detect my signature. You must hurry. You have to leave before they arrive." And then Althon was gone again, presumably to the ship's cockpit again.

"We have to stay and help him," Laura insisted.

"What good will we do against his people, given their technology?" Jimmy argued.

"We have to try!" Laura said.

Then Althon appeared again. "I have set us moving as quickly as I can. This will buy time, but we must load the items you wish to take aboard your ship and send you on your way."

"What if we stay and help you talk to them?" Laura asked.

"This will only make them angry," Althon said. "And I cannot guarantee your safety."

"They already tried to destroy Shortcut to keep us from having it," Jason pointed out. "What would happen if they found us with more tech?"

"Yes," Althon agreed. "You must go."

"But if you moved and you are cloaked—" Laura protested.

"They will come," Althon said. "I cannot put you at risk. To endanger others also violates my mission."

"We're grateful for all you have done for us," Jason said. "Especially for Laura."

"Come," Althon said. "I will help you load the objects on your ship."

An opening appeared in the wall nearby and Althon led them down a series of mysterious passageways again. In moments, they were back in the room filled with amazing technology.

"Where in your ship do you store cargo?" Althon asked.

"Near the front," Jimmy said.

Althon went silent a moment as if thinking, then said, "I believe I have found it. I can use the smaller Shortcut to transport whatever you need."

"They cannot detect that?" Jason asked.

"If they are close, but it does not send radio signals like the larger one," Althon said. "And in any case, they are already coming."

"So you're asking us to choose items then?" Jimmy asked, confused. "I mean, we want them all, right?"

"Laura has been here longer," Jason suggested, looking at his wife.

"Yes," she began leading Althon around the room and pointing to several devices. "This and this and this." She pointed out the garbage machine, *Voyager 1*, and a couple others, and Althon began transporting them via Shortcut to *Starship 30's* cargo hold, Jason presumed.

"I'd better go back and supervise," Jimmy said. "How do I get to our ship?"

"I can send," Althon says, his voice tense from concentrating, and in moments, Jimmy's form went black, almost an outline, and he disappeared, reminding Jason of Arroyo Seco Park when Laura disappeared. He'd been Shortcutted.

"Can he move things on his own?" Jason asked.

"There are lifters to help," Laura said.

Having never been in a cargo hold on a spacecraft, Jason took her word for it though he did wonder if SpaceX provided the same equipment NASA astronauts were used to. Oh well, Jimmy would figure it out.

For the next twenty-five minutes, they transferred devices to their hold, with Jimmy coordinating from inside *Starship 30* and Althon doing the Shortcuts. When they had finished,

Althon led Jason and Laura back to their ship to check the cargo hold. They stood beside Jimmy and viewed the hold through large thick, transparent windows. Although the hold could be accessed by crew, most of the time this occurred in EVA suits with the cargo doors open to space, so there were several steps one had to take to actually move from the passenger and crew areas into the hold, and they didn't need to do so. Jimmy had operated the hold's cranes remotely from the observation spot where they stood and they could see that everything had been securely stowed for the voyage.

"I can't believe you're just giving us these wonderful tools," Jason said, a tingling warmth in his limbs and his heart feeling full. "We owe you so much."

"You have saved my life and repaired my ship." Althon extended his hand-like appendage to shake. "I must go. Thank you and safe journey."

Instead, Laura pulled him to her in an embrace. "Thanks for taking such good care of me, for all you taught me. I hope we'll be in touch again," she said, her eyes sparkling, then pulled away.

"We will," Althon said, then shook with Jason. To Jason's surprise, the alien's grip was firm, despite the fuzzy nature of his form. What passed for his hand was warm, almost human-like.

"Words can't even begin to thank you," Jason finally managed, surprised to find he was close to choking up.

"We will meet again," Althon assured him. "I feel certain." Then Althon hurriedly shook Jimmy's hand and stepped away from them. He touched the wall of the ship and began fading to shadows, then there was a bright flash of light, and he was gone.

Jimmy moved toward the cell. "Let's get to the cockpit and start flight prep," he said and turned to open the door leading to the main compartment. As it opened, a figure similar to Althon appeared. It was shorter but like Althon had no discernable facial features: no eyes, lips, nose, ears, mouth, or hair. In seconds, it raised an object with one of its arm-like appendages and a beam shot out hitting Jimmy straight through the suit and into his abdomen with the smell of burning flesh. He cried out and fell back, and then the figure went black with a flash and disappeared. Had Althon Shortcutted him?

Laura and Jason ran to Jimmy's side.

"Jimmy, are you alive?" Jason asked.

Jimmy mumbled, then cried out as Laura pulled his hand away from the wound. "Burning, laser, I think," she said. "No way to know the depth of damage for sure but it looks deep."

"What do we do?" Jason asked, in shock.

Then, just as it had aboard his ship, Althon's voice came from overhead. "I'm sorry. The scout came aboard, but I have detained him. Are you okay?"

"He shot Jimmy," Laura said.

With a flash, Althon appeared beside them. He leaned over Jimmy and held out some sort of long thin device, moving it over his body. "His wound is to an internal organ. I can give medicine for pain and infection, but he will need a doctor. I don't know human anatomy."

"Do what you can, thank you," Laura said immediately.

Althon fiddled with the device a few moments, then waved it over Jimmy several times in odd patterns. Jimmy stopped groaning and his breathing eased. "I have done what I can,"Althon said. "You must go. The scout ship has a homing device. They will be coming quickly."

"How did they find you so fast?" Jason asked.

"I don't know,"Althon admitted, "but if the scout ship was close, there are ways."

"Will he survive?" Jason asked, looking at Jimmy.

"We need to move him to the cockpit so we can keep an eye on him," Laura said.

In one smooth motion, Althon bent and picked up Jimmy with his arm-like appendages, looking toward the door. "Where?"

Laura led the way and Althon followed, with Jason bringing up the rear. They moved through the passenger bays and into the cockpit where four seats sat behind the pilot and copilot for other crew.

Laura motioned to one of the four. "Let's put him here please."

Althon gently set Jimmy down as Laura hurried to a large metal First Aid kit on the wall marked with a large red cross sign and pulled it open, grabbing a syringe, bandages, and a bottle of antibiotics. She set them down on the spare seat beside Jimmy.

"Thank you," she said and hugged Althon again.

"I must go prepare," Althon said, then he was gone again.

"How do we know the alien medicine won't kill Jimmy?" Jason asked.

"We don't," Laura said. "I didn't think of that until after. But I can give him some antibiotics and bandage the hole, and we'll just have to watch him as best we can."

Jason nodded.

"Make sure the Shortcut system is charging," Laura said as she set to work on Jimmy's wounds. "I'll be there in a moment."

Six minutes later, with a lurch, they had detached and were drifting away from Althon's ship. Jason wondered if he'd ever see Althon or an alien ship again. Regardless, he knew his life would never be the same. Jason felt a surge and the spacecraft began accelerating a safe distance away from Althon's ship before they initiated the first Shortcut. Fortunately, Laura was a skilled pilot, allowing her to fly *Starship 30* as readily as Jimmy had, and she quickly began firing up systems and going through the pre launch checklist with Jason. After all they'd been through for months, the culmination was a few hours aboard an alien craft. Jason could have spent centuries there. But he was doing what he'd worked so hard for—he was bringing Laura home to Heather and their family. And ultimately, Jason found he couldn't feel anything but gratitude.

CHAPTER 21

LAURA WALKED THEM through the checklist and engaged the engines to move them a safe distance away from Althon's ship before they made their first jump. Both were strapped into their seats at the console with visors down just in case.

As Althon's ship faded in the distance, Jason caught a glimpse of a smaller spacecraft docked to one of its airlocks—the scout ship. He couldn't help but worry what would happen to his new friend, but he felt helpless to do anything about it. The scout had taken Jimmy out of it in seconds. He and Laura would stand no chance. Jason wished Althon had come with them, but he was a man of principle and pride, and another part of Jason had great admiration for that—a trait they shared.

"Okay, this is your moment," Laura said. "We're ready to jump." She looked at Jason. "Did you recalculate the jumps?"

Jason nodded. "The computer did, and I checked it. It will take us six jumps to be back in range of SpaceX mission control."

"Okay, well, you're in charge of this part, babe," Laura said. "Take us home."

Jason entered the first jump point coordinates into the *Starship 30*'s navigation computer and started counting.

"Jumping in ten...nine...eight...seven..." He punched the button to power up the lasers as Laura continued,

"...six...five...four..."

"Lasers powering up," Jason confirmed.

"Three...two...one," Laura counted and Jason hit the button to initiate the first jump.

Once again everything around them turned to shadows as a bright light flashed outside; the spacecraft vibrated around them and then his vision grayed. Jason was thrown back against his seat, the ship spinning. Laura scrambled beside him, steering and manning the brakes with her hands and feet. So much of what she did seemed to be pure instinct, the finely honed skills of an experienced astronaut. Jason had watched tapes of her training but had never gotten the chance to observe her in this environment as her copilot. She was so at home, so focused, so confident. He really admired it.

After a few minutes, as they slowed, Laura instructed, "Confirm next coordinates."

They went through the process again. Five more jumps, this time with only moments between, instead of the ten minutes they'd allowed on the voyage out. It was a heavier strain on them because of the repeated spinning and stress from G-forces, but would get them there faster, and Jason was anxious to land and get Jimmy the medical attention he badly needed.

When they'd completed the six jumps and were back in communications range with mission control, Laura paused and went back to check on Jimmy.

"How's he doing?" Jason asked.

"Unconscious but stable," Laura said. "No noticeable

change."

"I hope that's a good sign," Jason said.

"We'll let SpaceX know we need a medical team to meet us," Laura said. Her eyes met his, her eyebrows drawing together as her brow wrinkled. "There's a chance we won't be talking to Space X."

"I know," Jason said. By now the government would have discovered they were aboard *Starship 30*, and there would probably be agents or Military Police waiting for them when they landed. But they had to land, whatever the consequences. And then they'd figure out what to do, whatever they faced.

Laura keyed the comm, taking them out of the communications blackout. Immediately, there was a message broadcasting on repeat *"Starship 30* this is SpaceX, over... *Starship 30* this is SpaceX, over..."

She responded with "SpaceX, this is *Starship 30*. Do you read?"

"Go ahead, *Starship 30*," the mission control comms desk replied. It was a voice Jason thought he recognized from NASA though, not SpaceX.

"All systems nominal," Laura said as she checked over the indicators and controls.

"Shortcut system active and standing by," Jason said.

"Uh, *Starship 30*, this is Phil Cline," the familiar voice said, sounding worried. "Vandenberg and NASA control will be handling your landing."

Laura and Jason exchanged a look. As expected.

"Roger, Vandenberg," Laura said. "We need to inform you to have a medical team and ambulance standing by.

Colonel Burnette was wounded and will need immediate attention."

"What happened to Colonel Burnette?" Phil asked.

"Colonel Burnette was injured, but his vitals are holding steady," Laura reported and Jason imagined the worried looks and comments being exchanged on the other end.

"*Starship 30,* verify coordinates," the comm controller, Bob Cooper, said after a second or two.

"Okay, double check the coordinates," Laura instructed and punched a series of buttons with amazing speed and confidence—almost like second nature. The spacecraft began vibrating as thrusters fired outside causing it to turn and adjust course again.

Jason flipped through laminated cards attached by a hinge to the dash and found the return coordinates and codes, then checked the first one against the LED then keyed his comm. "Coordinates confirmed." Jason read them off to the controller.

"*Starship 30,* what is your mission status?" the CAPCOM asked. Jason thought he recognized the voice of Stacey Crowder from NASA.

"Three crew aboard," Laura replied. "No further injuries acquired. We're in emergency mode, Vandenberg, but we're safe."

Then the blue-green 3D Earth was there, slowly turning, filling the windows again. The next few moments flew by. Moments later, there was air friction as they entered the Earth's atmosphere. Jason alternated between looking out the windows and glancing at the readouts and controls. At this point, without pilot training, it was all on Laura. He was just along for the ride. He watched her in action again—the total professional—and had never felt more proud and amazed at the woman who'd chosen to share his life.

"Jets firing," the Propulsion controller, Leti Najera, said.

"Jets fired," Laura confirmed from beside Jason.

Jason watched as Laura made the quick adjustments then reported, "Altitude is now sixty-eight miles."

"Roger, *Starship 30*, we have you at sixty-eight miles," the Nav controller, Jamal Ammar, confirmed.

The angle was to control heating as the spacecraft descended into the atmosphere. Next, they would perform a series of four banks in order to dissipate speed as they descended toward landing. The first bank to the right, then back to the left, then back to the right, and then a final bank to the left as they approached Vandenberg and the runway.

Jason saw swirl patterns outside the windows that resembled the inside of a blast furnace. The heat from friction, he knew, was boiling the outside of the ship, but they were well protected.

"Re-release balloon deployed," Ammar said.

"Confirmed," Laura replied. "I have twenty-two, ten, sixteen."

"Twenty-two, ten, sixteen at forty-eight thousand feet," Matt D'Aunno at Flight confirmed, indicating they were on proper coordinates and at proper altitude to start banking.

"Rolling right," Laura said as she started the banks and pulled on the joystick.

The movements jerked them around quite a bit, but the straps held them against their seats and to Jason, it was far less stressful than what he'd experienced in the Centrifuge at Johnson Space Center. After four different twists and turns, the spacecraft settled again into a normal trajectory and its speed had slowed quite a bit.

"Normalizing speed and angle," Laura said, and Jason realized she'd handled the ship as smoothly as Killan and Jimmy despite it being her first time at its controls. His amazing wife truly could do anything.

"Roger, *Starship 30.* We have you normalized," Ammar confirmed.

And then Jason could see the landing pad come into view ahead and below them as the spacecraft leveled out and he felt the thrusters firing to slow them down as the rocket lowered rear end first toward the pad.

"Thrusters fired," Laura said.

"Thrusters confirmed," D'Aunno said.

"*Starship 30* is on target for LZ-4," Nav said and Jason found himself staring up at clouds and a blue sky as Laura lined the spacecraft up with the runway and guided her down. By the time they felt the familiar lurch as the rocket touched down and bounced, then settled into position on the pad, Jason felt a mix of relief, pride, and joy.

"*Starship 30* down," D'Aunno said.

"*Starship 30*, welcome home," Crowder added as cheers erupted behind her.

Laura took a deep breath beside him. She'd done it. She'd gotten them safely back to Earth. "Thank you, Vandenberg."

Laura clapped him on the shoulder, grinning, as Phil Cline called out congratulations to them both over the comm. But Jason knew the hard part was hardly over. They would probably be arrested and questioned, who knew for how long, and then they still had to explain themselves to Phil

Cline and many others, and tell them about Althon.

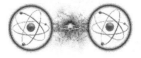

WITH THE PRESS there to cover Laura Maxx's safe return, Jason and Laura were welcomed like heroes, no sign of federal agents or Military Police until they'd crossed the tarmac from the landing pad elevator, waving at the press, as Phil Cline called out, "Press Conference at 1900!"

Then they entered the building and everything changed.

"Arrest them!" yelled a balding man in his early fifties with glaring green eyes and graying hair whom Jason had never seen before. He was powerful based on how everyone around them responded—Capobianco and his team moving in to surround Jason and Laura and slap them into cuffs, while shouting orders.

"Hands behind your back!"

"No sudden moves!"

"You're under arrest by the United States Navy!"

And so on.

The cuffs were tight and chafed Jason's wrist, but then he was grabbed by the arm and shoved forward with the command, "Walk!"

And so he kept his mouth shut and complied, Laura being pushed along beside him.

As they were led past him, Jason could tell Phil Cline was not happy about the treatment, but he refused to meet their eyes and kept his mouth shut as they were led past and into a garage on the opposite side of the building from where they landed, then shoved into black SUVs and driven away.

An hour later, after stewing alone in a nondescript small room with a table and four chairs, one of which he was handcuffed to with his hands behind his back, Jason finally learned the man's name.

A digital clock on the wall over the only door read 6:30 p.m. as the man strode into the room followed by an Asian woman in her late twenties. Both wore suits, but the older man's was clearly designer and far more expensive as were his shoes, watch, and everything else. The woman stood to his left, a step behind at all times, and she constantly consulted an iPad in her hands while the man carried nothing.

"Bring us coffee and leave us," the man snapped.

The aide nodded and turned to go, but Jason said, "Water for me, please."

She stopped and turned back, looking at her boss. He nodded, and then she whirled and was gone.

The older man glared at Jason for a moment before walking over and noisily pulling out the chair opposite him and sitting down.

"We have a press conference in thirty minutes, don't we?" Jason asked.

"Don't speak unless you're spoken to," the man snapped. "You won't be going."

"The press will love that," Jason replied with a defiant look.

"You're in a lot of trouble, Dr. Maxx," the man said with a complete lack of emotion. "I suggest you do as you're told."

"What do you want?" Jason asked.

"Do you have any idea who I am?" the man asked.

"Government suit, although yours is hardly government issued," Jason said.

"I'm the most important man you've ever met," the man said. "I'm the man who determines what the rest of your life is going to look like. You can call me Mister Rohner."

Jason smiled. "Did we get transported to Russia then after we landed? I thought this was the land of the free."

"Not for traitors like you." The man simply stared at him from across the table until Jason sunk down in his chair and waited.

A few moments later, the aide returned and set a bottle of water down on the table in front of Jason and a mug with a spoon sticking out for her boss, then turned without a word and disappeared again.

"My wife was missing," Jason said. "I spent months doing everything I could to find her and bring her back. I have no regrets."

"You endangered the entire world," Rohner said after a sip of coffee. Then he fiddled with the spoon noisily, stirring the contents around a bit.

"How?" Jason demanded.

"By putting us at risk from dangerous beings," Rohner replied.

"You mean aliens?" Jason said. "You can relax. The one we met came in peace."

"If he came in peace, how come Colonel Burnette is in surgery?" Rohner snapped. He sipped his coffee again and his face took on a more satisfied look as he removed the spoon and set it quietly on the napkin his aide had left beside the mug.

"That was someone else," Jason said.

"Explain," Rohner said. It wasn't a request.

And so Jason did, starting from when they docked with the alien spacecraft and continuing on through the arrival of the scout ship and their hurried exit.

"So this alien just came and gave you this technology?" Rohner asked skeptically, when Jason had finished.

"Did you check our cargo hold?" Jason asked. "See for yourself."

"Colonel Burnette was armed," Rohner said.

"Yeah sure, the three of us took on an entire ship of aliens and stole their technology," Jason replied, shaking his head.

"You said there was only one," Rohner replied. "Surely Colonel Burnette could handle that."

"He didn't have to," Jason said.

"I don't believe you," Rohner said.

"I don't care what you believe," Jason replied, holding his stare as he grabbed the water bottle, twisted off the lid, and took a long sip. He'd always hated arrogant government hacks like this guy. Avoided involving himself with them at any cost. But here he was. And to his surprise, instead of intimidating, he found the man annoying. He was a barrier to what Jason really wanted to do—so much science and research could come out of their trip. He couldn't wait to tell Jack, Li, Phil, and Peter Edtz all about it. Swallowing, he licked his lips and added, "Ask Laura. Ask Colonel Burnette."

"We will be, believe me," Rohner said.

"Good," Jason said. "Then you can let us go so we can get

on with what matters. We have lots of life changing science and research to begin."

"That may not be your problem," Rohner said as he stood, taking his mug with him.

"You can't just imprison us!" Jason protested, his throat tightening as he tensed in his chair.

"I can do whatever I want, Dr. Maxx," Rohner said, "and if you don't believe that, you soon will." He turned and marched for the door, his aide opening just as he reached it, and both disappeared outside, leaving Jason alone.

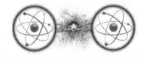

JASON WAITED IN that room for two hours alone before he started worrying. "Hey!" he yelled, hoping to be heard outside. "Did you forget about me in here? Where's my wife? I want to see Laura!"

When no one answered, he stood, chair and all, and walked over and kicked the door several times. "Rohner! Let me out!"

When he got no answer again, he sighed and dragged the chair back a bit, before sitting down, facing the door to wait.

Five minutes later, the door opened, but instead of Rohner, Capobianco and Killan appeared.

"You can't keep me handcuffed to a chair," Jason snapped. "It's cutting into my skin."

"I'm bleeding for ya, Doc," Capobianco said with a grin.

"Take them off!" Rohner boomed as he appeared behind them. Then as Capobianco grunted and Killan walked over and knelt, fiddling with the handcuffs, he looked at Jason. "I hope you're more ready to cooperate now that we've given you time to consider your position."

"Where's Laura? I want to see her," Jason replied as the cuffs came off and he pulled his arms forward, rubbing his sore wrists. Killan. Walked back to join Capobianco, standing guard on either side of the door.

"Tell us how you fucked up our spacecraft," Capobianco demanded.

"And then you'll let me see my wife?" Jason asked.

"We'll consider it," Rohner snapped.

Jason sighed. "It's a kill-switch I built into the system so I can always remotely deactivate the Shortcut mechanism. It was meant to counter corporate espionage, but I never thought it'd actually be that useful. It can be reversed."

Capobianco stepped forward, glaring. "You think you can just fuck with sensitive top secret equipment with no consequences, civilian?"

"You think you can endanger my wife with no consequences, Colonel?" Jason replied.

Capobianco stepped forward but Rohner stopped him with a hand on the chest.

"You will fix it. Like it never happened," Rohner ordered, staring at Jason.

"Does that mean you'll let me out of here?" Jason replied, holding his stare. He was sick of their games.

"Tell us how to fix it," Rohner said.

"I can do it or call my people," Jason said.

Rohner turned and nodded to Killan, who pulled out a cell phone and walked over, handing it to Jason.

"You're telling me your people can't handle a little computer problem?" Jason said with a smirk. But they all knew it was more complicated than that. The fact they were bringing it up meant their top people had been working on it with little success. This would be a lot faster.

"Make the call, sir," Killan said coldly.

Jason dialed Peter Edtz, knowing he would know just what to do, but he wasn't about to let on. "Peter, I need you to help some men clean up an issue with the Shortcut system on the X-39B," he said when Peter answered, then listened a moment before adding, "They seem to have a virus."

Jason hung up the phone and said, "A team can meet you." He tossed the phone to Killan, who caught it. "Now stop the intimidation crap and let me out."

"Do you really think the public will ever know anything about this?" Rohner replied. He was emotionless, tense, but Jason sensed something—as if the last thing Rohner wanted was the public knowing about this.

"These kinds of things don't stay secret for long," Jason said. "Too important."

"We keep a lot of important secrets," Rohner said.

"You're welcome to try," Jason said and continued staring at Rohner. It was a challenge and from the tendon that stood out in the man's neck when he said it, Jason knew he'd read him correctly. "Let me see Laura."

"When we're ready," Rohner said, then turned and walked out, Capobianco on his heels. The door slammed shut behind them.

ANOTHER TWO HOURS passed during which Jason thought about Althon, hoping his new friend was okay. He wished he knew of a way to contact him and ask how he was and hoped maybe Laura did after so much time aboard the ship. He'd begun wondering what was taking so long when the door opened again. This time, Jack Matthews and Li Chin walked in, hurrying to Jason as soon as they saw him.

"Jason! Thank God you're back safe!" Jack said.

"What are you two doing here?" Jason asked, surprised.

"They brought a lot of us here when they found out what you did," Li replied. "To question us."

"Did they handcuff you, too?" Jason said, through gritted teeth, his nostrils flaring. He was tired of this treatment. He'd done what he had to do, and in doing so he'd helped change the world. This was not the kind of welcome he deserved.

"Phil got us in, but we don't have long," Li said.

"Have you seen Laura?" Jason asked.

"She's fine," Jack said. "Looks great. In another room down the hall."

"Without the handcuffs," Li said.

"I want to see her," Jason said.

"Of course," Jack said.

"There was an alien," Jason said.

"Laura told us," Jack replied with a nod.

"So much to tell," Jason continued. "We brought back

technology that could change everything. We have to get it from them. Make sure it gets to scientists and engineers who can take advantage."

"They won't tell us anything," Jack said. "We asked already."

"We think they're gonna keep it," Li said, exchanging a look with Jack.

"And never share it, right?" Jason said. He'd already come to that conclusion, but they nodded. "Do you have a smartphone with you?"

Li looked puzzled. "Sure."

"I need you to help me make a video," Jason said. "Quickly before they come."

Li shrugged. "Okay." He pushed a few buttons then held up his phone aimed at Jason. "Whenever you're ready."

Jason straightened in the chair. "This is Doctor Jason Maxx of Caltech. I recently went on a top-secret rescue mission to Mars to bring home my wife, astronaut Laura Maxx. While there, we met an alien named Althon, who provided us with technology he wanted to share with the Earth under the supervision of the United Nations." The idea had just come to him. "The purpose is to help push us toward membership in the intergalactic community by advancing our technology. This technology has many purposes but it includes the ability to create enough energy from garbage to end Earth's energy crisis for good. There are agricultural tools, advances to help with astrophysics, and so much more. We want to share them with you as soon as possible. But men named Rohner and Capobianco have confiscated this material and held us prisoner. And I fear they may never release it." He took a breath and looked right into the camera for the last part. "Don't let this happen. I urge all of you to demand its release and ours immediately. This technology belongs with the UN, where it can be evaluated and properly analyzed and then distributed to where it can make the greatest difference. We can save the world together, but only if we help each other. I promise to explain more fully as soon as I'm free. Thank you."

Then he nodded.

"What do you expect us to do with this?" Jack asked.

"Get that on the internet, as fast as possible," Jason said. "They'll do the rest. I promise."

"We'll try," Li agreed.

Jason's eyes softened as he met theirs. "Thank you."

"We'll talk to Phil about making sure they treat you the way you deserve," Jack said. "But this Rohner is tough."

"He's an asshole, I know," Jason said.

Li and Jack each reached out and squeezed his shoulder, then they turned and knocked on the door. It opened and they were gone. Jason said a silent prayer his improvised plan would work. All he could do now was wait.

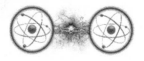

JASON SPENT THE night in an actual cell. It had bunk beds, a toilet in the corner, and a small desk and chair—everything bolted down—but it was basic and bland just like the food they slid through a slot in the door on trays. He still hadn't seen Laura. And he didn't sleep well, but he did try.

It was early morning when Rohner stormed in, looking

Shortcut | Bryan Thomas Schmidt

furious as usual. "If you're thinking that video stunt will matter, you're mistaken. You sabotaged a top-secret military vessel and will be brought up on full charges, believe me."

"I'm ready to face whatever consequences are necessary," Jason said. And as long as the technology Althon had gifted them was released to the UN, he was pretty sure he meant it.

Then he heard a commotion outside the door, and Rohner turned, looking annoyed. In a few moments, the door burst open and Phil Cline strode in, followed by six MPs.

"Jason, come with me," Phil said, "you're going home."

"What?! You don't have the authority!" Rohner raged.

Phil slapped a folder against Rohner's chest, allowing the government hack to grab it, as he said, "Presidential order. This comes from a higher authority."

Two MPs moved across the cell as Jason climbed from his bunk.

"Do you have your possessions, sir?" an MP with sergeant's stripes asked.

Jason chuckled. "Believe me, there's nothing here I want." He looked at Phil. "Where's my iPad?"

"It's waiting for you," Phil said, "and the technology you brought with you is being loaded onto trucks. It will be handed over to the UN."

"What?!" Rohner's face turned red.

"Read the paperwork," Phil said smugly.

"Bullshit!" Rohner snapped. "He defied my orders and incapacitated my starship. Mutiny, dereliction of duty, insubordination... No way he walks out of here." He began flipping through the paperwork in the folder Phil had handed him.

"...Don't forget failure to conceal technology that may save the world," Jason snapped back. "Surely that's a military crime."

"You're not funny," Rohner replied, scowling.

"No, just absolutely right," Phil replied. "That alien saved two lives: Jason and Laura Maxx both. And none of your soldiers were so much as hurt, other than their pride. Plus we have technology that may change our world for the better."

"It's not your call, Mister Cline," Rohner barked. "It was mine. My oversight. My spacecraft."

"Our mission," Phil said. "We invited you in."

Rohner waved a hand dismissively. "Maybe on paper."

"Absolutely in fact, no maybe about it," Phil said, glaring at him. "As the order states, it's not your oversight anymore. Jason, Laura, and Jimmy are heroes who performed to the best of their abilities, in the best interests of their mission and the entire world. That may not meet your standards, but it sure as hell meets mine."

"Well, we'll see what the panel thinks at Colonel Burnette's Court Martial," Rohner replied, looking away.

"Court Martial?! You've got to be kidding!" Jason protested.

Before Rohner could reply, Phil raised a hand to cut them all off. "Court Martial him if you want. He did what needed to be done. His job with NASA is secure."

"In the meantime, we'll be calling the president, and I wouldn't be surprised if Congress calls us to testify about the mission," Jason said. "We'll be sure to tell them exactly what role you played in all this and how it risked the entire mission."

Rohner just glared at them, but Jason knew they had him.

Phil smiled. "I think we're done here."

Rohner grunted, stood, and marched out, the door rattling closed behind him.

"Asshole," Phil muttered.

Jason laughed. "I don't think I've ever heard you talk that way, Phil. I like it."

Phil grinned. "I'm turning a corner...on my attitude toward bullshit."

"Glad to hear it," Jason said. "Does that mean we'll get less of it from you?"

Phil laughed. "Goes with the job, my friend."

"Can we get out of here so I can see my wife now?" Jason asked. He knew Laura just wanted to rest and get on a plane back to Houston to see her parents and daughter as soon as possible.

"I'm afraid you've got one more meeting first," Phil replied. "In Washington, D.C. The president wants more than a phone call. He wants to see you three personally," Phil said with a nod. "Thank you for your services and heroism and all that."

"Can't that wait until after we see our daughter?" Jason asked.

"The order says we're to bring you there immediately," Phil said. "I think he's a little pissed about your decision to turn that alien technology over to the UN."

But Jason had no regrets. He wanted the technology to be

made available as quickly as possible to all nations. So every country could send teams to study the technology, test it, and take pictures, then return home with the blueprints to make their own. If he'd given it to the U.S. government, he figured it would have been tied up in bureaucracy indefinitely, perhaps forever, and that would defeat Althon's purpose in sharing it with them. Whatever objections the President or anyone else might have, it was too late. The United Nations had surely applied pressure along with world leaders around the globe. Just as Jason had hoped when he'd made the video.

Jason smiled and motioned toward the door. "Get me outta here."

Walking out of that cell into the corridor was the freest Jason had ever felt in his life.

CHAPTER 22

AT 1 P.M., JASON and Laura joined Phil and Jimmy on NASA's plane headed for D.C. Whatever Althon had done to help Jimmy, it had wrought miracles. He spent one night in the hospital after they got back, recovering from surgery that turned out to be mostly about cleaning his wound and sewing him up, rather than major repair. Whatever Althon's device was, it had created some kind of force field over the hole the laser left in his gut. The beam had punctured his lower intestine, but by the time he got to base hospital at Vandenberg, that was already healing. The doctors were truly amazed. They cleaned the cavity and sewed up the wound, but other than bandages around his torso, he needed no recovery. The surgeon stopped short of using the term "medical miracle"and went with "unexplained phenomenon" instead.

Laura and Jason called Heather from the plane.

"Hi, baby," Laura said.

Jason couldn't recall the last time Heather had sounded so much like a little girl. "Mommy!" she said joyfully. "I missed you so much!"

"I missed you, too, baby," Laura said, her voice filled with a mother's deep love.

"I missed Daddy too!"

"I'm right here, sweetheart," Jason said, and after a few minutes reassuring her, he just sat back and listened as mother and daughter chatted for an hour, catching up on so many months apart. Their daughter peppered her mother with nonstop questions until they finally reminded her they were on a plane and would be landing soon and said their "goodbyes."

Laura leaned her head on Jason's shoulder and hugged his arm. "God, I missed you guys," and Jason didn't reply so he could choke back the tears forming in the corners of his eyes.

Four hours after they left Vandenberg, Jason found himself in the Oval Office facing the president, who started out by scolding them. "That technology is the rightful property of the United States Government and her people," he said, his voice surprisingly low volume despite his anger.

"No disrespect, Mister President, but that technology was given to us to benefit all the citizens of Earth," Jason said, not intimidated in the least. He'd done the right thing. And the President and Congress would just have to learn to live with it. "Not just the United States."

"The United States paid millions to fund your mission and rescue your wife!" the President snapped back.

"Well, until SpaceX bills you, that's not actually true," Jason said, earning a sharp look from Phil.

"We're grateful," Laura said, more soft and diplomatic than Jason. "But we felt we needed to honor the visitor's intentions and spirit, and the United Nations was in the best position to make it widely available to all as soon as possible."

The President shook his head. "The United Nations isn't a

superpower charged with keeping the world safe. That's our job." He looked at Phil. "I want detailed reports on how this mission went off course on my desk in two days."

Phil nodded. "Yes, Mister President."

But when the president excused them to take a call, Phil winked at them as they walked out.

Jimmy grinned. "Politicians put more carbon in the atmosphere with their bullshit than the rest of us combined," he joked.

For a minute, Jason, Jimmy, and Laura discussed Althon, wondering what had happened to him. Laura wasn't sure how to contact him any more than Jason, but she wanted them to try as soon as possible.

Ten minutes later, the President joined them again for photo ops and a press conference. The president was all smiles as he presented Jason, Laura, and Jimmy each with the Presidential Medal of Freedom, then praised their "generosity of spirit and heroic effort to make the world better for all its citizens" to loud applause from the assembled audience and press. He also took complete credit for giving the alien technology to the UN, saying, "It was our obligation to the world as the sole superpower to ensure that such life changing resources would be made available to everyone on the planet as quickly as possible." Of course, they applauded this too.

"That was relatively painless," Jason commented as they headed back into the White House afterward.

"I wish Heather could have been there," Laura said as she wrapped her arms around Jason's arm.

"Me, too," Jason agreed.

Moments later, they were in a car headed for the airport

and the NASA jet that would take them back to Houston at last.

"He was a little unhappy," Phil said, "but we'll survive it."

"Hell, he'll be distracted by the next crisis by the end of the day and forget all about it," Jimmy said.

"I'm counting on it," Phil said and they all laughed as they settled into their seats on the NASA jet. Overall, Jason was surprised and proud of Phil for the bold stand he'd taken with Rohner. Phil truly was growing.

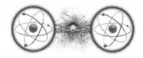

BY THE NEXT afternoon, Jason watched as Laura and Heather raced across the airport to embrace each other at Bush International in Houston and had to fight back his own tears and their obvious joy.

Then Laura hugged Roger and Susan, who were openly weeping, and Jason got a hug from his own daughter, who looked up at him grinning ear-to-ear. "I knew you'd keep your promise and bring her home."

"I couldn't let you down," he managed as he choked up a bit.

"Never. I believe in you," Heather said, sounding just like her mother.

That night, they had a family dinner, just the five of them, and it was the best family gathering Jason could remember. Susan hugged him warmly at the airport and again after dinner, and then Roger himself took Jason into his den and pulled his son-in-law into an embrace.

"If you tell anyone I did that, I'll deny it," Roger growled.

"Our secret, I swear," Jason said, smiling as he raised crossed fingers—Scout's honor.

"I heard a man almost died getting her back," Roger said.

"I suppose it could have gone that way, but he got the help he needed," Jason said. "And he's fine."

"Well, we're relieved," Roger replied. "But promise me you'll give us a year or two without such drama. I don't know if Susan can take it." From the look in his eyes, Jason could tell he was really referring to himself.

"Okay, I'll do my best," Jason said and they shook hands.

"Why don't you two just say 'I love you' and get it over with," Laura teased and they turned to find Heather, Laura, and Susan watching them from the doorway, grinning.

Roger grunted and put his hands on his hips. "We knew you were watching and wanted to put on a show." He looked at Jason, faking disgust. "A man can't even get privacy around here these days."

The ladies laughed and Laura swooped in to put her arms around Jason's and Roger's shoulders and pull them close. "I love you, too, Daddy," she said.

From that moment on, Jason no longer felt he had to earn Roger's approval. His father-in-law treated him like his own son, a surprising transformation, but one that touched him deeply.

The next day, Jason addressed an assembly of Shortcut team members at Johnson Space Center, the Caltech team looped in via Zoom.

"Twenty years ago, at this very campus," Jason said, "I gave a speech about why I love mathematics. A lot of people think it's just a bunch of numbers and scary figures and formulas. But I love mathematics because it is the most powerful tool that human beings have in our possession. It allows us insight into the world around us and because you can take any real world situation and solve it. From understanding the orbits of the planets, to sending spacecraft hundreds of millions of miles to specific locations; from designing a steel building or a bridge or an airplane with confidence it will work to decoding the mysteries of human DNA and preventing disease and so much more. I've always believed mathematics is the key to unlocking the mysteries of the universe, and today the evidence of that is sitting at the United Nations in New York City, paving the way for the success of entire nations in solving not only the energy crisis but possibly even poverty, hunger, and peace."

He paused and smiled, looking out over the faces in the crowd. Some he knew, some he didn't, but for the first time, all looked to him like family, and he felt an overwhelming gratitude and love for them.

After a moment, he continued, "In his final book, *Brief Answers to the Big Questions*, Stephen Hawking writes: 'One of the great revelations of the space age has been the perspective it has given humanity on ourselves. When we see the Earth from space, we see ourselves as a whole. We see the unity, and not the divisions…one planet, one human race.' Years earlier, Galileo said, 'The universe is written in the language of mathematics.' And I love being a coauthor of the universe." The crowd applauded and cheered, but Jason raised a hand to stop them. "But the greatest lesson of these past few months, really this past year, for me, is not just that humans are not alone in using that language, but that I, as a man, am not alone because I can count on so many like you to help me solve these problems and work toward a better future. We are not just an I, but a we. We are not singular humans but a whole, united humanity. That lesson, for me, is a profound insight, and I thank you for teaching it to me with patience and understanding, even when I made it hard."

He looked at Laura and took a deep breath. "My beautiful, beloved wife is back here with us today because of your faith and dedication as much as my own, and for that, you'll forever have our gratitude and our hearts. So thank you."

Again the crowd applauded and cheered but Jason's eyes were locked on Laura's and Heather's as they wiped away tears. Roger and Susan were beaming beside them. And Phil, Jimmy, and even Dr. Kim looked happier than he'd ever seen them. They'd done it. They'd really done it. And despite his own tunnel vision, he'd never had to do it alone. He'd had an entire team of friends supporting him, Althon too, and he'd always be grateful for the chance to know that. He considered it the most important discovery of his life.

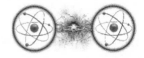

ON MONDAY, WHEN they got back to Pasadena, Jason and Laura celebrated with the Caltech team late into the night. Alice arrived the next day, and that meant several days of getting Heather to calm down and settle back into her routine. But the celebration was short-lived. As a first order of business, Jason had to address a Caltech faculty review board over conduct violations related to his actions surrounding the rescue mission for Laura.

They called him to a conference room on Wednesday morning in the George W. Downs Laboratory at 9 a.m. They were seated around an oval table, and Jason took the one open chair, facing them.

"Jason, we appreciate your making time to meet with us," the committee chair, Dr. Sheldon of the Physics Department said. "For reasons that are obvious, we have concerns about your recent behavior. Not only your seemingly defiant attitude toward authority, but government authority and institutions in particular, as well as a disconcerting lack of regard for how your actions and decisions reflect on this university. This university has always valued its close partnerships with government agencies and support that allows us to do the research we do not only better but in more meaningful ways. We cannot allow our faculty to jeopardize that, no matter what the reasons."

"That wasn't my intention," Jason said.

"What was your intention?" asked Dr. Rajesh of Astrophysics.

"I wanted to avoid involvement with a mission that might include reckless or unnecessary use of force," Jason began explaining.

"We know the mission was top secret," Dr. Sheldon said, raising a hand to stop him. "As such, there are details you're not at liberty to discuss. And while we understand, even share your concerns about violence, we do have a long history of military applications of our research and we value our close relationship with military organizations."

"Those relationships have been essential to this institution's success," added Dr. Howard from the Engineering Department.

"Faculty Members have special responsibilities as representatives of the Institute," said Dr. Leonard of

Astronomy reading from the Faculty Handbook. "These obligations include, but are not limited to, fairness and integrity, lack of bias or prejudice, respect for the opinions of others, support for academic freedom, and concern for the welfare and reputation of the Institute as a whole. Do you remember reading that? You made certain promises when you were hired."

"Of course," Jason said. "And I've done my very best to keep those promises."

"We know the circumstances were exceptional," Dr. Howard said.

"In fact, to my recollection, no faculty member during my tenure here has ever faced such dire circumstances," Dr. Sheldon added. The others nodded.

"But we would be neglecting our responsibilities if we did not hold you accountable and remind you of your responsibility to Caltech and to uphold the Eleven Principles," Dr. Leonard said.

"Of course," Jason replied, "and I assure you I am willing to accept in full the consequences of my actions."

"Good," Dr. Rajesh said.

"We are required to review this carefully and render a decision about whether discipline or other action is necessary," Dr. Sheldon said. "We will do so over the next few days and then meet with you again to tell you our decision."

"But before we do, why don't you tell us what you can about this mission and these alien life forms," Dr. Leonard said, leaning forward with a look of real eagerness. Jason had the impression this was less of an official request and more personal curiosity, but he was happy to comply.

AFTER MEETING WITH the committee, Jason met with Jack, Li, Laura, Purva, and Peter Edtz in Jack's office.

"How'd it go?" Laura asked anxiously as she stood with one arm holding the other elbow.

"It went fine," Jason said. "They wanted to know all about Althon. I told them what I could."

"Well, you seem in good spirits," Purva said with a smile. "That's encouraging."

"How much trouble do you think he's in?" Laura asked.

"Well, we're pretty sure the university has never faced a situation quite like this one," Li said.

"That actually works in your favor," Jack added. "But the potential for embarrassment and damage here was significant."

"But none of that occurred, did it?" Laura asked.

Jack shook his head. "No. Jason's video worked wonders."

"Between the international pressure and huge public support," Li said, "you're being hailed as heroes around the world."

"The university can't be too upset about that," Peter said.

"No, but they may have certain misgivings," Jack said.

"About what?" Laura asked.

"About whether Jason is someone who can be controlled," Purva said.

"In other words, will he comply with the university's standards for faculty or will he get a big head and think he's above it all," Li said. "That sort of thing."

"I did what I had to do," Jason said. "And if I had to do it again, I would. But I hope I never have to."

Jack grinned. "That's exactly what we expected you to say."

"I'm really sorry if my actions caused you any problems or put you in a bad light with the university or anyone else," Jason added.

Li brushed it off with a wave. "It's nothing we can't weather. You insulated us well."

"But please," Purva said, "try to stay out of trouble for a while."

They all laughed.

"I'll try," Jason said.

"He promises," Laura added, hugging Jason.

Jack got sober again for a moment. "We'll just have to wait for their decision, but we expect the reception you've received and the great benefits you've brought to the world community will be big factors in their decision making."

"Fingers crossed," Purva said, holding up her fingers and smiling.

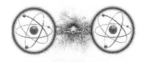

THE COMMITTEE CALLED him back the following Saturday.

After they'd all shook hands, Dr. Sheldon said, "Dr. Maxx,

your actions the past few weeks have been risky and reckless, and not in line with the highest ideals this institution expects from its faculty, staff, and students. As such, it is our duty to warn you that if you wish to continue on a tenure track at Caltech, you must do better moving forward."

"Most particularly," Dr. Leonard added, "we will uphold integrity in all we do."

"We fulfill the obligations of our role and we are responsible stewards of the institute resources entrusted to us, including the environment, equipment and facilities, money, and *people*," Dr. Rajesh said.

"We obey the law and comply with institutional policies," Dr. Howard said. "We protect the interest of those who place their trust in us. We are forthright with our students, their parents, employees, managers, and people who rely on us for leadership and accountability at all levels. We are open and honest in all our dealings with the government, external agencies, taxpayers, and donors."

"We are scrupulous in all business dealings," Dr. Leonard said. "We adhere to local, state, and federal laws and regulations. We deal honestly with the government in all matters."

"Do you recognize and agree to abide by these principles moving forward?" Dr. Howard asked.

"I do so promise," Jason said.

"Very good," Dr. Rajesh said with a thin smile.

"That having been said and agreed to," Dr.Sheldon went on, "it is the decision of this committee that you be officially congratulated by this university for your heroic efforts on behalf of all mankind in not only rescuing Dr. Laura Maxx but in making first contact with beings from another world and bringing back technology and knowledge to the benefit of all mankind. Congratulations and thank you."

And then, to Jason's great surprise, all four men applauded him.

ANOTHER WEEK PASSED before Jason finally settled back into a normal routine in his office at last. He was finding it harder than he expected to return to a normal pace. Just coming down off the adrenaline surges that had been driving him for over six months felt a bit like detox, but then figuring out where to go from here was another problem. He had to slow Shortcut down. NASA seemed in no rush to jump into more missions immediately, so he had time, but the success and the highly publicized results, particularly of the rescue mission, had made him a celebrity again and the pressure would return soon enough.

Truthfully, Shortcut had been his life for so long that he felt rather lost. There were options, of course. Other theories. And advances in laser technology Althon had given Laura that they both could develop. Those were already benefiting Caltech, which had given her a position as a Professor of Laser Optics in their Physics department, and they would benefit Shortcut in the long term, too. But nothing was far enough along it had truly caught his passion yet. And that left him feeling an emptiness he hadn't experienced in years: the emptiness of starting over.

It happened that night, after he'd gone home and stepped out into the yard to help Heather with the new telescope her parents had bought her for her birthday. She'd asked to see

Mars and Jason had taken care locating the planet and focusing the telescope in for the best view he could. Satisfied, he pulled his eye away from the viewfinder and motioned for her to take a look. "That's the best I can do at the moment," he said.

Heather gently squeezed past him and locked her eye to the scope, cooing with amazement. "So beautiful."

"Yes, yes, it is," Jason agreed, picturing the planet far more up close and viewed with his naked eyes.

"Daddy," Heather said after a few minutes as she pulled her eye away and looked at him. "What's it like up there?"

"In space?"

She nodded.

"Amazing," he said, at a loss for the words to describe it.

She made a face. "Cheater."

Jason laughed. "Okay, well, the thing is it's kind of hard to put into words. It is amazing... and it's big... it's daunting... it's awesome. It's so many things."

"Were you scared?"

"Only about your mother. Not about being there."

Heather went back to the telescope, looking at Mars again. "What about the aliens?"

"They weren't scary. Just different."

"Because there was only one?"

"Because he was kind and peaceful and trying to help." He thought of Althon and again wondered if they'd ever see him again.

"But he took Momma."

"Yes," Jason agreed. "That part was wrong. He didn't know what to do. We're aliens to him, too."

"So he was scared of us?"

"I don't know. Maybe." Jason figured anyone would be. But Althon had much more to fear from opponents amongst his own people at the moment.

After that, Heather stared at Mars for a while, studying its features and Jason just sat quietly beside her. But then he heard it.

Althon's voice in his ear.

"My friend, I am sending you a gift—some information I never had time to share. I hope you and Laura are safe at home and well. We have much to talk about when we speak again. And I look forward to it. Be at peace. I too am well. And grateful."

After they put Heather to bed, an hour later, Jason and Laura opened his laptop together and found an email from an unknown sender.

My friends,

I hope this finds you well. Another concern with your Shortcut process I did not have time to mention is that there are consequences to using this method of which you must be aware and careful. Since every particle pair has a finite zero-point energy, that energy must be borrowed from the quantum field. This energy is not limitless. Because your current Shortcut technology relies on short ventures into the quantum field, the amount of energy you are borrowing for each Shortcut is uncertain and the resulting energy fluctuations may do long-term harm to the fabric of our shared universe. But, once you learn to balance time and energy properly, there is little danger. So, enclosed is our math to get you started Shortcutting more safely. This also includes a communication method I believe you will find most useful and enlightening. Developing the technologies to accomplish this may take years, but by then, with what I have provided, perhaps humans will be ready to join the intergalactic community fully. I hope so. As I believe we need you.

With affection, your friend,

Althon.

Scanning the information Jason realized that Althon had just resolved the cosmological constant problem, a disagreement considered by some to be "the largest discrepancy between theory and experiment in all of science." John Wheeler and Richard Feynman had been right when they posited that there is enough zero-point energy in the vacuum inside a single light bulb to boil all the world's oceans. Later experimentalists had found that zero-point energy was one hundred twenty orders of magnitude weaker, but their experiments must have been incomplete. The energy was there. Enough to power civilizations.

They read on and got to the communications system. "This is how he whispered in our ears," Jason said, trying to wrap his mind around the brilliant details. It involved using quantum entanglement to project one's voice through space to another.

"This is amazing," Laura said.

Jason smiled. "Astounding is what it is. It will change everything."

Laura grinned. "I guess we know what your next projects will be."

Jason nodded as she hugged him again. "Plus, your father seems to like me now," he added.

"I know," she said. "He told me."

"That's astounding, too," Jason added.

"A miracle is what that is!" Laura laughed and cuddled into him, leaning her head on his shoulder as they stared at the screen.

Althon had just given Jason things to focus on for many years to come. And the potential applications had his head spinning. He was far from finished with Shortcut and Althon. Jason now saw this was only the beginning. He'd barely cracked the door to a world of endless possibilities, and the future posed only more questions, more possible discoveries, and more roads to hope with each step. The discoveries would truly never stop.

"You'd better get started improving those lasers," Jason said. "We're going to need them."

Laura pulled her head away and shot him a look. "You're not going to help me?"

"I have my own work, woman. Do I have to do everything?" he teased.

Laura punched his arm and he reached around to tickle her. As she laughed and leaped out of the chair to dodge him, he stood and grabbed her arm, pulling her to him, and they kissed again like newlyweds. He felt happier and more at peace than he'd ever felt in his life, and he hoped that would never stop.

THE END

ACKNOWLEDGEMENTS

For the record, whenever possible the science, math, and medical science used in this story is real. Quantum Entanglement is very real as is the laser science and mathematical formulas used herein. So too are polaritons and the technical aspects of communications between *Voyager* 1 and NASA, and of course details of various spacecraft from *Orion* to X-37B to Delta IV rockets. Also true is the astronaut training and medical regimen and the medical concerns astronauts face, as well as the medical science surrounding Jason's injuries and recovery. Frequent departures were necessary, most in the form of extrapolating what-ifs that are not yet possible and may never be, others more along the lines of poetic license which stretch well outside the bounds of what's possible. These were necessary choices to tell this story well, but none were undertaken lightly. I am forever indebted to a number of technical experts who gave of their time and knowledge to help me get as much correct as I did.

First and foremost, my "Personal Sheldon" who walked with me through the trenches and stressed and strained like it was a second full time job during the ten weeks we wrote this book, is Jonathan Madajian, Science Advisor Extraordinaire. An engineer employed by a top secret defense contractor somewhere on the west coast, as a graduate student he was involved on the fringes of Breakthrough Starshot, which gets a mention in the opening scene and is, indeed, a very real project. He prepared sometimes multiple scientific memos for me nightly on all sorts of topics, revising, expanding, and adding to them as necessary throughout the course of the project. These we hope to gather later into a nonfiction effort about the science of Shortcut, provided the movie comes to fruition.

Hunt Lowry and Patty Reed of Roserock Films for a fun collaboration, and Dr. Louis Friedman, whom I have not met but who founded the Planetary Society with no less than Carl Sagan, amongst others, served as Roserock's Science Advisor, and was the first to suggest polaritons, which are very real. And Emily Honey and Jack Bell, interns and proofers extraordinaire, with gratitude for covering my butt.

Dr. Kelly Cline, Profession of Math at Carroll College in Bozemon, Montana loaned me his "Why I Love Math" speech, which I modified a bit and present as Jason's. The passion is his as are many of the words and ideas, and I thank him. Here's a guy I'd love to study math under. Professors with this kind of passion and excitement about what they do are worth their weight in gold. So if your future plans include an academic career in mathematics, you could do worse than to look him up.

Dr. Dominick D'Aunno is a specialist in Space Medicine and Physiology, trained as an Air Force and NASA Flight Surgeon and performed research for a number of years at the Cardiovascular Laboratory at the Johnson Space Center in Houston, Texas. He helped develop much of the regimen and approach used in this book. He's also written pioneering research in several areas. He was also helpful with the hospital medicine as well.

Marianne Dyson and Les Johnson for help with the

Mission Control stuff. Both are NASA employees and fellow authors, and I recommend their books, especially Marianne's book A Passion For Space about her time as one of NASA's first female Mission Controllers.

Also assisting with hospital medicine was my father, Ramon W. Schmidt, M.D., now retired, who spent a career training paramedics and emergency room personnel in trauma in addition to his General Surgery practice and helped me develop the hospital scenes as well. It was my first time involving him so heavily in my book research and we enjoyed it, so I hope we can do it again.

Otis Carlisle, a computer guru, gave me advice on how one might theoretically hack an iPad. Though he makes no official claim to its viability, he did once work at Apple, according to his social media profiles. So he knows his stuff.

For the military training sequences, Tim Hightshoe, a training officer and police officer in Colorado Springs, Colorado was a great help as he has been before and really helped me capture authentically how such folks would prepare to assault and breach an unknown building or ship to rescue hostages. Thank you for your service.

Michael Capobianco, space enthusiast and fellow science fiction writer, gave great beta notes with a bit of snark that helped me gauge potential pitfalls with readers and fix them before they happened. Jace Killan, another fellow writer, also offered notes when he could.

Jonathan Maberry, Scott Sigler, and Marc Cameron, author friends for the blurbs; Guy Anthony De Marco, my publisher, Audra Redington for another great cover, Aniana Graciano, intern extraordinaire for great proofing, and my attorney, Brandon Chabner.

To the friends I tuckerized in here, many by mix and

match, enjoy the little cameos. None of these characters are in any way intended to represent any of you exactly. I am using your names only and creating characters all my own, so good or bad, no worries. You are still held in the highest opinion by the author.

Gratitude and love as always goes to my partner, May Restullas, and our kids Kishi and Kenjie, who weren't here when this project started but have been great support as I worked hard to finish it and finally get it out into the world.

This is the hardest work I have ever had demanded of me yet in writing a novel. The complexity of plotting and detail required much of me I didn't know I had. I thank the community that rallied around me despite the secrecy, the NDAs, and the lack of total forthrightness which I brought people in only as "need to know" dictated and nonetheless aided my efforts with enthusiasm and great kindness. Of course, any errors are ultimately mine and mine alone. The glories, however, they fully deserve to share.

AUTHOR BIO

Bryan Thomas Schmidt is a #1 bestselling author and Hugo-nominated editor. As an author, his novels include the SAGA OF DAVI RHII space opera series, the JOHN SIMON thrillers, and SHORTCUT, which is his 7th published novel of 11 written. As an editor, he has edited or co-edited 22 anthologies, including official entries in PREDATOR, and ALIENS VS. PREDATORS, Jonathan Maberry's JOE LEDGER, and Larry Correia's MONSTER HUNTER INTERNATIONAL series. His most recent anthology is ROBOTS THROUGH THE AGES, co-edited with SFWA Grandmaster Robert Silverberg. He's also written dozens of short fiction pieces including official tie-ins to The X-Files, Predator, Aliens Vs. Predators, Joe Ledger, Monster Hunter International, and Decipher's Wars. He can be found online at https://bryanthomasschmidt.net/ or on Facebook and X as @bryanthomass. He lives in Ottawa, KS with his two dogs, and two cats.

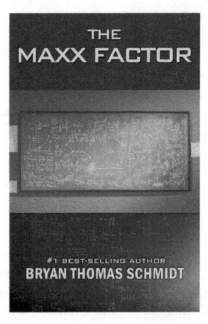

Please don't forget to support the author and other authors by reviewing SHORTCUT on Amazon, BarnesandNoble.com, Goodreads, or anywhere else you leave reviews. It has a huge impact on sales and visibility in searches so we sell more books and can keep on writing. Thanks.

For further adventures of Jason and Laura Maxx, sign up for my newsletter using the link or QR code below and get my prequel story THE MAXX FACTOR in which Laura helps Jason discover polaritons and build the first solar laser. I'll also send updates out 3-4 times a year on appearances, latest releases, giveaways, and other news, including your chance to be tuckerized in one of my future stories or novels.

https://mailchi.mp/088437a3c3a9/signup-page

Printed in the USA
CPSIA information can be obtained
at www.ICGtesting.com
LVHW040213270823
755618LV00004B/62/J